Praise for the New
Charmed Pie

Pecan Pies

"If the fanciful strikes your . . .
rabbit hole."   *Richmond —*

"Third in the series and, I believe, the best one yet . . . There's more action, romance, and a sense of completion after the buildup in the first two books."   —*Kings River Life Magazine*

"Riveting . . . Adams continues to build her name as an author whose mysteries feature strong, determined women who have to deal with secrets in their lives . . . An engrossing story that will only enhance Ellery Adams's reputation."
                                          —*Lesa's Book Critiques*

"Pies, magic, murder, and arson . . . [A] well-written and interesting book that will appeal to those who love mysteries and the paranormal."   —*Debbie's Book Bag*

"Adams takes the usual murder mystery boundaries and creates something special by not just including a murder mystery but a strong magical plot as well . . . [She] has us gasping and sighing at every turn."   —*Cozy Mystery Book Reviews*

Peach Pies and Alibis

"An original, intriguing story line that celebrates women, family, friendship, and loyalty within an enchanted world, with a hint of romance, an engaging cast of characters, and the promise of a continued saga of magical good confronting evil."
                                          —*Kirkus Reviews*

"Adams permeates this unusual novel—and Ella [Mae's] pies—with a generous helping of appeal."   —*Richmond Times-Dispatch*

continued . . .

"I love the world of Havenwood that Ellery Adams has created and every single one of her characters is fantastic. She fills each book with warmth and humor, and still manages to ground the magical elements within satisfying human conflicts."

—*Badass Book Reviews*

"A great book . . . The mystery kept me guessing but it was the relationship between Ella Mae and her relatives in this character-driven whodunit that made me feel like I was right there as they sought out a killer with an unexpected result."

—*Dru's Book Musings*

"A magical story, closer to urban fantasy or magical realism than mystery, although it still has murders and mystery . . . It's absolutely perfect, and left me eager to read the next book when it comes out. It's deep, and dark in spots, with references to Arthurian legends."

—*Lesa's Book Critiques*

Pies and Prejudice

"[A] delicious, delightful, and deadly new series! Full of enchanting characters in a small-town setting, this Charmed Pie Shoppe mystery will leave readers longing for seconds."

—Jenn McKinlay, *New York Times* bestselling author of the Cupcake Bakery Mysteries

"Enchanting! . . . Ellery Adams brings the South to life with the LeFaye women of Havenwood. This new series is as sweet and tangy as a warm Georgia peach pie."

—Krista Davis, *New York Times* bestselling author of the Domestic Diva Mysteries

"[A] savory blend of suspense, pies, and engaging characters. Foodie mystery fans will enjoy this."

—*Booklist*

"A little play of Jane Austen with a nod to Arthurian legend gets this new series from veteran author Adams . . . off to an enchanted start. A sensory delight for those who like a little magic with their culinary cozies."

—*Library Journal*

"Charming characters and a cozy setting make this mystery, the first in the series, warm and inviting, like a slice of Ella Mae's pie fresh from the oven."

—*The Mystery Reader*

Praise for the Books by the Bay Mysteries

"Not only a great read, but a visceral experience . . . Visit Oyster Bay and you'll long to return again and again."

—Lorna Barrett, *New York Times* bestselling author of the Booktown Mysteries

"Adams's plot is indeed killer, her writing would make her the star of any support group, and her characters . . . are a diverse, intelligent bunch." —*Richmond Times-Dispatch*

"I could actually feel the wind on my face, taste the salt of the ocean on my lips, and hear the waves crash upon the beach . . . AMAZING!" —*The Best Reviews*

"A very well-written mystery with interesting and surprising characters and a great setting." —*The Mystery Reader*

Lemon Pies and Little White Lies

Ellery Adams

BERKLEY PRIME CRIME, NEW YORK

THE BERKLEY PUBLISHING GROUP
Published by the Penguin Group
Penguin Group (USA) LLC
375 Hudson Street, New York, New York 10014

USA • Canada • UK • Ireland • Australia • New Zealand • India • South Africa • China

penguin.com

A Penguin Random House Company

LEMON PIES AND LITTLE WHITE LIES

A Berkley Prime Crime Book / published by arrangement with the author

Berkley Prime Crime Books are published by The Berkley Publishing Group.
BERKLEY® PRIME CRIME and the PRIME CRIME logo are
trademarks of Penguin Group (USA) LLC.

For information, address: The Berkley Publishing Group,
an imprint of Penguin Random House,
375 Hudson Street, New York, New York 10014.

ISBN: 978-0-425-27602-0

PUBLISHING HISTORY
Berkley Prime Crime mass-market edition / April 2015

PRINTED IN THE UNITED STATES OF AMERICA

10 9 8 7 6 5 4 3 2 1

Cover illustration by Julia Green.
Cover design by Diana Kolsky.
Interior text design by Laura K. Corless.

To Paige Bennett, my sweet-as-pie friend

Baked a lemon meringue pie,
cooled lemon custard & crust
on cold bathroom windowsill,
stirring in black night & stars.

—Sylvia Plath

Chapter 1

Ella Mae pressed chocolate cookie crumbs into the bottom of a springform pan with deft, quick motions. She then moved to her commercial stovetop and gave the marshmallow creme simmering in the saucepan a gentle stir. Satisfied, she turned the burner off and set the saucepan in a stainless steel bowl filled with ice. When the marshmallow creme was sufficiently cooled, Ella Mae reached for the liqueur bottles on the worktable and poured small amounts of crème de menthe and white crème de cacao into the fluffy mixture. Next, she squeezed in four drops of green food coloring and watched the white and green spiral around the tip of her wooden spoon before the green finally overpowered the white. She continued to stir until all traces of white were gone.

"Green as an Irish meadow," she declared to the empty room.

Ella Mae's mind began to wander. She thought of all the

things she needed to accomplish that day and of the endless list of tasks still awaiting her. She glanced down at the saucepan again and frowned. She couldn't remember if she'd added the crème de menthe.

Shrugging, she grabbed the glass liqueur bottle and added a generous splash to the mixture. After giving it a good stir, she leaned over the pan and inhaled deeply.

"Minty fresh," she murmured to herself and wiped at a drip running down the liqueur bottle with the hem of her apron.

Feeling pleased with her morning's work so far, Ella Mae hummed as she entered the walk-in freezer to fetch her beater attachment and a large mixing bowl. The cold air permeated the warm cocoon of marshmallow and mint that enveloped the entire kitchen and Ella Mae shivered. She didn't want to feel. She didn't want to think. She just wanted to bake, cook, and plate and repeat those steps over and over until it was time to close The Charmed Pie Shoppe for the day. After that, she could collect Chewy, her Jack Russell terrier, from doggie daycare and go home. HGTV and The Food Network awaited her there. As did her cooking magazines and page after page of glossy photographs and new recipes.

The oven timer beeped and Ella Mae backed out of the freezer, dropped the cold beaters and bowl on the counter, and pulled on a pair of oven mitts. She transferred six shepherd's pies, a trio of potato and green onion pies, and a dozen corned beef hand pies to the cooking racks. The scent of hot, buttery crust and fresh spices settled on her shoulders like a shawl, but she didn't pause to savor the aromas.

Instead, she poured heavy cream into the chilled bowl, attached the beater to her commercial mixer, and switched on the appliance. She stared at the white liquid as it frothed and churned in the bowl while her right hand involuntarily slid into her apron pocket and touched the letter nestled inside.

"No! I can't," she said, withdrawing her hand with the swiftness of someone whose fingers have come too close to a fire. "I have a business to run. I'm on the Council of Elders. Everyone's looking to me for answers. I need to stay focused."

Ella Mae's stomach growled and she removed one of the steaming shepherd's pies from the cooling rack and cut herself a thick wedge. While the mixer whirred, she savored every bite of pie. She had so little time to sit and enjoy a meal these days that she decided to take a few, precious minutes to enjoy this one. When her pie was done, she raised her coffee cup to her mouth and drained the tepid liquid. She then reached out to set the cup on the table, but her eyes had strayed to the window above the kitchen sink and she missed. The cup fell, and when it struck the kitchen floor and smashed into pieces, Ella Mae shouted, "*Opa!*" She'd survived so much over the past two years and wasn't about to let a broken cup bother her.

Turning her attention back to the whipped cream, she cursed. She switched off the mixer, dipped the beater in the cream, and raised it again. In lieu of stiff peaks, the mixture was grainy. For the first time in her life, Ella Mae had over-beaten the cream.

"I'll just add a little sugar," she said, heading for the dry-goods shelf. Grabbing the sugar container, she pried off the lid and scooped out a heaping tablespoonful. "A spoonful of sugar helps the medicine go down," she sang and dumped the sugar into the cream. She turned on the mixer again and finally achieved the desired result. At last, she folded the rescued whipped cream into the green marshmallow mixture and then poured the whole thing over the chocolate-cookie-crumb crust.

She carried the pie to the freezer and placed it at the end of a row of a dozen green pies. "That should be plenty for takeout orders and afternoon tea. I hope I made enough four-leaf clover cookies."

Back at the worktable, she saw that Reba or Jenny had left her an order ticket and had also dumped a pile of dirty dishes in the sink. The lunch rush was over, but there were still customers in the dining room. The Charmed Pie Shoppe had become so popular with locals and tourists alike that people often had to wait until two o'clock for a table. And since afternoon tea service started at three, Ella Mae baked and plated for hours in a row. She rarely left the kitchen, taking brief coffee or meal breaks perched on a stool next to the dishwasher. From this vantage point, she could stare out across the small rear parking area and over the Dumpster to the block beyond. On a clear day, she could see the roof of the fire station, its shingled gray gable rising a few feet above the brick building housing Havenwood Insurance. At certain times, the sun would hit the fire station's Dalmatian weathervane just right and it would wink like a star. Ella Mae would gaze at the glowing copper and think of Hugh.

"Hugh's gone," she told herself, and read the order ticket once more.

She plated a generous wedge of shepherd's pie with a side of field greens and was just spooning charred corn salad into a bowl to go along with a serving of corned beef hand pie when she heard the blare of a car alarm.

Ella Mae didn't pay much attention to the wailing until a second alarm sounded. And then a third. The noise was fairly loud and Ella Mae guessed that the cars were parked nearby. She barely had time to register this thought before voices raised in angry shouts added to the cacophony. Ella Mae couldn't tell what had made the people so upset, but she knew either Reba or Jenny would inform her sooner or later.

She didn't have to wait long.

Reba burst through the swing doors and cried, "Do you hear that devil's racket outside?" She put her hands on her hips and surveyed Ella Mae. "Mr. Jenkins just drove on the wrong side of the street. He scraped four parked cars from bumper to bumper, takin' off their side mirrors as he passed, and then plowed through the Longwoods' picket fence, flattenin' their collection of garden gnomes as he went. Mrs. Longwood is fit to be tied."

Ella Mae glanced toward the window. "Oh."

"That's all you have to say?" Reba pulled a red licorice stick from her apron pocket and shook it at Ella Mae. "What did you put in that Leprechaun Pie? Mr. Jenkins had two pieces."

Ella Mae feigned great interest in the parsley on the cutting board. "Are you asking if I enchanted our Saint Patrick's Day dessert?"

"You know damn well I am!" Reba snapped. "Seein' as you transfer your emotions into the food you make, I'd like to know what you *put* in those pies."

Shaking her head, Ella Mae said, "Nothing. I've been deliberately trying not to use magic when I'm . . ."

"Down in the dumps?" Reba narrowed her eyes and bit into her licorice stick. "Or just plain drunk?" In a flash, she closed the space between herself and Ella Mae just in time to catch Ella Mae's next exhalation. "You smell like a Peppermint Pattie dipped in paint thinner. How much of that mint liqueur have you had?"

Ella Mae felt her cheeks grow warm. She walked to the sink, turned the faucet on, and held a dirty dish under the water. "I haven't had a drop. I wiped the bottle with my apron, which is why I smell like I do."

Reba grabbed the plate and loaded it into the dishwasher. "I hope so. You've always been a glass of vino after work kind of girl."

"I still am. Though sometimes I have two, but that started when Hugh left," Ella Mae said.

"I know you miss him, but it's not like you two broke up. He told you he needed to travel—to search for a way to reclaim his lost powers—and you said you understood. It's only been a month and he's sent you letters. I see you readin' and rereadin' them." Reba frowned. "Is that why you put too much booze into your pies? I'm assumin' that's what happened because you've been real distracted lately."

"It was a mistake, and I only made it with a few pies. Not all of them. I didn't think I'd added that much more. I guess my magic somehow amplified the effects," Ella Mae said and continued to wash dishes. The steam from the water rose in diaphanous plumes around her face, masking her anguished expression.

"I'm going to deliver those orders and then I'm coming back here to pinch you," Reba warned.

"You already pinched me for luck today. And guess what? It didn't work."

Reba left with the food. When she returned, she turned off the faucet and took Ella Mae's red, water-wrinkled hands in her own. "What's got you so sad?"

With a resigned sigh, Ella Mae withdrew Hugh's letter and placed it in Reba's palm. Reba had just unfolded it when Jenny Upton, The Charmed Pie Shoppe's newest waitress, entered the kitchen.

"Where are those chocolate coins?" She frantically scanned the room, her gaze passing right over Ella Mae and Reba. "The ones wrapped in gold foil. I need them and I need them now."

Ella Mae heard the note of desperation in Jenny's voice. "I thought we made plenty of Saint Patty's Day gift bags for the customers." She pursed her lips. "But let me think. I ordered those gold-wrapped chocolate coins in bulk and they came packaged inside a cardboard treasure chest. That's where I put the extras."

"Then lead me to that treasure chest. And they're not for a customer. They're for me," Jenny added. "I had to give *every* customer a zap of energy before they left. They all had the Leprechaun Pie and were as tipsy as sailors on furlough. I was afraid to let them drive or cross the street on foot." She jerked her thumb toward the front of the store. "Look what happened when Mr. Jenkins got behind the wheel. Unfortunately for him and a hundred lawn gnomes, he paid his bill and slipped outside before I could touch him. And if I don't eat some chocolate, I won't be able to zap *you*, Ella Mae."

Ella Mae scowled. She was Jenny's boss, not some naughty child who could be pinched by one employee and given magical doses of energy by another. She whipped her head around to chastise Jenny, but was overcome by wooziness and stumbled to the closest stool. Putting both hands on the seat to steady herself, she suddenly remembered having placed the extra chocolate coins between containers of cocoa powder and confectioner's sugar. Plunking down onto the stool, she waved at the dry-goods shelves. "The treasure chest is on the second shelf from the floor."

By this time, Reba had finished reading the letter and had placed it on the worktable where Ella Mae did most of her prep work. Two sharp knives were resting on the wooden surface and Reba's hand closed over the paring knife. Her lips were compressed into a thin line and Ella Mae knew she was angry.

Jenny drew alongside Reba and dumped the treasure

chest on the table. "Here," she said, handing Reba a chocolate. "You look like you could use some candy."

"I never leave home without it," Reba said, taking a fresh
licorice twist out of her apron pocket. She tore off an end
and chewed furiously while Jenny unwrapped a dozen coins
as if her life depended on it.

While the two women devoured their confections, Ella
Mae stared at Hugh's letter. She then slid off the stool and
fetched a ball of dough from the walk-in. Shoving the knives
and letter to the side, she dusted the surface of the worktable
with flour and reached for her rolling pin. She freed the
dough from its plastic wrap and began rolling it out, forcing
it to grow wider and thinner, wider and thinner.

"Okay. Between the chocolate and the three cans of Mountain Dew I chugged on the front porch, I'm starting to feel
like myself again," Jenny said. "Are you ready, Ella Mae?"

"Just clear the fog in the poor girl's head," Reba said.
"She's had some discouragin' news and I want to talk it over
with her."

Before Ella Mae could protest, Jenny put a hand on her
shoulder and squeezed. A jolt shot through Ella Mae's body.
For a brief, delicious moment, her blood turned to liquid
sunshine—white hot and radiant—and hummed in her
veins. Her fatigue evaporated like chimney smoke swept
away by the wind and her mind was sharp and focused.
"Thanks, Jenny," she said, smiling gratefully. "I'm still in
awe of your gift."

"Yours isn't too shabby either." Jenny pointed at the
round circle of dough. "By influencing people's emotions,
you can alter their behavior. Talk about powerful." She
smiled. "So what's going into this pie?"

Ella Mae transferred the dough into a buttered pie dish.
"My heart."

Reba and Jenny exchanged worried glances as Ella Mae placed the dish in the oven.

"What happened?" Jenny asked.

"Hugh wrote that he hadn't found what he was looking for in England or Scotland so he's heading to Ireland. If that doesn't pan out, he's going to Greece. He's put his assistant manager in charge of Canine to Five, informed the fire department that he's no longer available to volunteer, and said that I shouldn't wait for him—that he's not coming back until he's the man he was before I . . ." She trailed off.

"Before the source of his power was taken and used for the common good," Reba finished for her.

Ella Mae threw out her hands in exasperation. "But he doesn't know that! He doesn't know what I am. I couldn't sit him down and say, 'Hugh, you're in love with a magical being. Not only can I make charmed pies, but I can also command butterflies. And according to some ancient prophecy, I'm the Clover Queen, a position that means I'm responsible for the safety and well-being of lots of enchanted people.'"

"Of course you couldn't tell him." Reba tenderly brushed a strand of hair off Ella Mae's cheek. "He isn't like us. Sweetheart, he never will be one of us."

Ella Mae nodded. "I know that, but I love him. I've loved him for most of my life. Since I knew how to love. And no matter what he said in this letter, I'll wait. If it takes twenty years, then so be it. I have to hold on to the hope that, one day, I can be completely honest with him and he'll be able to forgive me for what I did to him."

"What kind of existence will you have pining for him for twenty years?" Reba asked very softly.

Ella Mae faced her friends. "I don't plan on pining. You see, I'm going to bury everything I feel for Hugh into this pie. And then, I'm going to freeze it. I hope it'll be like pausing a movie—that it'll give me the freedom to focus on work and the rest of the people I care about."

Jenny looked doubtful. "Is that possible? Can you really transfer enough of your feelings that you actually stop, well, feeling?"

"When it comes to these particular emotions, I have to try," Ella Mae said, sounding like her strong, determined self again. "Hugh's wasn't the only letter I received in today's mail. The township committee has accepted my proposal to have The Charmed Pie Shoppe sponsor Havenwood's Founder's Day celebration."

Reba arched a brow. "Why would we want to do that?"

"Because it gives us an unprecedented chance to gather our kind from all over the country. If I can convince Elders from other communities to meet, we can discuss how to unite, grow stronger, and break a very old curse."

Jenny pumped her fist in the air. "Yes!"

"Founder's Day is the first of May. Beltane. Our biggest party. A celebration I dream about all year," Reba said, her eyes gleaming. "And with all these visitors, we'll have hundreds of magical people in our grove. Good-lookin', half-naked men from all over the country dancin' around a bonfire. Tall Texans with cowboy hats, bronze-bodied surfers from California, men from the Dakotas who know how to keep a girl warm at night." She grinned at Ella Mae. "This is your best idea ever."

"Make sure to leave a few half-naked men for me," Jenny said, and then issued a wistful sigh. "Too bad May is weeks and weeks away."

Ella Mae waved her hand around the pie shop. "Don't worry. With all we have to do to prepare for this event, the time will pass with lightning quickness."

"Speaking of which, I'd better zip back to the dining room and check on our customers," Jenny said and rushed off.

Ella Mae removed the pie dish from the oven and set it on a cooling rack. She then retrieved raspberries, heavy whipping cream, and a bar of white chocolate from the walk-in. She dropped the items on the counter and went to the dry-goods shelves for a bottle of orange liqueur, a package of unflavored gelatin, and a jar of currant jam.

Reba eyed the liqueur bottle warily. "What are you doin' with that?"

"Mixing it with the gelatin, cream, and chocolate. And I'm not serving it to our patrons." Ella Mae crossed the first and second fingers of her right hand and held them over her heart. "Promise."

Satisfied, Reba crossed the room and opened one of the swing doors a crack. "Only two tables are occupied," she said. "I think the rest of the customers raced outside to watch Mrs. Longwood soak Mr. Jenkins with her garden hose."

"That poor man," Ella Mae said, pausing in the act of breaking the bar of white chocolate into small pieces over a heated saucepan. Stirring in the rest of the filling ingredients, she said, "I'm responsible for the damage to the parked cars and to Mrs. Longwood's gnomes, not him. What if he's given a Breathalyzer test? He could be in big trouble. He might lose his license. Or worse."

Reba shook her head. "I called Officer Wallace and told her exactly what happened. She's going to help us out. Her report will make it sound like Mr. Jenkins's car malfunctioned. Leak in the brake line or that sort of thing. His insurance company will cover the damage and my buddy at the body shop will mess with those brake lines long before the insurance rep shows up."

"Thank goodness for Officer Wallace. I never realized

what an advantage it could be to have one of our kind on the police force."

"She's not the first person to relocate to Havenwood because of you," Reba said. "Thousands of folks would give half a lung to live in a place where they can renew their powers anytime they want. You've changed the rules, honey. And I have a feelin' you're just gettin' started." She picked up the bottle of orange liqueur. "You can't afford to be distracted. Your life isn't your own anymore."

Ella Mae knew Reba spoke the truth. "You're right," she said. "On both counts. Let me finish with this pie and then I'll be fine. Really, I will. But I have to do this alone, okay?"

Reba searched her face. "Okay, then. But remember, Jenny and I are just on the other side of those doors if you need us."

When she was gone, Ella Mae placed Hugh's letter in the pie dish. She unfolded it so she could see his familiar handwriting on the thin airmail paper. She traced the letters of his name, one at a time, silently pledging to love him as long as she lived. "But the part of my heart that you claimed needs to hibernate. I don't know when I'll see you again, and like Reba said, my life isn't my own. It belongs to the people of Havenwood, and they don't need a lovesick girl leading them. They need a woman. Fierce and fearless."

Ella Mae beat more cream, creating picture-perfect stiff peaks before folding the whipped cream into the chocolate mixture. As she gently worked her rubber spatula through the pie filling, she closed her eyes and thought of Hugh. Memories flashed through her mind like a high-speed slide show. There were images from the recent past: Hugh asleep in her bed, his Great Dane stretched out across his feet; Hugh frying bacon; Hugh frowning over a crossword puzzle; Hugh leaning in to kiss her. And then she went back further in time, to the first moment she'd seen him. He was still a boy then, and she, a shy and awkward girl. Despite her youth, Ella Mae's heart had tripped over itself when Hugh had turned his bright blue-eyed gaze in her direction. She'd felt a rush of heat, of terror, and a longing she hadn't fully understood.

"I understand it now," she whispered and then poured the creamy white filling over the letter.

While waiting for the filling to set, Ella Mae tidied the kitchen and washed the raspberries. She then melted a small bowlful of red currant jam and dropped the berries into the ruby liquid. Using her fingertips, she tenderly coated each berry and then removed the pie dish from the refrigerator. Gingerly pinching a raspberry between her fingers, she inhaled the sweet scents of white chocolate and jam, and as she gently pressed the berry into the filling, she willed her memories of Hugh's touch to enter the fruit. She repeated this act over and over, transferring into each berry the feel of his hands, the sound of his voice, his musical laughter, the hunger in his kisses, the glint of humor in his brilliant blue eyes, and the way his body moved when he danced. She pictured how he swam like a dolphin, the way he rolled on the ground when he played with his dog, and how he stood, taut and rigid as a steel beam, directing water from a fire hose at a wall of angry flames. She put all the things she felt about this remarkable man—the man she'd loved for most of her life—into the pie.

Feeling oddly vacant, Ella Mae dropped a handful of dark chocolate morsels and two tablespoons of butter in a glass bowl and cooked them in a microwave. Pouring the melted chocolate into a pastry bag, she piped dark hearts over the surface of the berries. The hearts overlapped until they were unrecognizable, but if Ella Mae looked very closely, she could follow the path of the lines and see the shapes she'd created.

She continued to pipe until the chocolate was gone. With a weary sigh, she sealed the pie in an airtight container and put it on a high shelf in the freezer.

By the time Reba returned with the first of the teatime orders, Ella Mae was ready to work again.

"Are you all right?" Reba asked.

"I will be," Ella Mae said and smiled.

Reba nodded. "I believe it. While you plate this order, why don't you tell me what you have in mind for this Founder's Day event? We should focus on the future now."

"Yes," Ella Mae agreed. Taking a deep breath, she prepared to leave the past behind. "My idea is for us to host a one-of-a-kind celebration of pie. It'll be called History in the Baking. We'll invite cooks from across the nation to participate and encourage them to bring friends and family along. There will be pie bake-offs, presentations, lectures, cooking classes, and large cash prizes."

Reba's brows shot up her forehead. "Where's the cash comin' from? Not from my salary, I hope."

"No." Ella Mae laughed. "We'll charge every contestant a registration fee, and I've already asked the manager of Lake Havenwood Resort about using their kitchen for classes and their auditorium for the presentations. He was willing to waive the fee for these facilities, seeing as our event is likely to ensure new bookings and plenty of advertising for his hotel."

"I don't get the history part," Reba said and started to slice a Leprechaun Pie into even wedges.

"Pies have a long and rich history," Ella Mae began. "Ancient Egyptian bakers made a form of pie dough, but the Greeks were the first civilization to produce a real pie. Of course, the pies were of the savory variety for centuries. The dough was just a container to hold a protein-packed filling. It wasn't until the fifteen hundreds that the bakers began experimenting with fruit pies."

Reba still looked puzzled. "So the contestants bake an old recipe—a really old recipe—and then talk about that country's culture?"

"Exactly. You could make a Roman mussel pie, for example. Of course, only the wealthy Romans could afford mussels, so you'd have to explain what the different classes of that period would use as their filling. For extra impact, you could dress like a Roman."

Shaking her head, Reba said, "Not a chance. You can't hide enough weapons under a toga. Give me a kimono. Or one of those medieval gowns. Do you know how many throwing stars I could tuck inside those bell sleeves?"

Ella Mae laughed again and was surprised by the levity of the sound. She felt much lighter, as if a burden had been lifted. With a shock, she realized the transfer had worked. She'd used her gifts to store her longing for Hugh in a white chocolate mousse raspberry pie. She could think of him now without feeling that needle-sharp ache in the center of her chest. Her love was intact, but it was a love without pain. It was more like the memory of love. Pure, sweet, and distant.

"Anyway," she continued animatedly. "The contestants don't have to restrict their recipes to foods made in ancient times. America has a storied pie-making history. Pie has always been very important to this nation."

Reba loaded her serving tray with the completed orders. "Shoot, everybody knows that. I bet there wouldn't have been an America if the pilgrims hadn't made pumpkin pie for the natives durin' the very first Thanksgiving."

"There wasn't any pumpkin pie," said Jenny, who'd entered the room in time to catch Reba's last remark. "That's a total myth. They ate fowl and venison at the inaugural

Thanksgiving. There might have been a savory pie, but definitely no pumpkin."

"All right, Einstein. You stay here and trade history lessons with Ella Mae. I need to serve my customers." With a scowl, Reba left the kitchen.

When she was gone, both Ella Mae and Jenny stifled laughter behind their hands.

"She really hates being corrected," Jenny said. "And I don't dare press a point with her. The woman has a whole arsenal of weapons concealed under her clothes. She might be smaller and older than me, but she could kick my butt from now until Tuesday."

Ella Mae retrieved a plastic bag filled with sugar-cookie dough from the walk-in and began to roll it out on the work-table. "Reba's been my bodyguard since I was born. I've never seen anyone fight like her. She's almost fifty, but her reflexes are quicker than those of a pissed-off rattlesnake."

"I'm glad she saves her venom for our enemies," Jenny said. "Though it would be nice if we didn't have enemies for a spell. I'd like to enjoy a peaceful spring."

At that moment, one of Ella Mae's aunts burst through the swing doors, leaving them to flap wildly in her wake.

"You need to come with me!" Aunt Verena bellowed.

Ella Mae was unfazed by her aunt's tone and volume. The oldest of the famed LeFaye sisters didn't possess an indoor voice. She was also accustomed to people leaping to obey her. When Ella Mae didn't, Aunt Verena pointed at the cookie dough and said, "Put down that rolling pin. We need to go!"

"It's the middle of tea service," Ella Mae protested. "I can't just—"

"Yes, you can!"

Reba entered with another order ticket. "What's goin' on?"

"Can you take over for Ella Mae for a few minutes?"

Though Verena towered over Reba and was nearly double her girth, she spoke to her with deference and affection. Reba might not have been a LeFaye, but she was still family. "There's something she needs to see."

Reba nodded and turned to Ella Mae. "You'd best listen to your aunt."

Knowing that Aunt Verena wouldn't insist unless it was extremely important, Ella Mae untied her peach apron, hung it on a wall hook, and quickly washed her hands. "I hope you aren't the bearer of bad news," she said, reaching for the dish towel. "It's a holiday, after all. We're supposed to wear green, pick four-leaf clovers, and look for pots of gold at the end of rainbows. We're supposed to be merry."

Verena looked pained. "Honey, there's nothing to be merry about. And there's nothing to celebrate. This news is beyond bad. And things are about to get worse."

And with that, she turned and pushed on the swing doors with such force that Ella Mae thought they'd fly right off their hinges.

Chapter 2

Ten minutes later, Verena opened her front door, and called, "She's here!" Stepping aside, she shooed Ella Mae into the foyer, and said, "They're all in the sitting room."

Ella Mae hurried through Verena's large kitchen into the sitting room. Usually a bright, cheerful space filled with soft chairs, colorful art, and music, the room was now shadowy and quiet. The plantation shutters had been closed. Uncle Buddy's vintage record player had been silenced. The television, normally hidden from sight inside a large cabinet, was on. Scenes flickered rapidly across its flat screen, casting an eerie blue-and-white glow on the faces of the women gathered before it.

Ella Mae's mother and her other aunts, Dee and Sissy, turned to look at her. Their grim expressions were unnerving. Ella Mae saw something in their eyes she wasn't used to seeing. Her aunts were afraid.

"What's going on?" she asked.

Her mother grimaced. "There's a terrible storm off the

coast of Scotland. It's gaining wind strength and speed by the hour and is expected to make landfall by tonight."

Ella Mae was drawn to the image on the television screen. As she watched, a massive spiral of dense clouds rotated in slow motion over the North Sea. A man was speaking, but his voice was too muted for Ella Mae to understand him clearly. "Could you turn up the volume, please?"

Aunt Sissy, headmistress of the Havenwood School of the Arts, nodded and pressed a button on the remote control.

". . . bearing northwest," the meteorologist was saying. "This storm breaks all the rules, and is behaving like the winter storm of 1953. We're expecting high wind speeds— one hundred and twenty miles per hour or more—and significant flooding. Evacuations are underway, especially in the north. Those in and around the Orkney Islands have been ordered to evacuate. There will be no place to hide when this storm makes landfall." The man pivoted, and a map of the United Kingdom filled the screen. He lifted his hand, tracing the Scottish coastland north until he came to what Ella Mae had always thought of as the tip of the rabbit's ears—the northernmost point of the landmass—and then circled a collection of islands off the coast with his index finger.

"Is this a live broadcast?" Ella Mae whispered.

Aunt Sissy shook her head. "We recorded it thirty minutes ago. That's when our weather channel airs the European forecast. But this story is *so* big that it's bound to be on every news station by this evening."

"Since you've all listened to the report already, could someone please tell me why I had to leave work for this? I don't mean to sound insensitive," Ella Mae added quickly. "I feel for the people in the path of that monster—"

"That's just it," Aunt Dee said in her soft, gentle voice. "This thing is a monster."

"It's bound to destroy at least *three* ancient magical groves," Aunt Sissy said. She tended to use dramatic pauses, emphasis, and gestures when she spoke. "Long ago, groves weren't necessarily built on high ground. Our kind didn't have to hide as completely as we do now." Her eyes were filled with sorrow. "No ash tree, not even a magical one, can withstand the force of this wind."

Ella Mae's mother took the remote from her sister's hand. "Losing groves is tragic enough, but there's more to this story. The Scots have named this storm after a figure in their folklore. An evil figure."

"Nuckelavee!" Verena cried. "A terrifying and gruesome creature that lived in the sea, only coming ashore to devour humans. According to legend, it had a huge head and a protruding mouth that hung open in a terrifying grin. The monster was skinless, so its yellow veins and slime-covered muscle were visible to the naked eye. And if that isn't horrible enough, Nuckelavee's poisonous breath could wither crops and kill livestock. It's his destructive power and supernatural strength that influenced a Scottish paper to name this super storm after him."

"In the old tales, all one had to do to escape this mythological creature was cross over a body of fresh water," Aunt Dee said. "That won't help the Scots tonight. This storm is a swirling mass of water and wind. It will sweep across rivers, causing them to overflow as it moves inland. As you heard, the experts are calling for massive flooding. The entire coastline of northern Scotland may be forever altered."

Verena took an atlas off the coffee table and pointed at a map of Scotland. "The storm will sweep from east to west. The groves in its projected path are here, here, and here." She tapped the map in three places. "Nuckelavee will rip the ash trees right out of the ground, leaving thousands of our kind without a safe haven."

Now Ella Mae understood why her family was so upset about the news. Her mother took her hand and gave it an encouraging squeeze. "There's more." Her mother pressed the play button on the remote. "They're going to show a satellite photo of the storm. It'll repeat over and over again, and then the meteorologist will point out the unusual shape of the storm's eye. That's why we're all gathered here. And it's also why we called you to join us. Because of the shape of that eye."

Perplexed, Ella Mae focused on the screen as the map was replaced by a satellite image. Ella Mae didn't understand all the meteorological jargon, but it was clear that Nuckelavee was massive. The camera view changed, zooming closer and closer to the center of the rotating clouds.

"And if this storm weren't unusual enough, take a look at this eye," the weatherman said, his voice filled with wonder. "In this image, the eye appears to take a familiar shape—one closely associated with today's holiday."

Ella Mae's mother paused the program again. "Do you see it?"

Cocking her head slightly, Ella Mae approached the television. She kept her gaze fixed on the center of the screen, frowning in concentration.

And then, she saw it.

"It can't be," she whispered. She stretched out her hand, silently asking for the remote, and then hit the rewind and play buttons several times, causing the storm to rotate from right to left with agonizing slowness. "It's a clover," she said in astonishment. "The eye is shaped like a four-leaf clover. And not just any clover either." She raised her palm and turned it toward her family, inviting them to compare the puckered skin near her wrist to the frozen image on the television screen. The storm's eye was a perfect match to Ella Mae's burn scar.

"The eye shifts by the end of this segment," Aunt Dee

said. "When it reforms, it's circular again. Maybe it doesn't mean anything. Maybe it's just a freak occurrence."

There were no noises or murmurs of assent following this remark. None of them believed in coincidence.

Ella Mae crossed her arms over her chest, tucking her trembling hands out of sight. Icy dread chilled her blood, and every cell in her body trilled with the same wordless message: *Danger*.

"What does this mean?" Ella Mae gestured wildly at the screen. "Our kind can't be responsible for this. Why would someone or a group of people deliberately destroy our groves—the source of our power?" She looked from her mother to her aunts. "No one is capable of creating a storm of this magnitude. Maybe a group could increase the intensity of a storm, but to manipulate it until the eye looks like a clover? That can't be the result of magic." She hesitated, thinking of all the earth-shattering discoveries she'd made over the past year or so. "Or can it? Is it possible?"

Her mother frowned. "We don't know, Ella Mae. We have as many questions as you."

"That's why we called you!" Verena declared. "Nothing will stop this storm from its current course of destruction, but if a group of our kind is truly capable of manipulating the weather, these people pose a threat of catastrophic proportions."

"We must discover exactly who they are and what they're after. And *quickly*," Aunt Sissy added. "You remember what happened when we all joined hands. Consider the havoc we created, and there were only five of us."

Ella Mae thought back to the summer night when she, her mother, and her aunts had grasped hands. A fireball of light had formed in the center of their circle. It had been a swirling, gaseous sphere—like they'd taken a scoop out of the surface of the sun. It had dangled in the air for half a heartbeat before shooting through the window in a burst of dazzling light and broken glass. "A meteor? A bomb? I'm not sure what we made, but judging from the state of the sunroom window and the way the lake steamed where it struck the surface of the water, it definitely had destructive powers."

"You and Suzy need to see if this has happened before. Search through as much of our recorded history as you can," Verena said.

Ella Mae's mother nodded. "Not only do you have the use of all the materials at Partridge Hill, but Opal Gaynor is also offering access to the library at Rolling View. She's never shared resources before, and I'm glad to see that she's sticking to her vow to serve her community. I doubted your decision to make her an Elder, but you were right, Ella Mae. We need her."

"I'll call Suzy as soon as I finish watching this and set up a time to meet," Ella Mae said, and sank into one of Verena's club chairs to listen to the rest of the special report. Nuckelavee churned over the North Sea, beating the waves into a frenzy. The wind bent the treetops along the coastline until they looked like dancers bowing before an audience.

The next group of images showed scenes of people in line at hardware stores, putting sandbags around their homes, and loading possessions into their cars. The segment ended with footage of an old woman shooing her chickens inside a henhouse. The wind ruffled the birds' feathers, and a galvanized bucket rolled across the muddy yard. The woman's hair, which had been fastened in a bun, suddenly came loose and floated above her head like a dollop of whipped cream. Seeing this, Ella Mae was reminded of another woman. A local woman who'd once given her a recipe for banoffee pie.

"Fiona Drever is from the Orkneys," she said, turning off

the television. "Her daughter still lives there. I should pay Fiona a visit. It must be terrible for her to watch this monstrous storm bear down on her childhood home. I think I'll make her a pie before closing shop and head up the mountain to deliver it. Suzy won't be able to help until she gets off work anyway."

"That would be a nice thing to do." Aunt Dee smiled in approval. "What will you put in Mrs. Drever's pie?"

Ella Mae paused to consider the question. "Chocolate, pecans, and comfort. I'll serve it warm with a cup of strong tea." She glanced at her watch. "Speaking of tea, I need to get back to the pie shop. Reba and Jenny can serve the dessert pies, but they can't bake cookies and take care of customers at the same time. I'll let you know if Suzy and I discover anything useful."

"Until then, all we can do is pray for our brothers and sisters in Scotland," Aunt Sissy said, clasping her hands together. "May they all get out of Nuckelavee's way in time."

Verena drove Ella Mae to the pie shop in silence. It was only when she pulled up to the back door that she turned to her niece and said, "You seem different today. More clear-headed. I haven't seen you like this since before Hugh left."

"I found a way to put my feelings for him on hold," Ella Mae said, opening the passenger door. "Thank goodness I did too. If that clover in the middle of the storm was meant as a threat, then no one in Havenwood is safe. Isn't that why you're all so frightened? Because of that clover-shaped eye? Because it matches the burn on my hand?"

Verena nodded, her mouth pinched with worry.

"I have no idea what the presence of that clover means, but I do know that I have to be sharp as a knife's edge until I solve the mystery behind the storm."

"Cha ghéill sinn gu bràch!" Verena cried.

"Cha ghéill sinn gu bràch," Ella Mae echoed with slightly less gusto. Her mind had already turned to future tasks.

When she entered the kitchen, Jenny was loading a tray with servings of Leprechaun Pie. "What did you just say?"

"It's a Gaelic war cry," Ella Mae explained. "It means 'We'll never fall back.' Reba and I have shouted it a few times before, always in moments of trial."

Jenny rolled her eyes. "Let me guess. We're not going to have that peaceful springtime I was hoping for."

Ella Mae gave Jenny an encouraging smile. She didn't want to discuss the storm with anyone other than Suzy yet. "Maybe we just need a bit more luck. Speaking of which, I don't see any green on you today. Has anyone pinched you yet?"

Jenny glowered. "Yes, and once was enough, thank you very much! Mr. Ledbetter had half of my butt cheek between his fingers. I swear he's been waiting to do that since I started working here."

Despite the fact that Mr. Ledbetter had been way out of line, Ella Mae laughed. The man had pinched many a female bottom in Havenwood. Seeing as he was on the far side of eighty-five and legally blind, it was difficult to admonish him. "With all the squats you do, he probably couldn't grab an ounce of fat."

Looking pleased, Jenny said, "I won't have buns of steel if I keep eating pie twice a day. Anyway, I don't think old Mr. Ledbetter will pinch anyone ever again."

Ella Mae, who'd been gathering ingredients for the chocolate pecan pie, froze. "He didn't go after Reba, did he?"

Grinning, Jenny nodded. "She wrapped his fingers in duct tape and told him if he couldn't learn to keep his hands to himself, she'd be delighted to apply that tape to other parts of his body."

Both women were doubled over with laughter when Aiden Upton entered the kitchen through the rear door.

"Oh, I see how it is," he muttered crossly. "I'm sent off on deliveries while you ladies live it up without me."

Jenny walked behind her brother, jerked her thumb at his backside, and smiled at Ella Mae. "What do you think? Would Mr. Ledbetter like a piece of that? We could put Aiden in an apron and parade him next to Mr. Ledbetter's table."

Aiden waved his hands in protest. "No aprons! It's bad enough that I have to drive a pink mail truck. I draw the line when it comes to peach-colored aprons. My reputation as a ladies' man suffers enough doing this job, thank you very much."

Ella Mae tried to speak, but the image of Aiden bopping around town in her pink truck, which was emblazoned with images of pies and silver stars, had her laughing all over again. What made it so funny was that Aiden Upton could be the poster child for masculinity. Measuring well over six feet, he towered over the rest of The Charmed Pie Shoppe staff and was as brawny as a bull. His arms and legs were tree-trunk thick and his chest was as solid as a boulder. He wore tight T-shirts featuring soda or junk food logos that emphasized his incredible physique. Today's was a faded green Mountain Dew shirt.

"Come on, Aiden," Ella Mae said once she had herself under control again. "You look like the Incredible Hulk's younger brother. You could dress in a tutu and people would still find you manly." She gestured at his T-shirt. "At least you wore green. Your shirt probably saved you from being pinched by half a dozen bank tellers during your last delivery."

Aiden shook his head. "Nah. They know I'm off the market. Even so, the manager gave me such a nice tip that I'll be able to take Suzy to the Wicket tonight for green beer and pub food."

"See? Working here has its perks," Jenny said. She gave her brother's shirt a tug. "You're changing before your date with Suzy, aren't you?"

While Jenny teased Aiden about his limited wardrobe, Ella Mae was on the verge of telling Aiden that Suzy might not be free this evening when she stopped herself. Why should she ruin her best friend's date? She could start researching on her own and include Suzy tomorrow. One glance at Aiden's dreamy expression told her how much he was looking forward to celebrating Saint Patrick's Day with his girlfriend. Suzy and Aiden hadn't been dating long, but all of Havenwood knew that Aiden Upton was completely smitten with the lovely and clever bookshop owner.

"You two are going to have a great time," she said, feeling a mild stab of envy. She'd love to spend the evening at Havenwood's only pub listening to Irish ballads and exchanging bawdy limericks with the locals, but she had work to do. Grabbing a ball of dough and her rolling pin, she started rolling out the crust for the chocolate pecan pie.

"I have one more delivery on the schedule," Aiden said. "It's not far from Partridge Hill, so should I just head home afterward?"

When Jenny and Aiden had been forced to leave Oak Knoll, a small town in Tennessee, Ella Mae had offered them temporary lodging in her mother's large house. At the time, her mother had been trapped in the grove. After her release, she invited the siblings to stay with her at Partridge Hill as long as they wished. She told them multiple times that she enjoyed their company and would be sad to see them go, especially since Ella Mae lived on her own in the renovated guest cottage at the back of the property.

"Yes, go on home." Ella Mae said and then glanced at Jenny. "What are your plans for tonight?"

Jenny shrugged. "They're not as cool as Aiden's. I'm taking Miss Lulu out for a run, and then I'm heading to a friend's house—someone I knew from Oak Knoll—to gorge on mint chocolate chip ice cream while watching *Waking Ned Devine*. I love that movie. You should join us. It'll be a whole bunch of single gals wallowing—oh!" She stopped abruptly. "I didn't mean to imply that you were . . ." She trailed off.

"Open your mouth, sis. I'll help you stick your foot in it." Aiden chucked Jenny in the arm.

"I'm not offended." Ella Mae slid the pie dish into the oven and then smiled at Jenny. "I know what you meant. Normally, I'd jump at the chance to eat a pint of ice cream, but I'm going to stay here and make a treat for a woman named Mrs. Drever. She lives in the hills above the lake, and I haven't seen her around lately. It'll do me good to pay her a visit." Catching sight of the keys to her pink mail truck, she added, "Jenny, you should head out with Aiden. Reba can handle the rest of the tea service, and you'll be needing your car later anyway."

Jenny hesitated. "Are you sure? Aiden can always swing back here and pick me up." She held up her index finger. "Then again, if he has a date, he could be primping for two hours. The man takes longer to get ready than a girl going to her senior prom."

Aiden reddened but didn't refute the accusation.

Ella Mae laughed and shooed them both out the door.

Alone in her kitchen, she added pecans, brown sugar, corn syrup, eggs, and vanilla extract to a bowl. Gently stirring the filling, Ella Mae closed her eyes and called forth memories from her early childhood. She remembered being helped out of the bathtub. Shivering with cold, someone—it must have been

Reba—had wrapped Ella Mae in a big, fluffy towel and held her until she was warm. She flashed on another image. She was in her bed and had just had a terrible nightmare. Her mother appeared by her side, drying her tears with the corner of her robe while humming a lullaby. Ella Mae could almost feel the soft, ocean-blue comforter from her childhood bed and smell her mother's perfume of roses and moonlight. She poured these images and feelings of comfort and love into Mrs. Drever's pie.

"You look like you're makin' somethin' special," Reba said, startling Ella Mae from her reverie.

"I am. And I've sent the Upton siblings home. You and I need to talk." She pointed toward the dining room. "How many customers are left?"

"Half a dozen. They're all about done too." Reba narrowed her eyes. "But I can't wait to hear what you have to say. I can tell it's serious because you keep touchin' your burn scar."

Ella Mae hadn't realized she'd been doing that. Sticking her hand into her apron pocket, she said, "Yes, it's serious." And then she gave Reba an abbreviated version of what she'd seen at Aunt Verena's house.

"What does any of this have to do with Mrs. Drever?" Reba asked.

"Her daughter lives in the Orkneys, so she must be worried sick. I just want to check on her."

"She's the one who gave you that recipe for the banoffee pie." Reba raised her eyes to the ceiling and moaned. "I have dreams about that pie." Shaking her head as if to clear it, she looked through the window to the dining room and back at Ella Mae again. "Okay, so we'll drop by her place after work and then hit the books. I might not have Suzy's ability to memorize everythin' I read, but I can do my best to help you find what you're lookin' for."

Ella Mae smiled at her. "What would I do without you?"

Reba peeked through the window leading into the dining room. "Have a bunch of unsatisfied customers, I suspect. Be right back. It looks like everyone's finishin' up at once."

An hour later, the two women were in Ella Mae's truck heading north. They passed the newly paved streets leading to the mansions overlooking Lake Havenwood and continued upward. The road narrowed, winding its way higher and higher into the blue-green hills to where the forest became denser and tiny lanes sprang off the main thoroughfare like streams branching off a river.

"They all look the same," Ella Mae said, slowing down in front of a gravel road. "And half of them are missing signs."

"It's the next one," Reba said, her eyes eagle-sharp even in the fading afternoon light.

Ella Mae drove carefully over the bumpy lane. She didn't want to pass Mrs. Drever's driveway, and she'd only been to the secluded cottage once before. Last month, she'd accompanied Aiden on his delivery round, providing him with a short tour of the homes, trailers, and cottages dotting the hillside. Mrs. Drever's was one of them.

"This is it," Ella Mae said, turning into a driveway flanked by pine trees and mountain laurels. "I remember the faded violets on the mailbox. Mrs. Drever told me that her daughter painted those. She also asked me to call her Fiona the last time I was here, but it just doesn't feel right."

"It'd be like callin' one of your schoolteachers by their first name," Reba agreed.

Ella Mae pulled in front of a fairy-tale cottage. The snug, two-bedroom home was made of gray stone and had a periwinkle door with matching shutters. Every window featured a window box crowded with multicolored pansies, and the tidy garden was filled with birdhouses and spring blooms.

"Mrs. Drever must have gotten a new car," Ella Mae said, gesturing at the Ford sedan in the parking nook. "She used to drive a green Subaru. It had a Scottish flag decal on the back window."

Reba glanced at the Ford. "She traded down, then. This car's at least ten years old and the frame is startin' to rust. The only sticker is on the side window. See? It says, 'My Shih Tzu Is Smarter Than Your Honor Student.'"

Ella Mae frowned. "Mrs. Drever doesn't have a dog. At least, she didn't have one last month." Moving to the door, Ella Mae knocked three times. She waited, hoping to hear sounds from inside the house, but all was still. She knocked again. There was no answer.

"I don't think she's here," Ella Mae said.

Reba put her ear to the door. Her senses were far keener than Ella Mae's, so when her eyes widened slightly, Ella Mae felt a stirring of alarm.

"Do you hear something?" she asked.

"Not hear. Smell." Reba inhaled deeply and then tried the door handle. "Damn. It's locked."

Ella Mae touched Reba's arm. "What are you doing?"

"We need to get inside," Reba said. "I smell gas. Lots of it. Enough gas to put a person to sleep and make sure they stay that way forever."

Chapter 3

Ella Mae quickly moved to the nearest window and peeked in. Though the living room was stuffed with books and knickknacks, everything seemed to be in its proper place.

"I'll try the back door," she told Reba. "Can you pick this lock if need be?"

"I can kick the thing right in," Reba said. "I'll give you a minute to check other doors and windows, but if you don't find a way in, I'll make us one. Somethin' isn't right. I can feel it in my bones."

Ella Mae ran around the side of the house and mounted a small flight of steps leading to the kitchen door. She could now smell the gas too. She tried the knob. To her immense relief, it turned easily and the door swung inward with a slight groan.

"Mrs. Drever!" Ella Mae called as she entered the kitchen. She scanned the room, seeing a teapot on the stove and a mug and sugar bowl waiting on the counter. A plate with bits of bread crust sat nearby, and there was a jam jar and a crumpled napkin on the kitchen table.

Rushing to the front door, Ella Mae unfastened the dead-bolt. Without waiting for Reba to catch up, she continued into the living room. "Mrs. Drever?" Her calls were softer, more hesitant. The gas smell was growing stronger as she and Reba moved deeper into the house, where the bedrooms and small sunroom were located.

"The hairs on the back of my neck are standin' straight up," Reba whispered.

Ella Mae was experiencing the same sensation. There was an ominous silence in the back of the house that neither the ticking of the living room clock nor the birdsong from the garden was able to penetrate.

Stepping into the sunroom, Ella Mae instinctively covered her nose and mouth with her hand. The room was unaccountably warm, and she was surprised to see a fire burning in the hearth.

"Gas logs," Reba said, hastening to examine them. "This is definitely the source of the smell. You'd better open a window before we lose consciousness."

Ella Mae opened all four, inviting the spring air to sweep inside and do its best to dilute the invisible cloud of gas.

"The vent was closed," Reba said after she'd switched off the logs. "If Mrs. Drever sat here for more than an hour or so, she would have gotten real sleepy." She pointed at a splayed paperback resting on the arm of the sofa. Judging from the cover, it was a romance novel. "Especially if she was readin' the slow bits in between the steamy scenes."

"She might be passed out in another room!" Ella Mae cried. Racing into the hall, she poked her head into the first bedroom. The bed was made and unoccupied. The second bedroom, which was smaller than the first, was also empty.

However, a pair of pants and a green sweater had been laid out on the bed, and a suitcase was propped open on the blanket chest beneath the window. "It looks like she was about to get dressed. She could only be in one place."

In the hallway, Reba stood in front of the closed bathroom door. "Let me go first. We don't know what we'll find in there."

Though frightened by the possibilities, Ella Mae shook her head. "I came here to check on her and I'm going to do just that." And despite the ridiculousness of the action, she knocked on the door. It was one thing to wander uninvited through an acquaintance's house and quite another to burst into her bathroom. "Mrs. Drever? It's Ella Mae LeFaye. I'm coming in, okay?"

She slowly opened the door and for an instant she thought the room was vacant. But then she noticed the folded towel on the closed toilet seat and the drawn shower curtain. Her stomach knotted with dread. "No," she whispered and tiptoed across the tile floor.

Before she could protest, Reba sprang in front of her, pulled the shower curtain aside a few inches, and peered into the tub. Her face went taut and she made a hissing noise. And then she frowned. Her shocked expression was suddenly replaced by one of confusion.

Ella Mae reached for the curtain, but Reba grabbed her hand.

"Someone's in here, but it's not Mrs. Drever," she said. "And the poor thing isn't a pretty sight. I'd say this lady's been in the tub for quite a while."

Thinking of the uneaten toast in the kitchen, Ella Mae hesitated. "Do you recognize her?"

"No," Reba said.

"Maybe I will." Steeling herself, Ella Mae took Reba's

place and stared down at the figure in the water. It was difficult to look at the naked, submerged flesh without flinching, and Ella Mae's initial reaction was one of shame. This person, whoever she was, didn't deserve to be gawked at, but Ella Mae forced her gaze to travel up the woman's doughy body and until it came to rest on her bloated face.

"I think I've seen her before," Ella Mae said, taking in the curls of dark gray hair floating around the woman's head like a tarnished halo. She studied the thin lips, the mole above the left eyebrow, and the flaccid skin of her cheeks and chin, which was as colorless as bread dough.

"She takes care of her nails," Reba said quietly. "A French manicure on her fingers and fuchsia on her toes."

Ella Mae backed away and closed the shower curtain. "I'm guessing that's her car out in the driveway and her suitcase in the second bedroom. If so, she must have a handbag somewhere in the house."

Ella Mae was ready to get out of the bathroom. The woman's bloated visage was terrible to behold, and though Ella Mae was tempted to release the drain plug and let the water disappear down the pipes so she could cover the stranger with a towel, she knew she had to leave her be.

"I'll call for help," Reba said as Ella Mae headed into the second bedroom.

It didn't take her long to locate the woman's floral handbag. Inside was a matching wallet containing three credit cards, a library card, a blood donor card, forty-four dollars in cash, a photograph of a handsome, sandy-haired man in his thirties, and a Georgia driver's license.

"Her name is Joyce Mercer," Ella Mae told Reba after Reba had placed the call to emergency services. "I recently saw her at Canine to Five. She was picking up her dog, a Shih Tzu, from the groomer's. I remember because the hot pink ribbons in the dog's fur were the same shade as Mrs. Mercer's toenails."

"So why is she taking a bath in Mrs. Drever's house?" Reba wanted to know.

"I can't even begin to imagine." Ella Mae shook her head. "And where is Fiona Drever?"

The women retreated to the kitchen, where the remains of Joyce Mercer's breakfast sat on the table.

"Looks like she was about to fix herself some tea," Reba said. "Maybe she planned to have another piece of toast with her tea and that's why she didn't put the jam away."

Using the dish towel, she picked up the kettle by its handle and gave it a little shake. It was almost empty.

"She must have gone back into the sunroom to read while waiting for the kettle to boil," Ella Mae said. "It would have whistled when it was ready. Mom has one just like this."

"So Mrs. Mercer returns to her book and her cozy couch," Reba continued the narrative. "The fire's been on for a while because the sunroom's on the chilly side, but not long after she gets all comfy and starts readin', Mrs. Mercer feels the need to close her eyes for a spell."

"The chimney vent isn't open, so the gas from the logs must have made her very sleepy. But then the whistle from the kettle roused her." Ella Mae abruptly shook her head. "No, this reconstruction doesn't work. If Mrs. Mercer got up to return to the kitchen, why didn't she make her tea? Why suddenly decide to take a bath?"

Reba pursed her lips in thought. "She must have been pretty far gone when she got in that tub. She filled it all the way up, and then it looks like she settled into the water and blacked out. Slid under the surface and wasn't even aware of it."

"You think she lost consciousness because of the gas fumes and then came in here and drowned?"

"The whole thing seems crazy, but the cops will come and do their thing and then we'll have a clearer picture," Reba said.

Ella Mae glanced around the kitchen again. "Before they arrive, we should search for a clue as to where Mrs. Drever's gone. If I was worried about her before, it's nothing compared to what I'm feeling now. She's missing, and there's a dead woman in her bathtub."

"We can dig around, but we'd better not touch anythin'. You never know what the cops will look at." Using the dish towel again, Reba began opening drawers and cabinets while Ella Mae entered Fiona's bedroom.

The room had been done in shades of lavender and moss green. Like the living room, it was filled with keepsakes, but there was an order to the objects Fiona Drever had collected over the years and there wasn't a speck of dust in sight. Framed photographs covered the dresser, books and several porcelain figurines of barn animals occupied the nightstand, and a tartan blanket was folded across the end of the bed. Ella Mae opened the closet, feeling a prick of guilt for invading Mrs. Drever's privacy, and saw gaps in between the clothes where items had been removed and empty hangers left to hold their place.

"Your car and purse are gone. Some of your clothes are missing, and another woman is staying in your house. What's going on?" Not finding any obvious answers, Ella Mae took a moment to study the photographs. She'd never been to Scotland, but she guessed that the images were from the Orkney Islands. There were weather-hardened men posing by their fishing boats, school-age children standing on rocks overlooking the sea, and a lovely young woman waving from the doorway of a whitewashed cottage. Ella Mae recognized the woman as Mrs. Drever's daughter, Carol.

She was in her forties now, but her face hadn't changed much since the picture had been taken.

"Any luck?" Reba asked from the hall.

Ella Mae joined her in the living room. "I wish we could find an address book or a day planner. Maybe she's gone on a trip. Some of her clothes are missing, but I didn't rifle through the drawers. Someone must know why Joyce Mercer is here. If we can discover that, we'll know where Mrs. Drever went."

At the sound of car tires crunching over gravel, Ella Mae and Reba moved to the front door, which Reba had propped open to allow more fresh air into the house.

Officer Jon Hardy passed through the doorway and raised his cap in greeting. "Are you ladies all right?"

"We are," Ella Mae said, and stood aside to allow room for Officer Wallace to enter. The pretty policewoman, who had thick brown hair and a round, freckled face, smiled briefly at both women.

"Mrs. Mercer is in the bathroom," Ella Mae said in a quiet voice, and pointed down the hall. "We opened a bunch of windows and turned off the gas logs."

"Good," Hardy said, and strode off.

Wallace lingered behind. When Hardy was out of earshot, she asked, "Is she one of us?"

Ella Mae shook her head. "No. Neither is Mrs. Drever. I think this is just an accident. A tragic accident. It doesn't really make sense to me, but I'm not sure exactly how carbon monoxide poisoning effects people's behavior."

Taking out a notebook, Officer Wallace led them into the kitchen and invited them to sit.

"I know a bit about the symptoms," she said. "A person can start off with a headache or dizziness. Next, they feel nauseated. If the exposure continues, they become weak and confused, have blurred vision, and finally lose consciousness."

Ella Mae gestured at the teapot and glanced at Reba. "Maybe that's why Mrs. Mercer never made her tea. She no longer felt like eating or drinking."

"But why soak in the tub?" Reba asked. "Why not just curl up in bed?"

"If she was feeling foggy, maybe she thought a bath would clear her head," Ella Mae said. "If she felt dizzy, she wouldn't risk standing in the shower, so it would make sense that she'd take a bath instead."

Officer Wallace interrupted their speculations by having them recount their movements from the time they arrived at the house. While they were relaying their statements, an ambulance pulled in behind the police cruiser. Two EMTs jumped out and pushed a gurney to the base of the front steps.

Leaving Ella Mae and Reba in the kitchen, Wallace led the men to the bathroom. A short while later, the body of Joyce Mercer, covered by a damp white sheet and strapped securely to the gurney, was wheeled out of the house.

"Poor thing," Ella Mae said.

Officer Hardy, who'd been holding the door open for the EMTs, turned to her. "Did you know Mrs. Mercer?"

"No, but I feel terribly sorry for her family. This could have been avoided, right?"

Hardy nodded. "The vent was closed tight, leaving no place for the gas to go but into the room. Modern gas logs have an oxygen sensor and will cut off if there isn't enough oxygen, but these logs were made before the sensors became a requirement. There's a warning label near the power switch cautioning not to use the logs for more than four hours, but it's partially covered in soot and the print is quite small. It's likely Mrs. Mercer never saw the warning."

"It was probably chilly in the sunroom early this morning," Ella Mae said. "If Mrs. Mercer was reading there before breakfast, she could have been breathing carbon monoxide for hours."

Hardy jerked his head toward the bathroom. "I found preloaded insulin pens inside Mrs. Mercer's medicine kit. The EMTs believe she may have suffered a diabetic seizure while in the bathtub. It was probably that, or the carbon monoxide poisoning, that led to her drowning. We won't know until the ME sees her, but it appears that Mrs. Mercer's death was an unfortunate accident." He looked grim. "I have to inform her family as soon as I locate them."

Ella Mae couldn't imagine how difficult that conversation would be. She'd been involved in Hardy's investigations before, both voluntarily and involuntarily, and she held him in high esteem. He was a dogged police officer and a good man, and even though she'd been under suspicion of murder when they'd first met, he'd never failed to treat her with fairness and respect.

"This might sound silly, but if her family lives in town, would you give them the pie I made for Mrs. Drever? It was meant to be a gesture of comfort," she added when he gave her a curious look. "I thought Mrs. Drever might need it because an enormous storm is about to hit her hometown in Scotland. Her daughter still lives there, though I hope she evacuated days ago."

"I saw the storm footage earlier today," Hardy said. "A nasty beast. Reminds me of Hurricane Sandy. I have cousins in New Jersey who lost everything because of flooding. They could have used one of your special pies." He took the pie from her and wished her a good evening.

The ambulance drove away, and Ella Mae and Reba followed shortly afterward.

"Where to now?" Reba asked as they headed back down the mountain.

"Canine to Five," Ella Mae said. "I want to see Chewy."

Ella Mae wasn't the only dog owner waiting to collect a four-legged family member from daycare. There was a long line at the reception desk, and handlers were appearing from the back, leashed dogs in tow, at a steady clip.

Ella Mae never grew tired of seeing the daily reunions between humans and their dogs. As Ella Mae watched, a smiling yellow Lab strained at his leash, whining in anticipation as he drew near to a slim woman in a tailored suit. The moment he was close enough, he stood on his hind legs and licked her chin, nearly knocking her over in the process. Laughing, she scolded him and then knelt down to give him a big hug. Clumps of yellow fur clung to her navy jacket and pants, but she didn't seem to care.

Chewy's favorite handler, a young man named Max, waved to Ella Mae and hurried over. "Hi, Ms. LeFaye. Sorry about the wait. We should have Chewy out any minute now."

"I'm not in a rush. Just standing here puts me in a better mood," she said. "This is always one of the highlights of my day."

"Mine too," Max said, and headed to the back.

When he returned with Chewy, Ella Mae scooped her terrier off the ground and buried her face in his neck. "Hello, my sweet boy! Hello!" Chewy wriggled in her arms until he was able to bathe her cheeks with his tongue. Finally, she set him on the floor and reached out to grab Max by the shirtsleeve. "Could I talk to you for a quick sec?"

Max darted a nervous glance at Chewy. "Is this about Chewy's behavior report? Because we're still working on his—"

Ella Mae grinned. "It has nothing to do with that, though if Chewy lost any gold stars, I'm sure he deserved it. Actually, I was wondering if you knew a woman named Joyce Mercer. She owns a Shih Tzu."

Max nodded. "Coco Chanel. That's her dog's name. We all call her Coco for short."

"Have you seen Coco lately?" When Max didn't respond right away, Ella Mae added, "I'm not trying to be nosy. I just need to make sure that someone's looking after her. Mrs. Mercer is, um, not going to able to do that anymore."

"Really?" Max frowned in concern. "Because Coco's here. Mrs. Mercer is having her kitchen redone, and she told us the noise was bothering her dog. She paid for two weeks' worth of daycare and said she'd be staying at a friend's house. Her friend is allergic to pet hair, so that's why Coco's with us."

"I'm going to need to speak with Leslie about Coco. Is she in?"

"She's in her office. Go on back."

Ella Mae hadn't been in Hugh's office in over a month, and it was surreal to find Leslie Conrad sitting behind his desk. Stranger still were the feminine touches in what had once been a masculine space. Ella Mae glanced from the scented candles, potted fern, and floral cup holder and matching desk blotter to the wall calendar featuring puppies in the countryside.

Leslie looked up from her computer screen and, seeing Ella Mae, pretended to be upset. "What? You've come empty-handed? I'm afraid I'll have to charge you double this week."

Ella Mae laughed. "You wouldn't have wanted my Leprechaun Pie. Didn't you once tell me that you weren't fond of mint?"

Leslie grimaced. "No, I'm not. Mint makes food taste like chewing gum. And you know I'm just teasing. You've spoiled us rotten for months now." She pointed at the computer screen. "I just got an e-mail from Hugh. He left Scotland, thank goodness, and has arrived safely in Ireland. It sounds like he's having quite an adventure." She gazed at Ella Mae sympathetically. "You must miss him."

Ella Mae thought of the three letters she'd received since Hugh had left Havenwood. They'd been sent via airmail and, though Ella Mae enjoyed the novelty of receiving a real letter, she would have preferred more frequent contact. She suddenly wondered how many e-mails Leslie had received, and a dull ache bloomed in her chest. Ignoring the sensation, she nodded. "I definitely do. But you and the Canine to Five team seem to be handling his absence well. I know Chewy is a satisfied customer."

"That's sweet of you to say. In all honesty, the dogs are the easy part of this job. It's the owners that give me fresh strands of gray hair every day." She gestured at the empty chair on the other side of the desk. "Not you, of course. Would you like to sit down?"

Ella Mae took a seat and invited Chewy to hop up on her lap. She scratched him behind the ears and returned his toothy smile before focusing on Leslie again. "I wanted to talk to you about Coco Chanel, the Shih Tzu."

Leslie looked surprised. "Coco? Was there an incident between her and Chewy?"

"No, nothing like that. I'm afraid Coco's owner, Mrs. Mercer, has met with a terrible accident." Ella Mae hesitated, searching for the right words. "She passed away earlier today."

"How awful! Poor Coco!" Leslie's hand flew to her mouth.

"I was hoping you'd continue to board Coco until someone from Mrs. Mercer's family can come get her. At least she'll be looked after here and it'll probably take time for the Mercers to absorb what's happened and turn their thoughts toward Coco. I'd be glad to cover the cost—"

"That won't be necessary." Leslie waved off the suggestion. "We'll give Coco lots of extra love until her family
comes for her. It sounds like she's going to need it."

Thanking Leslie, Ella Mae took Chewy out to the car.
Reba hugged him and kissed his black nose and rolled down
the window for him. The terrier immediately stuck his entire
head out of the window, sniffing the air in anticipation of
the ride home.

"I think we should swing by the police station before we
settle down for an evening of research," Ella Mae said, and
explained why Mrs. Mercer's dog was in daycare.

"If she was stayin' at Mrs. Drever's house because her
kitchen was being redone, then it sounds like she lives
alone," Reba said glumly.

An image of Joyce Mercer's submerged face entered Ella
Mae's mind and she gripped the steering wheel, trying to
push aside thoughts of the woman's naked flesh filling the
tub basin or the bright pink of her toenails in the clear water.

"You okay?" Reba asked.

"I'm going to need a glass of wine tonight," Ella Mae
said as she backed out of Canine to Five's parking lot. "Just
one. It's been a helluva a day and it's not even six yet."

Leaving Chewy in the mail truck with the windows
cracked, the women entered the police station, where they
were told that Officer Hardy was busy and that Officer Wallace would meet them in the conference room.

Ella Mae groaned. "I hate that room."

"It's the artwork," Reba said. "A bunch of pictures of
grouchy-lookin' men in uniform and ugly landscapes."

"I think it has less to do with the paintings and more to
do with the fact that I spent a morning in that room believing
I was about to be arrested for murder," Ella Mae said.

As it turned out, the room was almost unrecognizable.

The walls had been painted a warm taupe, the metal chairs had been replaced by leather desk chairs on casters, and both the artwork and the portraits of former police chiefs were gone. Framed nature photographs occupied the longest wall while the state flag of Georgia hung between the room's two windows. The drab, brown curtains had been removed, and the blinds were open.

"This is a transformation worthy of HGTV," Ella Mae told Officer Wallace, and began to examine the photographs more closely. She was drawn to a nighttime image of Lake Havenwood. A full moon had cast a glimmering path across the surface of the water, and it was both inviting and eerie. Next to the image of the lake was a photograph of the rocks at the swimming hole. There were also photos of the stream in the park, the narrow waterfall in the mountains, and several snapshots of a deserted beach. "These are wonderful." She peered at the signature in the bottom corner of an image of a wave curling onto the shore. "M. Wallace. Are these your work?"

The pretty officer blushed and nodded. "I got into photography about a year ago. It took me half as long to talk the chief into letting me spruce up this room and hang my prints here."

"They're real nice, but how will you intimidate the bad guys when this place feels like a coffee bar?" Reba asked.

"Never fear. We still have a cold, gloomy, claustrophobic interview room down the hall," Wallace said, her dark brown eyes twinkling with amusement. "For now, I just need to review your statements and have you sign them. No interrogations necessary."

While Reba examined the paperwork, Ella Mae told Officer Wallace what she'd learned at Canine to Five.

The policewoman nodded solemnly. "Mrs. Mercer is a widow. Her son, Finn, lives out-of-state, but he's en route to

Havenwood. I was in Officer Hardy's office when he had to tell Mr. Mercer what happened to his mom." She shook her head, clearly saddened by the experience. "I don't think I could do that."

"You could if you had to," Reba said. "Our kind is made of stern stuff."

Officer Wallace's gaze slid to the row of photographs on the wall. For a moment, she looked acutely vulnerable. In a blink, she was no longer a confident policewoman in her late twenties but a lost and frightened child. But then she shook her head and became herself again. "I hope our people in Scotland are made of stern stuff. The storm will make landfall in two hours. It's going to be a nightmare come to life."

Ella Mae could almost hear the sound of the hurricane gale sweeping over roofs along the Scottish coast. In the starless night, the water would climb up beaches. Its liquid black fingers would creep over docks and claw at the shore. The fingers would quickly turn into hands. These would smash into fences, cars, and buildings. Thinking of the flooded streets, ruined groves, and evacuated towns made Ella Mae angry. She hurriedly signed her statement and pushed it across the table.

"I'm sorry about what happened to Mrs. Mercer." She stood up to leave. "Please let me know where Mrs. Drever has gone and if she's all right. You can call me as late as you'd like. Reba and I have hours of work ahead of us. We're going to make sure we're ready to battle a Nuckelavee should such a storm come our way."

Officer Wallace's eyes grew round as buttons. "That's impossible. We're way too far inland. Not only that, but our grove is way above sea level. It's a veritable fortress. A castle with boulders for walls."

Ella Mae paused in the doorway, and said, "No castle is impregnable."

"Maybe not." Reba gave her a little nudge, propelling her forward. "But think of all the cool weapons used to defend them. Arrows. Catapults. Vats of burnin' pitch. Maybe I need to add a few of those goodies to my arsenal." Reba sounded gleeful at the thought.

Her merriment was soon dimmed. By the time Reba and Ella Mae had prepared a quick meal of spaghetti Carbonara and salad and turned on the TV in Ella Mae's living room in search of news about the storm, they were shocked to learn that a cruise ship off the coast of Britain had been hit by a rogue wave and had foundered.

"Rescue efforts are underway," a reporter in foul weather gear shouted over the driving rain as the dark sea roiled behind him. "But conditions are making it nearly impossible to search for survivors. Relatives of those on board fear the worst."

"We're going to need more than pitch and arrows," Ella Mae said in a low and dangerous voice. Her appetite gone, she laid down her fork and turned to Reba. "It's time to learn what power is behind this killer storm."

Chapter 4

Ella Mae and Reba crossed the lawn and walked through the back garden to the main house. Ella Mae carried a glass of wine into the library while Reba went off in search of whiskey.

The lights in the library were blazing and a stack of books and scrolls waited on the large mahogany table in the center of the room. Ella Mae's mother sat on the leather sofa with a pile of loose documents on her lap. She wasn't looking at them; she was staring into the middle distance, as if lost in a memory.

Ella Mae stumbled upon her in this state more and more often. Even though her mother told her not to worry, she found it disconcerting.

"It's almost like a dream state," her mother said a week ago. "I've always been in tune with plants and flowers, but my bond to the natural world is far stronger now. Even though you separated my body from the ash tree, I am somehow still connected to it. Those roots ran deep. Very, very deep."

Ella Mae realized that it had been foolish to hope that everything would go back to normal after she'd freed her mother. Even before her mother had volunteered to become the Lady of the Ash, she'd been taciturn. Now, she rarely spoke. Her dark hair had gone silver, she no longer needed reading glasses, and she fell into one of her "lapses" several times a day. It was as if she were listening to music that no one else could hear.

Setting her glass on the table, Ella Mae quietly moved to her mother's side and touched her shoulder. "I'm here," she whispered.

Her mother blinked. "Good. I laid out what I could find on groups of our kind combining forces, but there must be more information than this. Is Suzy coming over?"

"No, she has a date. Reba will keep me company." Ella Mae noted the bags under her mother's eyes. "Why don't you turn in early tonight?"

Her mother smiled. "Do I look that bad?"

Ella Mae shook her head. "You're more beautiful than ever."

It was true. The LeFaye sisters were famed for their beauty. Though no longer young women, they still possessed radiant skin, lustrous hair, and captivating pewter-gray eyes. Adelaide LeFaye, the tallest of the four sisters, had always had the bearing of a queen. To Ella Mae, her mother's regal air hadn't diminished, but she'd become a bit of a recluse. She seldom left Partridge Hill, preferring to spend most of her time in the garden. She'd sit for hours among the plants, her hands turning the soil as she hummed the same melody to the roses and the rest of the budding flowers.

Her mother straightened the documents in her lap and handed them to Ella Mae. "I don't think I'll get much sleep tonight knowing what's happening in Scotland, but I'll try. I'll open the windows." Her voice sounded distant. "That way, I can smell the phlox and Solomon's seal blossoms. And if I gaze at the sky long enough, the stars look like clusters of white rue anemone petals growing in rich, black soil."

Reba entered the room and, after studying Adelaide's weary face, ushered her upstairs to bed.

When Reba returned, she took a gulp of whiskey and sat at the table across from Ella Mae. "Her senses don't turn off like ours do. It's like part of her is always tuned in to the natural world. Even when she sleeps."

"I know. She feels things and they influence her mood, but she can't put those feelings into words. They're too intangible, like a dream you can't remember no matter how hard you try." Ella Mae stroked the supple cover of a book bound in vellum. "Some days she's perfectly normal, but there are moments when I barely recognize her. I feel like I didn't really save her. Only part of her."

"She said it would take time," Reba reminded Ella Mae, and then gestured at the stack of reading material. "So will this. Just look at all these books. This is *not* my forte."

"Luckily, it's mine!" declared a voice from the doorway.

"Suzy?" Ella Mae smiled in surprise and delight. "Aren't you supposed to be with Aiden?"

Suzy shrugged. "I met him for a drink, but I'm not a big fan of beer, green or otherwise, and the pub is way too rowdy. Plus, Verena stopped by The Cubbyhole this afternoon. Ever since she mentioned your evening plans, I've been dying to come over and hit the books."

"That wasn't nice of her," Ella Mae said, and made a mental note to chastise her aunt. "Aunt Verena forced you to divide your loyalty, and it wasn't even necessary. I planned on recruiting you tomorrow anyway." She placed her palms on a thick tome. "You should be out enjoying yourself. These can wait."

Ignoring Ella Mae, Suzy turned to Reba. "I can take it from here."

"You won't hear any protests from me." Reba practically leapt from the chair and, grabbing her whiskey, raised it in a toast. "May the hinges of our friendship never grow rusty."

And with that, she was gone.

Suzy pointed at Ella Mae's untouched glass of wine. "One shouldn't drink or research potentially dangerous subjects alone."

"There's an open bottle in the kitchen. Feel free to bring it in here. This might be a long night," Ella Mae said.

Suzy covered Ella Mae's hand with her own. "You've had your fair share of late nights lately, haven't you? I'd say you've been through trial by fire this year. Just when you got your mother back, Hugh took off. I don't know how you've handled things as well as you have. If I were in your shoes, my pies would taste of disappointment and bitterness. Yet your food is still infused with good cheer. Verena said that you have so many wedding requests that you need to hire a catering manager."

"I offered the position to Jenny, but she said that the odds of her slapping the first bridezilla she came across were on the high side."

Suzy laughed. "No wonder she and Reba get along so well. Let me pop into the kitchen, and then I'll start reading. Just push a pile of materials my way."

Ella Mae complied and then opened to the page her mother had bookmarked in *Women of Arthurian Legend*. She began to read the chapter on the women of Avalon.

She instantly became absorbed in the author's description of life on Avalon, which was also known as the island of apples. Because the book was over two hundred years old, the author's florid descriptions enhanced the mystical nature of the isolated community of magical women. For several minutes, Ella Mae was transported from the library at Partridge Hill to a mist-veiled island.

"The author calls them priestesses," she murmured to herself, and began to jot notes on a memo pad. She continued to read about Avalon's hierarchy and how the Lady of the Lake ruled over dozens of women. Until now, Ella Mae had never heard of a group of people coming together to pool their magical talents. What the book didn't say, however, was what the priestesses did with their combined abilities.

"The Lady of the Lake is a title given to the most powerful woman of Avalon," she told Suzy after finishing the chapter. "Centuries ago, the first woman to become Lady of the Lake was a priestess called Nimue. According to this book, she was also Merlin's lover."

"And his nemesis. See?" Suzy gently pivoted an illuminated manuscript page so that it faced Ella Mae.

Ella Mae couldn't read the Latin penned so carefully in ink on the parchment, but she could decipher the meaning behind the exquisite images drawn in the wide margins. On the left-hand side, a bearded man was instructing a lovely young woman. He showed her scrolls in one scene, pointed out a bird in a tree in the next, and stood over a reflecting pool in the third. On the right-hand side, the older man and woman were caught in a passionate embrace. The last drawing showed Merlin being absorbed into a tree as lightning bolts flew from Nimue's fingers and tears dripped down her cheeks and fell on her pale blue gown.

"It's just like our curse." Ella Mae stared at Merlin and the tree. "He was trapped inside. Not dead, but no longer human."

"That's just one version." Suzy tapped on another piece

of parchment. "According to this author, Merlin is sealed inside a cave, but I've also read other interpretations claiming that he was imprisoned in a large rock or locked away in a glass tower. And while Nimue is angry and grief-stricken in the document you're examining, she's power-hungry and triumphant in the version I have here."

"Nimue." Ella Mae couldn't stop staring at the illustration. "The Elders told me about a woman named Nimue a few months ago. Apparently, she was an enemy of Morgan le Fay's. Though Morgan put Nimue under a sleeping spell hundreds of years ago, rumors have been circulating across the UK claiming that Nimue is awake and bent on revenge." Ella Mae shook her head. "Of course, that's ridiculous. Some crazy woman is using the name to scare people. She probably read the same books we're reading."

Ella Mae returned to her reading. After finishing the segment on Avalon from *Women of Arthurian Legend,* she reached for a tattered book of indeterminate age entitled *The History of Water Spirits: From the Greeks to the Celts.*

She and Suzy read in silence for over an hour. Other than the crackle of the fire and the whisper of turning pages, there were no other sounds. Finally, Ella Mae looked up from her book, and said, "According to this, Morgan le Fay was also the Lady of the Lake. She left Avalon to offer her services to Arthur following Merlin's disappearance. When Arthur refused to listen to her counsel, she retired to her castle on the coast. Both she and Nimue are referred to as powerful water spirits. The priestesses of Avalon all seem to have some connection to water."

"I stumbled across a passage about that too," Suzy said. "In this sixteenth-century poem, the Lady of the Lake is known for being as changeable and destructive as water, but then the poet adds half a dozen stanzas describing how these women could heal and stimulate crop growth using water. So, depending on what you choose to believe, these ladies either worked together to help their community or they used their magic to flood whole villages."

Ella Mae closed the book she'd been reading and sighed. "These stories are always contradictory. I remember how shocked I was when I first learned that Morgan le Fay wasn't evil. She was merely portrayed that way by male writers who didn't approve of her wealth, intelligence, or influence. The same could be said of Nimue. Is she, along with the other priestesses of Avalon, being rewritten as villain because she's a woman? And if water is their strength, then what's their weakness? What overcomes water? Fire? Earth?"

Suzy drained the wine from her glass and shrugged. "All I've found is a cryptic hint about alchemy. Not the turning-stone-to-gold kind, but ancient alchemical charts and recipes alluding to defeating a person who is able to control a particular element."

"Element," Ella Mae whispered the word. "What if there's an entire group of women who are also water elementals? What if they're like Hugh?"

Suzy pulled a face. "We shouldn't leap to any conclusions. We're just gathering information right now, remember?"

Ella Mae motioned for Suzy's laptop and searched for the footage of Nuckelavee that showed the clover-shaped eye. "I don't think this is a random occurrence. I think it's a message, and I believe it's meant for me."

Suzy stared at the image on the computer screen. "If I'm not helping customers, I'll do more research at the store tomorrow." She failed to stifle a yawn. "There are a few rare-book databases I can check out. I've never read about a group of our kind creating storms. In the meantime, what will you do?"

"Throw myself into work. Founder's Day will be here

before we know it, and if I can gather enough of our people in one place, we might be able to change our future for good. I'll keep researching too, but right now, I need to focus on all things pie."

"Is that realistic?" Suzy asked softly. "Can you just flip a switch and turn your other emotions off?"

Ella Mae thought of the chocolate raspberry pie in the freezer of The Charmed Pie Shoppe. "I have no choice." Her mouth curved in a humorless grin as she pointed at the wine bottle. "At the moment, however, I think I need a few more ounces of liquid courage. Being a queen kind of sucks."

Suzy laughed and filled Ella Mae's glass. "I'll drink to that."

The next day, Ella Mae turned on the television and was horrified by the damage Nuckelavee had done. By the time the storm had passed and a timid sun had shone down on the Scottish coast, the landscape was nearly unrecognizable. The waters of the North Sea had swept farther inland than anyone had imagined, flooding towns and villages and causing millions of dollars in damage. Livestock had drowned, crops were obliterated, and houses had been torn from their foundations. Fishing trawlers, ripped from their moorings, ended up on high hills, and cars were scattered throughout saturated meadows like lost sheep. People had been lost too. How many the experts could only guess, but the number was over a hundred and rising.

Ella Mae watched the coverage until she was too sickened and saddened by the sight.

In need of solace, she went to church and bowed her head alongside her fellow townsfolk. The congregation prayed for the victims of the storm, but neither the comforting

words nor the hymns nor the sunlight streaming through
the stained glass windows alleviated Ella Mae's anxiety.

What if it is *possible?* she thought on her way home after
the service. *What if that storm was made to serve a purpose? To destroy groves and create destruction? But why
would anyone do such a thing?*

With no answer to these questions, Ella Mae tried to find
a release by running for six miles. When she finally stopped,
her legs aching and her lungs burning, she felt almost human
again. Back at home, she took a very long, very hot shower,
ate a huge egg-and-cheese omelet, and played catch with
Chewy on the lawn.

When her terrier grew tired of fetching balls and sticks,
she made herself a chicken salad sandwich, wrapped it in
wax paper, and drove to the pie shop.

She entered through the kitchen, pushed through the
swing doors leading into the dining room, and gasped.

There was a jagged hole in the front window and shards
of glass were strewn across the pine floor. Resting at the
base of one of the café tables was a red brick. Ella Mae
quickly scooped Chewy into her arms and carried him back
into the kitchen. She then grabbed a broom and returned to
the dining room to examine the brick.

Moving carefully, she cleared a path with the broom and
then squatted down next to the brick. She picked it up, feeling its weight, and then flipped it over.

"What the hell?" she cried, and dropped the brick as if
she'd been burned.

There was a chalk clover drawn on its porous surface.

She retreated to the kitchen and called the police. After
asking Office Wallace to come to the pie shop to investigate
a case of vandalism, Ella Mae stroked Chewy. Her agitation

was contagious, and he began to whine and shift back and forth on his feet.

"It's all right, boy. It's all right." As Ella Mae soothed her dog, her own fright slowly morphed into something else. Anger.

Unable to sit still while she waited for Officer Wallace, Ella Mae brewed a pot of coffee. She poured herself a mug of hot, strong coffee, gave Chewy a treat, and was just composing an invitation for the upcoming History in the Baking event when there was a knock on the kitchen door.

"I saw the broken window," Officer Wallace said.

Ella Mae led her into the dining room. "Here's the projectile."

"Not very original," the policewoman said, turning the brick over in her hands. Seeing the clover, she added, "It could have been a Saint Patty's Day prank. We made a number of arrests last night. Several townsfolk had too many pints of green beer. A few of them are still sleeping it off in our holding cell."

When Ella Mae didn't respond, Officer Wallace touched her arm. "Do you have any known enemies?"

"Loralyn Gaynor and I have disliked each other since birth, but this isn't her style."

"Do you want me to write this up? I'm not sure there's much to investigate, but—"

"No." Ella Mae shook her head. "I'm sorry I even called you. I was scared at first, and then furious. But it's just a window."

Officer Wallace dropped the brick into an evidence bag. "I'll keep this just in case, and I'm going to file a report as soon as I return to the station so you can get an insurance claim started. I hope you know someone in the glass business."

"Reba does." Ella Mae reached for the broom. "Thank goodness we're closed tomorrow." She smiled. "Thanks for coming, and good luck dealing with the guys in lockup."

When Officer Wallace was gone, Ella Mae swept and vacuumed the floor, and then she and Chewy moved to the front porch. Ella Mae opened her laptop, took a sip of coffee, and tried to concentrate on creating an invitation again.

"How can I word this so that it sounds like more than a bake-off?" she asked Chewy. "Because it's so much more than that. It's a dynamic, multifaceted celebration of pie."

Chewy responded by releasing a contented moan and then rolling onto his back, his paws dangling limply over his belly. His eyes remained shut, but his nostrils were quivering.

"You keep chasing those dream squirrels." Ella Mae smiled down at him.

But Chewy was unable to sleep for long. A police cruiser pulled to a stop at the curb and Officer Hardy alighted from the car. Seeing Chewy, the two boxers in the passenger seat launched into a round of frenzied barking. Chewy bolted to his feet, his bark of surprise high and shrill.

"Shhh!" Ella Mae scolded. "He's one of the good guys." Setting her laptop aside, she gestured at the empty rocking chair next to her. "I see you brought your K-9 units with you," she teased, knowing full well that the boxers were Hardy's beloved pets, and then her smile vanished. "Is this an official visit? Because Officer Wallace already responded to my call about this." She jerked her thumb at the broken window.

He frowned and moved closer to the jagged glass. "When did this happen?"

"I don't know. I came in at lunchtime and found a brick in the dining room."

Hardy released an exasperated sigh. "If I discover any more evidence of last night's tomfoolery, I'll have to ask the mayor to impose a curfew for our next Saint Patrick's Day." He turned to Ella Mae. "I'm sorry that you have to deal with this, but I hope I can cheer you up a little. I was able to locate Mrs. Drever."

"Thank goodness!" Ella Mae exhaled in relief.

"She's in Edinburgh with her daughter," Hardy continued. "They're both safe, but Mrs. Drever was understandably shaken by the news about Mrs. Mercer. She and her daughter have booked flights and should be in Havenwood by tomorrow evening."

"And Mrs. Mercer's son?"

Hardy looked pained. "He arrived late last night. His mother's death has hit him hard. She was all the family he had."

Ella Mae fell silent. Here on the front porch, with birds flitting in the dogwood trees and clumps of cheerful tulips and daffodils swaying in the mild breeze, it seemed hard to believe that so many people were grieving. Finn Mercer. And countless people overseas.

In her mind, she saw the clover in the center of the storm. She thought of the clover drawn on the brick and couldn't help but glance at the identical shape burned into her palm. Closing her hand into a tight fist, she said, "Mrs. Mercer had a dog. Coco. She's at Canine to Five. Maybe seeing her would bring a measure of comfort to Mrs. Mercer's son."

"I'm sure it would. I'll let him know," Hardy promised. "He asked me to spread the word that his mother's memorial service will take place Wednesday morning. He doesn't really know who her friends were, and I'm afraid I'm not much help . . ."

Ella Mae waved her hands as if to dispel his worry. "Between my aunts and Reba, we'll pack the church." She paused. "I wonder if he's planning to serve food. If so, I could lend a hand."

"Apparently, some of his mother's cousins—people he's never met—are driving down from Pennsylvania and made it clear that they expected to be served funeral pie. Mr. Mercer has no idea what they're talking about, but I suspected you might."

"I do indeed, though it's definitely not a popular pie among my customers. You really have to like raisins to enjoy that pie. And I mean *really*."

When Hardy's mouth twisted in a grimace, Ella Mae had to laugh. "Are you the victim of a childhood raisin trauma?"

"I never cared for them. Despite that, my mama put them in everything. Cookies, bread, oatmeal, cakes, chicken, casseroles. Even in the meatloaf."

"Meatloaf?" Ella Mae shuddered for Hardy's benefit. "Well, if Mr. Mercer's relatives want a funeral pie, I'll make them one. Please tell him that I'll take care of the refreshments. No charge. With relatives like that coming to pay their respects, he'll need as much kindness as we can offer. I'll also add a few shoofly pies to the menu to mollify his mother's cousins. It's Hugh's favorite, so I've made it. . . ." she trailed off.

Hardy, who was adept at reading people, gave Ella Mae's hand a paternal pat. "He won't stay away forever. He can search the far corners of the world and not find anything better than what he has here." He gave her shoulder a reassuring squeeze and stood up. "I'll tell Mr. Mercer about your generous offer. Thank you, Ms. LeFaye."

After saying good-bye to Hardy, Ella Mae went into the kitchen to dig through her recipe box. She hadn't made a funeral pie in a very long time and wanted to make sure she had an authentic Amish or Pennsylvania Dutch recipe. Uncertain as to the origin of her recipe, she ended up searching the Internet for the history of funeral pie.

"The idea was to use shelf-stable ingredients," she told

Chewy, who appeared to be listening raptly. He sat on his haunches, his ears perked and his head cocked to one side, and gazed up at her. "Things that don't spoil," she continued. "Like raisins, sugar, allspice, cider vinegar, and flour." She clicked a link and was taken to another site. "According to this woman who posted her family's Depression-era recipe, the funeral pie was supposed to be so cloyingly sweet that the grieving family would forget their sorrow while having a slice. Do you think that would work?"

Chewy wagged his tail in reply.

"Shoofly pie is really sweet too. I'd better make some savory tarts to offset the heaviness of all those raisins and molasses. And we need something really special for Finn Mercer. Anything with melted cheese is comforting, right?"

Chewy barked in agreement.

"Yes, a triple cheese pie with a biscuit crust. I'll imbue it with the same warm and cozy memories I used for Mrs. Drever's pie."

Ella Mae jotted down a shopping list and ushered Chewy into her pink truck. After a visit to the grocery store and the farmer's market, she stopped at the hardware store for plastic sheeting and a staple gun. She returned to the pie shop, covered the broken window with plastic, and then spent the rest of the day making balls of dough.

On Monday, while waiting for the glass repairman to arrive, she e-mailed invitations to Elders across the country. Ella Mae didn't want to limit the attendees to her kind, so she sent a press release to cooking and baking magazines, pastry shops, culinary arts schools, and popular foodie blogs.

By day's end, she had a new window and her inbox was filled with messages. People were clearly interested in the event and in winning one of the handsome cash prizes, but reading through the e-mails became quickly overwhelming.

Ella Mae picked up the phone and called Aunt Verena. Her aunt had vast experience in organizing grandiose charity events and would know how to handle the array of inquiries.

"Just forward everything to me, dear!" Verena boomed. "You have enough on your plate, and I love the idea of luring folks to Havenwood. Your press release was so appealing that I'm looking forward to Founder's Day myself. It sounds very exciting!"

"We could use a different kind of excitement around here," Ella Mae said. "I don't want to find any more bricks in my dining room."

"The best response to a threat is not to let it bother you. Keep on keeping on," Verena advised, and hung up.

Ella Mae got to the pie shop early on Tuesday and began to roll out dough for piecrusts. She planned to make the food for Joyce Mercer's memorial service before working on pies for the shop, but she had barely lined two pie plates when Reba entered the kitchen with uncharacteristic reserve.

"There's a ridiculously hot guy on the front porch askin' to see you. Says he's Mrs. Mercer's son."

"Would you ask him to come through?" Ella Mae said, wiping her hands on her apron. "He probably wants to talk to me about the food I offered to make for his mother's memorial service."

Reba smiled. "We raised you right, your mama and me. Be back in a tick."

A moment later, Reba pushed open one of the swing doors and led a man wearing jeans and a leather jacket into the kitchen. "Go on in, darlin'. I'll brew us some coffee."

"Thanks, Reba." Ella Mae moved forward and pulled out a stool. "Would you care to sit?"

Finn Mercer ran a hand through his sandy hair and nodded. "I really wanted to thank you in person. Before tomorrow, that is. Complete strangers have been incredibly kind to me. Yourself included. No wonder my mom loved this town so much." He dropped his gaze and Ella Mae felt a rush of sympathy for him. She knew how it felt to lose a mother. She'd walked around like a hollow shell for months. And unlike Finn, she had the tiny flicker of hope that her mother could return to her one day. Joyce Mercer was truly gone, leaving her son alone in the world.

Ella Mae also understood loneliness. She knew how it ate away at a person's dreams, how it became a black hole inside the heart, devouring light and laughter.

"I'm sorry about your mom," she said gently. "That's what everyone says, but I know what you're going through. It's like a constant ache that only goes away when you sleep. It weighs you down and empties you out. But it *will* ease up. Not right away, of course. Things will be absolute crap for now, but it'll get better. And if you ever need to talk with someone . . ." she gestured around the kitchen. "I'm easy to find."

Finn gave her a small smile. He was attractive in a rugged, outdoorsman sort of way. She could picture him wearing a flannel shirt and striding into the forest to chop trees for firewood. In fact, he smelled faintly of wood chips. She glanced from his scarred and weathered hands to his wide chest to his face. His eyes were a golden brown and when he smiled, the spark of warmth in his glance reminded Ella Mae of Chewy.

"Officer Hardy told me that you and Ms. Reba found my mom. I'm glad you were there. I just wish that . . ." He paused to collect himself. "Anyway, thanks for checking on Coco too. She's back at my mom's place even though the guys are still working." He shrugged. "I figured my mom wanted that new kitchen, so they should go ahead and finish it."

"How's Coco handling the noise?"

"It's all detail work now, so there isn't much. I might

not be cooking for weeks in any case. The neighbors have brought more food than I know what to do with."

"That's the South for you," Ella Mae said. "Where do you live?"

"Baltimore. Mom used to be just down the street, but after Dad passed she went on a cruise just for widows and met Mrs. Drever. The two of them hit it off and started visiting each other. My mom fell in love with Havenwood and moved here." He traced circles in the flour dust on the worktable. "I thought she was crazy to leave Baltimore, but not anymore." He shrugged again. "There's something really peaceful about this place. Peaceful but not boring. Sorry, I'm not making much sense."

"Sure you are." Ella Mae began to roll out another ball of dough. She wanted to look at something other than Finn Mercer. He was so easy on the eyes that she was gazing at him a little too keenly. "We're so isolated that visitors often assume we're a sleepy little hamlet, but there's tons to do in Havenwood. However, it's when I don't feel like doing a thing that I like this place the most. You won't find more comfortable rocking chairs, hammocks, or porch swings anywhere."

Finn's brow creased and he spoke very quietly, as if afraid the tremors in his voice would prevent the words from escaping. "Mom used to spend every morning on her porch. Coco keeps going out there and staring up at the rocker near the door. She keeps looking for Mom. I do too . . ." Ella Mae saw Finn's face crumple in pain before he hid it in his hands. Without warning, he got to his feet and turned toward the door.

Hurriedly wiping her hands on her apron, Ella Mae came around the worktable and stood in front of Finn. Wanting to comfort him, to ease his ragged grief if only for a few seconds, she put her hands on his shoulders and gently pulled him toward her. "It's okay. Don't be ashamed to cry over losing someone you loved. Don't ever be sorry."

Finn's body was stiff beneath her touch, but then he suddenly gave in and his chin sank against Ella Mae's shoulder. His arms slid around her back and she echoed the motion. They held each other for a long moment. Finn silently cried and Ella Mae whispered to him. She breathed in his woody scent and tried to ignore how good it felt to be embraced by this stranger.

Eventually, Finn stepped back and dried his eyes with his jacket sleeve. "This isn't the impression I was hoping to make." He managed a wry smile. "I'd better go before I totally lose it. But seriously, thank you for everything. Especially that hug. That's the best thing that's happened to me in weeks."

Me too, Ella Mae thought. Aloud, she reminded Finn to stop by if he needed anything and, stealing a quick glimpse at his blotchy face, let him out the back door.

As soon as he was gone, Reba burst into the kitchen and placed two coffee mugs on the counter. "The coffee was ready five minutes ago, but when I peeked through the window and saw that you two were cuddlin' like a pair of—"

"I was just comforting him," Ella Mae interjected. She was about to elucidate when someone knocked on the door.

"Maybe that glorious man is back for another dose of 'comfort,'" Reba said. "Well, I'll be! It's Mrs. Drever!"

Reba hurried to let the older woman in. "I'm real sorry about your friend," she said, and touched Mrs. Drever lightly on the arm. "Such a terrible accident."

"That was no accident," Mrs. Drever declared firmly. "Joyce Mercer was murdered."

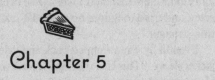

Chapter 5

"Murdered?" Ella Mae stared at Mrs. Drever. "What makes you say that?"

"For starters, my chimney damper was open the day I left," Mrs. Drever said. Her anger made her Scottish burr more pronounced. "I've been burning hearth fires for decades, and I'd never close the damper knowing Joyce would use the gas logs. She was cold-natured, same as me. Whenever she visited during the evening, we'd take our books into the sunroom. We'd read, eat chocolate, and drink wine. It was lovely."

Ella Mae heard the pain in Mrs. Drever's voice. "Maybe Mrs. Mercer closed the damper by accident."

Mrs. Drever shook her head. "I showed her how to turn the logs on and off. Joyce was a sensible woman. Too sensible to mess with the damper or take a bath with a foggy head." She jabbed her finger at the air. "Listen to me. I looked through Joyce's things. She's missing insulin, and there's no way Joyce would have given herself an extra dose. I think someone shut the damper, injected her with her own pre-loaded syringes, and dumped her in that tub. As soon as I saw the teapot, I knew she'd been killed."

Ella Mae and Reba exchanged concerned glances.

"We thought the scene was strange too, but with no signs of struggle and no clear motive, we assumed Mrs. Mercer's passing was an accident." Ella Mae studied Mrs. Drever. "Why would someone want to murder your friend?"

"Don't answer that yet," Reba commanded gently. "You look wrung out. Take a seat while I get you somethin' hot to drink." She briefly left the kitchen and returned bearing a steaming cup of coffee for Mrs. Drever.

"Thank you, dear." Mrs. Drever's face was etched with sorrow. "I think I was the intended target. I believe the killer didn't know what I look like, so he or she simply attacked the woman in my house, assuming Joyce was me."

Stunned, Ella Mae placed a sugar and creamer set in front of Mrs. Drever. "Why would anyone want to harm you? And if that's truly the case, the killer might return to correct his mistake. You should be talking with the police right now. I'm just a baker."

At this, Mrs. Drever let out a dry chuckle. "You are far more than that, my girl. You're the stuff of legends—the stories I heard when I was a child. The tales that helped us survive the long winters when the wind raked the rooftops and water froze in the blink of an eye. We passed the time hearing about people like you."

Ella Mae looked at Mrs. Drever in alarm. There was no point pretending. It was clear that the older woman couldn't be fooled. "How could you know? You're not one of—"

"You think I'm not *sìth* because you've never seen me in the grove," Mrs. Drever said, using the ancient Scottish term for magical entities. "I never entered because I gave up my gift many years ago. I let it burn down like a candle." She snapped her fingers. "And now it's gone."

Reba gasped. "Why would you do that?"

Mrs. Drever gave her an indulgent smile. "Once, I was like you. I had my own Ella Mae to protect. Someone we believed might save our kind from Myrddin's curse." Mrs. Drever cradled her warm cup and frowned. "We were wrong, of course. And because of that mistake, the girl I loved died. After that, I never wanted to use my abilities again. I wanted to hide. To forget. But you can't escape your past. You can never run far or fast enough. You can't distance yourself from something you carry with you."

Suddenly, without the slightest warning, Reba grabbed a knife from the cutting board and hurled it at Mrs. Drever.

It happened so fast that Ella Mae didn't even have time to scream. Her mouth opened in a wide O of horror as she waited for the blade to pierce the older woman's sternum, but Mrs. Drever's hand shot up, quick as a striking snake, and caught the knife by the handle. Then, as if nothing unusual had happened, she calmly placed it beside the sugar bowl and took a sip of coffee.

Reba grinned in delight. "Hot damn. Who would have guessed? Sweet little Mrs. Drever—"

"It's Fiona. Now that you've thrown a knife at me, there's no sense in being formal." Fiona gestured at the untouched piecrust. "You should keep working, dear. I don't want you to fall behind, especially if those are for Joyce's service. I heard that you offered to donate the food. That's very kind of you."

"Was Joyce one of us?" Ella Mae asked while transferring the crust to a dish.

"No. She was just a nice lady who loved dogs, sugary treats, romance novels, and her son. She was generous and loyal and funny. She was my dearest friend, and I have to find out who did this to her." Fiona picked up the knife and studied its sharp edge. "If Finn demands an autopsy, I'm sure they'll find too much insulin in Joyce's system. The police might still rule her death an accident, but *I* know that isn't the truth."

"There's no evidence—" Ella Mae began but Fiona drove the knife into the wooden countertop with such force that Ella Mae's words died in her throat. For a short, small-boned woman in her late sixties, Fiona was incredibly strong.

"You asked why someone would come after me, so I'll tell you. The woman I followed like a shadow for her whole life gave birth to a daughter. The father of this child, who cared about nothing but where his next bottle of whiskey was coming from, died the night of her sixteenth birthday. He was a fisherman. He drowned in a freak storm that came out of nowhere. Waves as tall as mountains sprang up, smashed his boat to bits, and disappeared again as if they'd been a mirage. Men fishing nearby said they'd never seen anything like it. The sea turned smooth as glass the moment his boat was gone. They also swear that they heard the sound of a girl's laughter being carried by the wind. Her mother and I knew then that she was very powerful."

Ella Mae was certain she already knew the identity of the child, but she asked all the same. "What was this child's name?"

"You know her name. I can see it in your eyes."

Gripping her rolling pin, Ella Mae whispered, "Nimue."

"Yes." Fiona pushed her coffee cup aside. "She must have found out that I was living in Havenwood. That I was living in the same town as you—the one person who could shatter her dreams."

"What does she want?" Reba's voice was nearly a growl.

"To restore the old ways," Fiona said. "To bring magic out into the open."

Ella Mae gaped in astonishment. "That's insane! We'd all be put in jail cells or psych wards. We'd be hunted."

"Or worse. We'd become people's weapons. Their lab rats," Reba said, her voice laced with venom.

"Our people are ruled by laws. We pay a terrible penalty for using our gifts in public," Ella Mae continued shakily. "So how is it possible for Nimue to disregard the rules? Is she above punishment?"

Fiona pulled a face. "More like immune to it. She's as strong as you, dear, and she also wants to unite our kind. But her means of accomplishing this are to destroy groves wherever she goes, forcing people to be dependent on her. She will rule our kind by fear. But that's nothing compared to what she wants to do to non-magical people."

Ella Mae raised her chin, her hazel eyes flashing defiantly. "Is she partially responsible for the storm that swept through Scotland? Or is she here in Havenwood, throwing bricks through my window?"

"I don't know where she is," Fiona said. "And I can't tell you the extent or limitations of her powers. I haven't seen her for years. But I have an inkling of what she wants."

"Which is?"

"Nimue believes she is the true Clover Queen and you are a false one. She will not rest until she proves that to our kind." A flicker of pain surfaced in Fiona's pale eyes. "I'm a threat because I know things about her that she wouldn't want shared. I'm a reminder of the life she left behind. Anyone near me is in danger, and I wanted to warn you."

Ella Mae walked to the dry-goods shelves and began to gather ingredients for the funeral pie. Taking hold of a box of raisins, she wondered how many more funeral pies she'd be making in the future.

"None," she whispered resolutely. She spent a moment

in front of her spice tins and ran her fingers across the tubs filled with sugar, flour, and nuts. Only when she felt calm again did she return to the worktable.

Reflecting on everything Fiona had said thus far, Ella Mae measured out raisins and dumped them into a saucepan along with two cups of water. Turning on the gas, she watched the blue flame spring to life and thought of Joyce Mercer. Had someone truly closed the damper, injected Joyce with too much insulin, and then dragged her into the tub to drown? If so, where was her killer now? Could this deranged woman named Nimue be responsible for Joyce's death?

When the raisins were simmering, Ella Mae focused on Fiona Drever again. "Tell me more about Nimue."

"I only knew her as a child," Fiona said. "She'd barely come into her powers when her mother died. I left Scotland shortly after that and never saw Nimue again. I heard she went to a boarding school in England where she disappeared along with a handful of other young women."

Ella Mae raised her brows in question. "Was she recruiting them?"

"I don't know." Fiona looked worried. "The women were declared missing by their families. Incidentally, they were all water and wind spirits."

Reba paled. "Sounds like trouble to me."

Fiona slowly got to her feet. "I should be going now—let you get back to work."

"Wait," Ella Mae said. "Will you be safe?"

Fiona shrugged. "I can take care of myself. My daughter, Carol, is staying with me now as well. She lost her home in that storm."

"I wish . . ." Ella Mae trailed off and then suddenly smiled. "Weren't you once the wedding coordinator for the Methodist church?"

"I was, but the job kept me from visiting my daughter. I wanted to go to Scotland during the spring and summer months and that's when most weddings take place."

Ella Mae studied the older woman, her eyes glimmering. "Seeing as Carol is in Havenwood now, would you consider working here on a part-time basis? I need a catering manager and—"

For the first time since she'd entered the pie shop, Fiona Drever smiled. The smile transformed her. Her face glowed and her blue eyes sparkled. "I accept your offer, Ms. LeFaye." She held out her hand and Ella Mae shook it heartily. "When do I start?"

Glancing at the raisins simmering on the stovetop, Ella Mae's delight in having Fiona Drever join her staff was instantly dimmed. "You've just lost your friend," she said softly. "You should take as much time as you need—"

"I'd like to help with the food for Joyce's service. It's the least I can do for Finn. It's my fault his mother is dead." Fiona raised her hand to stave off Ella Mae's protest. "We can't escape the past. Mine has caught up with me and it has cost Joyce her life." Her eyes turned hard. "I will avenge her death. With your permission, I'll go to the grove tonight and restore what's left of my gifts."

"Of course," Ella Mae said, still unaccustomed to granting requests.

Fiona left and Ella Mae concentrated on the funeral and shoofly pies. Once they were in the oven, she started making the day's savory pie—sausage and Swiss chard. She chopped onions and garlic and sautéed them in a frying pan. She was just adding a handful of crumbled Italian sausage to the mixture when Aiden entered the kitchen.

He sniffed the air. "Is that breakfast?"

"It could be," Ella Mae said. "How about a sausage, onion, and garlic omelet?"

Aiden grinned and patted his flat belly. "This job *does* have its perks."

"It's the least I can do. I feel like I ruined your date with Suzy."

He shook his head. "That was all me. I was acting like a frat boy at the pub. Pounding back green beer and shooting darts." He sighed. "I'd love to show Suzy that there's more to me than bluster and brawn. If I don't, I'm afraid she'll get bored with me."

"Nonsense. Suzy's crazy about you." Ella Mae cracked eggs over a mixing bowl. She whisked them rapidly until the yellow liquid was a froth of tiny bubbles and poured them into a frying pan. She then gave the sautéing sausage, onion, and garlic mixture a quick stir.

"I hope so," Aiden mumbled. "Anyway, I know you need her as much as I do. For different reasons, of course." He held out his massive hands. "But I want to help you too. You saved Jenny and me. We owe you big-time."

A sheen formed over the surface of the cooked eggs, and Ella Mae deftly flipped the pale yellow disc in the air. It fell back into the pan in perfect alignment, and she scooped the sausage filling into its center, folded the sides of the omelet, and slid the finished product onto a plate. She added a garnish of fresh parsley and a fan of sliced tomatoes.

"I do have an assignment for you," Ella Mae said as Aiden dug into his meal. "After work, I need you to get together with Reba to conduct some weapons research for me."

"Now you're talking!" Aiden exclaimed, his mouth stuffed with omelet. At times, he was boyishly charming, but there were times when he was simply juvenile. Ella Mae decided that he was right to be concerned about his relationship with Suzy. If he wanted to take it to the next level, Aiden Upton would need to put aside his youthful habits and become the man Suzy deserved. Someone who was not only strong and brave, but responsible and dependent too.

The oven timer beeped, and Ella Mae grabbed a pair of potholders and started transferring the funeral and shoofly pies to the cooling racks. Every crust was golden brown, and Ella Mae inhaled a whiff of buttery dough mingled with the syrupy scent of warm molasses and cooked raisins, an exotic hint of cinnamon and cloves, and the sweet tang of cider vinegar.

As Ella Mae gazed at the row of pies, she remembered the day Hugh had stood in this kitchen and told her about his grandmother—the one who'd made shoofly pies for him—and of how he loved to watch her cook. She recalled the affection with which he'd spoken of this merry, apple-cheeked woman. Ella Mae, who'd been rolling out a piecrust at the time, had been overwhelmed by feelings of tenderness for him. That longing still lingered in the depths of her heart, and though she sensed its presence, it didn't overwhelm her as it had in the past.

Ella Mae grabbed a fresh ball of dough, sprinkled more flour on the worktable, and drew the design of a wave in the center of the flour. "Fire is the opposite of water," she said to Aiden. "Electricity can travel through water, right? You're an experienced electrician. Help me find a weapon to stop water."

Aiden looked pensive. "Like harnessed lightning?"

"I'm not sure," Ella Mae admitted. "Something that can counteract both wind and water. Recruit anyone you know who has a gift for weaponry and brainstorm ideas."

"I'm on it," Aiden said without a moment's hesitation. "But what's this all about?"

Ella Mae shrugged. "You know that whole the-best-defense-is-a-good-offense theory? It has to do with that, and a water spirit. I'd go into more detail, but I have neither hard evidence nor facts."

"No worries. Messing around with electricity is my idea of fun." After saluting her, Aiden went to help his sister set up the dining room.

Doing her best to shut out thoughts of a killer prowling around Havenwood, Ella Mae dropped a handful of Swiss chard on top of the sautéed sausage, onion, and garlic. Once the leaves had wilted, she poured the contents of the pan into a large baking dish and added milk, beaten eggs, and Gruyère cheese to the mixture. After covering the entire dish with a lattice crust, she slid the entrée into the oven and started to prepare the filling for a large batch of chicken-and-mushroom pies with dill-flavored crusts. It was one of the shop's best-selling savory pies, and people called for it all year long.

The morning passed quickly. The Charmed Pie Shoppe was busier than ever, and two newly engaged women begged Reba for the chance to convince Ella Mae to make the desserts for their wedding.

"Tell them to stop by on Thursday and ask for Fiona," Ella Mae said.

When Aiden returned from his lunch deliveries, Ella Mae asked him to pop down to The Cubbyhole and purchase a day planner for Fiona. "Suzy can pick it out. And take her a generous helping of today's special. I'll pack sides of broccoli slaw and fruit salad for her as well."

Aiden darted into the dining room to add the money he'd collected on his deliveries to the till and then hustled back into the kitchen. He gathered Suzy's food and then paused at the door. "I have to ask. Why are you so worried about a water spirit?"

"Lake Havenwood is both wide and deep," Ella Mae said. "There's enough water in that lake to wipe this town off the map. I was in grade school during the Flood of Seventy-nine. Havenwood had an unusual amount of snowfall that year and during the spring thaw, all that water ran down from the mountains into the lake. And then it rained like crazy. The lake rose higher and higher until it turned into a hundred rushing rivers. Schools closed because the kids were needed to help line the downtown streets with sandbags. It was crazy. People traveled by rowboat for days. I'll never forget how Loralyn Gaynor decorated her boat like it was a parade float and got boys from our class to row her around."

Aiden looked thoughtful. "Come to think of it, I haven't seen Loralyn lately. It's been ages since she stopped in to complain about the food, criticize the décor, or insult the staff."

In the past, Ella Mae would have added a disparaging remark, but she felt only pity for her childhood enemy. Loralyn's father had been sent to prison, and her family's reputation, which she prized over anything else in the world, was forever sullied.

We both lost someone this winter, Ella Mae thought sadly. *Loralyn lost her father, and I lost Hugh. They're not dead, but they're gone.* She glanced at a postcard Hugh had sent from London. *Maybe our pain will bring us closer.*

Ella Mae would have a chance to make friendly overtures toward Loralyn sooner than she expected. To everyone's surprise, Loralyn resurfaced the very next day at Joyce Mercer's memorial service. Dressed in an impeccably tailored dove-gray skirt suit, Loralyn entered the church without fanfare and took a seat near the back of the sanctuary. She bent her head as if in prayer, but her eyes remained open.

"What's she doin' here?" Reba whispered.

"I'm going to sit with her," Ella Mae said. She was just about to make her way over to Loralyn when Finn Mercer walked down the center aisle and enfolded her in a powerful hug.

"Thanks for coming," he said.

"Hey, you're welcome to hug me too," Reba said when he released Ella Mae. "I can show you what Southern comfort really means."

Ella Mae elbowed Reba, but Finn already has his arms open. "Mom turned me into hugger when I was a kid. Guess I never grew out of the habit."

"A fine quality for any man to have," Reba said, resting her cheek against Finn's chest. "Is all this muscle from work or workin' out?" she asked.

Finn gently detached himself from Reba's grasp. "I'd have to say both because my job is a workout. I design and build custom wood furniture." He cast a mournful glance toward the front of the church, where a framed photo of his mother smiled out at the mourners. "Mom has a few of my pieces, but in general, my designs are too modern for her taste." He swallowed hard. "I can't seem to talk about her in past tense. I keep expecting her to show up and ask us what we're all doing here."

Ella Mae saw the sorrow in his eyes. "In a way, she is here. She'll always be with you, Finn. Some bonds can never be broken."

Finn nodded in reply. Fighting to regain his composure, he turned to greet Fiona and Carol Drever while Ella Mae made her way over to Loralyn's pew.

"May I join you?" she asked.

Loralyn didn't look at her. "Aren't you supposed to be polishing your crown or baking subpar pastries?"

"I decided this was more important than our tea service. I put a note on the front door inviting our customers to come to the service. This way, they can enjoy free food and support Finn Mercer at the same time."

"Always swooping in to save the day, aren't you?" Loralyn said with a sneer.

Ella Mae fell quiet. She watched people she'd known for
most of her life file into the church, exchanging hugs and
handshakes and then waiting in line to pay their respects to
Finn. Minister Davis stood at Finn's side, making introduc-
tions and bestowing his gentle smile on all the attendees.

Eventually, the thrum of organ music filled the sanctuary
and the minister took his place at the pulpit. Latecomers squeezed
into back pews as the organist launched into the opening strains
of "A Mighty Fortress Is Our God." Minister Davis asked the
congregation to stand and sing. Throughout the church, hymnals
were opened and people got to their feet. Except Loralyn. She
sat with a ramrod-straight spine and an implacable look on her
face. She didn't sing, she didn't utter any prayers, and she didn't
react to Finn's moving eulogy. She didn't even respond when
he picked up a guitar from the first pew, and said, "This one's
for you, Mom," before belting out her favorite song.

Ella Mae didn't recognize it at first, which wasn't surprising, since she hadn't heard it in a decade. She also wasn't used
to hearing it performed by one man instead of three. By the
time Finn reached the chorus, everyone came to realize that
he was singing "How Deep Is Your Love," by the Bee Gees.

The song transported Ella Mae to the carefree summers
of her childhood. She was suddenly a gawky preteen in a
Bee Gees T-shirt and denim cutoffs again, riding her bike
to the swimming hole or to buy a Coke at the gas station.
Her whole life had been in front of her then. She hadn't
known about magic. It was just something she read about
in books. And the books never mentioned the downside of
magic, the price that practicing it exacted. Storybook magic
was all about granting wishes, traveling to fantastical lands,
and defeating evil creatures with star-spangled wands.

If only it were that simple, Ella Mae thought.

Finn had nearly reached the end of the song, but he lost control of his voice in the middle of singing, "Keep me warm in your love and then softly leave."

He stopped abruptly. Tears streamed down his cheeks and dripped onto the guitar. He lowered his eyes and shook his head as if apologizing to his mother's friends and neighbors.

Fiona Drever rose to her feet. Very quietly, in a voice that was more whisper than song, she sang the next line. Her daughter joined in and by the time mother and daughter had completed the stanza, most of the congregation was standing, including Ella Mae.

They sang the last line, "We belong to you and me," over and over again until the words and the quiet melody wrapped around everyone like a soft, warm blanket. At that moment, Ella Mae had never been so proud to call Havenwood home.

Later, the guests filed into the fellowship hall to enjoy the food Ella Mae had prepared. She knew she should oversee the slicing and serving of the pies, but she lingered behind. Reba, Jenny, and Fiona could handle the food. Ella Mae felt that it was her duty to break through Loralyn's stony façade and at least try to offer her some comfort.

"Loralyn," she began in a quiet voice, "I know you don't want to talk to me right now. Or ever, maybe."

"What gave you that idea?" Loralyn asked acerbically.

Ella Mae took a deep breath and quelled her annoyance. "I'm really sorry about your dad, and I know that nothing I say can ease your pain, but believe it or not, people miss you."

Finally, Loralyn turned to face Ella Mae. Her mouth curved into a malicious grin. "Do they? Well, when I decide to fully reenter society, it'll be with a bang."

Ella Mae didn't like the sound of that. "What do you mean?"

Loralyn's grin morphed into a twisted smile. There was a cold, maniacal light in her eyes and her long nails dug into the soft cover of the hymnal. "If I were religious, which I'm not, I'd pray for this whole town to be torn apart."

Accustomed to Loralyn's hatred and scorn, Ella Mae was unfazed by her icy fury. "Then what are you doing here? Did you even know Joyce Mercer?"

"I attend all the funerals now." She flashed that damaged smile again. "It's my favorite form of entertainment. No one pays me any attention, but I get to sit here and witness people's agony. It's the only thing that makes me feel human these days."

Shocked by how deeply wounded Loralyn was, Ella Mae reached out to touch her hand, but Loralyn snatched it away. Without saying another word, she tossed the marred hymnal on the pew, stood up, and left the sanctuary.

Ella Mae watched her go, feeling a mixture of anxiety and pity, and then looked up to see that her mother was waiting by the entrance to the Fellowship Hall.

"What was that about?" she asked when Ella Mae joined her.

"Loralyn's taken to crashing funerals these days."

Adelaide LeFaye darted a quick glance over her shoulder to where Opal Gaynor was conversing with Sissy and Dee. "Her mother told me that she's been having a difficult time. You seem especially troubled though. Why?"

"Loralyn's a siren," Ella Mae whispered. "And my oldest enemy. I don't trust her, especially since she's acting so unstable."

"Opal will keep her in line. She's on our side now."

Reba waved at her from across the room and Ella Mae signaled that she'd be right over.

"We'll talk about this later," Ella Mae said. "At the moment, I have the unhappy honor of having to serve funeral pies."

Chapter 6

Weeks passed. March turned to April, and all of Havenwood seemed to burst into bloom. The dogwood trees were a riot of white blossoms, and the town's garden beds overflowed with blue speedwell, lavender larkspur, and prim lily of the valley. A sea of purple iris and periwinkle cornflowers crowded the patio garden of The Charmed Pie Shoppe, and a playful breeze tickled the wind chimes. Ella Mae's customers vied for seats at the café tables, and the waiting list Jenny oversaw grew longer and longer each day.

Ella Mae's mother tended the plants every morning. She fed and watered them, weeded and pruned, and hummed haunting melodies while touching the petals with her fingertips. As a result of her ministrations, the pie shop's patio garden was an enchanting place. The scent of fresh herbs mingled with the perfume of hundreds of flowers. Butterflies drifted from bloom to bloom, crossing paths with hummingbirds and honeybees.

Whenever Ella Mae took a break to chat with her customers, she found that all they wanted to talk about was the upcoming Founder's Day celebration. Lake Havenwood Resort was fully booked for the entire first week of May, and every hotel, motel, and campground within a fifty-mile radius reported an identical lack of vacancies. Locals had begun advertising rooms for rent, and these were snapped up almost as soon as the ads were printed. Adelaide LeFaye offered rooms at Partridge Hill to some of the Elders from other states, and her sisters quickly followed suit.

"You wanted our kind to come from all over the country? Well, I think you got your wish," Reba said one afternoon as she reviewed the History in the Baking guest list.

"I just hope I'll be able to put such an impressive assembly to good use," Ella Mae murmured to herself.

Ella Mae's days passed in a blur. She worked at the pie shop, attended countless meetings concerning the separate History in the Baking events, and tried to ignore the fact that Hugh had only sent her one letter in almost a month. He'd written that he was still in Ireland and had fallen under the country's spell. He described the geography of the small rural village where he was staying in detail, but said nothing of his future plans. Ella Mae pictured him strolling over green hills dotted with sheep and down narrow lanes lined with stone walls until he reached the pub. She could see him buying pints for the gruff, salt-of-the-earth men within. Once the ale had loosened their tongues, he'd ask them to share their local lore. He'd listen to their tales while trying not to look too eager. Too desperate.

Hugh had embarked on a quest to find a magical object that could restore his gifts. Ella Mae didn't think he'd succeed, but she also knew that he wouldn't come home until he'd exhausted every possibility.

"By then, you might forget where home is," she said, sliding his letter into her apron pocket.

"Which man are you daydreamin' about?" Reba had entered the kitchen with the stealth of a cat, causing Ella Mae to jump. "The hunky fireman or the hot carpenter?"

Ella Mae fixed her attention on the wedding checklist Fiona Drever had given her before she'd left for the day. The bride wanted an assortment of two-bite tarts, including lemon meringue, chocolate silk, raspberry and white chocolate mousse, key lime, and bourbon pecan. "Neither," she lied. "Besides, why would I be daydreaming about Finn?"

"Let me think." Reba tapped her lips with her index finger. "Oh, I've got it. Because he's a stud. Seriously, I'd let him smooth my rough edges any time, but the boy's clearly smitten with you. His face lights up like a Fourth of July sparkler whenever he sees you. Word has it that he's decided to hang his hat in Havenwood. He put an offer on that empty warehouse near the lumberyard. It'd be a great woodshop, don't you think?"

"The last thing I need right now is a distraction," Ella Mae said. "Especially the male kind. Finn's funny and sweet and, yes, he's very attractive, but I can't even think about men right now. I have to pour all my energy into my business and ensuring that History in the Baking is a success."

"I know that you're dealin' with lots of stuff, hon, but I also hate that you're all alone. More than ever, you need a partner. Someone to stand beside you and help you face the challenges life keeps throwin' at you." Reba frowned. "You've probably been too busy to watch the news lately, but the storm that flooded half of Ireland has moved on to Iceland. Rogue waves are poundin' her shores, and they've lost a dozen fishermen. Roads are impassable, and hundreds of homes have been damaged."

"Is there a grove in the storm's path?" Ella Mae asked.

"The only one in Iceland. It's at the base of a volcano, and the storm's triggered a glacier flood. The grove doesn't stand a chance."

Ella Mae was stunned. "How can this be happening?"

"If there's an explanation, you'll find it." Reba took out a licorice twist and bit into it as if she didn't have a care in the world. "Speaking of which, Suzy's out front. She wants you to go to the Gaynors' house. Says they have an ancient scroll that talks about water spirits. Maybe it holds the answers about these killer storms."

"I hope so, but I'm not feeling very confident," Ella Mae said. "After all, I've made no progress in identifying the person who murdered Joyce Mercer. *If* she was murdered, that is. No one's bothered Fiona, and Carol said that she hasn't seen a single suspicious visitor within a mile of her mother's house." She sighed. "And the research we've conducted on super storms has only led to more riddles. Cryptic metaphors in Latin, Greek, and Aramaic."

Ella Mae had a pile of water-spirit references at home. Her kitchen table was covered with photocopies and scribbled notes, and her head was filled with imagery from the epic poem *Beowulf.* She and Suzy had been reading dozens of scholarly articles on the poem because one of its villains, Grendel's mother, was often called a water witch. In every translation, this powerful and dangerous woman lived in or near a lake and possessed a magic sword.

"She sounds like the Arthurian Lady of the Lake," Ella Mae told Suzy one evening during a research session. "Except that she's described as a warrior too. The only way to kill her is by striking her with a sword made by giants."

"I think that's code for enchanted," Suzy said, and signaled for Ella Mae to pass her the article. Ella Mae was comforted by the knowledge that Suzy's photographic memory would store every word of the fifteen-page article.

By the third week in April, they'd exhausted their references on the Lady of the Lake and magical swords. They'd examined all known local sources as well as those they'd purchased from rare bookstores or found online. Finally, Suzy asked Opal Gaynor if they could examine the oldest documents in the Gaynors' library. These were not books, but sheaves of parchment, vellum, or animal skin kept in airtight containers and hidden in a small room behind one of the polished mahogany bookcases.

Not only did Opal grant them full access, but she also brought them sandwiches and cups of strong coffee. Her manner was still standoffish, but Ella Mae didn't expect warm and fuzzy from Opal Gaynor. That just wasn't in her nature.

Tonight, however, it was Loralyn who came into the hushed room bearing a silver tray. She placed it on the table where Ella Mae and Suzy were studying the crude illustrations on a cracked and faded scroll. Because it was encased in a glass box, Opal had lent them jeweler's loops. They were both so fixated on the strange images that they didn't realize Loralyn had entered the room until the thud of the tray being dumped on the table made them jump in their seats.

"Hot tea and ham and cheese sandwiches, compliments of my mother," Loralyn said with forced civility.

Suzy smiled at her. "This is such a lovely surprise! It's been too long since we've seen you, hasn't it, Ella Mae?"

"It has. Thank you for the hospitality, Loralyn." Ella Mae put down the jeweler's loop and rubbed her sore eyes. "I'm sorry we had to invade your privacy, but we're hoping the gems in this library will lead us in the right direction."

"Perhaps there are no answers," Loralyn said.

Loralyn sat in a leather armchair and gestured at the main

room behind her. "Every rug, painting, and stick of furniture that my father bought for that space is gone. My mother has replaced it all. My father's been replaced too. She's going to divorce him and marry that cretin, Robert Morgan."

"I wish you hadn't been caught in the middle of your parents' drama," Suzy said. "I wish they'd both put you first."

Loralyn shrugged. "I guess it's up to me to look out for me." A wistful expression crossed Loralyn's face. "It would have been nice to have had a sister. Look at your mother and your aunts, Ella Mae. Thick as thieves."

"Why do I have the feeling that you're up to something, Loralyn?" Ella Mae asked suspiciously.

Loralyn leaned forward and tented her fingers. "I have a major decision to make. I have to decide which Clover Queen to back." She turned her cold stare on Ella Mae. "It would be nice if I knew which one of you was the real deal."

Ella Mae couldn't conceal her irritation. "Do you plan on selling your services to the highest bidder?"

Loralyn's eyes flashed and, for a moment, she looked like her old self. Fearless and arrogant. "I would, but there are other people to consider. My employees, for example. And those who work for Gaynor Farms. Most of them have shown me more affection than my own parents. I can't turn my back on them."

Ella Mae's inclination was to distrust everything Loralyn had to say. After all, she'd always been a skilled actress and a master of manipulation. She stared intently at Loralyn. "The only person you've ever cared about is yourself, so why don't you tell me the real reason you're sitting here right now?"

"Ella Mae . . ." Suzy began, clearly shocked by her friend's rudeness.

Loralyn's mouth curved into a sickle-shaped smile. "I'll

pledge my loyalty to you on one condition. You must restore my father's gifts." When Ella Mae raised her hand to protest, Loralyn narrowed her eyes and lowered her voice to a dangerous hiss. "You need me, Ella Mae. If you ever come face-to-face with Nimue, she will crush you beneath her feet. She has something you don't."

"Which is?" Suzy asked breathlessly.

"A magic weapon," Loralyn said, pointing at the drawing in the margin of the ancient scroll. "The first sword ever forged, as legend would have it."

Ella Mae and Suzy exchanged astonished glances. "What legend?" Suzy shot to her feet in her eagerness to hear more.

"Give me your word, and I'll tell you all I know," Loralyn said, her gaze locked on Ella Mae.

It sounded so simple, but Ella Mae knew she couldn't accept Loralyn's offer. Jarvis Gaynor was a fire elemental. He'd committed murder. He deserved neither the return of his powers nor his freedom.

"Why are you trying to rescue your dad?" Ella Mae spoke very gently. "He betrayed you. He threatened to kill you. On the other hand, your mother protected you. She wanted you to see your father's true colors so you'd realize that your loyalty for him was misplaced. She loves you, Loralyn. Help us for her sake."

"I've been my mother's puppet for far too long," Loralyn said flatly. "I'm done with that now. My father never recognized my full potential. If I give him what he wants most, he'll see that I'm just as much *his* daughter as hers. We can build a new relationship. Make up for lost time."

Ella Mae's heart ached for Loralyn. Like everyone else, she just wanted to be loved and accepted for who she was. And like all children, she wanted her father to be proud of her. And though Ella Mae sympathized, she couldn't agree to Loralyn's terms. "I can't restore his gifts even if I wanted to," she said, hoping Loralyn would drop the subject. "If I were capable of such a feat, Hugh wouldn't be thousands of miles away searching for a way to restore his own."

"You'd succeed if you had the sword Nimue carries," Loralyn said. "With it, you could save both men. Because Hugh and my father bear little resemblance to their former selves. They're hollow shells. And Hugh will never come back to you the way he is now. Even if he does, do you really think he could love you again after what you did to him?"

Though the words punctured Ella Mae's veneer of confidence, she remained composed. "I'm sorry, Loralyn. I can't give you what you ask. Your father is volatile. He'd set things on fire to escape from prison and would undoubtedly hurt innocent people in the process."

Loralyn rose to her feet and turned to Suzy in appeal. "Talk to her, Suzy. You two can examine this scroll for days and still not find what you need."

"I will not agree to your terms," Ella Mae said tersely. "Not now. Not ever."

"In that case, prepare for heartbreak, Clover Queen." Loralyn's glare could have frozen water. "Your only hope of reuniting with Hugh Dylan just slipped through your floury fingers."

Loralyn's threat haunted Ella Mae through the rest of the night and into the next day.

"I need a joyful memory," she told Chewy on the way to Canine to Five the following morning. Chewy had his head out the window and was smiling his biggest doggie smile as his ears flapped in the wind. His eyes glimmered in the spring sunlight and his tail thumped against the passenger seat like it was a bass drum. At the first red light, he pulled his head and front paws back inside the Jeep's cab and pressed his body against Ella Mae's side. It was the equivalent of a Chewy hug, and Ella Mae scratched his neck and kissed his black nose in gratitude. He then licked her right on the lips and she laughed. Seconds before the light turned green, she glanced to the left and saw a little girl on her bike staring at them in delight. The little girl shouted, "Your dog is *so* cute!" before riding off toward the park.

"If only I could keep you in the kitchen, my heart would definitely be lighter," Ella Mae said to Chewy when they reached Canine to Five. "But I don't think the health inspector would approve." She nuzzled him once more before leading him inside and then drove the short distance to the pie shop.

In addition to the wedding order, Ella Mae also had to prepare pies for a birthday celebration. The administrative assistants from an accounting firm had chipped in to purchase treats for their boss and his partners and Ella Mae wanted to make sure they got their money's worth.

"He should be payin' for their lunch, not the other way around," Reba grumbled while Ella Mae assembled the ingredients for the birthday pies.

"At least these are easy," Ella Mae said. "Strawberry muffin pan pies topped with fresh whipped cream. I'll make extra for those sweet ladies who are surprising their boss. His name is Franklin Boggs. I don't think I've ever met the man."

Reba rolled her eyes. "I have. He walks around with a black cloud over his head all the time. An agin' bachelor who thinks of nothin' but numbers. Apparently, Ginny over at the Piggly Wiggly tried to tell him a joke once, and he told her she should stick to baggin' groceries because she had no future in comedy."

Ella Mae grabbed the sugar canister. "It's high time Mr.

Boggs lightened up. And I know just how to make him
smile."

Reba turned on the radio and then went outside to hose
off the patio and sweep the front porch. Ella Mae hummed
along to a Beach Boys song as she washed and chopped a
bowlful of glossy strawberries. Next, she gently tossed them
in granulated sugar. As her fingers carefully moved the berries, she closed her eyes and thought back to the moment
she'd first met Chewy.

She'd been walking home after a particularly challenging
culinary class, in which she and the other students had been
asked to make a *croque-en-bouche*. This French dessert was
made of cream-filled puff pastry balls stacked into a cone
and then covered with a caramel glaze and spun sugar. The
confection required a delicate touch and frustrated the most
accomplished pastry chefs. Ella Mae's creation had been
progressing nicely until she'd burned the caramel. Rehash-
ing her mistake all the way home, she'd nearly tripped over
a homeless man sitting near the entrance to the subway.

"Miss?" he called to her. "Please. Would you buy my dog?
I can't feed him no more, and you look like a nice person."
And then he took a squirming ball of fur from inside his coat
and offered it to her.

Reacting instinctively, Ella Mae cupped her hands
together to receive the precious bundle. The puppy whim-
pered and gave her palm a timid lick. And then he looked
up at her with eyes the color of melted chocolate and whined.
Ella Mae immediately cradled him against her chest.

"Does he have a name?"

The man shook his head.

The puppy started to shiver, and though Ella Mae's husband had told her time and time again that he never wanted
pets, she thrust her hand into her purse, pulled out all the

cash she had, and gave it to the stranger. "Can I do anything for you?"

"No, miss. Just give that dog a good life."

Ella Mae promised that she would. She took the puppy home, where he proceeded to piddle from one end of the apartment to the other. Despite the mess, Ella Mae cherished that first evening with Chewy. She recalled how she'd fed and bathed him and how he'd fallen asleep in her arms.

"I loved you from the moment I saw you, Charleston Chew," she said, opening her eyes and focusing on the pie filling. "Love is a risk worth taking, Mr. Boggs. If you rescue someone, they may rescue you right back."

Ella Mae lined several muffin tins with circles of dough, covered the dough with scoops of filling, and then sprinkled a crumble topping over the sugared strawberries. She then slid the pans into the oven and turned to her next task.

The day passed in a rush of activity. It was almost closing time when Jenny came racing into the kitchen, a big smile on her pretty face.

"Come quick! You have to see this!"

Wiping her hands on her apron, Ella Mae followed Jenny through the dining room and out onto the front porch. She arrived just in time to see a small parade of men in business suits and women in skirts and heels march by the shop.

Each person wore a sparkly party hat, and the procession was led by a beaming man holding the leash of a rambunctious border collie. He kept pausing to pet the dog and coo at him. His middle-aged face was completely transformed, and Ella Mae could see the boy he'd once been. He couldn't stop grinning, and there was a skip to his step that only joy could produce.

"Is that—?" she began.

"The birthday boy, Mr. Boggs," Reba said. "I just got off

the phone with Dee. She was at the shelter when all these folks wearin' party hats came in to adopt pets. Apparently, five cats and four dogs found new homes today, and Dee figured you had somethin' to do with their good fortune."

"So the border collie is one. And there's a Yorkie." Jenny pointed at one of the administrative assistants. "See his head poking out of that lady's bag?"

Aiden gestured at a tall man near the front. "And that guy with the red party hat is holding a wiener dog. He looks like a kid on Christmas morning."

"That man at the end has a chocolate Lab," Ella Mae said. "Look how happy they are together."

Reba frowned. "But what happens when the magic wears off? Will all these critters be returned to the shelter tomorrow?"

Picturing Chewy's sweet face, Ella Mae smiled, and said, "Don't worry. This kind of magic never wears off."

With the accounting firm's parade fresh in her mind, Ella Mae decided to pay Aunt Dee a visit.

Aunt Dee lived at the end of a long, narrow, tree-lined lane in a clapboard house at the edge of the woods. In addition to the dogs and cats she'd adopted from the shelter over the years, she fed and provided sanctuary to a number of strays. These animals scattered like autumn leaves when Ella Mae parked next to the enormous barn Dee used as her studio. Ella Mae let Chewy out of the Jeep, and he bounded away with a cheerful bark to play with the other dogs.

Blue-white flashes through the windows signaled that Dee was working on a sculpture. Slowly, Ella Mae slid open the massive barn door, stepped inside the vacuous space, and froze. Aunt Dee wasn't alone. There was a second metal artist, face completely obscured by a welder's mask, working alongside her aunt.

Moving into Aunt Dee's field of vision, Ella Mae kept her attention on the stranger, who was wielding a blowtorch. The visiting artist was male—he had the strong, stocky body of a bull and powerful-looking hands. Ella Mae was hypnotized by his movements. She watched, unblinking, as he deftly fused a metal wing to a bird's body. And then, her aunt switched off her blowtorch, pushed her mask off her face, and pointed at the ceiling.

"If you think that's impressive, look up," she said.

Ella Mae raised her eyes and gasped. There, hanging from thin wires, were hundreds of birds.

"You usually make a life-sized version of an animal who's crossed the Rainbow Bridge to help assuage the owner's grief," Ella Mae said. "Did someone lose an entire flock of birds?"

"It's just an experiment. We thought we'd create a huge kinetic sculpture. If it works out, we plan to donate one just like it to the new bird sanctuary. It would help make their opening night memorable. It's too hard to explain, so let me just show you what I mean." Aunt Dee signaled for her partner to turn off his torch.

"Ella Mae, this is Kyran Marravar. His name means 'warrior of light.' Though he lives in India, he has a visiting-artist position at a local college and agreed to pay me a visit and help with this project."

Kyran removed his mask, took a few steps forward, and held out a calloused hand. Ella Mae shook it while taking in the man's striking dark eyes and blue-black hair. Like Dee, he was in his early sixties, but his physique was that of a much younger man. A fierce light danced in his eyes, and his direct gaze made Ella Mae a little nervous, but then he looked at Dee and his face changed. All the hard lines softened and a glow came over his features.

"Kyran and I trained together many years ago. He's the only person I know who could create such an exquisite bird or such a unique light display." She gave Kyran a small smile. "Should we show her?"

Nodding, Kyran drew the thick privacy curtain over the room's only window. He then passed Ella Mae a pair of goggles, and he and Aunt Dee put their welder's masks back on. Reaching inside the metal bird in his hand, he pulled a lever and threw the sculpture into the air. It spiraled upward, its metal wings outstretched, and slowly flew toward the ceiling. "Get ready," Kyran warned. "In three . . . two . . . one . . ."

Suddenly, a flash of blinding light exploded from the bird. It was so bright that Ella Mae felt as if she'd been staring directly at the sun. Moments later, when the light had faded, Ella Mae's vision was still filled with sunspots. It was like trying to see past a wall of headlights.

"What was that?" she asked once her senses returned to normal.

"Directed energy," Kyran explained. "But I think I used too much. I hope that wasn't uncomfortable. Dee and I thought it would be wonderful to create a light show in the sky using these birds."

"It would be incredibly beautiful at night," Ella Mae said. "But you'll have to dial the intensity back quite a bit."

Kyran nodded and jotted a note in his sketchbook.

Taking a seat near her aunt's tools, Ella Mae watched the pair of metal artists until it grew dark. But as mesmerizing as it was to witness the delicate birds being crafted, Ella Mae knew she needed to return to her own work. Suzy had dropped off more books at the pie shop, which meant another long night of reading and note taking.

Waving good-bye to Aunt Dee and Kyran, Ella Mae left the barn and called for Chewy. On the way home, she wondered if her aunt and the handsome artist from another continent were more than former classmates. Ella Mae had always known that Dee, the youngest of the four sisters, had had her heart broken so badly that she vowed never to love another man. Had Kyran been the source of her heartache? Or was he the man who could make Dee's heart burst into life again— who could send it soaring like a bird freed from a cage?

Later that night, after she read until the letters became fuzzy, black blobs of ink, an exhausted Ella Mae climbed the stairs and dropped onto her bed. She hugged a pillow to her chest and gazed at the starry sky. She thought of Hugh, imagining him staring at the same stars, and was dismayed by the emptiness she felt inside.

Aren't I just like Aunt Dee? I've baked my feelings into a pie—trapping my heart within layers of chocolate and raspberry.

Eventually, she went into the bathroom to wash her face. After scrubbing off the day's dirt and makeup, she studied the quote she'd hung on her mirror frame, which came from a book of Native American legends. As rivulets of cool water ran down her bare skin, she spoke the line aloud, "You must become the rock the river cannot wash away."

Turning away from her reflection, she climbed into bed and fell, heavy as a stone, into sleep.

Chapter 7

The next day, as Ella Mae drove by The Charmed Pie Shoppe, she saw a man sitting in one of the porch rockers, a bouquet of flowers in his hands.

Her heart cried out, *Hugh!* but then the sun illuminated the man's sandy brown hair, and Ella Mae knew she'd been mistaken. Still, Ella Mae smiled as she turned the corner. Finn Mercer had that effect on people.

Entering the shop through the kitchen, Ella Mae switched on lights and ceiling fans and then unlocked the door leading to the front porch.

"Good morning," she said to Finn.

He jumped out of his seat, and his momentum caused the rocker to smack against the wood siding next to the window. Finn instantly dropped to his knees to search for signs of damage.

"I'd love to make you a set of patio gliders," he said, running his fingertips along the wall. "The porch is kind of narrow for these rockers. Look at all these dents." He pointed at the wall and then gazed around the space. "I can picture a row of gliders along the front and built-in benches at either end. I've seen your customers lining up at lunchtime. It would be nice to offer them more places to sit while they wait."

Ella Mae was just about to agree when Finn suddenly glanced down at the flowers and grinned. "I've had too much coffee. Can you tell? These are for you. They're, um, kind of a bribe."

"Oh?" Ella Mae accepted the arrangement of pink peonies, bearded iris, white hydrangea, and lilac branches. "These are beautiful."

"They're from my mother's garden," Finn said, looking pleased.

Ella Mae held open the front door. "Come on in. I'll put these in water, get the coffee going, and listen to your proposition."

"It's nothing indecent." Finn followed her inside. "Unless you'd like it to be." He quickly raised his hands and laughed. "Just kidding! I'll shut up now and let you work. And I can help. These hands aren't good at being idle."

Taking advantage of the offer, Ella Mae had Finn set tables in the dining room while she preheated ovens, started the coffeemaker, and removed balls of dough from the walk-in. By the time the coffee was done, the dining room was ready for lunch service. Finn had even distributed the bud vases Ella Mae's mother had prepared.

"Who does your flowers?" he asked, pointing at a narrow vase containing a peach-colored rose and several sprigs of ivy green Hypericum berries.

"My mom. She comes in early to tend the garden and refresh the bud vases." Ella Mae picked up the coffeepot and held it over an empty mug. "Would you like a cup?"

Finn shook his head. "No, thanks, I've had too much

already." He gestured at the wall clock. "Your mom and I must be on the same schedule. I keep waking with the sun. I feel strangely wired, and then I just can't go back to sleep."

"Does this have anything to do with the warehouse for sale? The one next to the lumberyard?"

For a moment, Finn was stunned, but then he laughed. "Nothing stays a secret for long in a small town, right? I'll have to get used to how fast word travels around here. But yes, the warehouse is a part of my excitement. In fact, I bought it. I'm going to move my business to Havenwood."

It was a nice change to hear happy news. "That's wonderful, Finn," Ella Mae said, and she meant it. "Your mother would have been tickled to know that you've fallen under the town's spell."

He nodded. "Now I understand why she called Havenwood magical. Tourists come here because it's beautiful and quaint and all that, but I want to live in Havenwood because of its people. I expected a few old ladies to attend my mom's memorial, but the church was packed. Every person made a point of sharing a kind word or story about my mom. And their thoughtfulness didn't end after the service. Folks stop by the house all the time to check on me and to bring me food. A guy I've never met before mowed my lawn yesterday."

Ella Mae could listen to such anecdotes all morning, and Finn's timing couldn't have been better. His praise of the place she loved redoubled her resolve to protect it.

"I'm glad I found you on my porch this morning," she said, smiling at him warmly. "I was feeling a bit down, and you saved me from sinking deeper into the mire." She took a sip of coffee and then pointed at the bouquet Finn had given her. She'd placed it on the counter next to the register so that everyone who came into The Charmed Pie Shoppe could enjoy the lovely blooms. "You mentioned bribery?"

"I did, and here I am talking your ear off about everything else." He shrugged as if it he couldn't help himself. "But I like talking to you. I'd like to get to know you better, and I could also use some business advice. I was hoping to share some of my ideas with you over dinner. You see, I'm used to selling directly to high-end furniture stores and boutiques, but I'd like to open a retail store in Havenwood. Hang up my own shingle, for once. I have tons of questions about how to do that, and since you're a small business owner, and the best-looking one I know, I was hoping you'd advise me over a decent meal and a better-than-decent bottle of wine."

Before Ella Mae could reply, Reba called out a cheery hello from the kitchen. After pushing through the swing doors with a flourish, she came to an abrupt halt. A licorice twist dangled from her lips while both hands were busy tying her apron strings.

Reba took the candy from her mouth. "Isn't this a pleasant sight? Everyone's all smiles this mornin'." She turned to Finn. "I hear you got a deal on that warehouse, and I hope you get your workshop runnin' real soon, because I need a new bed. A custom job. Mine is too small for certain acrobatic feats. For example, I can—"

"I'd love to have dinner with you," Ella Mae said hastily, ushering Finn toward the front door. "I'm off Sunday, so Saturday night works for me."

"Saturday it is, then. Oh, and dress comfortably." His brown eyes twinkled and he flashed her another winsome smile. "We're not eating in a traditional restaurant."

Finn had barely closed the door when Reba pressed her hands together as if in prayer. "Lord in heaven, this is good! I like that boy, Ella Mae. Goin' on a date with him is just what you need. You can't bake and research and talk about weapons every second of the day. It's not healthy."

"We're just having dinner. It's not a date." Ella Mae felt the need to correct Reba. "Finn wants business advice, that's all."

Reba rolled her eyes. "He brought you flowers. And I assume he set the tables too?" When Ella Mae nodded, Reba threw out her arms. "There you have it. Men don't set tables unless they want somethin'. In this case, that somethin' is you. Why not give him a chance?"

"We're ten days away from History in the Baking. Cheating on my boyfriend is *not* on my radar," Ella Mae snapped. Her anger was misdirected, she knew. She was mad at herself for responding to Finn's charms when her heart was supposed to belong to Hugh Dylan. Perhaps there was a drawback to putting her feelings for Hugh inside a pie. Maybe it was so easy to forget her cares in Finn's company because she'd emptied out her heart. She had to admit that she was looking forward to spending an evening with a handsome man who smiled often, laughed with gusto, and knew nothing about magic.

"Hugh told you not to wait," Reba said softly. "You think a distraction would be bad right now, but I think it's just what you need. Have a little fun before History in the Baking starts."

Ella Mae searched Reba's face. "Is that what I'm looking for? A few, carefree moments before I try to change the world?" She glanced at Finn's bouquet. "Maybe it is."

"Who knows what tomorrow will bring?" Reba took another licorice stick from her apron pocket. "Eat candy, smell the roses, and be romanced while ye may."

And with that, she folded the licorice stick in half, popped it into her mouth, and went outside to sweep the front porch.

On Saturday, Aiden and Fiona loaded the Jeep with the mini pies and tarts for the wedding and then drove off to the reception site to assemble the dessert buffet. Watching the Jeep pull out of the parking lot, Ella Mae sighed with satisfaction.

"Fiona seems to have The Charmed Pie Shoppe's burgeoning catering business well under control," she said while plating three lunch orders. It seemed like months had passed since Fiona Drever had lost her best friend. Neither Fiona nor Ella Mae mentioned Joyce Mercer, but sometimes she hung in the air between them like a ghost.

"Maybe she should join Jenny and me." Reba scowled and jerked her finger toward the dining room. "Because things are totally nuts out on the other side of those doors."

By the end of tea service, Jenny was echoing Reba's complaint. "No amount of Red Bull could have prepared me for today. People are already in town for History in the Baking. I spoke with a lady from Michigan and a gentleman who came all the way from Oregon. He went into great detail about how Oregon produces most of the nation's hazelnuts, and swears that he has a recipe for a chocolate hazelnut pie that can make women swoon."

"They're swoonin' because he looks like Grizzly Adams," Reba said with a cackle. "Did you hear the Michigan lady's speech on cherries? If she can't beat the other guest bakers with her cooking skills, she can just talk them to death."

Jenny dropped onto a kitchen stool and polished off her second can of Mountain Dew. "Forget about bake-offs and long-winded ladies, what are you wearing tonight?"

As tired as she was, Ella Mae felt a thrill of anticipation over her dinner with Finn. "He said we wouldn't be eating in a regular restaurant, so I won't get too dressed up."

"I bet he takes you on a picnic," Jenny said. "He obviously likes the woods."

A shadow of alarm surfaced in Reba's eyes. "Don't go

anywhere too isolated, Ella Mae. We still don't know who threw that brick. Or what really happened to Joyce Mercer."

"I won't." Ella Mae sighed, her merriment dimmed by the thought.

Jenny crumpled her soda can and frowned. "What about Fiona? Is it wise to trust her? I've spent plenty of time with her, and she keeps things close to the chest. If someone murdered Joyce Mercer in a case of mistaken identity like Fiona claims, then why hasn't the killer gone after her? Why would the murderer just vanish?"

Ella Mae and Reba exchanged befuddled glances.

"Maybe the killer learned that Fiona's gifts have been restored and she's no longer vulnerable to attack," Ella Mae said after a moment's consideration. "Fiona said the magic in our grove is like nothing she's ever experienced. Every blade of grass, flower petal, and tree leaf radiates power, and she's stronger now than she was in her prime."

"Thanks to you," Jenny said.

"If only I could use magic to bring justice to Joyce Mercer," Ella Mae murmured.

Jenny dropped her soda can in the recycling bin and smiled at Ella Mae. "You see yourself as an inept leader, but we all know that you're constantly working behind the scenes to improve our lot." She reached across the worktable and touched the clover-shaped burn scar on Ella Mae's palm. "I see what you do for us on a daily basis, and the sacrifices you've made over the past few months are written all over your face. You're worth following, Ella Mae. I know it, and they know it."

Ella Mae was so humbled by Jenny's words that she was afraid she might cry. Before she could say thank you, Jenny threw her arms around her shoulders and hugged her with all her strength. Not only was Jenny very strong, but she also possessed an extremely useful gift. When Ella Mae felt a rush of warmth and heat flow through her body, she knew that Jenny was using magic on her—infusing her with energy.

"There's your daily dose of skip-in-your-step," Jenny said and released her.

Ella Mae felt like she'd slept for twelve hours. "Liquid sunshine. That's what I call it."

"I didn't use it on any of my customers today. I figured you needed it more." Jenny made a shooing motion at Ella Mae. "Get out of here. Reba and I will close up shop. You need to take a long bath and make yourself pretty."

"When you're with Finn tonight, forget about your responsibilities. Just enjoy a beautiful spring night with a beautiful man," Reba added. "And I expect to hear all the details tomorrow."

In the hours leading up to Finn's arrival, Ella Mae and Chewy strolled through the gardens behind Partridge Hill. Jenny let Miss Lulu out to play, and the two dogs raced over the lawn and down to the lake's edge where they splashed about in the shallows and played tug-of-war with sticks.

Ella Mae left them to their games and meandered around the rose garden. Ever since her mother's return, the roses grew in riotous mounds of color and scent, forming walls of flowers and thorns that reminded Ella Mae of the illustrations from her *Sleeping Beauty* storybook. Taking a seat on a stone bench, she held out her hand and smiled in delight when a zebra swallowtail butterfly landed on her palm. The black-and-white butterflies were uncommon, and Ella Mae knew this one had found her for a reason.

"Show me," she whispered, and shut her eyes.

Suddenly, she was flying through a mass of dense gray clouds. She could feel the sting of a sharp wind and hear a deafening roar. Below her, she saw a large ship. A freighter, perhaps. Women in white dresses tied with braided belts of red and gold stood in a semicircle on the deck. Their attention was fixed on the woman at the bow. She wore a floor-length crimson dress secured by a belt made of gold scales. The buckle was shaped like a serpent's head and the snake's mouth was open. It was swallowing its own tail.

Ella Mae recognized the ancient symbol. It signified the eternal repetition of cycles and served as a reminder that the life force of certain living things could never truly be extinguished.

She wears red, the color of magic, Ella Mae thought. *And her belt is a constant reminder of her ancient title, Lady of the Lake. And of her authority.*

At that moment, the woman lifted her face to the sky. Her eyes were swirling gray storm clouds, and locks of her long, red hair writhed around her head like Medusa's snakes. Her beauty was both wondrous and terrible. Her mouth curved into a chilling smile, and she raised her hand in the air, as if in greeting.

In a flash, the vision disappeared. Ella Mae opened her eyes and looked down at the butterfly in her palm. It was dead.

"Are you all right?" Ella Mae's mother was suddenly at her side. She slid an arm around her daughter's waist. "You've gone very pale."

"I saw Nimue," Ella Mae whispered hoarsely. "And she saw me."

Her mother took the butterfly and carried it away. She returned a moment later and drew Ella Mae in close, like she did when Ella Mae was a child. She then stroked Ella Mae's hair and hummed the strange, haunting tune she hummed whenever she was tending the plants.

"I can sense her too," her mother said after a while.

"She's just like water—changeable and fickle. A woman with a frozen heart. Something must have happened to her to make her so numb. Find out what happened and you may discover her weakness."

Ella Mae raised her head and stared at her mother. "I deliberately sought numbness, so maybe I'm not so different from her."

"You are different, because you are loved. Where there is love, there is hope. These emotions are greater than any magic. Most of us don't live for power or fame or wealth. We live for one another. For friends and family. Husbands and wives and children. Sisters and daughters." She pressed her forehead against Ella Mae's, and Ella Mae smelled roses and moonlight.

Ella Mae thought of Loralyn and her desire for love. What lengths would she go to in order to be loved? Or at least valued?

Lifting her head, Ella Mae gently pinched a new rosebud between her fingers. Her mother put a hand over her daughter's and the bud began to swell. Ella Mae pulled her hand away and the rose slowly unfolded. Petal upon petal spread outward until the flower was the size of a salad plate.

"That's amazing," Ella Mae whispered.

Her mother touched the center of her chest. "Everyone has a heart as magical as that rose. Hearts can be changed. Healed. Restored. Remember that."

Just then, Ella Mae heard the sound of a car approaching. This was followed by a chorus of excited barking by Chewy and Miss Lulu. After giving her mother a quick hug, Ella Mae hurried out to the driveway to meet Finn.

"So, where are we going?" she asked once they'd left Partridge Hill behind.

"A place in town," he replied, a smile playing around the

corners of his mouth. "It's not known for its ambiance, but the food's good. And if not good, at least it'll be hot."

Ella Mae laughed. "What a ringing endorsement."

As Finn drove, he told Ella Mae how he'd spent the day cleaning out the house and bringing his mother's clothing to the church thrift store.

"That must have made you sad," Ella Mae said sympathetically.

"I was okay until one of Mom's purses fell out of a box I was handing to a volunteer. I picked up the purse and just stood there holding it. It was very manly. Me, clutching a pink leopard-print handbag and thinking of all the crazy stuff my mom wore. Yep. Very manly indeed."

"Everyone looks good in leopard print," Ella Mae assured him. "And I'm glad you brought her things to that thrift store. A few months ago, we had an influx of people from a small town in Tennessee. Most of these folks were let go when the town's biggest company suddenly decided to downsize, so they came to Havenwood to start over. Because it took a while for many of them to find jobs, they couldn't afford new clothes and household goods, but they *were* able to buy lots of nice stuff from the thrift shop."

Finn brightened. "That's what the volunteer told me. She said that not only would other women treasure my mother's things, but the proceeds from the sales would also be divided among several local charities, including the animal shelter. Mom would have loved that. Coco has to be the most spoiled dog in all of Georgia. And she's not helping my manly-man image either."

Ella Mae laughed again. "I think you should start carrying her around in a purse. Maybe a Chanel knock-off?"

"You're killing me." Finn mimed being stabbed in the heart. "If I ever get a second dog, I can see that it'll have to be a rottweiler or a bullmastiff. I'll get him a camo collar and we'll ride around town in a commercial grade pickup with a gun rack. No one will mistake me for a sissy after that."

"You're built like a lumberjack," Ella Mae pointed out. "I doubt anyone would dare to call you a sissy."

"That's high praise, considering that your deliveryman looks like Hercules. Where did you find that guy? At a strongman competition or a cage-fighting match?"

Ella Mae smiled, but she felt a familiar pang of regret that she'd never be able to tell Finn the truth about her employees, her family, or herself. To change the subject, she described Aiden's abhorrence of driving around town in a pink Jeep.

"Coco and I need to hang out with that guy," Finn said, pulling into the empty parking lot of a warehouse building. "I can bring the leopard-skin purse."

"Isn't this your new place?" Ella Mae asked when she was done laughing.

Finn's eyes sparkled with pride. "Welcome to Mercer's Furniture Design Studio. At least, that's what I went by in Baltimore, but I want the store to have a hipper name. I was hoping we could bat a few ideas around while we ate."

"Sure." Ella Mae glanced in the backseat. "Do you need me to carry anything?"

"Nope, I'm all set," he said, jumping out of the car and racing around to the passenger side to open Ella Mae's door. "Milady." He offered her his arm.

They walked to the front door, where Finn released her because he needed both hands to unfasten the padlock and open the heavy door. He then took two steps into the cavernous space and turned to Ella Mae. "The ambiance calls to mind a haunted airplane hanger." Picking up a battery-powered lantern near the door, he switched it on. "I'll hold the light. You follow the rope." He indicated a thin piece of rope disappearing into the gloom.

Ella Mae hesitated. Reba wouldn't approve of her stumbling around in the dark with someone she didn't know, but then again, Ella Mae had her revolver in her purse. She slid her right hand into the bag, touched the gun's cold reassuring metal, and used her left hand to grasp the rope. "This is very mysterious," she said, trying to sound casual.

"That's me. Finn Mercer. International man of mystery and owner of a pocket dog."

Ella Mae walked slowly, her body tense and her senses on high alert, but the second she saw what was at the end of the line, she relaxed.

"This was the best I could do without my full workshop," Finn said, hurrying forward with the lantern. "I thought you could use it as a staff table. Maybe put it out back behind the kitchen."

"This is way too wonderful to be tucked between the shop, the parking lot, and the Dumpster!" Ella Mae declared, running her hand over the café table. Finn had carved four plates into the circular top. Each plate held a slice of pie, and each slice looked incredibly lifelike, right down to the lattice crust and dollop of whipped cream. "I could put it on the front porch in between those gliders I'd like you to make for me." She stared at the table. "But I can't accept this as a gift. It's too much, Finn. I insist on paying for it."

Finn waved off the idea. "Not a chance. Trust me, you'll have earned it by the end of the evening. I have a whole list of questions for you." He pulled out his cell phone and glanced at the screen. "Ah, that should be our pies!" When Ella Mae raised her brows in question, Finn grinned. "Pizza pies. Nothing tastes better in an empty warehouse than pizza and cheap wine. Have a seat. I'll be back in a sec."

Finn returned carrying three pizza boxes and a paper grocery store bag. "I had no idea what toppings you like, so I told the pizza guy to surprise us." He put the boxes on the table and handed Ella Mae a paper plate. "I hope you're willing to live dangerously."

"Just this once," Ella Mae said, lifting the lid of the first box to reveal a buffalo chicken–and–bacon pizza. She showed it to Finn. "What's in box number two?"

He peeked inside, "Half Hawaiian, half Margherita. This *is* an adventure. You open the last one."

"Looks like an Italian buffet. There's salami, pepperoni, onions, and banana peppers." She sniffed. "And loads of garlic."

Finn held out his plate. "Perfect. Did I mention that this warehouse is home to several vampires? They should be dropping from the ceiling any minute now." He examined his watch. "Yep. It's officially feeding time."

"In that case, I'd better have a slice of that Italian fest too." Ella Mae pointed at a small piece. "It's a good thing I have a full pack of gum in my purse."

"Pffft!" Finn reached into the grocery bag. "That's what the wine is for. The better to smell you with, my dear." Using the Swiss Army knife on his key chain, Finn deftly removed the cork from the wine bottle and passed it to Ella Mae. "Can I start bombarding you with questions, or should I be a gentleman and let you eat first?"

Ella Mae poured wine with one hand and held a slice of pizza with the other. "I can multitask. Fire away."

Completely at ease with each other, the pair enjoyed their food, drank red wine from Solo cups, and talked.

Finn was in the middle of asking Ella Mae about payroll taxes when he stopped mid-sentence. A deep furrow appeared in his forehead as he stared intently at something over Ella Mae's head.

"Is it the vampires?" she asked, turning around to peer into the gloom.

Rising slowly to his feet, Finn grabbed the lantern off the table and raised it. When the light illuminated the shifting shapes, Ella Mae sucked in a sharp breath.

"Are those butterflies?" Finn murmured.

There were hundreds of moths and butterflies darting about. Monarchs, swallowtails, skippers, satyrs, admirals, and emperors flitted among tiger, sphinx, and luna moths. Ella Mae could tell they were agitated, so she closed her eyes and waited for them to deliver their message.

She saw smoke first. Smoke curling into the night sky. Smoke snaking through tree branches. Smoke hovering above a roof. The roof was burning. From the air, she had no idea what building the roof belonged to, so she willed the butterflies to show her more. And when she recognized the structure, she cried out. Her eyes flew open and she bolted from her chair.

"Finn!" she shouted, her voice shrill with urgency. "I need your keys! My aunt's barn is on fire!"

To Finn's credit, he handed her the key chain without hesitating. And he was right behind her as she sprinted for the door.

Ella Mae barely registered his presence. She couldn't think. Her mind was filled with the butterflies' final vision. In the midst of the hungry orange flames, she'd seen the body of a metal bird—wings crumpling as they melted—fall to the barn floor.

And next to where it fell, she'd caught a glimpse of a human hand. The fingers were curled like a claw, the skin bubbling and blackening.

Inside Dee's barn, someone was burning.

Chapter 8

Ella Mae drove at a reckless pace through the bustling downtown. Her dangerous speed earned her a plethora of angry horn blasts and hand gestures, but she didn't notice. Her entire focus was on getting to her aunt's place as quickly as possible.

She was so intent on her destination that she nearly forgot Finn was in the car. He hadn't spoken since they'd left the warehouse, and Ella Mae was grateful for his silence. Her mind was consumed by the image of the curled hand and the horrific thought that her aunt was lying unconscious and helpless inside a burning barn.

Motivated by desperation and fear, Ella Mae increased her speed even more.

The moment she rounded the final curve of Dee's driveway, she saw flames stretching into the night sky. She brought the car to a screeching halt as close to the barn as she dared and leapt out without bothering to turn off the ignition or shut the driver's-side door.

The barn windows were far off the ground. Someone could escape from the inside by climbing on a chair or a workbench and hauling themselves up to the sill, but seeing that they were still intact, Ella Mae feared that she was too late to save Aunt Dee.

"Break the windows!" Ella Mae shouted at Finn over her shoulder.

She then bolted to the front of the barn, taking in a potent chemical odor and the industrial-sized spray canisters scattered around the ground, only to discover that a heavy metal chain had been looped around the handles of the main doors. In the middle of the chain hung a massive padlock. Someone had deliberately locked Dee inside.

Ella Mae's cry of rage and anguish mingled with the wail of approaching sirens.

She pounded on the door for several seconds, screaming Dee's name and listening for a reply.

None came, so when she heard glass shattering, she ran back to the side. Finn had found a shovel and was using it to smash the windows. Shards of glass rained down on his head and shoulders, but he didn't stop. He raised his arms and swung the shovel like a kid clouting a party piñata, but the confetti falling around him was jagged and dangerously sharp.

"Someone locked the doors!" Ella Mae yelled as smoke billowed through the holes in the glass. "I need a bolt cutter, but all Aunt Dee's tools are in there!" She gestured wildly at the burning barn.

Finn pointed at the car. "We have a battering ram. Stay here and warn anyone inside to move away from the door."

As he rushed back to his mother's sedan, Ella Mae called out to her aunt. Fear made her voice hoarse, and it was hard to make herself heard over the violent noises of the fire. Just as Ella Mae paused to listen for a response from inside, there was a roar of crashing wood as the fire chewed through one of the rafters, and a chunk of roof collapsed.

Ella Mae was about to urge Finn to hurry, but there was no need. He already had the car aligned with the barn door and was reversing from the building as fast as possible in order to give himself room to build up a decent amount of speed. He paused only to switch gears and then hit the accelerator. The sedan slammed into the wooden doors, and they broke apart with a sickening crunch. The hood of the car was immediately engulfed in angry orange flames.

While Finn backed out of the splintered cavity he'd created, Ella Mae darted in, her gaze desperately sweeping the barn's interior as she continued to scream for her aunt.

And then she saw Dee.

Huddled in a far corner with a cat in her arms, Dee looked like a frightened child who'd tried to hide, to make herself as small as possible so that the nightmarish flames couldn't reach her.

Disregarding the heat and the fire raging all around her, Ella Mae picked her way over charred wood and lumps of melted metal until she was at her aunt's side. She didn't bother trying to rouse her. Instead, she attempted to pull Dee upward so she could get her over her shoulders, but there was no way to move Dee without dislodging the cat.

"I'll have to carry you both!" she cried to her unresponsive aunt.

She wrapped her arms around Dee's waist and gave a mighty heave, groaning with the effort. Suddenly, her burden became lighter, and Ella Mae realized that Finn was lifting Dee from behind.

"I've got her. You take the cat!"

The second the cat was safely pressed to Ella Mae's chest,

Finn draped Aunt Dee over his shoulders and headed for the exit.

As they drew closer to the fractured doorway, Ella Mae could feel the heat roiling over her. The smoke burned her skin, eyes, mouth, and throat. She thought she heard men calling out to one another, but it was difficult to tell above the crunching and cracking sounds of the insatiable fire. All she could think about was getting out and breathing pure air again.

To her immense relief, two firemen appeared in the space where the doors once stood. One aimed a jet of water at the flames threatening to lick at Finn and Ella Mae while the second darted forward to help Finn carry Dee to the waiting EMT truck. Cradling the cat in her arms, Ella Mae followed behind, her thoughts divided between a bone-chilling dread over her aunt's condition and the image she'd seen of the blackened hand. Dee's hands were red—too red—but not black.

"Someone else might be inside!" she told the fireman once he and Finn had carefully set Dee on a gurney.

"Got it," he said, leaving Dee in the hands of the paramedics.

Ella Mae watched one of them place a cushioned mask over Dee's face. As soon as it was in place, the second paramedic began pumping a bag, sending precious oxygen down Dee's throat and into her lungs.

"Pulse is thready. Starting an IV."

Ella Mae watched in mute horror. Her aunt had been reduced to a human doll. The paramedics pumped her unresponsive body with oxygen and fluids. Glancing down at the cat in her arms, Ella Mae saw that she'd wet the animal's fur with her tears.

Dropping to her knees, she laid the cat on its side, reached under its arm, and put three fingers to its chest. She was so happy to feel the feline's rapid heartbeat that she nearly cried out, but she still wasn't sure if the cat was breathing. Without asking for permission, she reached into the paramedic's kit and grabbed a piece of gauze.

Holding it under the cat's pink nose, she saw it move a little and knew the cat was breathing.

"Is she pregnant?" Finn asked, and Ella Mae looked at the cat's belly.

"I think she's nursing." She stroked the soft fur on the cat's neck. "There's an emergency vet on the road heading south out of town. You've already done so much, but would you bring her there? I need to be with my aunt."

Finn nodded. Helping himself to one of the emergency blankets stored in the side of the nearest fire engine, he tenderly transferred the cat onto it and wrapped it around her body as if he were swaddling a baby.

"They're both going to okay," he said as he got to his feet. "I promise."

Ella Mae swallowed a sob and squeezed Finn's arm. "I'll never forget what you did tonight. Thank you."

There wasn't time to say anything else. The paramedics loaded the gurney into the ambulance, and Ella Mae hopped in next to Dee. It was only when they were underway that she noticed the dreadful burns marking Dee's legs, arms, and hands.

"No, no, no!" she moaned, letting the tears fall freely. She wanted to touch Dee, to offer her comfort, but she didn't want to cause her more pain, so she grabbed the side of the stretcher.

"Is she conscious?" Ella Mae asked the paramedic who was rhythmically squeezing the oxygen bag.

He shook his head. "That's probably a mercy, miss. Hopefully, when she wakes, her burns will be cleaned and dressed and she'll be hooked up to a morphine drip. We doused the burns with water, but there's not much else we can do."

"Heaven help her," Ella Mae murmured miserably and stared at her aunt's chest. As long as it was rising and falling, there was hope, and Ella Mae clung to that hope with every fiber of her being.

The trip to the hospital seemed to last forever. The wailing of the ambulance echoed Ella Mae's anguish, and she longed for silence. Trying to block out the rhythmic shriek of the siren, she leaned over and whispered into Dee's ear, assuring her that everything would be fine and that she was in good hands.

Without her purse, which she'd left behind at Finn's warehouse, Ella Mae couldn't call her mother, her aunts, or Reba.

She needn't have worried, however, because they were all waiting outside the hospital's double doors when the ambulance pulled into the bay reserved for emergency vehicles.

Ella Mae's family stood shoulder to shoulder, gray-faced and silent with fear. The paramedics wheeled Dee into a restricted area, and a nurse with a kind but no-nonsense manner prevented Ella Mae from entering.

"Sorry, sugar. You need to go through those doors to the waiting room. I'll come out and talk with you just as soon as I can."

The automatic doors closed with a soft hiss, and Ella Mae stood inert, listening, until her mother put her arm around her shoulders and gently pulled her away. She led her to where the rest of the women stood. They all proceeded into the waiting room and stared at the plastic chairs. No one sat. No one spoke.

"How did you know?" Ella Mae whispered, looking from one grim face to the next.

"My police scanner," Reba said. "I was relaxin' after our

crazy day when the dispatcher used the code for fire followed by another code requestin' EMTs. I thought I must have had too much to drink when the woman gave out Dee's address, but when she repeated it a second time, I knew it wasn't a mistake. I called your mama from the car and Verena phoned the dispatcher. She told us they were bringin' Dee here."

Aunt Sissy balled her hands into tight fists. "Tell us, Ella Mae. How bad is it?"

"She's alive," Ella Mae said. Her voice trembled and she fought to keep it steady. "The EMTs were giving her oxygen, so I'm not sure if she can breathe on her own. And they said her pulse was thready."

Verena shook her head in dismay. "That means it's weak. Oh, my sweet, gentle Dee. You need to be stronger than you've ever been."

"Can't we do anything?" Ella Mae asked. "Don't we know someone with healing abilities?"

"We do," her mother said. "In fact, he works at this hospital and is with her now. But there are limits to what he can do." She swallowed hard. "Was she burned very badly? Was that man, Marravar, with her? He—"

"Adelaide!" Verena's tone was harsh. "This is *not* the time!"

Ella Mae gazed into the middle distance. Once again, she saw the curled and blackened hand. "If Kyran Marravar was inside that barn, then he's dead. Before I even left for Dee's, the butterflies showed me an image of someone long past the point of rescue." Picturing the chain and padlock on the barn door, she let loose an animalistic growl. "Someone locked them inside! Doused the barn with an accelerant and struck a match."

Sissy released a shrill cry. "The fire just needed to reach the bird sculptures. There were *so* many of them. All those birds would have created light pulses."

"Yes," Verena agreed, her voice cold with rage. "They would have blinded the two people who created them."

"They would have been too confused to react," Ella Mae's mother continued in a voice that was nearly a moan. "How did Dee survive at all?"

"The important thing is that she did," Reba declared fervently. "And she'll recover." She pointed at the door to the restricted area. "As soon as that nurse comes back and fills us in on Dee's condition, I need to go look at what's left of the barn."

"If Kyran was inside, the whole area will be a crime scene now," Sissy said, and then her lips began to tremble. "What about Dee's animals? I hope they weren't injured. Those poor creatures!"

Ella Mae told them about the cat she'd found in Dee's arms and then went on to describe Finn's heroics.

"He should be at the emergency clinic by now, but I can't even call to ask him about the cat." She grabbed Reba's arm. "My purse is back at his warehouse. I have to get to it before Finn does. My gun is in that bag."

"We'll get it," her mother said. "But not now. I'm not leaving this room until I know how Dee is doing."

They didn't have to wait long before the nurse who'd taken Dee into a trauma room stepped through the automatic doors leading to the restricted area.

"Are you with Delia LeFaye?" she asked.

Ella Mae was unaccustomed to hearing Dee's full name. In that moment, it sounded especially beautiful. Delicate as wedding lace. As gentle as a summer rain.

"We're Delia's family," Verena replied. "Please. How is she?"

"She's stable." The nurse gave them a reassuring smile. "The doctor is recommending that she be moved to the Grady Burn Center in Atlanta. Their facility is excellent and their complicated-wound management is second to none. Ms. LeFaye would definitely benefit from their hydrotherapy tables, and she'd be more comfortable in one of their private rooms. They have zoned-air surface beds that adjust to the patient's weight, and lots of other specialized equipment. And they offer physical and occupational therapy too."

Everyone looked at Verena. "If her doctor thinks she can be moved, then we'd like her to go to Atlanta." She searched the nurse's face. "This sounds very serious. Can we see her?"

"Not yet, I'm afraid." The nurse gestured toward the registration desk. "The faster we can get the paperwork completed, the faster we can transfer Ms. LeFaye to Grady. We've already talked to them, and they have a bed available, so that's good news. I'll meet you at the counter when you're ready."

When she was out of earshot, Verena turned to Reba. "Go to Dee's and look around. I want to know what happened." Her eyes blazed with fury. "If the cops are there, then watch them from a distance. Try to learn what they know. Use that exceptional hearing of yours. And once they've gone, conduct your own search. Look inside Dee's house. Examine everything. Dee's privacy isn't as important as her life. There must be some clue as to who tried to murder her."

"Adelaide, you should take Ella Mae home," Aunt Sissy said after Reba left. "She's covered in soot." Studying Ella Mae, she frowned. "Your shirt is full of holes. Maybe we should have a doctor examine you."

Ella Mae glanced down at her ruined shirt with a feeling of complete detachment. "My eyes and throat hurt from the smoke, but I didn't get burned. The fire hadn't reached the corner where Dee was huddled. Luckily, the metal storage unit where she keeps her tools had fallen at an angle that created a buffer against the flames."

"I'll give her herbal tea and chicken soup to soothe her

throat. And I have eye drops at home as well," Ella Mae's mother said, but she didn't move. "I don't want to leave Dee. She's my baby sister."

Sissy was about to respond when Officer Wallace and a second policeman Ella Mae recognized but didn't know by name appeared in the waiting area.

"We just came from Ms. LeFaye's." Officer Wallace's brown eyes were filled with concern. "How is she?"

"In stable condition," Ella Mae's mother said. "They're making arrangements to transfer her to the burn center in Atlanta."

Officer Wallace seemed taken aback by the news. "Already? Is she awake and lucid? Officer Bristol and I need to speak with her."

"No one is allowed to see her," Aunt Sissy said curtly. "Not even us, and we're *family*."

Officer Bristol turned to Ella Mae. "I understand you were on the scene before the fire department. Could you tell us everything that happened from the moment you arrived at Ms. LeFaye's residence? Please include as many details as you can. You never know what might be important."

Ella Mae shot a quick glance at Officer Wallace, who gave her the briefest of nods, as if granting her permission to provide an edited version of events to her non-magical partner. "Before I do, would you answer one question?"

"If I'm able," Bristol said.

"Why are you here? Isn't this a case for the fire investigator?"

Bristol stiffened as if he'd been insulted. "He's involved, of course, but this isn't just about arson, miss. It's also a murder investigation. The fire and police departments are working in conjunction."

Ella Mae's throat grew dry, increasing the soreness and

discomfort she already felt. "Murder," she croaked. "Who's the victim?"

"My daughter is not giving a statement until she's had something to drink," her mother said, glaring at the two officers.

"I'll get her some tea from the cafeteria," Aunt Sissy offered, and hurried down the hall.

Ella Mae pointed at the water cooler behind the registration desk. "I'll ask the nurse if I could have a cup of water."

"Allow me," Officer Wallace said. She returned shortly with a cup in each hand.

The first few sips stung Ella Mae's raw throat, but by the time she'd finished the first cupful, the soreness had abated somewhat. "The murder victim? Who is it?"

"We don't know. We were hoping that either you or your aunt could shed some light on his or her identity," Officer Bristol said.

Ella Mae decided not to mention Kyran. It was up to Dee to determine what she wanted the police to know about her friend. "I didn't even notice another person when I went into the barn. I only saw my aunt." She raised her hands. "But I'm getting ahead of myself."

"Take your time," Officer Wallace said, and handed Ella Mae the second cup.

"I'll talk until it hurts too much to continue, okay?" Ella Mae said, speaking very softly. She explained that she'd been having dinner with a friend when Reba sent her a text about the fire. The last part was a lie, of course, but a necessary one. "My friend's name is Finn Mercer, and he was the hero of the night. He broke the barn windows and drove his mother's car through the doors, because they'd been chained and padlocked."

Because neither officer seemed surprised by this revelation,

Ella Mae assumed that the police had already conducted a preliminary search of the crime scene.

"Where is Mr. Mercer now?" Bristol asked.

"At the emergency animal clinic. At least, that's where he was headed. I don't know if he's still there."

Officer Wallace looked stricken. "Was an animal injured in the fire?"

Ella Mae nodded. "A cat. Dee had her in her arms. I think she was a new mother, but I didn't see any kittens. I hope . . ." She trailed off, unable to complete the horrible thought.

"Oh no!" Officer Wallace suddenly buried her face in her hands. "That's awful!"

Bristol was obviously stunned by his partner's reaction. "Get a grip, Wallace," he murmured. "We have an unidentified body in the barn and an injured woman in the hospital, and you're losing it over a cat?"

"I'm sorry." Wallace struggled to collect herself. "I'm really sensitive when it comes to animals. I can't stand to think—" She stopped, inhaled deeply, and then exhaled loudly through her mouth. "I'm good now. I apologize for the outburst, Miss LeFaye. Please continue."

"There isn't much more to tell," Ella Mae said wearily. "Finn helped me carry my aunt out of the barn, and then the firemen and EMTs took over. I rode with Aunt Dee, and Finn took the cat to the clinic."

Aunt Sissy returned with the tea and immediately shooed the officers away from Ella Mae. "That's *enough*. My niece needs rest. Can't you see that she's been to hell and back?"

Ella Mae's mother was quick to agree. "My sister's right. I'm taking my daughter home now. If you have more questions, they can wait until tomorrow. Ella Mae, we're leaving." Turning her back on the police officers, she hugged Sissy tightly, and whispered, "Will you come to Partridge Hill when you're done here? It doesn't matter how late. I want us to be together."

"I can't," Sissy said. "Verena and I need to be with Dee when they move her to Atlanta. But I'll call you. Until then, you take care of our girl."

After the sisters parted, Ella Mae and her mother headed for the exit.

Neither woman spoke as they stepped into the dark night, but in wordless synchronicity, they searched for, and found, each other's hands.

"I'll never let go," her mother promised in a choked voice.

They passed beneath a dim fluorescent light, and Ella Mae stole a glance at her mother. At that moment, the tears cascading down the slope of her mother's cheeks looked like falling stars.

Ella Mae showered, took three Tylenol, and drank a mug of herbal tea.

"Next up is chicken noodle soup," her mother said, placing a bowl on the kitchen table. "The nurse told me that tea and chicken soup will stimulate the cilia in your respiratory tract, thereby hastening your recovery. I also gave Chewy a snack. He was whining the whole time you were in the shower. I think he smelled the smoke on your clothes and it upset him."

Ella Mae ate half of the soup and then took the rest to the sunroom. She sat on the rug in front of the window overlooking the rose garden and invited Chewy to rest his head in her lap. After the tea and the soup, she thought she'd be more than ready to climb into bed, but she wasn't. She was too angry to lie down and too worried about her aunt to sleep.

"Has there been any news?" she asked when her mother joined her.

"Not yet."

Ella Mae set aside the empty soup bowl and wondered if she could do something constructive while waiting for an update on Dee and for Reba to report back on what she'd found at the crime scene.

As she stared out at the moonlit roses, she thought about Joyce Mercer and the fact that her killer had never been identified. Of course, the idea that Joyce had been killed originated from Fiona Drever. And despite how forthright Fiona seemed to be, Ella Mae couldn't help but feel that there was much she'd left unsaid.

Ella Mae got to her feet. "I'm going out," she told her mother. "I need to see Fiona Drever, and it can't wait until tomorrow."

Rather than objecting, her mother nodded. "I'm coming with you."

"Actually, I think you should pay a visit to the Gaynors. Loralyn has never hated our family as much as she does now. The idea that she set the barn on fire makes my stomach turn, but we need to know where she was tonight."

"You shouldn't be alone," her mother protested.

Ella Mae knew she was right. "I'll take Jenny."

Sensing the something was going on, Miss Lulu ran to the back door and started barking. She turned in small circles, barking and looking from the women to the door, her eyes lit with anticipation.

"Lulu!" Jenny chided from the top of the stairs and then noticed Ella Mae and her mother. "Are you two going out?" She was clearly surprised, especially since Ella Mae's mother preferred to meander through the garden until she was tired enough to sleep.

"Yes, and I'd like your company," Ella Mae said. "I'm going to see Fiona Drever and the visit could be unpleasant.

If Fiona's combat skills are anything like Reba's, we could be in for it."

Jenny didn't need to be asked twice. "Should we drop by Suzy's and get Aiden?"

Ella Mae shook her head. "I don't want to form a lynch mob. I just want some answers." She waited for Jenny to descend the stairs before saying, "Remember that dose of liquid sunshine you gave me this afternoon?"

Jenny nodded.

"I think it may have saved my life. And my aunt Dee's as well."

Blanching, Jenny drew closer to Ella Mae, studying her anxiously. "What do you mean? What happened?"

"I'll tell you in the car, but it's beginning to occur to me that our gifts might be more multifaceted than we realize. For example, my mother's abilities allow her to grow lush gardens, but she can also perform the Luna Rose ceremonies to determine whether or not a couple is meant to be together. I think all of our gifts have a secondary purpose, and I believe the energy you gave me acted like a force field. I went into a burning building and, though my eyes and throat were a little sore, I'm uninjured."

Jenny held up her index finger. "Whoa! You went into a burning building? You were supposed to be on a date with Finn, not taking over your ex-boyfriend's job. Why were you playing firefighter?"

Hearing Jenny refer to Hugh as her "ex" was like a knife twist in the heart, but Ella Mae didn't feel like arguing about her relationship status now. "I'll give you the short version on the way to Fiona's. After that, I'll need quiet to mull a few things over."

"Like what?" Jenny asked, shooing Miss Lulu away from the door.

"Like how to catch the person who deliberately set fire to my aunt's barn with two people trapped inside."

Jenny's eyes went wide. "When you find out who did it, will you turn them in to the police?"

Ella Mae's mouth tightened in fury. "If there's enough evidence to put them away for good. If not, I know someone with an abundance of sharp metal objects."

Ella Mae's mother understood at once. "You'd let Reba handle the punishment." She glanced up at the sky, her eyes locking on the sickle moon. "Whatever it takes, I will have justice for my sister. And if not justice, then I'll gladly settle for vengeance."

Chapter 9

Ella Mae parked in front of Fiona Drever's cottage and told Jenny it would be wise for them to wait by the truck for a moment. As expected, a living room curtain twitched, and seconds later, the door flew open. Fiona's daughter appeared in the threshold, a shotgun slung over her shoulder.

"It's late," she said with unconcealed distrust.

Ella Mae raised her hands to show that she was unarmed. "I need to see your mother. Jenny's just here to keep me company."

"Let them in, Carol!" Fiona called from somewhere deeper in the house.

Lowering the gun, Carol gestured for them to enter. She led them into the sunroom where Fiona sat in an armchair with a book splayed on her lap. There was a fire burning in the hearth, and the sight of it temporarily paralyzed Ella Mae.

"I thought you'd knock on my door long before now." Fiona motioned at the sofa opposite her. Her sharp gaze followed Ella Mae and Jenny as they perched on the edge of the cushions. "You're angry. Why?"

"It's not for you to ask questions," Ella Mae said. "Not tonight."

Carol, who'd taken up a position behind her mother's chair, stiffened.

"Fair enough." Fiona sounded unfazed by Ella Mae's abruptness. "I suspect you'd like to know what became of Nimue's mother because something's happened to cause Joyce's murder to return to the forefront of your mind. Am I right?"

Ella Mae nodded. "I want the whole story this time, and if I suspect you're omitting details, I'll return with my aunt Verena."

"I know of her gift. She can tell if a person is lying. A very useful ability, especially when one is married to a politician." She let loose a dry cackle and then glanced at the fire. Instantly, the humor disappeared from her face, and she seemed to age a decade. "Nimue's mother was a lovely woman named Cora. She was soft-spoken, graceful, and charitable. She could hold her breath for nearly an hour and swim in the coldest waters. She loved to swim with the seals when they came close to shore."

Carol shook her head in distaste. "A hundred little heads bopping in the shallows. They'd stare at us with those big, dark eyes. It was easy to believe they were all selkies."

Jenny cocked her head. "Selkies?"

"Shape-shifters. Seals that could shed their skin and take a human form," Fiona explained. "In many legends, they'd change into beautiful women."

"But not necessarily the smartest or strongest women," Carol added. "According to local lore, a selkie could be captured and enslaved. All one would have to do is grab their sealskin after they've changed into a human. They'll do anything to get their skin back, because they can't resume their true form without it."

At any other time, Ella Mae would have loved to listen to stories from the Orkneys, but she refused to be distracted by selkie legends, no matter how fascinating. "Back to Cora," she prodded. "How did she die?"

"Aye, let's get right to it." Fiona released an audible sigh, and the air was instantly tinged with the weight of loss and regret. Her daughter put a hand on her shoulder and Fiona reached up and gave it a pat. "It has to be said, luv," she whispered, and then looked at Ella Mae. "Cora drowned."

Jenny cast a dubious glance at Fiona. "Didn't you just tell us that she could swim like a seal? How could she drown?"

"That was the official ruling. Cora was found on the beach. Her back and head were covered with cuts and bruises, but the authorities said those occurred when her body struck the rocks close to shore." Fiona waved dismissively. "I knew the truth. Cora was murdered. By her own daughter."

Ella Mae saw the sorrow in Fiona's eyes. For a second, she regretted forcing the older woman to relive her heartbreak, but there was no avoiding it. "Why did Nimue kill her mother?"

"Nimue was a late bloomer. She didn't experience her Awakening until her sixteenth birthday. By then, she was already a shy and sullen child. I use that term because she looked and acted like a child. Not at all like a young woman." Fiona's gaze grew glassy, as if she was calling forth an image of the sixteen-year-old she once knew. "She was always thin. Never got those womanly curves all the popular girls had. Because of her awkward demeanor and looks, she was picked on by those girls and ignored by the boys. A teenage girl's worst nightmare. To those who mattered most, she didn't exist. And if they did notice her, it was only to ridicule her childlike body or the clover-shaped birthmark on her neck."

Jenny frowned. "You're saying that Nimue was bullied?"

"She wasn't treated kindly, that's for sure. And when she came into her powers, she got back at those girls." Fiona said. "You see, she could bend water to her will, so when those girls used the restroom, Nimue would make the sink water shoot into their faces, or they'd get completely soaked using the loo."

"Ew." Jenny crinkled her nose in disgust.

"Of course, word spread that Nimue was using her gifts far too openly," Carol said. "Because she disguised her antics as plumbing accidents, she was given a firm warning, but she refused to stop. She was hooked on power. She was fearless and reckless. Her pranks escalated until, one day, she flooded the school to avoid the term's-end exams. She was quite popular after that."

Ella Mae whistled. "But she'd crossed the line."

"Aye," Fiona agreed solemnly. "She was punished too— permanently banned from entering our grove. She was sent to school in England and told not to use her gifts at all. If she did, the director of the school would see to it that she faced the local tribunal of Elders."

Jenny put her hand over her mouth. "This must have been really hard on Cora."

Fiona nodded. "It was hard on both of us. We tried to steer Nimue in the right direction after her Awakening, but she was a very headstrong girl. In England, she somehow managed to renew her gifts, all the while pretending to be resigned to a life without magic. I should have known she wouldn't surrender her powers so easily."

"Nimue was in a different country," Carol reminded her mother. "She rarely wrote or visited. How were you to know what she was doing?"

"Cora was killed a week before Nimue was due to gradu-ate from university," Fiona continued as if Carol hadn't spoken. "I knew Cora didn't drown, and as soon as I heard what had happened, I rushed to the house, where I discovered that Nimue had taken anything of value and bolted. There were footprints on the rug in her room. Depressions made by bare feet. And when I bent down to touch them, my fingers came away damp and smelling of salt water."

Fiona got to her feet, grabbed the fireplace poker, and jabbed at a thick log with its sharp point. For a brief moment, Ella Mae feared that the older woman would sever the gas line, but then she noticed the basket of kindling next to the fireplace. Fiona must have removed the gas logs following Joyce Mercer's death and was burning real wood instead.

Ella Mae closed her eyes and allowed the fresh memories of the sounds and images of the fire at Aunt Dee's to fill her mind. She wanted to hold on to her anger, to fan its flame until every other emotion was suppressed.

"Did you go after Nimue?" she asked Fiona.

Fiona kept her eyes on the fire. "Of course I did. Despite what Nimue had done, Cora would have wanted me to look after her daughter. I don't know what would have happened if I'd succeeded in finding her. Part of me wanted vengeance, but I also remembered Nimue when she was just a wee lass. I remembered the days I'd rock her to sleep or tell her stories on a cold winter's night."

Fiona sounded so like Reba that Ella Mae felt a lump in her throat. Had she been wrong to come here at this hour and force Fiona to speak of her greatest sorrow?

You had no choice, she told herself.

Jenny, who was clearly riveted by Fiona's narrative, whispered, "Did you find her?"

"No." The word was infused with a lifetime's worth of shame and regret. "Though I learned a few things in my search. For example, Avalon isn't an invisible island off England's western coast. It can exist in the center of any lake." She turned and gestured out the window. Ella Mae followed the older woman's glance, peering through the dark woods until she was able to catch a glimpse of Lake Havenwood. It spread out below them like a black stain, and Ella Mae gave an involuntary shudder. She'd always loved the lake, but now she knew that bodies of water could be as secretive as people. There was far more lurking beneath the surface of that lake than anyone could ever fathom.

"So there *is* a real Avalon," Jenny said in awe. "Ella Mae told me about some of the research she's done on the place in hopes of figuring out where these storms are coming from, but I didn't quite believe it was real. What's it like?"

"That's the rub," Fiona said with a wry smile. "You can't get there unless you're a woman possessing powerful magic. And it's not a fixed location."

Carol came around from behind her mother's chair and coaxed Fiona into sitting down again. She pressed a glass of water into her hand and motioned for her to drink.

"What my mom is trying to say is that the island moves."

"What?" Ella Mae and Jenny exclaimed in unison.

Carol gave a little shrug as if to say that she could barely believe it either. "Avalon is wherever the Lady of the Lake is. It flourishes when she flourishes. The two are intertwined. A strong Lady can create Avalon in any lake. Mom believes Nimue has become that Lady."

"I chased after her for years, but eventually, I gave up. I couldn't help someone who didn't want to be found. I'd failed as a guardian. I failed Cora, and I lost her daughter." She looked pained. "Because of these failings, I swore to renounce my gifts and start over in a place far from my home. I chose Havenwood, and I've been here ever since."

Ella Mae was still trying to wrap her head around the notion that Avalon wasn't a fixed place when Jenny got up and moved to the window. "What about Excalibur? Does it exist, or is it really a jeweled letter opener or some giant's toothpick?"

Fiona laughed. "Ah, Jenny. Thank the stars for you. Things were getting way too serious. And Ella Mae is sitting there trying to picture Avalon as if it were Jules Verne's floating island." She shook her head. "It's not. The Lady and her priestesses inhabit an island, cloak it in mist, and work their magic in secret."

"Lake Havenwood has an island," Ella Mae said. "I can see it from my house."

Nodding solemnly, Fiona focused on Jenny again. "Excalibur is a relatively modern name for a very old sword. Long ago, the people of Britain used to cast treasure into the water in exchange for bountiful crops, victory in battle, good health, and whatever else their hearts desired. Excalibur was thrown into the water centuries before Arthur was born. The Celts called it *Caladbolg*."

"That explains why Loralyn believes the sword can restore her father's gifts," Ella Mae said. "She has an old text containing information on *Caladbolg*."

"Did you see the text?" Carol wanted to know.

Ella Mae frowned. "Briefly. Loralyn won't show it to me again though. She wanted to barter in exchange for her support and I couldn't agree to her terms, so she's undoubtedly trying to find a way to contact Nimue. Loralyn wants that sword, and she'll do anything to get it." Ella Mae saw the flames devouring Dee's barn and clenched her fists. "Anything."

"Foolish girl." Fiona frowned. "I hope Opal Gaynor can talk sense into that daughter of hers."

"It may be too late for that." Ella Mae flashed on an image of Aunt Dee's raw, red skin. Suddenly, she was back in the ambulance, watching the paramedic squeeze the oxygen bag over and over again. "Earlier tonight, Loralyn might have committed a terrible act of betrayal."

Jenny gave Ella Mae's hand a squeeze, silently offering to do the talking for her. She gave the Drevers a brief account of the fire while Ella Mae studied both women closely. Carol's reaction was a combination of surprise and horror, but Fiona's face tightened with rage.

"We have to capture this vile person," she muttered darkly.

"My mother is at the Gaynor house as we speak," Ella Mae said when Jenny was done. "She'll find out if Loralyn set the fire."

"Can't you just get the butterflies to show you who started the fire?" Jenny asked Ella Mae.

Ella Mae sighed. "I tried. They showed me a figure silhouetted against the trees. The person was dressed all in black. Black pants, black hoodie, black sunglasses. It was as if he or she knew they might be seen."

Carol waved at the hearth. "What about Joyce? Could Loralyn have killed her?"

"I don't think so," Ella Mae said. "It wouldn't have been a case of mistaken identity. I'm certain Joyce had her nails done at Perfectly Polished, Loralyn's nail salon. Loralyn wouldn't confuse her with your mother." Ella Mae knit her brow and continued. "Besides, what would she gain from Fiona's death? I think someone else took Joyce's life. Someone who hasn't been here long enough to know the difference between the two women, though I still don't understand the killer's motive. Why are you a threat, Fiona?"

"A small part of Nimue might fear me," she said.

"Are you trying to tell me that Joyce's murderer acted on Nimue's wishes?" Ella Mae didn't bother to conceal her astonishment. "That a woman who lives an ocean away has an agent in Havenwood?"

Setting aside her glass, Fiona stood before Ella Mae. "I know nothing for sure. At one time, the people of my village believed that Cora had given birth to the Clover Queen. Nimue had a clover-shaped mark. She came to her magic later than other girls, and though she was not the product of two magical parents, we still thought she could be the one the legend spoke of. We were wrong." Fiona knelt and laid her palms on Ella Mae's knees. "I am on your side. From the moment I heard what you did to save your mother and liberate your people, I vowed to offer my life and my loyalty should you have need of either. Now that my gifts are restored, they are yours to command. My daughter's too."

"Thank you." Ella Mae rose and pulled Fiona to her feet. "And for what it's worth, I believe Cora would want you to let go of your guilt. You couldn't have known what Nimue would become. Nor could you have changed her. She chose her path. As you've chosen yours."

"Wisely put," Fiona said with a weary smile. "Has this visit helped you at all?"

"I have a better sense of who Nimue is. I know that she carries a powerful weapon and thinks she's the rightful Clover Queen because she was raised believing it. And though I hate to ask if there are other versions of the Clover Queen legend, I must. Could Nimue possibly be right? Could *I* be the imposter?"

Fiona got a distant look in her eyes again. "Your ancestor, Morgan le Fay, is a descendant of Boudica, a Celtic queen who rebelled against the Romans. Boudica put the welfare of her people above all else. She went to war in hopes of securing their freedom. Gold coins minted in her honor bear a clover flower and three leaves. My granny used to say that a Clover Queen was born when her people needed her most. That's you, my dear." She led Ella Mae to the front door and stepped outside with her. Gazing up at the night sky, she said, "You should try to get some rest."

An owl hooted somewhere in the darkness and a winged shadow blotted out the starlight for several seconds before disappearing into the trees again.

"You're done in, child," Fiona whispered, and signaled for Jenny to start the car. "Go to bed. Things will look better in the morning."

Too exhausted to argue, Ella Mae dropped into the passenger seat and pressed her cheek against the cool leather headrest. She desperately wanted to believe Fiona—to wake tomorrow and learn that Aunt Dee was on her way to a full recovery, that Reba had discovered the arsonist's identity, and that Loralyn was no longer a threat.

"One can dream," she murmured drowsily as Jenny drove down the mountain. Below them, the lights of downtown shone like distant beacons and the moon escaped from behind a veil of clouds to lay a pale pathway over the surface of the lake. Before she closed her eyes, Ella Mae couldn't help but wonder if the trail of moonlight was meant for her, or for another woman. A woman born with water magic.

No. This is my *home*, was Ella Mae's last thought before the motion of the car lulled her to sleep.

When Ella Mae woke, she was momentarily confused by her surroundings. She wasn't in her bed in the guest cottage, but curled up on a sofa in Partridge Hill's library. Someone had stuck a pillow under her head and covered her with a blanket, and Chewy was asleep on the opposite sofa. His mouth was curved into a smile, as if he were fully aware that he'd been granted a special dispensation to nap on the furniture just this once.

"Good morning, boy," Ella Mae whispered. She patted the cushion next to her and Chewy opened his eyes and leapt up to join her. He covered her face with tender little licks, his tail thumping wildly against the sofa back. Ella Mae buried her nose in his fur, which smelled of garden soil and cut grass.

She snuggled with her dog for a few minutes, wishing she didn't have to move. But then she remembered the fire, and she gently pushed Chewy to the floor.

Her body was stiff and sore from a night on the sofa. Rubbing her neck, she shuffled into the kitchen and heard voices coming from the sunroom. Her mother and Reba were seated at the table looking tired but purposeful.

"There's coffee." Reba began to fill a mug. "Are you hungry? I could fix you somethin'."

Ella Mae shook her head. "How's Dee?"

"Out of danger," her mother said. "She was safely transferred to the burn center in Atlanta. Verena told me that Dee's doctor had to use every ounce of his gifts to heal her internal injuries." She gazed out the window, but not before Ella Mae saw the worry in her eyes. "Unfortunately, her external burns are still quite serious. And very painful."

Absently, Ella Mae poured cream into her coffee and watched the dark liquid become light and cloudy. She didn't stir the cream with the spoon pinched between the fingers of her right hand. Instead, she stared at her own burn. "Two violent crimes have occurred in Havenwood and I have no idea who committed them. What kind of leader am I?"

"Don't be ridiculous." Using her own spoon, Reba stirred Ella Mae's coffee and told her to drink it. "A skilled criminal can make himself invisible. Can become a member of the community. I keep a close eye on anyone who comes near you, and so far there haven't been any red flags. We're all on the lookout. Jenny, Aiden, Suzy, your aunts. Everyone.

For some reason, we just can't see behind this person's mask."

Ella Mae sipped her coffee and told Reba and her mother what she'd learned at Fiona's. When she was done, she looked at Reba. "Did you find any clues at Aunt Dee's?"

Reba frowned. "I had to wait forever for the firemen and the cops to leave. My night vision is pretty good, but I couldn't spot any clues that would reveal the arsonist's identity." She glanced at Ella Mae's mother, who issued a reluctant nod. "But I did see this. Someone burned the grass to create this design." She handed Ella Mae a cell phone.

At first, Ella Mae wasn't sure what the lines of scorched grass were supposed to be, but then she rotated the screen and gasped. "Another clover. It's the same shape that was drawn on the brick! The same we saw in the eye of the storm. How is this possible?" She felt a fresh burst of rage. "Could Fiona be right? Could this Nimue have an agent in Haven-wood? And is that agent Loralyn?"

Reba pointed at her phone. "That's not all. I called Officer Wallace, and she said the accelerant used to start the fire is sold at any hardware store. There are no prints on the containers either. And when I mentioned the clover in the grass, she sent me a photograph from Joyce Mercer's crime scene. Of course, the official ruling was that it was an accidental death, but Wallace no longer believes that's the case. Not since she saw this when she pulled Joyce's file last night to see if she'd missed anything. Scroll to the next image."

Ella Mae stared at a glowing clover drawn on the tile wall above Fiona Drever's bathtub and released a savage growl. "Why didn't we see this?"

"It was drawn with Irish Spring soap and only showed up under the black light. The officer who took the photo-graphs didn't think anything of it, and since Officer Hardy was in charge of the investigation and ruled the case closed, Officer Wallace didn't read through the whole file until last night," Reba explained. "She was able to review every piece of information without Hardy wondering why. His mother is gravely ill, and he's left town."

"Two reprehensible acts," Ella Mae whispered. "When I get my hands on the person who committed . . ." She fought to think clearly, to rein in her fury and decide what should be done next. "What else did Officer Wallace say?"

Reba glanced down at Chewy, who was sitting on his haunches next to Ella Mae's chair like a perfect gentleman. "Not much. She was real worried about Dee's animals. She went on and on about how they'd all end up in the shelter or that the wilder ones would run away."

"I'm anxious about them too," Ella Mae said.

Her mother shook her head. "Don't be. A pair of Canine to Five staff members was kind enough to meet Reba at Dee's very early this morning. Between the three of them, they rounded up any animal tame enough to be boarded, including the litter of kittens they found safe and warm inside a cardboard box in Dee's bathroom."

"Thank goodness." Ella Mae was relieved to hear this.

Reba gave her hand a reassuring pat. "Another employee will drop by Dee's place twice a day to put out food and fresh water for the feral animals, so you can strike that item off your worry list."

"I'd like to cross out a few more," Ella Mae said gravely. "Have the police identified the burn victim?"

"No, and if it's Kyran, the authorities probably won't be able to identify him. Since he's from India, I doubt he'll show up in our databases," her mother said. "When Dee is able to talk, she'll tell us who was in the barn with her."

Ella Mae finished her coffee and poured herself another

cup. The fog in her head was beginning to dissipate. She looked at her mother. "What happened at Rolling View?"

"There's nothing positive to report, I fear. Loralyn is gone. She left Opal a curt note saying that she was tired of being treated like a second-class citizen and that she was determined to restore her family's reputation and secure her father's release from prison."

It was strange to think that Opal was completely alone in her stately mansion. She had hired help, of course, but no family. Within the space of a few months, she'd lost her husband and her daughter.

"Loralyn and Nimue are frighteningly similar," Ella Mae said. "They'd both roll over anyone who dared to stand in their way. Loralyn is vain and mean-spirited, and Lord knows I never liked her, but I never truly thought she was capable of murder. Until now. Is she the arsonist?"

Her mother looked grim. "It's possible. Opal didn't notice Loralyn was missing until she knocked on her bedroom door to tell her that she was leaving to have dinner with Robert Morgan. When Loralyn didn't answer, Opal entered the room and found the note on the dresser. Neither she nor the household staff had seen Loralyn since breakfast, so Opal has no idea whether she's responsible for the fire or not."

"And you believe her?"

"I do, because Verena does. I had my phone on speaker throughout the entire conversation so Verena could listen in. Opal was telling the truth. She's very frightened by what Loralyn may have done and by what might happen to her now that she's run off."

Through the sunroom window, the garden was a leafy paradise of lush blooms, fragrant herbs, and droning insects. Ella Mae opened the French doors and felt the sunlight fall across her face. She smelled roses and basil, gardenia and mint, honeysuckle and rosemary. If this were a normal Sunday, she'd take out her food notebook and jot down savory pie recipes that she could make using her mother's fresh herbs. The instant she thought of the pie shop and her bright, sunny kitchen, she felt stronger, more grounded. If she wanted to have a normal Sunday ever again, she'd have to earn it.

"The first History in the Baking event starts tomorrow," she said as Chewy shot past her and into the garden. "Despite everything that's happened, I have to make certain that it's a success." Ella Mae ran her hands through her tangled hair. "I need to show our guests that nothing will interfere with my determination to unite our kind. I can't let anything distract me from that goal."

"Then I'd best not give you this," Reba said, brandishing Ella Mae's cell phone. "Finn's left a bunch of voice mails, and you have a dozen new text messages." She pointed at Ella Mae's purse, which was on the empty chair beside her. "I got your bag out of the warehouse without incident. Your gun is safe and sound, but your cell phone battery is about to die."

Ella Mae accepted the bag and the phone and examined her text messages. "Finn wrote that the mother cat is going to be okay. In fact, he brought her home. He's offered to keep her until Dee can take her back."

It was clear that no one wanted to speculate on when that would be. While Ella Mae scrolled through her messages, her mother shared how Dee had drifted in and out of consciousness during the transfer to Atlanta. Whenever she woke, she was in so much pain that the nurses increased her medicine until she was finally coaxed into a morphine-induced sleep.

"We'll get another healer," Ella Mae said as her phone vibrated, signaling a new text message. "I'll spread the word among our visitors. Someone must know who can treat her burns, and then—" She glanced at her phone screen, and whatever she meant to say flew out of her head like a startled bird.

"What is it?" her mother asked.

Ella Mae stared at the single sentence, which floated in the center of her screen like a buoy in a silver ocean. "It's from Hugh," she said in voice tight with emotion. "He's coming home."

Chapter 10

Ella Mae didn't receive any more texts from Hugh.

She wrote several of her own asking when he'd be coming home, but he didn't reply. His one-line text had her head spinning. Was he really returning to Havenwood? And why now? Against all odds, had he found what he'd been looking for?

"I can't obsess over this," she chided herself after checking her phone for texts the tenth time that morning. "I have too much work to do."

In fact, her list was longer than usual. Due to the History in the Baking events, The Charmed Pie Shoppe would only be open for tea the following week, but Ella Mae still had to prepare enough dough for teatime pies and tarts. She also had to shop for ingredients for the fillings. That meant a trip to the farmer's market followed by an afternoon in the kitchen making balls of dough until her hands ached.

"At least it's Sunday, so you can come along," she told Chewie. "I'll put you on security detail."

When Ella Mae pulled into the lot behind the pie shop, she was surprised to see a row of familiar cars. Inside, her family and friends were gathered in the kitchen. Her mother and two aunts were wearing the shop's official peach aprons embroidered with the phrase "That's How I Roll," while Reba and Jenny had to make do with aprons from home.

"What's going on?" Ella Mae asked, hanging her purse on a hook near the door.

Before anyone could reply, Suzy and Aiden came into the kitchen through the dining room. Aiden carried a coffee carafe in each hand and Suzy held a pitcher of sweet tea.

"We're here to work." Suzy placed the pitcher on the counter and smiled at Ella Mae. "We might not have your magic touch, but all of us are capable of operating small appliances, chopping fruit, or washing dishes."

"I volunteer Aiden for dishwashing duty," Jenny said with a snigger.

He nudged her in the side. "Make my sister slice the onions. I like it when she cries like a baby."

"We don't need onions, you big, lumbering oaf. We're making desserts for the tea menu." Jenny swatted her brother with a potholder. "Or did you think Ella Mae would serve her customers an onion meringue pie?"

Reba held up a warning finger. "Don't make me put you two over my knee. Aiden, the front porch and patio need to be swept. I'd recommend you do the job with your shirt off, but seein' as your girlfriend is standin' right next to me, I'll keep my randy thoughts to myself."

"That would be a first," Verena said and winked at Ella Mae. "As for Sissy and me, we caught a few hours of sleep and would rather be here than moping around our houses."

Ella Mae smiled. It was a balm to see the circle of familiar, beloved faces, but she felt that someone else was far more deserving of company and comfort. "What about Dee? Shouldn't someone be with her?"

"Sissy, Adelaide, and I have already worked out a schedule," Verena said. "But we can't spend eight hours a day in Atlanta, sweetheart. Dee knows that you need us too."

"All of Havenwood seems to be buzzing," Sissy said. "Everyone's bright-eyed and chatty. There's so much *energy* in the air. It's like a late spring fever."

"Well, my Buddy is jumping out of his skin with excitement over the History in the Baking events." Verena chuckled. "I swear that whenever that man closes his eyes he envisions a giant coffer filled with gold coins. I bet we'll see several town beautification projects this summer."

Sissy pried the lid off the flour container and waved it around. "Every hotel, motel, and spare room from here to Atlanta is booked, and the shops and eateries are packed with people. As mayor, it's no surprise that Buddy's thrilled." She gestured at the commercial mixer. "Tell us what to do with that intimidating contraption, Ella Mae."

As Ella Mae got Sissy and Verena started on the dough, her mother washed the fruit from the farmer's market. Reba was tasked with measuring out nuts for the bourbon pecan and chocolate hazelnut tarts Ella Mae planned to make and then freeze for later in the week. There'd be no cream or meringue pies on the menu. To make up for this, Ella Mae decided to bake a large batch of cream cheese–and-peach hand pies. These treats would freeze well, and she knew a warm, creamy, and delectably sweet hand pie topped with a scoop of cinnamon vanilla-bean gelato would delight her customers.

After Aiden headed outside to clean, Jenny washed her hands and volunteered to grease pie dishes and roll out dough for crusts. As soon as she was set, Ella Mae had Suzy boil peaches on the stovetop and then, once they were cool enough to touch, remove the skin and pits.

"I never knew you could skin a peach this easily," Suzy said, her eyes round with wonder. "It's almost like magic."

The women worked and chatted and moved around one another like synchronized dancers. The kitchen was filled with sunlight and the scent of roasting nuts and freshly brewed coffee. Reba switched on the radio. Over the seductive crooning of Michael Bublé, Ella heard occasional bursts of laughter or squeals of dismay as a peach rolled onto the floor or an egg broke in a drippy mess on the worktable.

While she gently stirred chunks of semisweet chocolate in the double boiler, Ella Mae felt the invisible threads binding her to each woman in the room. They seemed to thrum like living things, and Ella Mae knew that she wouldn't need to infuse her food with magic today. It was all around her, filling the air with music and transforming the sunlit dust motes into fairy dust.

This is where my strength comes from, Ella Mae thought. *When I need it most, I'll just close my eyes and remember this feeling.*

Hours later, both the cooling rack and freezer were loaded with tarts and pies. Ella Mae stood back and admired the results of their combined efforts. Since The Charmed Pie Shoppe was closed on Mondays, she was now fully prepared for a café filled with customers on Tuesday.

"Even with the events taking place at the resort, I still expect to be mobbed at teatime," Ella Mae said. "After all, talking about pie will make people hungry for it."

"Not to worry. Your aunts and I plan to be here all week." Her mother touched her apron and smiled.

Verena nodded. "That's right. When we're not with Dee, we'll be with you. Fiona and Carol Drever are in the rotation too. After Adelaide told me about your late-night visit, I wanted to speak with Fiona myself. She's an honest woman, Ella Mae. A good and loyal woman."

Ella Mae frowned. "What about Opal Gaynor? She must be in pain right now."

"Adelaide asked her to help you with some of the History in the Baking events," Verena said. "Opal has incredible organizational skills and she excels at crowd control. We also like the idea of keeping her close."

Ella Mae studied her aunt. "Why? You don't trust her?"

Verena hung up her apron and took both of Ella Mae's hands in her own. "I don't have a child of my own, but when you were born, I claimed you as belonging partly to me. We all did. And if you were to raise your hand against me for whatever reason, I wouldn't fight back. I couldn't. Your life is far more precious than mine. Knowing you're in the world brings me joy."

"If Opal feels the same about Loralyn—and despite her icy exterior, I suspect she does—then she's vulnerable." Sissy brushed Ella Mae's cheek with her fingertips. "So, for the first time in our history, a LeFaye will protect a Gaynor. You will keep Opal safe and show all our visitors that the two clans can stand together. This is your destiny, my dear."

Ella Mae thanked everyone for helping her and then shooed the women out of the kitchen, telling them to go home and relax. She even had her mother take Chewy, knowing he'd rather play in the garden with Miss Lulu than spend another hour snoozing on the porch.

Alone in the pie shop, Ella Mae removed the white chocolate raspberry pie from the freezer and placed it in the middle of the counter. She was just about to unwrap it when there was knock on the back door.

"Don't tell me you're working," Finn said, shielding his eyes against the spring sunlight. He made no move to enter. "I came to see if you were okay."

Ella Mae glanced at the pie on the worktable in confusion. She'd been thinking of Hugh, but it was Finn who stood in her doorway. It was Finn who'd been utterly selfless last night. He'd helped rescue Aunt Dee and the cat in her arms. He'd ruined his car taking down the barn door and risked his life rushing into a burning building after Ella Mae. And how had she repaid him? By sending him a text message thanking him for being her hero. She hadn't even spoken to him in person.

Feeling deeply ashamed, she walked toward him. "Finn," she began before stumbling over a bulge in the floor mat by the sink. She pinwheeled her arms as Finn leapt forward. He clamped a hand on either side of her waist, and she fell against his chest with an "umph."

Making no attempt to let go, Finn smiled at her. There was so much kindness in his big brown eyes that she had a powerful urge to kiss him. And before she knew it, her lips were on his. Instantly, his arms encircled her. He pressed her closer. And closer still. She could barely breathe, but she longed to be made breathless.

But Finn's kiss didn't feel right. It wasn't Hugh's kiss. Finn's lips were soft and wet and warm, but they weren't Hugh's. For all his fine qualities, Finn was a stranger. A charming and attractive stranger, but he wasn't Hugh. And Ella Mae wanted Hugh. She loved Hugh.

She backed away. "I shouldn't have done that." She touched her lips and then shoved her hands in her apron pockets. "I'm sorry, but I'm in love with someone else. When he left, he told me to move on with my life, but I can't. I tried to put him out of my mind, but I can't." She shook her head in apology. "I really like you, Finn, and I owe you a huge debt of gratitude, but I shouldn't have kissed you."

"I'm not sorry," he said hoarsely, his eyes locked on hers. "And I'll never stop hoping we can repeat the experience. By the end of next week, I'll officially be a Havenwood resident. I'm going to stick around, Ella Mae. Your guy might have been crazy enough to leave you, but I wouldn't. If you were mine, I'd never let you go." Lifting her chin, he stared down at her, and whispered, "I'd run into the fire for you a million times over, but I won't interfere with your relationship. If you need me, you know where to find me. Until then . . ." He pressed a kiss on her palm, smiled at her, and then left the shop.

She watched him go; wishing her hot skin would cool and the rapid beating of her heart would slow. When Finn vanished from view, Ella Mae poured herself a big glass of water and gulped it down. She then moved back to the worktable and slowly removed the layers of aluminum foil from around the frozen pie. When the last piece came free, her eyes widened in surprise.

The overlapping hearts of melted chocolate she'd piped in February were broken. In the cold quiet of the walk-in freezer, every single heart had cracked, the thin squiggles of dark chocolate mysteriously separating into jagged halves.

Hands trembling, Ella Mae rewrapped the pie in foil and shoved it back into the freezer. In the empty kitchen, she touched her lips again, as if the ghost of Finn's kiss could offer her warmth and comfort. But she felt chilled, as though winter had sunk deep into her bones. She left the pie shop and headed home, where sunlit roses and flights of butterflies awaited her.

The next day, Ella Mae arrived at Lake Havenwood Resort well before the first event. Mr. Brandon, the manager, greeted her in the lobby. He pumped her hand with gusto while predicting that the weeklong festivities would be a rousing success.

"I certainly hope so." Ella Mae smiled at him. "And I'm glad our first activity is indoors. It's rather gloomy out today."

"Not to worry," Mr. Brandon said. "It's the ideal weather to pack the auditorium, the restaurant, and most importantly, the bar."

Ella Mae laughed. While Mr. Brandon moved off to speak with a guest, Ella Mae proceeded into the auditorium to conduct a microphone test. After mounting the stage, she spotted a couple in the third row gazing up at her with a look she could only interpret as wonder.

"Hello. I'm Ella Mae LeFaye," she said into the microphone. Her voice sounded foreign to her own ears, so she switched off the mic, exited the stage, and approached the couple.

They immediately jumped to their feet. "This is such an honor," began the woman, who was at least twenty years older than Ella Mae.

The man removed his baseball cap and performed an awkward little bow. "An incredible honor, ma'am. She's even more beautiful than the tales tell, isn't she, Linda?"

"I expected no less. After all, she's our . . ." The woman trailed off and glanced around. "Forgive us. We're just a bit starry-eyed. We're the Shermans from North Dakota, I'm Linda and this is my husband, Bill."

Ella Mae recognized the names. "Of course. You're the beekeepers. It's lovely to meet you, and I can't thank you enough for baking the samples for this morning's event."

Bill waved off her thanks. "The honor's ours."

"Can we do anything else to help?" Linda asked.

"I need to get the word out that I'm holding a meeting in our grove tonight," Ella Mae said. "I'd like the chance to talk to everybody about changing our future."

The Shermans exchanged gleeful smiles, and then Linda took a hesitant step forward. "I know this is terribly rude, but we've traveled so far and, well, would you mind showing us the mark?"

For a moment, Ella Mae didn't understand, but when she realized what Mrs. Sherman was asking, she nodded and held out her palm. The Shermans both whispered an awe-filled "ahhhhh."

At that moment, the double doors in the back of the room were opened, and the audience began filing inside.

"I know you need to go," Bill said in a low voice. "But Linda and I made up a sign so you'll have a way of knowing who's loyal to you. We figured out how to make a clover shape with our hands. See?" He curled his thumbs into his index fingers as if he were making a pair of shadow rabbits and then folded his remaining fingers on top of one another, creating a roundish hollow above the two roundish hollows he'd made with his thumbs. He raised his hands so the beam of an overhead spotlight shone through the gaps between his fingers. Ella Mae saw the shape then. It really did resemble a three-leaf clover. Linda repeated the movements with her hands, smiling shyly as she did. "We'll spread the news about your meeting."

Ella Mae returned to the stage, feeling slightly dazed by the Shermans' demonstration of fealty and by the number of people filling the auditorium.

I hope I'm worthy of their trust, she thought, and gazed out at the sea of faces before her. She wondered how many of the audience members were magical and how many she could count on to join her in breaking their centuries-old curse.

"Welcome to History in the Baking," she said once every seat had been taken and an expectant hush had fallen over the room. "Food is magical. It nourishes our bodies, but it also feeds our souls. It connects us to other people. Our memories are, forgive the pun, peppered by food."

"I get it!" exclaimed an elderly man in the front row. "Peppered! Like salt and pepper!"

The crowd laughed, and Ella Mae gave him a thumbs-up

and continued. "Our mental scrapbooks contain images of a father carving a Thanksgiving turkey, a mother baking chocolate chip cookies, a grandmother pouring a cup of tea, and a grandfather frying the fish he caught that morning. We're more communicative when food is present. How often do we chat with friends over a cup of coffee? Or gather around the family dinner table, passing the breadbasket or the mashed potatoes, to share something about our day? And of course, we celebrate with food. We mark milestones with food. And we mourn our losses with food."

There wasn't a sound in the room. Every eye was trained on Ella Mae, but she wasn't nervous. She'd wanted to be a pastry chef ever since she could remember, and here she was, living her dream. With or without enchantment, she'd become a skilled pie maker. Amid the craziness and confusion of being magical, she always had pie to keep her sane. Pie was her tether to a normal life, and she was overjoyed to be able to share her passion for it with others who understood its importance.

"Pie has existed for centuries. It's been a part of our human culinary narrative since the ancient Egyptians rolled out the first dough and cooked it over hot coals. The Greeks and Romans made meat pies. For hundreds of years, the piecrust was merely a container to hold the filling. The crusts were often called coffins and were typically discarded." She grinned at the audience. "Piecrusts have come a long way since Plato's day. I've seen examples of some amazing recipes on your websites." She made a sweeping motion with her arm to include the whole of the room. "Crusts made of cheddar cheese, pistachios, fennel seeds, dried onions, cinnamon buns, pretzels, potatoes, cookies, cereal, and, of course, chocolate. Any chocolate lovers out there?"

A round of clapping, several whoops, and a few shouts of "Me!" greeted this question.

"Fortunately, Wednesday's agenda includes several demonstrations involving chocolate. Thursday is the Best in the Nation event, in which our judges will taste samples from states around the nation and then bestow prizes on the top three entrants. We have an incredible number of states being represented. After trying a bite of Kentucky Chocolate-Nut Pie or a Hoosier Pie from Indiana, you can decide if a sweet cherry pie from Iowa can truly trump Michigan's famous tart cherry pies."

Several boisterous cries of "Iowa!" and "Michigan!" followed this remark.

"Today's highlight will be the Pie Through Time presentations. And on that note, I'd like to offer my warmest thanks to Bill and Linda Sherman from North Dakota. They've generously re-created one of the oldest recorded pie recipes. This Roman savory pie has a rye crust and a goat cheese–and-honey filling. The Shermans, skilled bakers and beekeepers, have samples of this special pie for everyone. The resort waitstaff will now distribute your tasting plates as well as small cups of honeyed wine, in keeping with our Roman theme."

The curtains behind Ella Mae parted to reveal a row of waiters dressed in togas and sandals. The audience burst out in appreciative applause and whistles. The waiters marched off the stage with as much dignity as they could muster and collected forks, napkins, and small plates bearing two-bite pies from the buffet tables lined up on both sides of the auditorium.

Waitresses in more modest Roman-style robes streamed in through the rear doors carrying small glasses of honeyed wine. Murmurs of anticipation rose from around the room, and Ella Mae was thrilled to see the responses as people took their first bites of goat cheese–and-honey pie. She suspected the Sherman's honey was unlike any honey in the world, and she invited the couple to stand so that they might receive a well-earned round of applause. Next, she informed the audience that it was time for the presentation on the history of pie.

"This entertaining and informative video, called *The Pie Chronicles*, was produced by one of my dearest friends, Suzy Bacchus. Suzy owns The Cubbyhole Book and Gift Shop, one of my favorite places in all of Havenwood. Make sure you stop by while you're in town, and Suzy can show you her collection of rare cookbooks."

Suzy was out of sight, no doubt making last-minute adjustments to the projector, so Ella Mae signaled for the lights to be dimmed and left the stage. A large screen was lowered from the ceiling, and the audience tittered in excitement.

The first slide featured a cartoon of a flock of blackbirds bursting from inside a baked pie. This was followed by a series of facts on pies and pie makers from the ancient world. Suzy had used Photoshop to add slices of pie to famous works of art. She'd inserted a wedge of a pecan pie into an Egyptian tomb painting, a lemon meringue into a Chinese scroll, a chocolate silk into a Greek amphora, and Michelangelo's David statue appeared holding a slice of cherry pie in his left hand. A checkered napkin covered his private parts.

Laughter resonated throughout the large space and intensified with the introduction of medieval pie baking. A portrait of Henry VIII filled the screen and included a very contemporary buffet table loaded with a cornucopia of pies. Suzy had somehow managed to place a dollop of whipped cream on the tip of the corpulent monarch's beard.

As the show continued, Ella Mae watched the light from the screen flicker over the faces in the crowd. The darkness and the brief flashes of illumination gave everyone an alien appearance. Ella Mae felt a prick of unease, and she had to remind herself that she didn't know any of the audience members, whether locals or visitors, well enough to trust them.

On-screen, the image changed to the famous painting of George Washington crossing the Delaware. Suzy had enhanced the blue and gray tones, and the colors seemed to ripple over the spectators like water. The effect reminded Ella Mae of Joyce Mercer. She looked out into the crowd and saw Joyce's face, eerily still and pale, submerged in the water of Fiona Drever's bathtub.

Unable to focus on the slides highlighting the importance of pie in American history, Ella Mae's eyes darted from row to row. Having seen the clover in Fiona's bathroom and burned into Dee's lawn, Ella Mae was positive that Joyce's murderer and the arsonist were one and the same. She couldn't help but wonder if that person was in the room. Was he or she sitting in the dark, watching her?

Tonight, I'll ask the others to help me find this person. The villain must be brought to justice before anyone else is hurt.

The Pie Chronicles came to an end to the sound of raucous applause. The lights came up, and Ella Mae stepped behind the podium once more. She outlined the rest of the day's events—a lobster potpie luncheon and chef's demonstration in the resort dining room, a walking tour of Havenwood, and the World's First Pie Makers presentations—and then thanked Suzy again for treating them to such an entertaining film.

"I hope you enjoyed this introduction to History in the Baking and that this week will be a memorable one. If you should need me for any reason, I'll be attending most of the morning and evening events. In the afternoon, I'll be in the kitchen of The Charmed Pie Shoppe, so feel free to come by for tea and a bite of something sweet. Thank you, everyone. Have a wonderful rest of the day, and I look forward to seeing you later on."

She replaced the microphone in its cradle and smiled at

the crowd. They returned her smile and then, in swift unison, several people in every row raised their hands in front of their hearts and formed the clover symbol the Shermans had shown her. With this brief, covert movement, men and women of all ages honored her with the silent gesture.

Tears burned in the back of Ella Mae's eyes, but she blinked them away. These people needed her strength and courage. They'd traveled far from home in hopes of finding a worthy leader, and she would not disappoint them. Raising her chin, she stood tall and proud, accepting their wordless homage.

Ella Mae remained in this posture until the last person left the room. When she was finally alone, she released the breath she hadn't known she'd been holding and glanced down at her right hand. The clover-shaped burn on her palm was glowing. Like a star trapped beneath her skin, it shone with a blinding light for a long moment before abruptly winking out.

When Ella Mae lifted her gaze again, she saw someone sitting in the first row. Someone who hadn't been there earlier. Someone she'd been longing to see since he'd gone away.

Hugh.

Chapter 11

Hugh had barely gotten to his feet when Ella Mae threw herself into his arms.

"I can't believe it!" she cried. "You're really here!" She buried her face against his neck, anticipating the scent of damp sand and cool, fresh water, but he smelled different. Almost brackish, like he'd just emerged from a salty tidal pool.

Hugh put his hands on Ella Mae's shoulders and pushed her away.

"Let me look at you," he said, and smiled.

She smiled back and waited for the intense, exhilarating feeling of bliss to bubble up inside her. When it didn't come, she searched Hugh's handsome face in confusion. Something about him had changed; she could sense it before she saw it. But when she met his curious stare, Ella Mae went rigid in shock.

Hugh's eyes had always been a brilliant Aegean blue.

Guilelessly clear and beautiful. Now, gray mottled the blue, like storm clouds moving across a summer sky.

The tenderness she'd always found in his eyes was missing too. His gaze was friendly, but lacked warmth. Hugh seemed solemn, which was also atypical. He was known for his easy laughter and his unfettered playfulness. Now, his mouth was set in a firm line, as if he were reluctant to speak.

"You're . . . different," she said, a knot of dread forming in her belly.

He shrugged. "They say traveling changes a person."

Ella Mae was frightened by the sound of that. "In what way did it change you?"

"Leaving Havenwood allowed me to become myself again."

Ella Mae lowered her arms and stared at Hugh. "You did it? You found a way to restore your powers?" She looked him up and down, wondering if there was an obvious sign that he was a water elemental again. "I thought your quest was impossible, but I'm glad you succeeded. I really am. You have to tell me everything."

"That's why I'm here," Hugh said, visibly relaxing. He reached for Ella Mae's hand. "What I'm about to say will be difficult for you to hear, but I'm asking you to listen to me. To *really* listen."

Hugh's tone put Ella Mae on guard. Why was he being so stiff? Why hadn't he kissed her? This was not the reunion she'd imagined.

"A woman named Nimue helped me," Hugh said.

Ella Mae felt like the wind had been knocked out of her. The floor tilted crazily and she leaned to the side and grabbed the back of a chair.

"Are you all right?" Hugh asked.

Unable to speak, Ella Mae closed her eyes and concentrated on the simple act of breathing for several seconds. "Go on," she said weakly.

"I ran into her in Ireland. She heard from the locals that I'd been asking them to share their stories about objects of power." Hugh spoke casually, as if estranged couples chatted about such things all the time. "Nimue tracked me down and offered to lend me her sword. She told me that the sword had all the power I needed to reclaim the other side of myself." He paused and waited for Ella Mae to speak. When she didn't, he continued.

"While she looked on, I walked into an Irish lake until the water closed over my head. For a moment, I actually thought I might drown, but then the sword started to glow, and I could see and breathe and swim just like I used to! I could race alongside schools of fish, moving through that dark and secret world—a world that has more beauty and mystery than an ordinary person could ever imagine."

"Ordinary?" Ella Mae's feelings of hurt and betrayal were rapidly morphing into anger. "If you're referring to the non-magical, then let me remind you that those people run your business, grow your food, and fix your car. They stand beside you fighting fires and trust you with their pets. Just because they can't hold their breath for twenty minutes doesn't make them inferior. Is this *her* influence?"

Hugh let loose a dry laugh. "How can you say that? You of all people? I know who you are now. Nimue told me everything *you* should have told me." A strange light gleamed in his eyes. "You're the stuff of fairy tales. You are your family and friends. Was I the *only* person who didn't know the truth about you?"

Ella Mae realized that Hugh was also angry. She'd been responsible for the loss of his powers because she'd removed a magical object from the bottom of Lake Havenwood, but she'd also kept her own abilities a secret from him. He clearly resented her for more than one reason.

"There are the rules," she said defensively. "We can't reveal ourselves to people who aren't like us. It isn't safe. Or smart."

"Why should we hide in the shadows?" Hugh asked. "Any of us? There was a time when our powers earned us respect."

"Hundreds of years ago, people were more isolated. We live in a global community now. If we used magic in public, the whole world would learn about us, and that would put us all at risk." She threw out her arms in exasperation. "Think about it, Hugh. Scientists would pick us apart. Governments would use us as weapons. Or lock us up. Instead of taking that risk, we choose to be invisible. At least until we've broken Merlin's curse and can stand together as a united people. Has the all-wise Nimue told you about the curse too?"

He nodded. "Your dad died because you're the child of two magical parents, right? If two of your kind have children, there's always a price to pay."

"What about elementals?" Ella Mae asked. "Don't you have rules?"

"No," he said, his eyes flashing. "We're free to do as we wish."

Ella Mae felt her ire rise even more. "Oh, really? You intentionally lost swim races when we were kids. Wasn't that you trying to blend in?" When Hugh didn't answer, she pressed on. "Of course it was. You couldn't allow people to see how fast you were. I bet you had to remember to take a breath just so you'd look normal. We're not that different, Hugh. We have to keep that part of ourselves a secret."

Spots of color appeared on Hugh's cheeks. "But even when you found out what I was, you didn't share your secret. You kept right on deceiving me."

Ella Mae dropped her gaze. "I don't blame you for being angry. I didn't want to lie to you. I hated having to do it." She searched his eyes for a hint of affection, but saw only hurt and hostility. "Here we stand. I know what you are and you know what I am, but having everything out in the open doesn't bridge the chasm between us, does it? Judging from the look on your face, it's too late." A sob rose in her throat. She swallowed hard, forcing it down. "It's obvious that you can't forgive me for removing the source of your power, even if it meant saving my mother's life. Are you really willing to throw away what we had because of that?"

Hugh said nothing and Ella Mae took his silence as confirmation. There was a sharp pain in her chest, as if someone were sticking hot needles into her heart. She also felt dizzy. Dropping into a seat, the full force of what was happening slowly sank in. She was losing Hugh. He was standing right in front of her and she was losing him.

Was he ever mine? she wondered in despair. *Was what we had really love? How could it have been when both of us were leading secret lives?*

She looked up at Hugh. How many times had she thought of him and felt her heart flutter with longing? How many cumulative hours had she daydreamed about being with him? And at last, after what seemed like decades of waiting, he'd fallen for her. Their happiness had been fleeting, but Ella Mae treasured every moment she'd spent with him. Every memory. She couldn't picture a future without Hugh in it, but she couldn't see how they could start over either, especially now that Nimue had come between them.

And then, a terrible thought occurred to her. "What did you have to give Nimue in exchange for the use of her sword?"

Hugh seemed startled by the question. "Nothing."

Ella Mae arched her brow. "When you were done, she just took the sword back and continued on her way?"

Hugh took the seat next to her. "She asked me to speak to you. That's all. It was a simple request, and I never imagined it would be this hard. I thought you'd be glad to see me—that sitting and talking with you would be the most natural thing in the world. But you keep looking at me like you don't know me. You've seen every side of me, Ella Mae. It's *you*, the so-called Clover Queen, who's the stranger here."

How does he know these things? Ella Mae's blood ran cold. The fleeting thought she'd had earlier grew until it couldn't be ignored, and she had to consider the possibility that Hugh had fallen for Nimue. And as much as it sickened her to pursue that line of thought, she forced herself to wonder if he and Nimue had known each other long before he went to Ireland. It was possible that he'd only pretended to love Ella Mae to glean information about her and her kind. Handsome, charismatic, amiable Hugh. Dog lover, volunteer fireman, business owner, and gentleman. He'd make an ideal spy.

But was he a murderer? Surely he knew Joyce Mercer, seeing as her dog was frequently taken to Canine to Five's grooming facility, so he wouldn't have killed her believing she was Fiona Drever. However, he could have set fire to Dee's barn. No one would know how to get the job done better than a fireman. And he could have returned to Havenwood long before today. There were plenty of places he might have been hiding, living off canned food and washing in the lake.

Ella Mae rubbed her temples and tried to silence her disjointed thoughts. "I'm still the same girl you've known all your life," she said softly. "Yes, I can do unusual things, but my abilities don't define me, any more than your abilities define you. You know me. I love to cook for people, spend time with my family, run through the woods, stretch out on the rocks by the swimming hole, drink too much coffee, stay up watching British dramas, and kiss Chewie on the nose first thing each morning." She turned to Hugh. "You've known me since I wore my hair in pigtails. Look at me. I'm that girl, Hugh, and you can still talk to me. So go on. Deliver your message."

Hugh hesitated. His uncertainty was palpable, but after a moment he nodded. "Nimue wants an alliance. It's her hope that you'll join her and that, together, you can convince people to come out of the shadows. The two of you can change the future. Peacefully." He squeezed her hand, as if his touch could convince her.

Ella Mae studied his fingers, noting the clean half moons of his nails and the hundreds of tiny lines traversing his knuckles. The blue-tinged veins, the constellation of freckles near his thumb, and the two-inch scar leading from the back of his hand to his wrist, where he'd cut himself with a Swiss Army knife when he was ten, were so familiar. Why couldn't the rest of him be as she remembered?

"Tell me one thing," Ella Mae said. "Is she responsible for the storms? Has she gathered people like me together in the name of peace? Or destruction?"

Hugh didn't answer.

"She's wrecked sacred places, caused ships to sink, and flooded towns and fields. People have lost their homes, their businesses, and their lives." Ella Mae struggled to maintain an even tone. "Is she coming to Havenwood, Hugh? Is she coming for me?"

When Hugh didn't respond, Ella Mae thought of all the stories she'd read where a sympathetic character was rescued from enchantment by a kiss. She looked at Hugh, searching his face for any sign of affection. Seeing none, she pictured him on the night they'd swum together in a pool surrounded by candlelight. He'd gazed at her as if she were the brightest star in the sky. The most beautiful thing he'd ever seen. Love had shone from his whole being and swept over Ella Mae like a sun-warmed wave. If she could make him feel that way right now, she might be able to bring him back, to break Nimue's spell. It had to be a spell. Hugh could never have changed so completely unless he was under Nimue's thrall.

Ella Mae stood and tugged on Hugh's hands until he was on his feet. "Close your eyes," she whispered, and gently traced the curve of his brows. Wrapping her arms around his back, she pressed her chest against his, erasing the space between them. She wanted every inch of her body to make contact with his, to let her blood and bone and tissue speak to his in a language with no words. Shutting her eyes, Ella Mae returned to the memory of the night in the pool and placed her lips on Hugh's lips.

For a terrible second, he didn't react, but then slowly, so slowly that Ella Mae almost gave up, his arms slid around her waist and he kissed her back. His kiss was both tender and tentative. But when his fingertips dug into her flesh, she knew he was returning to her.

Ella Mae forgot about everything but Hugh. There was no Nimue, no magic, no pie festival. She wasn't the Clover Queen and he wasn't a water elemental. They were a man and a woman finding each other again. They were two people who loved each other.

Tears of overwhelming relief slipped from Ella Mae's eyes.

Hugh brushed his fingers over her cheek and captured a droplet on his skin. As he stared at it, a change came over him. It was like watching a mask fall into place. The tenderness in his eyes vanished and he stepped out of Ella Mae's embrace.

"I can't do this," he murmured, shaking his head as if to

clear it. "I can't choose between being with you and being who I was born to be." He started retreating, his hand held up to stop her from coming any closer.

"I'd never ask you to do that," she said, her voice pleading. "I love you just as you are."

He continued to back away. "I wish I could believe you. I really do. I trusted you once, but I won't play the fool again." Without another word, he turned and hurried from the room.

When he was gone, the large, empty room seemed to expand until it was as cold and desolate as a glacier.

Ella Mae dropped to her knees. She was too numb to cry. She couldn't move. Her body had turned to stone.

She stared up at the podium, where she'd stood with such assurance, and then lowered her eyes to the clover-shaped burn on her palm. The cost of being magical had always been high, but never so much as now.

Don't let this break you, she told herself. *Joyce and Aunt Dee and Kyran deserve justice. You must be strong for them.*

Ella Mae's saw the flames consuming Dee's barn and felt her anger burn as bright as fire. If Hugh was an arsonist, then he was also a spy and a murderer. If he was responsible for such terrible acts, of his own free will or not, she'd make him pay.

"I won't play the fool either," she rasped in anguish. She curled her hands into fists and pushed herself off the floor.

Steeling herself, she walked through the resort with her head held high. She then drove to the pie shop and took the white chocolate raspberry pie out of the freezer.

Setting the oven to broil, she cooked the pie until it was black and hard as coal. The kitchen filled with the acrid odor of burned chocolate and charred dough. It was so unlike the tantalizing aromas Ella Mae was accustomed to that she opened the back door, inviting the spring breeze inside. Catching a whiff of cut grass, Ella Mae thought of Hugh. She stood in the doorway for a long time; her face tilted to the sun, and wondered how many lies Hugh had spoken to her.

"Probably just as many as I told him," she whispered. Overcome by sorrow, she leaned her head against the doorframe and cried. She let the tears flow and the guttural groans of pain she'd held in check since Hugh left in February spill out. She hammered the wall with her fist and sobbed.

Eventually, her tears dried and she fell quiet. She closed her eyes. There was a pressure in her chest and a pounding in her head. It felt like drowning. But her lungs still filled with air. It was only her heart that wouldn't work right. There was a hidden fissure deep in its core. A jagged tear that would never heal.

Ella Mae didn't know how long she was lost in grief. When she opened her eyes again, she saw a butterfly perched on the back of her hand. It fluttered its wings, its delicate, dancing legs tickling her skin. Then it lifted off and flew north.

She followed its flight path toward the blue hills and the grove's secret entrance. When it was only a smudge in the sky, she washed her hands, locked up the pie shop, and went home to change her clothes. She wanted to take her time getting ready. Tonight, she planned to look like a queen.

Ella Mae walked up the mountain path leading to the boulder wall with sure steps. Around the last curve, when the trail appeared to come to an end, she raised her palms and pressed them flat against the massive rocks.

It felt like her body was being pulled apart cell by cell, but the discomfort only lasted a moment. And then she was in the grove, with the velvety grass beneath her bare feet and a sky streaked with tangerine and lavender. The air smelled of honeysuckle and fireflies drifted among the boughs of the apple trees. The apples were no longer gold and silver as they'd been in the autumn, but were blush-colored, the same hue as Ella Mae's dress.

She moved through the orchard on her way to the meadow. As soon as she passed beneath an arbor of vanilla-scented roses, she could hear the soft din of many people taking. Even when Ella Mae saw just how many had gathered at the base of the ash tree's hill, her steps remained steady and sure.

A hush fell over the crowd as she approached. Ella Mae had not decked herself out in her finest. Quite the opposite, in fact. She wanted people to see her for what she was, so she'd chosen a slip of a dress and nothing else. She wore no makeup or jewelry. Her hair was arranged in a low chignon.

Ella Mae could feel every eye on her. As she crossed the meadow, many people smiled. Some just stared. Others gazed at her with guarded expressions. Ella Mae had expected a host of different reactions and that was okay with her. She knew it was her job to convince these people to come together.

At the top of the rise, she stood next to the ash tree and gazed down at the throng of upturned faces. She was about to speak when a bear of a man detached himself from the front of the crowd. Well over six feet tall with a wide chest and generous belly, he had a thick, dark beard and a mop of black hair. Performing a theatrical bow, he spoke in a rich and resonating voice. "Lady, I am Alfonso Caprice, humble opera singer at your service. I can project sound over a large space." He gestured to incorporate the entire meadow. "Everyone will be able to hear you if I briefly touch your throat."

"Please." Ella Mae indicated the empty space beside her. "Join me."

Alfonso closed the distance in four giant strides. "I will put my fingers here." He showed her on his own neck. "Above your voice box. You might feel a little tingle."

Ella Mae nodded and raised her chin, exposing the length of her neck.

Alfonso placed three fingers on her skin and closed his eyes. He swept his free hand from left to right and the air shimmered like a heat wave, and then the shimmer rushed over the meadow. The whole thing had taken less than five seconds. Alfonso grinned. "You're ready now." After another gallant bow, he returned to his place.

Ella Mae felt a strange sensation in her throat, but when she said, "Welcome," in her everyday voice, she could tell by the crowd's attentive expressions that Alfonso's gift had worked.

"Thank you for coming to Havenwood," she continued. "I don't have a long speech prepared. I have a simple message to share with you. When I'm done, you'll all be faced with a decision."

She glanced around and couldn't help but grin when Alfonso gave her a thumbs-up.

"I never expected to be standing here, addressing a large crowd. I didn't expect to be marked with a clover or meet the criteria of the Clover Queen legend. I don't even know what it means to be a queen. What I *do* know is that we have been plagued by a curse for centuries, and I believe it's time to break that curse."

This statement was followed by several shouts of approval.

"But how?" someone cried.

"By uniting the descendants of Morgan le Fay and Guinevere, Queen of Camelot," Ella Mae said plainly. "Our enmity has kept us from rising to our full strength. We've never joined forces. We've never pooled our resources or our talents. We've spent centuries feuding when we should have united to improve our lives and those of future generations."

A woman standing near a lilac tree shook her fist, and

shouted, "I could never trust a LeFaye. How do we know you haven't gathered us here just so you could feed us a pack of lies?"

There was a murmur of agreement followed by several more rude outbursts.

Ella Mae was unfazed by the dissent. She'd expected it. "Opal, would you come forward and speak to the members of your family?"

Opal, who'd been standing in a cluster with the rest of the Havenwood Elders, was clearly startled by the request. But she smoothed her silk blouse and did as Ella Mae asked.

Alfonso used his gift again, and then Opal spread out her arms and said, "Look around you. This grove is pulsing with magic. A never-ending supply. There are objects of power, like the one used to transform this grove, hidden throughout the world. If we retrieve them, we can create permanent groves. There will be no more need of a Lady of the Ash. No more sacrifices. Your magic will never fade." Her eyes fell on the woman by the lilac tree. "Ms. LeFaye won my respect through her courage, for I was the guardian of the object she brought to this grove. I had to fail in my task to recognize that it had been a fruitless labor all along. My cousins, we've been taught since birth to undermine the LeFayes while elevating our own family, but we're getting weaker as a species because of this division. Our kind is dying. We cannot deny this awful truth."

A young woman near Alfonso burst into tears. "I'm afraid to marry the man I love! He wants to start a family, and though I'm willing to risk my life to have a child, I'm not willing to risk his."

"Nor should you have to," Ella Mae said fervently. "What if our private libraries contain the clues to break this curse? We'll never know until we work together. And we'll never trust one another until we have to stand together to defend our way of life. For those of you who are bold enough, brave enough, and open-minded enough, the time to make a change is now." Her gaze drifted across the crowd. She saw an array of expressions from fear to fury to conviction and knew she had a long way to go before convincing the majority to stand with her.

"I have an English aunt who is following the lead of a woman named Nimue. I like Nimue's idea of using our gifts out in the open! Are you for or against that?" Ella Mae couldn't tell who'd spoken until Leslie, the manager at Canine to Five, pushed her way to the front. "Many of us have been waiting for someone like her to come along," Leslie boldly continued. "Why should we hide when we could rule? What's the point of magic if you can't use it?"

Dozens of people shouted their opinions and Ella Mae felt her control slipping away.

"Why should we listen to you?" Leslie yelled over the din. "I heard that Nimue has the mark of the clover too. Maybe *she's* the genuine article. Can you prove to us that you're the real Clover Queen?"

Ella Mae was shocked by Leslie's hostility. She'd always been so friendly, but now she was trying to undermine Ella Mae in front of everyone.

Ella Mae focused on staying calm. She sensed the magic pulsing through the grove, its heartbeat echoing in her own chest. She only needed to reach for it and it would be there. Rising to her full height, she smiled at Leslie. "If a demonstration will help prove that I am who I say I am, then I'll give you one."

After placing her left hand against the ash tree, Ella Mae extended her right hand, palm facing skyward. Her burn mark began to glow and a beam of light shot out from her palm. A thousand stars winked to life in the empty sky. When they slowly began to float toward the ground, several people cried out in alarm. Still smiling, Ella Mae made a beckoning gesture and the stars soared toward her. When they reached the treetops, they suddenly changed. Their white light grew dimmer and they sprouted wings, leaving sparkles in their wake as they fluttered toward Ella Mae.

If I am the true queen, then crown me, Ella Mae whispered in her mind.

Hundreds upon hundreds of glittering, luminescent butterflies landed on her body. They covered her arms and legs, her head and face, and every inch of her dress. Within seconds, she was completely obscured by a mass of shimmering wings. And then they flitted onto the tree branches over Ella Mae's head.

There was a collective gasp from the crowd.

Ella Mae glanced down to find that she was wearing a dress made of starlight. The silver fabric pooled around her feet and glinted when she moved. The cuffs and sweetheart neckline were trimmed with tiny pearls and the bodice was embedded with small diamonds and iridescent moonstones.

In the hush, a groan came from deep within the ash tree and the butterflies scattered. Tree branches fell around Ella Mae like a leafy curtain, and the butterflies swarmed around her head. She felt a weight upon her brow and then the branches retreated and the butterflies vanished. Ella Mae didn't need to reach up and touch the object the grove had given her. She knew it was a crown.

She looked at the faces staring up at her and waited.

One by one, people dropped to their knees, forming the clover sign with their hands. Ella Mae watched in amazement as male and female, young and old, stranger and friend, bent their knees to her.

Of course, there were those who refused to pay homage. Leslie was among them. Staring straight at Ella Mae, she produced an object from the handbag slung over her shoulder. It was one of Dee's metal birds. Leslie tucked it under her arm and reached into the pocket of her jeans. When she drew out a lighter and produced a flame, her mouth curving into a wicked grin, Ella Mae pointed at her and shouted, "Grab that woman!"

In a flash, Officer Wallace had Leslie pinned to the ground. She wrested the bird from Leslie's grasp and, leaving Alfonso to stand guard, brought the sculpture to Ella Mae.

"Is this a trophy?" Wallace asked quietly. "Taken from your aunt's barn the night of the fire?"

Stifling her rage, Ella Mae took the bird and held it out to the crowd. "My aunt was gravely injured when someone set fire to her barn. Another Havenwood resident was murdered last month. The mark of a clover was left behind at both crime scenes." She let her words hang in the air for a moment. "Change often comes at a price. If you feel this is the time to seize our destiny, then stay. We will create a new future, and we can start by working together to apprehend a killer. If you don't want to be a part of this, then you can leave now, knowing that you'll always be welcome in Havenwood."

After a brief hesitation, groups of people hurried across the meadow toward the exit. With every person that left, Ella Mae felt a growing unease. Would they all abandon her?

Touching the cool metal of Dee's bird, Ella Mae glanced around at those who remained. More than half of the crowd stood firm. She looked to where Reba stood with Fiona and Carol Drever and then paused to meet Aunt Sissy's proud gaze. Finally, her eyes found her mother's. Her mother blinked back tears and nodded. It was a beginning. They stood a chance of breaking a centuries-old curse and seeking justice for Joyce, Kyran, and Dee.

Ella Mae smiled warmly at her people, overwhelmed by the trust they were placing in her.

She then fixed her attention on Leslie Conrad, and her features hardened in anger. *Before I can make any plans, I need to deal with this traitor.*

Chapter 12

Ella Mae signaled for Officer Wallace to approach.

"Will you take Leslie Conrad to the station for immediate questioning? If she's in an interrogation room, I can worry about one less suspect. Maybe she'll admit that she murdered Joyce Mercer and tried to kill two people by setting fire to Dee's barn. If she doesn't, you won't be able to hold her for more than twenty-four hours, right?"

Officer Wallace tugged on her braid. "That's right, but—"

"My aunt Verena is in Atlanta," Ella Mae continued. "Until she returns, we won't know how much of what Leslie tells you is a lie. Can you keep her as long as possible?"

"Don't you think I should be here with you?" Wallace asked. "I haven't been a cop long, but I'm useful in a fight, and I'm concerned about your safety."

Seeing the plaintive look in the younger woman's round, dark eyes, Ella Mae said, "Of your usefulness, I have no doubt. But knowing whether or not Leslie is a murderer is even more important."

Mollified, Officer Wallace set off to deal with Leslie.

Ella Mae waited until the two women had disappeared into the orchard before calling for a volunteer to record the magical ability of every person in the meadow.

"Even if we pool our resources," a man called out, "how will that help break the curse? We're all so different."

"I'm not so sure about that. Give me a minute and I'll show you," Ella Mae told the man. Her voice still carried across the space, cutting through dozens of animated discussions. Ella Mae was pleased to see the locals making an effort to introduce themselves and strike up conversations with the visitors. She hoped the friendly overtures would develop a tenuous bond between families who'd feuded for centuries.

Smiling, she beckoned to her mother, Aunt Sissy, and Reba. "Join me."

Alfonso bounded up the hill. When Sissy neared the top, he offered her his hand. "Miss Cecilia LeFaye. I have heard of your musical talent." He stroked his thick beard, admiring Sissy from head to toe. "If I should die in the coming days, it will be with a smile on my face and a song in my heart, for I have made the acquaintance and held the hand of a true muse." He gazed at Sissy with such overt adoration that she was rendered utterly speechless for the first time in her life.

"Oh!" she squeaked, unable to form a lucid word, and beamed at the opera singer.

"You are even more dazzling when you blush, madam," Alfonso said. "I will now release your hand, only to dream of the moment when I might hold it again."

While Sissy twittered and fanned herself with the end of her batik scarf, the people Ella Mae had called forward settled down on the grass. Ella Mae then asked all the Elders to join them. When everyone was assembled, she turned to her mother.

"I'm sorry to put you on the spot, but you're the only person to have merged with the ash tree. You know what it is to be human, but you also know what it is to be connected to the natural world like a thread in a complex tapestry."

"It's Adelaide LeFaye," someone murmured in awe. "The only Lady of the Ash to survive a separation from the tree."

Her mother leaned in close and whispered, "I told you that I don't remember specifics. Just feelings. Sensations."

"And a song," Ella Mae said softly. "You've hummed it every day since your return. Sometimes, I hear it in my dreams, but I can never repeat the melody. It's too elusive. I can't say why, but I believe it is a very old song—one that belongs to an age before we were cursed, when we were as numerous as the stars."

Her mother nodded. "Yes, it is a wordless reminder of what we once were."

"And can be again." Ella Mae couldn't contain her excitement. "Would you hum it now?"

"Of course." Closing her eyes and pressing both palms against the trunk of the ash tree, her mother grew very still. In her pale green dress, with her silver hair falling over her shoulders, she looked like a dryad. Beautiful and otherworldly.

Her mother began to hum. The notes danced in the air like dandelion seeds, and the tune was hauntingly familiar to Ella Mae. The music spoke to something deep inside her—a slumbering part of her being that had once been linked to the rest of world. Shutting her eyes, she saw the sun rise over an endless ocean, veils of glistening snow draped over tall mountain peaks, herds of deer leaping through primeval forests, and brilliant rainbows springing from majestic waterfalls.

The song was an invitation to remember another time. It was a reminder that magic was everywhere. It was the force that united their kind with the earth. That bound them to every element.

Ella Mae gazed at the small company seated around the tree. "If you could choose only one word to describe the feeling this melody evokes, what would it be?"

No one spoke. It was clear that each and every person was trying to put a finger on which word captured such a wide range of sensations and emotions.

Finally, one of the visiting Elders, a small man with a neat moustache and round spectacles, cleared his throat. "Home. It speaks of a home I've never known, but yearn to see. I feel foolish saying that out loud, but the song still echoes inside me. It is full of regret for what we have lost and hope for what we might rediscover."

"That's exactly how I feel," said one of the Havenwood Elders, a lady physician. She turned to Ella Mae with a quizzical expression. "Why didn't you share that song when we first entered the grove tonight? Those who left might have decided to join us if they'd heard it."

Ella Mae shook her head. "I wanted them to exercise free will. The song tugs at something deep within us, and I didn't want to manipulate them. However, I plan to use the melody to convince as many others of our kind as I can that we have the power to reclaim the past and reshape our future."

Alfonso threw out his arms. "What an evening! And here I thought you'd called us together to talk about pie." Laughing, he bowed once again and trotted down the hill.

An hour later, only Ella Mae and her family remained in the grove.

"I think that was *very* successful," Aunt Sissy said. "You are *full* of surprises, you clever girl."

Her mother tapped her watch. "You should rest while you can. This is going to be a very long and lively week."

"You and Aunt Sissy go ahead. I'll be along in a minute."

When they were gone, Reba stared at Ella Mae in confusion. "A little birdie told me that Hugh's back in town, so why aren't you in a rush to be with your man?"

Ella Mae removed her crown. She turned the thin circlet, which was made of hundreds of silver strands woven together, around in her fingers. Entwined among the strands were tiny gold clovers and butterflies.

"When I first moved back to Havenwood, you warned me that Hugh and I weren't a good match." Ella Mae placed the crown on the closest limb of the ash tree. A network of branches immediately closed around it, while Ella Mae ran her fingers through her hair, releasing it from the chignon. "You said that he and I would cause each other pain. And we have. We've cut to the quick. Inflicted wounds that can't be healed. We've become strangers to each other. And possibly— though I still can't wrap my head around it—enemies."

Reba's face grew pinched with worry. "Let's get you home. I'll fix my special mac and cheese. I used to make it when you'd had a rough day at school."

"I remember. It was the ultimate comfort food." Ella Mae managed a ghost of a smile. "You had me put on my pajamas before supper, and when we were done eating, we'd curl up on the sofa and watch TV with big bowls of ice cream on our laps. By the time I went to bed, I'd forgotten my troubles."

"I'll stop at the grocery store on the way home. It sounds like we're gonna need at least three pints: double chocolate chunk, peanut butter cup, and cookie dough." Reba hooked Ella Mae's arm in her own. "While I'm cookin', you can pour yourself a glass of wine and tell me what happened. You'll feel better if you let it all out."

Ella Mae plucked at the sleeve of her jeweled gown. "I'll feel better when I have my pajamas on. This is like wearing an entire Tiffany store's inventory."

"Fit for a queen, Your High and Magnificent Royalness." Reba performed an exaggerated curtsy and Ella Mae laughed.

Arm in arm, the women crossed the meadow and vanished into the silver shadows.

The next day, Verena appeared in the kitchen of The Charmed Pie Shoppe and settled her formidable rump onto a stool. She wore a white skirt covered with black roses, a black suit jacket, and heels the color of ripe mangos. Once she was comfortable, she slapped the worktable with her palms and announced, "Leslie Conrad is not a criminal. She didn't kill Joyce Mercer or start the fire. She's furious with you because she thinks you're to blame for the change in Hugh's demeanor. She believes you drove him from Havenwood months ago and that you've made him even more wretched following his return."

"Is she in love with him?" Ella Mae felt an instant surge of anger at the thought, but then she remembered that she shouldn't care who loved Hugh. He was no longer hers. There was a chance that he never had been.

"Leslie's gift is that she's able to tame wild animals, especially dogs," Verena explained. "The woman has a pack mentality. In her eyes, you hurt the alpha of her pack. She wants to avenge his wounded pride and restore the harmony that once existed at Canine to Five. Since Hugh came back, he's shown zero interest in his business and barely speaks to his staff."

At that moment, the oven timer beeped and Ella Mae turned to transfer two trays of tarts to the cooling racks. Verena watched her hungrily. "My, my! What tasty treat do you have there?"

"Peach blackberry tarts with a shortbread crust." Seeing the gleam in her aunt's eyes, Ella Mae pushed two miniature tarts onto a plate with the edge of her pot holder. "Give them a few minutes. You'll burn your tongue if you eat them right now."

"I'm sure a generous scoop of vanilla ice cream would speed the cooling process!" Verena declared and spread a clean dish towel over her skirt.

"Why didn't I think of that?" Ella Mae grinned and retrieved the ice cream from the freezer. After dropping a plump scoop on top of each tart, she watched the ice cream melt until it puddled on the plate. The solid lumps resting on top of the tarts looked like a pair of abstract doves. The shapes made Ella Mae think of Dee and Kyran's metal birds. "How did Leslie end up with that bird?" she asked. "And why did she bring it to the grove?"

Verena poked her fork into a tart and its ice cream dove collapsed. "A select group of Canine to Five staff members is tending Dee's animals. Leslie is one of them. Despite her hostile behavior last night, she's given those cats and dogs her very best care. She swore those animals would be kept happy and healthy until Dee returns and she meant it." Verena put a forkful of tart into her mouth, chewed, and moaned in ecstasy. "What kind of enchantment did you add to this divine dish?"

"None," Ella Mae said, pleased that the tarts were so good that her aunt assumed they were tinged with magic. "It's the freshness of the fruit, the buttermilk in the filling, and the shortbread crust. Can we get back to Leslie and why she had that bird?"

"Of course." Verena loaded her next forkful. "Leslie was in Dee's kitchen because one of the cats requires a daily dose of antibiotics and the medicine must be kept refrigerated. And before you ask, none of the kittens are sick. Another staff member has been bottle-feeding them, and they're all flourishing." She stole a bite of tart while Ella Mae took in the good news. "Dee had stuck a prototype of the bird on a shelf next to her cookbooks and teapots, and when Leslie noticed it, she decided to borrow it for a while."

Ella Mae scowled. "How did she know the bird would upset me?"

"Sweetheart, there was a front-page photo of a partially melted bird in the paper! That fire was big news. And I realize you've been far too busy reading other things to enjoy a Sunday morning drinking coffee and perusing the paper." Verena gave her a sympathetic look. "Anyway, Leslie knew the barn had been full of those sculptures, and when she realized that the only remaining bird might be the one in Dee's kitchen, she grabbed it." Verena glanced around. "I shouldn't have mentioned coffee, because now I want a cup."

"Finish telling me about Leslie and I'll ask Jenny to brew a fresh pot," Ella Mae said, folding her arms across her chest in a show of stubbornness.

"Unyielding, eh? Good!" Verena nodded in approval. "The long and the short of it is that Leslie wanted you to suffer. She liked the idea of upsetting you in front of hundreds of people, so she brought the bird into the grove and waited for just the right moment to reveal it."

Ella Mae held up a closed fist. "She certainly succeeded in upsetting me. If my abilities included shooting lightning bolts out of my fingers, the woman would be a pile of cinders and charred bone by now."

"Leslie's indiscretion may also prove useful." Verena's

expression turned smug. "I was able to convince her that Nimue is the real reason Hugh isn't himself these days. Leslie was quick to redirect her anger and vowed to pass on any information she can glean from Hugh, his computer, or his cell phone. In fact, she was so grateful to be released from police custody that she's already shared something."

Jenny entered the kitchen balancing a tray of dirty dishes on her shoulder. She set the tray near the sink, greeted Verena, and gestured at the remains of her dessert. "Would you like a nice cappuccino to go with that tart?"

"I most certainly would!" Verena exclaimed. "You're a gem, Jenny."

After loading the dishwasher, Jenny returned to the dining room to make Verena's drink, and Ella Mae cut one of the peach blackberry tarts into even slices. "What did Leslie share?"

"Hugh said that Nimue wants to meet you, Ella Mae. Sooner rather than later."

Ella Mae scowled. "He mentioned that to me as well. I hope she does come to Havenwood. I'd give her a welcome she'd never forget."

Just then, Reba pushed through the swing door and cheerfully slapped three new order tickets on the counter. She then perched on the stool next to Verena and bit into a licorice stick. "How's Dee?"

Ella Mae groaned. "What's the matter with me? I was so caught up with Leslie Conrad that I didn't even ask."

"You have so much on your mind, darling. Give yourself a break," Verena said. "But to answer your question, Reba, the doctors are pleased with Dee's progress. However, her healing is only physical at this point. She's not saying much. The nurse said that she's probably suffering from post-traumatic stress disorder."

"Who could blame her? She nearly died," Reba said angrily. "So you don't know who was in the barn with her?"

"As soon as I spoke Kyran's name, I knew it was him." Verena sighed heavily. "Dee's eyes filled with tears and she turned away from me. She wouldn't turn back for the rest of my visit."

Ella Mae hated the fact that her gentle aunt was suffering so acutely. "Can't we do anything to help her?"

"No magic can cure grief," Verena said. "Dee knows that better than most. She's spent her whole life creating art to ease the pain of loss, but its power is stronger than ours. What she needs now is for someone to show her an unfailing amount of quiet and selfless kindness. Someone who'll sit with her, read to her, and talk to her without expecting anything in return. Luckily, we're all very fond of a man who fits that bill."

"August Templeton!" Ella Mae nearly shouted their family attorney's name. "Of course. He's been in love with Dee forever."

"Yes, he has," Verena agreed. "August has taken a leave of absence from his practice, rented an apartment near the burn center, and collected a trove of stories and music to bring to Dee each day."

Reba wound a fresh licorice twist around her finger. "It sounds good for Dee, but what about August? He'll play Florence Nightingale and end up with nothin' to show for it. He's been tryin' to win her heart for years and never succeeded. Is it right to ask this of him?"

"He insisted." Verena's mouth curved into an enigmatic smile. "Besides, I have a feeling that she'll finally come to view August in a different light. He's no looker, but he has a kind and generous spirit. I think Dee will see that he's not unlike the strays she takes care of. They might be lost and lonely, but that doesn't mean they aren't worth loving."

Just then, Jenny stepped back into the kitchen. "My cousin Tyson is coming for a visit! He's putting on the fireworks show at a huge Kentucky Derby pre-party this Friday, and when it's over, he'll load up his pyrotechnic goodies and drive to Havenwood. He should be here in time for our May Day celebration."

"Your cousin does fireworks displays?" Reba grinned. "He sounds like someone I'd like to meet. Does he have a special talent?"

"He said he could create any shape you could imagine."

Reba pointed at the cooling rack. "How about a pie in the sky?"

"You can ask him yourself," Jenny said. "And speaking of pie, that order for table four is probably ice cold by now."

Pushing her uneaten licorice into her pocket, Reba hopped off the stool, collected the loaded tray, and rushed into the dining room.

Verena got to her feet. "I need to get going myself. I want to check on Opal Gaynor. She told Sissy and Adelaide that she hasn't heard from Loralyn, but I need to make sure she's telling the truth."

"Wait a sec." Ella Mae placed a few tarts in a pink bakery box and handed the box to her aunt. "Please give her my best."

Alone in the kitchen, Ella Mae stared at the cooling rack and thought about Opal. *She's hurting, but she won't show it. She'll lock her pain away and only acknowledge it in private. For the first time in my life, I need to follow her lead. I need to act like a Gaynor.*

After its eventful first day, the History of the Baking Festival looked like it had the makings of being a great success. People bustled between Lake Havenwood Resort, the public library, and the community park to attend panel discussions and participate in tasting sessions and contests.

By the end of the third day, however, Ella Mae heard just as much talk about the storm currently wreaking havoc along the Virginia coast as she did about the festival. The system was producing four inches of rain per hour, creating massive groundwater flooding, and causing every river, stream, and pond to overflow. Meteorologists across the nation were unable to explain the weather phenomenon. With the exception of hurricanes and nor'easters, storms just didn't move from east to west. A celebrity meteorologist even joked that such a rebellious storm should have a male name, and when he suggested Caliban, a character in Shakespeare's *The Tempest*, the name went viral.

"In the play, Caliban's the son of a witch," Ella Mae heard a woman say just before taking a bite of apple crumb pie during the Apple of My Eye bake-off. As one of the judges, the woman had the challenging task of picking the three best pies out of scores of entries.

"We live in Ohio, so we'll be on our way home before that mess gets here," the baker answered. "Thank goodness, because that storm is a nasty-looking beast."

Spotting Ella Mae, the judge dipped her chin in greeting. Ella Mae smiled in return and kept moving. Everywhere she went, people bobbed their heads in deference, and as the days passed and the nightly meetings at the grove continued, she began to feel more comfortable in her role as leader.

However, when she was at home, Ella Mae couldn't stop thinking about the clover symbols drawn in chalk and soap or the ones formed in storm clouds or burned into the grass next to Dee's ruined barn. At night, she barely slept, twisting restlessly in her bed until she managed to doze off for a few hours. Her dreams were filled with fragmented images of storms, swords, and Hugh.

Part of her was thankful for the frenzied pace and endless list of tasks, because it left her with little opportunity to think about Hugh. She didn't run into him in town, but that didn't stop her from looking for him. Whenever she moved through a crowd, she searched the faces for his. She missed Hugh. She missed their conversations, their intermingled laughter, and the way their bodies fit together as they slept. She missed his scent on her pillow, the sound of him singing in the shower, and the sight of his shoes by the front door. She missed all of it.

Even Chewy sensed something was wrong. He moved to Hugh's side of the bed and slept closer to Ella Mae, as if he knew she needed comfort. He no longer went to doggie daycare at Canine to Five; he now spent his days with Miss Lulu and Ella Mae's mother in the garden. He didn't seem to mind the change. He and Miss Lulu raced around the yard, dug holes in the rich soil, rolled around in the herb bed, and napped in the sunshine. Ella Mae envied them their freedom.

As she strolled among the festivalgoers, it struck her how much more she would have enjoyed the events if she'd just been a regular woman.

All I've ever wanted to do was cook good food, she thought. *Food that will make people happy. I don't need magic for that.*

She came upon a vendor tent and read the name stenciled on the yellow-and-white-striped awning. Sugar Pies—Lake Wales, Florida. Smiling lemons danced on little green feet on either side of the text.

"Best lemon pie this side of heaven," someone behind her said. Ella Mae turned to find a short, round-cheeked woman in a checkered apron standing before her. "I'm

Sugar." She waved toward the back of the tent. "Come inside, honey. You look all tuckered out."

Ella Mae stepped into the shade and watched Sugar move behind a long table and remove a pie with a whipped topping from a portable refrigerator. She cut a slice, plated it, and handed it to Ella Mae. "A little bit of Florida sunshine. Free of charge. One piece of my Sunshine Lemon Pie will chase your worries away."

"Thank you." Ella Mae took a small bite and her eyes widened in delight. The pie was simultaneously smooth, sweet, and tart. The crust was made of lemon sandwich cookies, and the whipped topping was garnished with a sprinkling of crushed lemon drop candies. The filling was creamy and flavorful and reminded Ella Mae of a carefree summer day. She polished off the rest of the pie and then licked her lips. She felt like laughing. She felt like skipping. She felt overwhelmed by optimism, and she owed it to a stranger who'd served her an amazing slice of pie.

"You look much happier now," Sugar said with a satisfied nod.

"Because you reminded me why pie matters." Ella Mae took Sugar's small hands in her own. "You reminded me that food can heal many ills. So can a stranger's kindness. Thank you."

Sugar's smile was as bright as the Florida sun. It warmed Ella Mae for the rest of the day.

Chapter 13

It seemed like a thousand people were lined up for the Parade of Nations event.

Ella Mae couldn't remember a time when Havenwood had been so crowded. She looked down the stretch of road leading from the public library to the Havenwood Community Center and saw a rainbow of awnings, tents, and food trucks. Pie makers from twenty different states were set up in kiosks along both sides of the street. Dispersed among the bakers was an assortment of food and merchandise vendors. Due to the warm temperatures and cloudless sky, Ella Mae predicted that the merchants offering cold treats would make a killing. After purchasing several pie samples, people would be more than ready for a snow cone, a tall cup of frozen lemonade, chilled bottled water, shaved ice, or Georgia Juice—a refreshing blend of peach juice, lime-flavored sparkling water, grenadine, and crushed mint.

Ella Mae and the rest of the judges started their tour of

the nation's pies an hour before the event opened to the public, and by the time they'd completed the first half of their tasting duties, they were all hot and thirsty.

"I can't eat another bite right now," one of the judges said, and wiped his glistening brow with a napkin.

"Why don't we take a break?" Ella Mae suggested. "We can catch our breaths at a picnic table and compare notes on what we've seen and tasted over cold glasses of Georgia Juice. I've chosen my favorites from the states we just visited, so maybe we can narrow down some of the entries before we proceed."

The rest of the judges thought this was an excellent idea. After delighting in a few sips of Georgia Juice, they took turns sharing which pie makers had made an impression with their costumes, presentation, and food.

"I loved the ginger-crumble pumpkin pie made by Mrs. Redman of Illinois," said one of the male judges. "Mr. Redman should get bonus points for dressing in that pumpkin costume. Did you spot his green tights? And the way those artificial vines curled around his arms and head?"

Another judge nodded. "The Redmans also used creative props to describe the history of pumpkins." She glanced down at her notes. "They made mats of dried pumpkin the same way the Native Americans did, and I was fascinated by Mrs. Redman's demonstration on how the colonists prepared pumpkins. She cut off the top, took out all the seeds, and then filled the inside with honey, milk, and several spices. She then baked the pumpkin in hot ashes. Did anyone else try a bite of the finished product? Delicious!"

"I also liked how they had printouts with pumpkin facts and activities for the kids attending today's event. However, I didn't care for their pie." The judge gave an apologetic shrug. "The ginger overpowered the rest of the flavors."

The group was in complete agreement that a contestant from Mississippi had designed a wonderful backdrop of paddleboats cruising down the mighty river, but had dropped the ball when it came to the mud pie. "It tasted like chocolate pudding topped with spray-can cream. There was no garnish and the crust was soggy. One shouldn't have to eat pie with a spoon."

Ella Mae felt guilty about placing an X next to Mississippi, because she knew the baker had devoted a great deal of time and energy to this event, but they had to move on.

"At this point, my favorite state is Kentucky," Ella Mae said. "The baker's excellent chocolate-nut pie followed the original nineteen fifties recipe from the Melrose Inn of Prospect, Kentucky. The walnuts were perfectly roasted, the bourbon gave the filling just the right amount of moistness, and the high-quality chocolate lent it a very rich flavor. The crust was perfect. It was as flaky as a Southern biscuit."

"The lady baker did an amazing job with her presentation too," agreed another judge. "I loved how the sampler plates were arranged on top of saddles and that she used a trophy to hold plastic forks and napkins. But the best part of her costume was that hat."

The judge next to Ella Mae laughed. "I don't know how she managed to serve us with that thing on her head. It must weigh twenty pounds. The whole racetrack is on that hat, including a Churchill Downs spire. And the horses actually move!"

"My top pick goes to the gentleman from Oregon. He promised that his chocolate hazelnut pie would make me swoon, and he wasn't kidding." The female judge shook her head in wonder. "I'm not even a big fan of hazelnuts, but he was very charismatic. I've never met anyone more passionate about nuts."

"He can trace his family's roots back to the pioneer days," another woman said. "When his great-grandparents emigrated from Germany, they brought filbert saplings with them. Apparently, his relatives have been growing *hasselnuss* ever since."

The man across from Ella Mae frowned. "Unfortunately, I liked the name of his bakery, In a Nutshell, far more than I liked his pie. It was overpoweringly sweet."

The woman who'd mentioned swooning looked annoyed. "You didn't care for the mud pie either. Maybe you just don't enjoy chocolate-flavored desserts."

"I love chocolate. The Michigan couple made a lovely chocolate cherry pie." He rubbed his jaw. "That pie would have gotten my vote, but there was a pit in my sample, which kind of ruined the tasting experience for me."

In the end, the judges decided that the top bakers from the first half of the Parade of Nations were Kentucky and Oregon.

"The second half will be even more difficult, I'm afraid," Ella Mae told the group. "We'll be tasting incredible apple pies from New York, key lime and lemon pies from Florida, sweet potato pies from North Carolina, blueberry pies from Maine, and peanut butter pies from Georgia."

The man next to Ella Mae was clearly confused. "Peanut butter? Why not peaches?"

"Don't tell anyone, but South Carolina produces more peaches than Georgia." Ella Mae spoke in a conspiratorial whisper. "They have for years."

"How scandalous!" One of the women chuckled and put her finger to her lips. "Don't worry. Your secret is safe with us."

As Ella Mae walked from booth to booth with the other judges, sampling pies and listening to brief presentations, she was able to put her worries aside. The event had a carnival atmosphere. The air was perfumed by the aromas of buttered corn, sausage on a stick, pulled pork sandwiches, and fried pickles. A man selling pie-shaped balloons passed the time by juggling oranges until the general public entered.

"I'm glad you included other food vendors," one of the judges said. "I never thought there could be such a thing as too much pie, but if I have any appetite later on—and I mean much later on—I'll be lining up for a pulled pork sandwich and fried pickles."

Their next stop was the Indiana booth, where they tasted Hoosier Pie. "Also called sugar cream pie," said a middle-aged woman wearing a plain dress and cap in the Amish style. She went on to explain that pies with similar ingredients existed all over the country. "Pies made using ingredients you'd find in the pantries of most farms are known as Desperation Pies. Buttermilk, shoofly, and vinegar pies are some examples. One thing that hasn't changed for a century is the tradition of stirring the Hoosier Pie filling with your finger instead of a spoon. This keeps the bottom crust from tearing."

Ella Mae, who'd popped her pie sample into her mouth while the women was speaking, paused midchew. She swallowed the intensely sugary bite and cleansed her palate with a sip of water.

She and the judges thanked the baker and moved on to the North Carolina booth. The adorable young couple representing the state ran a bakery called From Scratch. They told the judges that they'd only been married for two weeks and had signed up for the event as a wedding gift to each other. "We love this place!" the fresh-faced bride declared. "And Lake Havenwood Resort is so romantic. For two people who share a passion for baking, this whole trip has been a dream come true."

"We prepared two kinds of sweet potato pie," her husband said, stepping forward with samples. He wore an orange suit and his new wife wore a sundress in the same shade. "The first is baked in a pecan gingersnap crust, and the second is topped with a cinnamon-flavored meringue. My beautiful bride and I think sweet potato pie can compete with the rest of the entries here just fine on its own, but we try to incorporate layers of flavor into all of our pies. It's what our bakery is known for back home."

The young couple shared several interesting facts about the sweet potato. The judges were surprised to learn that it was one of the world's oldest known vegetables. "Evidence suggests that it may have existed during prehistoric times," the young man said. "That's why our backdrop shows a dinosaur eating a mouthful of sweet potatoes."

After thanking the enthusiastic newlyweds, the judges made their way to the South Carolina booth, where two bleached blondes tried to charm them with peach pie, dresses straight out of *Gone with the Wind*, and exaggerated drawls. Ella Mae was unimpressed by their pie, which was overcooked, as well as their presentation, which was thin on content. The Southern belles seemed to be relying on their pretty smiles and generous décolletage to win them a place among the finalists, but Ella Mae doubted that they'd be successful.

Besides, it would be hard for anyone to outshine Sugar, who was representing Florida. Entering Sugar's booth was like walking into the middle of an orchard of three-dimensional lemon and lime trees. Glittery fruit hung from every bough, and a yellow disco ball dangled from a wire attached to a metal frame concealed behind the highest branches. As the ball spun, fragments of light danced over the trees, and the fruit sparkled and glowed.

Sugar's Mother Nature costume was a grass-green dress trimmed with leaves, flowers, and benevolent insects. Her headdress was made of gold sunrays, and when she lifted her arms, plastic blue beads hanging from blue threads mimicked falling raindrops.

Her key lime pie was heavenly, and as the judges chewed

in silent appreciation, Sugar explained that her secret was that she only used juice from fresh-squeezed key limes.

"You can't get that Florida sunshine in a bottle," she said with a bright smile. "The same goes for lemons. And you need to pick them at the peak of their ripeness. I go into the orchard about an hour after dawn, when the fruit is covered in dew, and give it a good sniff. I can smell when it's ready." She gestured around the booth. "I focus on nature's role in cooking. The best food contains fresh ingredients. The fewer steps from ground to table is what makes a great dish, and the same is true of pies."

Ella Mae could tell that the judges had not only enjoyed both of Sugar's pies, but they were also taken with her sincerity and dedication. With only three booths remaining, Ella Mae wondered if anyone could top Sugar's Sunshine Lemon Pie. Still, she kept an open mind at the Maine and Georgia booths, but neither the blueberry nor the peanut butter pies could hold a candle to Sugar's.

At last, the judges reached the final booth.

"I hoped you saved some room!" shouted a man in a red apple costume. He removed his brown stovepipe hat and swept it from left to right. "We're the Bergers from the Big Apple. The Empire State produces more apples than any other state except for Washington." Beckoning the judges inside, he introduced his daughter and baking partner. "This is Nora. She designed and painted our whole backdrop."

Nora hobbled out from behind a table covered with a red-and-green checkered cloth and whispered a shy "Hello." She wore overalls, a white T-shirt, and a baseball hat embroidered with the American flag. She leaned heavily on a pair of crutches, and Ella Mae noticed that her legs were slightly bent and the toe of her left shoe dragged along the ground when she walked.

"CP?" asked a female judge softly.

When Nora nodded, the judge smiled. "My son has CP too. He's about your age, but he's more into video games than art. This is incredible!" She pointed at Nora's display, and the rest of the judges pressed forward for a better look.

Nora had painted the history of apple pie in America. Her timeline began with a motorized ship bearing colonists and apple trees across curled pipe cleaner waves. In the next scene, early settlers were harvesting fruit from the trees, which their pioneer descendants were baking into pies. The final scene showed a pie-eating contest followed by three rows of pies on display at a county fair. Naturally, the apple pie took the blue ribbon. As with the ship, certain pieces in each scene moved via a hidden motor. Apples dropped into baskets, the flames in an oven flickered, and a man in the pie-eating contest pushed a slice toward his mouth again and again. Behind the row of pies at the fair, a Ferris wheel turned in a steady rhythm.

"Don't tell me you bake too," said the female judge.

Nora's father answered for her. "She sure does! When this kid isn't at school, she helps out in the bakery. She's always coming up with new recipes. Two of our three samples are Nora originals."

"Stop bragging, Dad." Nora acted embarrassed, but the mutual affection between father and daughter was apparent.

After Nora's presentation on apple pies, her father passed out samples. "We have three pies for your tasting pleasure. The first is called America's Bounty, and it's your traditional double-crust apple pie. Next up is our Firecracker Apple Pie. The firecracker refers to the jalapeño pepper jelly, which gives this pie a little kick. The third sample is Nora's latest invention. It's called State Fair Apple Pie. This apple pie has a funnel-cake bottom crust and a topping of layered whipped cream, chocolate syrup, and a maraschino cherry."

Stuffed as she was, Ella Mae looked forward to trying

Nora's recipes. She found the sweet and spicy combination of the Firecracker Apple Pie most intriguing, and while the State Fair Pie was somewhat messy and a bit heavy for her taste, Ella Mae had to credit Nora for her inventiveness.

"You are a very talented young lady," she told Nora. "I'm so glad you and your father came to this event. It wouldn't have been complete without your apple pies."

Having visited every Parade of Nations booth, the judges gratefully retired to an air-conditioned conference room in the library to deliberate.

"I heard you talking to that sweet girl on crutches," a judge said to the woman who'd mentioned her son. "I hope you don't mind my asking, but what is CP?"

"Cerebral palsy. My Josh was diagnosed when he was three." The judge smiled. "He's the light of my life. Like Nora, he doesn't let his condition get in his way. And if I must confess, my vote for New York as one of the top three might be a teeny bit influenced by that plucky young woman."

"Fair enough," her colleague said.

It didn't take long for the group to pick the top six bakers, but choosing the first-, second-, and third-place winners set off an animated debate. Ella Mae was as fervent as the rest of the judges in fighting for her favorites, and she relished every second of the discussion. It was sheer joy to be among people who were so devoted to food and who took their judging roles seriously.

Eventually, they came to a consensus, and Ella Mae thanked the judges for their time and presented them with small gifts of appreciation. She then made a call to the print shop and told them the names to add to the oversized cardboard checks. After that, she phoned the bank to have the real checks drawn up.

Ella Mae barely made it to The Charmed Pie Shoppe for

the start of tea service, but there were no customers waiting
when she arrived. In fact, they only served one couple during the first hour of business.

"Can't say that I'm surprised." Reba said. "Everyone's at
the Parade of Nations. I know this borders on blasphemy,
but folks might not want pie for days after that event."

Ella Mae nodded. "You're probably right. I'm so full from
this morning that I can hardly look at a slice of pie."

Reba jerked her thumb toward the back door. "You should
go home. Take a long walk. Play with Chewie. Have a moment
to yourself. Jenny and I will hold the fort. If we don't get more
customers, we'll just close up shop."

"You both deserve a break too." Ella Mae untied her apron.
"But I'm not going home. I'm driving to Atlanta to see Aunt
Dee."

Reba frowned. "You can't go by yourself."

"I was going to ask Aiden to come along. Not only is he
a good bodyguard, but I also think he's tired of being my
delivery boy. It's time we had a heart-to-heart."

Aiden was more than happy to oblige. He even insisted on
driving so Ella Mae could relax. As they headed south, they
spoke of pleasant things. Aiden talked about the mischief he
and Jenny had gotten into when they were children, and Ella
Mae shared her own memories of growing up in Havenwood.

Eventually, Ella Mae shot Aiden a sideways glance, and said,
"I know you love being around your sister, and you've been
invaluable to me, but your true talent is wasted at The Charmed
Pie Shoppe. Have you been looking for electrical work?"

Aiden chewed his lip. "Actually, Finn Mercer and I have
been batting ideas around. We've been texting like teenage
girls."

"Really?" An image of Finn's friendly face appeared in
Ella Mae's mind and she smiled. "What kind of ideas?"

"Adding lighting to his custom furniture installs for starters. I told him I could do that—no sweat—but that he shouldn't stop there. Why not create a whole line of lighting? He's into natural materials, so I suggested he include light fixtures that replicate natural sunlight. Lots of people respond to light therapy, and I could give each and every piece of lighting an extra jolt of energy. Of course, I couldn't tell him about my magic touch, but I brought him a prototype I made a few months ago in your mom's garage. There was a bunch of scrap metal in there, and she said I could do whatever I wanted with it, so I made a floor lamp."

Aiden's enthusiasm for the project was contagious. Before long, Ella Mae was coming up with ideas too. "How about a chandelier with flower-shaped bulbs? Or a shade made from beads that light up? Like a string of pearls."

"Cool," Aiden said. "We need girlie pieces. Only so many women will want faux antler wall sconces or cowhide desk lamps." He eased off the highway and stopped at a traffic signal. "Would you be okay if I left the pie shop to work with Finn?"

"Absolutely." She smiled at him. "I want you to do what makes you happy. Pie isn't your passion. It's mine. Though my deliveries are sure to fall off. Lots of ladies placed orders just so you'd knock on their doors."

Aiden shrugged. "They'll have to get used to it, because this man only cares about pleasing one lady in particular."

"Does Suzy know about your plans?"

Aiden shook his head. "I wanted to talk to you first, but after I firm things up with Finn, I'll take Suzy out to dinner and tell her all about it. I bet she'll have tons of ideas. She's the smartest person I've ever met."

Ella Mae feared Aiden would spend the rest of the trip extolling Suzy's finer qualities, but as he wasn't familiar with Atlanta, he was forced to listen to the GPS. At the burn center, Aiden dropped Ella Mae at the front door, and said, "Tell your aunt that Jenny and I send our best. Call me when you're ready to leave and I'll meet you here. I'm just going to park, get in touch with Finn, and give him the good news. I know he's packing, but he won't mind being interrupted by his new best bud."

"Tell him I hope his move goes smoothly," Ella Mae said, thanked Aiden, and entered the lobby. She was suddenly very nervous. Her discomfort grew as she rode the elevator to Dee's floor. She didn't know what she'd find when she got there. What would her aunt look like? Would she speak to her? Or would she avert her eyes and refuse to say a word?

When Ella Mae reached Aunt Dee's room, she found the door ajar and heard a man's voice coming from inside. The voice belonged to August Templeton.

" 'Where you tend a rose, my lad, a thistle cannot grow,' " he said, and Ella Mae felt a thrill of delight. August was reading from *The Secret Garden*, one of her all-time favorite books.

Tiptoeing into the room, she saw that August had pulled his chair close to Dee's bed, and he had a hardcover spread open on his lap. He was showing Dee a colorful illustration when he spotted Ella Mae out of the corner of his eye.

"What a treat!" he exclaimed softly, set the book aside, and came forward to enfold her in a warm hug. August was a round man with a shiny pate and a pair of deep dimples on his round cheeks. He wore a seersucker suit, complete with a silk trifold handkerchief protruding from the breast pocket. August's impeccable manners, quick wit, and fastidiousness reminded Ella Mae of Hercule Poirot.

"Hello, August. It's wonderful to see you," she said, and then added, "How is everything?"

August took Ella Mae's hand and led her away from the

bed. "Your aunt is taking it easy after yesterday's skin graft surgery, but speaking with you will be a balm to her spirit." He gave Ella Mae's shoulder an affectionate pat and then glanced at Dee, who was propped up on two pillows, looking both alert and tired at the same time. "Delia, I'm off to get tea and a few magazines. I'm sure you've been dying to learn all about the latest celebrity scandals and fashion faux pas."

August left the room, and Ella Mae took his seat. Leaning over, she planted a feather-light kiss her aunt's forehead. Without warning, her eyes filled with tears. "I'm so sorry."

Dee gazed at her in confusion. "Why? You're not responsible for what happened."

"But I have yet to discover who set that fire." When Dee didn't respond, Ella Mae let the silence wash over her. She found it comforting after all the noise she'd been exposed to recently.

She touched a lock of her aunt's long, auburn hair. "I hardly ever see your hair loose. You always wear it in a braid. It's so beautiful, like sunlight hitting autumn leaves."

"Gets in the way when I work, though." Dee said. Her words were a mere whisper, and Ella Mae had the feeling that her aunt had been using speech sparingly. "And I will work again," Dee added, a little louder this time. "My nerves weren't damaged, and though these skin grafts look nasty, I was lucky. I survived, thanks to you and Joyce Mercer's son."

"Finn." Ella Mae nodded. "He was amazing. And he's taking care of the mother cat we rescued. All of your animals are doing well."

"I'm sure I miss them more than they miss me." Dee picked at a loose thread on her blanket. "August arranged to have a volunteer from a local shelter drop by before my surgery yesterday. She brought a pair of Siamese kittens for me to hold. They climbed around on my bed, purring and playing—it was the first time I've laughed since . . ."

Ella Mae wished she could think of something better to say, but there were no words of comfort to ease Dee's emotional pain. "Would you tell me about him? About Kyran?"

Dee glanced at the wall. For a long moment, Ella Mae feared her aunt was shutting down, but then she sighed and began to speak.

"Kyran and I met in art school. It wasn't love at first sight. Not at all." Her mouth curved upward, and Ella Mae could tell that she was lost in a memory. "I thought he was arrogant and he saw me as a flaky idealist. When a professor assigned us a joint project, we learned we had similar abilities. We slowly became friends and eventually spent all of our free time together. We worked in the studio after hours, went out to eat, attended lectures, took long hikes, and had picnics that would last for hours. By the end of the year, we'd fallen in love."

Dee turned back to Ella Mae and spread her hands in a gesture of helplessness. "Kyran told me from the very beginning that he had a fiancée waiting for him in India. After graduation, he'd return to his home country, marry her, and raise a family. His parents and her parents had signed a marriage contract when Kyran and his future wife were young children, so his future was planned without his consent."

"Did he have to marry this other woman?" Ella Mae asked quietly. "Especially after falling in love with you?"

"He was an honorable man," Dee replied. "He wasn't in love with his fiancée, but he was fond of her. He'd known her his whole life. Their union would please both families, and he felt duty-bound to go through with it." She shook her head. "We should have stayed away from each other, but we didn't. We were caught in each other's orbits. Perhaps our feelings were intensified because we knew we'd have to part. We tried to cram a lifetime into those four years." A light danced in her eyes as she spoke. "After graduation, I drove him to the airport. We kissed good-bye on the curb in the pouring rain, and he left. I've hated rainy days ever since."

Ella Mae stared at her aunt. "That was it? You never saw Kyran again?"

"Not until he came to Havenwood. A few months ago, I read about his wife's passing in our alumni newsletter. It was cancer. I sent Kyran a card and a little bird sculpture. A week later, he called me." Dee put her hand on her heart. "Hearing the sound of his voice again after all these years was like listening to a beautiful song. We talked for hours, and the next thing I knew, he was en route to Havenwood." She smiled shyly. "We were just getting to know each other again while making those birds. I thought they'd end up being the most memorable work of our lives."

"I have an idea of how they still can be," Ella Mae said. "I'll explain another time. Let's just say that the moment I get home, I'm going to call all of our people together and tell them how I think these birds can help put an end to these killer storms."

"To do that, you'll have to make peace with the people creating them." Dee touched Ella Mae's cheek. "Now, I have something to say to you. Verena told me about Hugh. I know what you're going through—perhaps better than anyone— but you mustn't surrender to your pain."

"I'm not." Ella Mae was instantly defensive. "I have too much going on to think about Hugh."

"You *should* think about him." Dee's voice was unusually firm. "You've loved that boy since you were seven years old. Since he climbed a tree to rescue your kite."

Ella Mae had completely forgotten about that incident. She suddenly flashed on an image of Hugh perched on a tree limb, his legs dangling in the air as he tried to extract her kite from where it had been trapped between a nest of branches. The kite had been Ella Mae's most prized possession. It had showed a glittery rainbow on a field of blue. The blue had been the same shade as Hugh's eyes. "How—?"

"You came home with a look on your face that we've all seen a million times since then. At the very mention of Hugh's name, you'd glow like the sun. Don't you dare convince yourself that what you two shared wasn't real—that it's not worth fighting for. Because it is. It's worth *everything*." She squeezed Ella Mae's hand. "He may have wandered, but you haven't lost him. Bring him back, my sweet girl. Because no matter how many others you save, you won't have a happy ending without him."

Ella Mae felt heavy with sorrow. "I don't think I believe in those anymore."

Dee let out a little laugh that sounded like the tinkling bells over the door of The Charmed Pie Shoppe. "Of course you do."

Chapter 14

The award ceremony that took place Friday morning to honor the prize-winning bakers was a jubilant affair.

The event was held in Lake Havenwood Resort's auditorium, and when Ella Mae entered the room, she tried not to glance at the spot where she and Hugh had kissed for the last time. Instead, she sat on the opposite side of the room and struck up a conversation with an elderly couple from Alabama.

Ella Mae was relieved that she didn't have to serve as master of ceremonies. That distinction fell to Havenwood's mayor, her uncle Buddy. He opened the program by thanking everyone for participating. "The residents of Havenwood certainly hope you'll come back and visit us again. Our town is home to so many delightful events!"

He then launched into a detailed description of the summer's Row for Dough race, the Autumn Harvest Fest, the Christmas Carnival, and the Winter Wonderland Festival.

He painted such a charming picture of each event that Ella Mae was certain the resort would soon be taking many new reservations.

The mayor finished his opening remarks by reminding the audience that the Founder's Day Ball would start at six that evening. He then asked Verena to join him onstage. "This is my lovely wife, the first lady of Havenwood," he said as she appeared in a curve-hugging houndstooth dress and a pair of cherry-red heels.

Taking the microphone from her husband, Verena's voice burst through the speakers. "I tell you folks, it takes a formidable woman to handle these formidable checks!" The audience cheered in response. "For the past week, you've treated us to incredible food. I hope you had a wonderful time and made lots of new friends. And none of this would have been possible without the efforts of my niece." Her eyes flashed with pride. "Ella Mae LeFaye, wherever you are, please stand. I'm sure these folks would like to express how much they enjoyed Havenwood's inaugural History in the Baking Festival."

Groaning inwardly, Ella Mae rose and turned to wave at the crowd. She was both pleased and embarrassed by the raucous applause.

Verena waited for the noise to abate before shouting, "Let's get to the prizes!"

From that point, the ceremony proceeded swiftly. Verena announced the winners of the Best Costume, Best Presentation, and Best Pie among the History of Pie contestants, and Ella Mae was thrilled to see the Shermans claim one of the oversized checks. Bill and Linda Sherman had been the first out-of-towners to offer their unwavering support, and she would never forget when they'd first shown her the clover symbol. She saw people flashing it to one another all the time now and knew it had become a gesture of unity.

After the History of Pie prizes were bestowed, her aunt and uncle introduced the winners of the pie-eating contests. The winner in the junior category was a slim teenage girl who told the audience she competed in eating contests throughout the Southeast in hopes of saving enough money to pay for college. The adult winner was a short man with fleshy cheeks and a protruding belly. After accepting his check, he congratulated the teenager and praised her for pursuing an education. The pair exchanged friendly hugs, and the audience released a collective "awww."

Prizes were presented to the chefs who'd given the best cooking demonstrations and lectures, and then it was time for the Parade of Nations awards. Ella Mae grinned as the honorable mentions were presented to the baker from Oregon, who'd been so zealous about hazelnuts, and to the couple from Illinois, who'd shared a passion for pumpkins. Third place went to Kentucky, and Ella Mae had to laugh as the lady baker took the stage wearing her Derby hat. She bounced up and down with such glee that some of the racehorses flew right off the brim and into the second-row seats.

Verena cracked a joke about "holding one's horses" and then beckoned to the mayor to come forward with the next oversized check. "The next winning bakers pulled out all the stops! The judges were impressed by their presentation, creative décor, and the uniqueness of the pie samples. How could one *not* be bowled over by a pie made with a funnel-cake crust? I'd like to congratulate the Bergers of New York. Joel and Nora, you're the apple of our eye!"

Ella Mae had asked the resort manager to save seats for the Bergers near the stage. Nora shrieked in happy surprise, and her father lifted out of her seat and swung her around in a circle. "We did it, my girl!" he cried.

When he put her down, Nora grabbed her crutches and

made her way onstage. As she approached Verena, Nora said, "My purse can't hold a check that big."

Verena laughed and pressed an envelope into Mr. Berger's hand. "Don't worry, honey. Your daddy can take this one straight to the bank."

As soon as the Bergers moved off to join the other winners, a hush fell over the auditorium. "The overall winner of the Parade of Nations showed the judges that fresh ingredients, purity of taste, and attentiveness to detail matter above all else. This baker created a backdrop that brought us closer to nature and a pie that brought us closer to heaven. It's an honor to present the grand prize to Sugar Jackson of Florida for her Sunshine Lemon Pie."

Sugar came jogging down the center aisle, whooping and hollering like a contestant on *The Price Is Right*. Instead of bounding up the stage steps, she turned left, barreled straight over to Ella Mae, and gathered her into a fierce hug. "Bless you, sweetheart," she said. "I've been dreaming of owning a little piece of land, and now I can buy one. This is just the extra bit of change I needed to top off my piggy bank. You and the other judges have made a lifelong dream come true."

Ella Mae smiled. "You earned it. Now, go claim that check before my uncle Buddy tries to add it to his campaign fund."

Sugar hurried to the stage and kissed Verena and Buddy before bursting into tears of joy. The mayor asked all the winners take a final bow and then thanked the audience again. The lights came up and people began to file out of the room. Ella Mae was the last to leave. History in the Baking was over. She could hardly believe it. The entire week had been a great success, and though she wanted to relish this moment, she knew that many of the people who'd just left the room would be meeting her in the grove tomorrow. They wouldn't be gathering to celebrate, but to discuss whether or not they dared to use their gifts to stop a storm.

For the storm was coming. It had been steadily moving toward Havenwood all week.

And with it would come a woman named Nimue.

Lost in thought, Ella Mae walked through the lobby and stepped outside. A tenuous cloud cover had moved in that morning, and it had grown markedly thicker throughout the course of the day.

"I wonder when we'll see the sun again," Ella Mae murmured, and headed to The Charmed Pie Shoppe. In the kitchen, she found Reba, Jenny, and Fiona staring at the small screen of a portable television.

"We thought we'd better keep an eye on how fast the storm is moving," Jenny said as Ella Mae hung her purse on a hook. "It's flying. Come see."

Peering at the tiny screen, Ella Mae saw a map of western North Carolina. A meteorologist pointed at the wide swath of green in the western part of the state. The mass was rotating south toward Georgia. Both man and map were replaced by an aerial shot of the flooded homes around Lake James. A reporter in foul-weather gear interviewed a bereft resident before the meteorologist returned on-screen. He gestured at a second map, circling a river with his pointer finger.

"This is the Broad River," he said. "It's completely unrecognizable to those who've lived along its banks for decades."

Footage of the churning rush of a river filled the screen. The water carried trees and other large pieces of debris in its feverish current and Ella Mae gasped when the roof of a car shot by in a flash of silver.

"Right before you walked in, they showed a town that looked like Havenwood," Reba said. "The water was up to people's knees. The whole business district was flooded.

It'll take years and Lord knows how much money to get the place up and runnin' again."

"It might never come back," Fiona said. "Sometimes, when a thing is too far gone, folks just walk away from it."

Jenny nodded. "That's what happened to my town. After our grove was burned, people wanted to start over elsewhere. Most of them didn't even try to sell their houses. They just loaded their cars and drove off."

Ella Mae stared at the screen. "The storm has really picked up speed in the last twelve hours. If I didn't know better, I'd say Nimue was in a hurry to get here."

"According to the weatherman, the system will hit our area tomorrow night, which is fine with me. I'm ready to rumble." Reba smacked her palm with her fist.

Ella Mae turned to Jenny. "I hope your cousin arrives ahead of the storm."

"He'll by here by noon, and he's looking forward to meeting you." Jenny switched off the television. "What else needs to be done to get ready for the gathering in the grove?"

The bell over the front door chimed. "For the moment, let's focus on our customers," Ella Mae said. "I'm afraid tomorrow's Beltane celebration won't be as merry as I'd hoped. We'll be lucky to have a dance and a cup of wine before the storm hits."

"All the more reason to eat, drink, and live it up!" Reba declared. "I plan to be the belle of the Founder's Day Ball." She elbowed Jenny. "Are you in?"

Jenny grinned. "Only if you promise to save some men for me."

Together, they pushed through the swing doors into the dining room.

"I invited a few of my own people to join us for Beltane—some Scots who'd like to get their hands on the woman who tried to ruin their lives," Fiona said. "If Nimue tries to mess with you, they'll be your first line of defense." She glanced at her watch. "They'll be landing in Atlanta in about an hour, so unless you need me, Carol and I will pick them up."

"You go ahead." Ella Mae put an apron over her head. "I'm all set."

"Until Beltane, then." Fiona said.

Ella Mac nodded. "Until Beltane."

Long ago, Beltane marked the unofficial beginning of summer. People would accompany their livestock to the summer pastures and then gather around an enormous bonfire to perform rituals encouraging a bountiful harvest. They'd also sing, dance, and feast beneath the open sky until night gave way to dawn.

In Havenwood, the festivities took place in the hidden grove in the mountains high above the lake. A traditional bonfire was lit, and everyone dressed in loose, flowing clothes bedecked with yellow and orange flowers meant to echo the bonfire's flames.

On the morning preceding the Beltane celebration, Havenwood woke to a pounding rain and a forceful breeze. Ella Mae hoped that people had listened to the mayor's announcement the previous evening. During the Founder's Day Ball, he'd advised visitors to get on their way as soon as possible the next morning and asked residents to prepare for the storm if they hadn't done so already. The locals who'd been around to witness Havenwood's last major flood had already stocked up on canned food and batteries, but Ella Mae knew that there weren't enough sandbags in all of Georgia to stop Lake Havenwood from overflowing once the rain started falling at four to five inches per hour.

Despite the downpour, someone had decorated the frame around Ella Mae's front door. When she opened it to give Chewie a chance to do his business before she headed to the grove, Ella Mae found garlands of marigolds and yellow primrose woven with rowan and hawthorn branches brightening her threshold. There was also a posy of buttercups, goldenrods, and fern leaves tied with a saffron ribbon on her welcome mat.

Once Chewie was ready to come back in, Ella Mae ushered him into the kitchen and toweled him off. She then spread an old blanket over the sofa, invited him to jump up, and waited until he was comfortable before kissing the top of his head several times.

"I'll be home soon, boy. You guard the house, okay?"

Chewie pricked his ears and cocked his head, as if he didn't quite believe her. He whined when she opened the front door, and she promised that she wouldn't leave him alone for long.

Stepping into the rain, she prayed she could keep that promise.

She ran to her truck and discovered another bouquet of gold and orange flowers on the passenger seat. The interior was redolent with their perfume. Ella Mae touched the silky petals and smiled. Only her mother could have cultivated blossoms that looked like flames. She sat there for several moments, the rain hammering against the metal of her truck, and thought of how fire could be both destructive and beneficial. That led to thoughts of Dee and her aunt's advice about Hugh.

"I don't know how to fight for him." But as she watched the rain stream down the windshield, she suddenly realized how much she wanted to try. There was no denying her feelings. She loved the man. No matter what he'd said or done, she loved him. She always had and always would. "I've hinged everyone's future on love, so it had better save the day. If I'm wrong,

Havenwood will fall and it won't matter what I feel for Hugh Dylan," she murmured, starting the engine and driving away.

As Ella Mae passed through downtown, she saw almost no signs of life. No cars lined the streets, and most of the shops were closed. She stopped at a traffic light near Perfectly Polished, Loralyn's nail salon, and fixed a worried gaze at the fluorescent Closed sign in the window. She and Loralyn had never been friends, but now Ella Mae truly didn't know what to think of her lifelong nemesis. Was Loralyn a murderer? Was she out there somewhere, plotting Ella Mae's demise and thinking of ways to welcome Nimue to Havenwood?

The rain increased in intensity and, though the wiper blades on Ella Mae's truck beat back and forth at top speed, she couldn't see to the end of the next block. The wind had also picked up and was whipping the groundwater into miniature tidal waves.

Ella Mae had checked the local radar map on her computer shortly before she'd let Chewie out and knew that Havenwood was getting its first taste of Caliban's fury. Still, she felt strangely calm. The time had come for Ella Mae to face the woman who called herself the Clover Queen. The woman who'd captivated Hugh Dylan. The woman who had likely convinced a resident of Havenwood to murder an old lady and set a barn on fire with two people trapped inside.

Leaving downtown behind, Ella Mae hit the winding mountain road and picked up speed. "Yes, the Lady of the Lake is almost here, and I'm ready to give her a greeting the likes of which she'll never forget."

The parking lot at the base of the mountain trail was already packed when Ella Mae pulled into a makeshift spot on a level patch of grass and hustled up the trail. She had to dig her heels into the sodden ground to make any headway.

The wind and slanting rain seemed determined to push her back down the mountain.

Once inside the grove, her dripping hair and saturated clothes dried immediately. She entered the orchard to find Jenny, Aiden, and Suzy with a man dressed in leather pants and a black T-shirt. He had shoulder-length hair the color of sunlit bronze and a close-cropped beard of a slightly ruddier shade. Ella Mae couldn't see his face because he was bent over, rifling through a backpack.

"We wanted to catch you before you headed through to the meadow," Jenny said, and pointed at the man. "This is Tyson Upton. We wanted to surprise you with a fireworks show. It's all set up and ready to be launched."

"Call me Ty." The man dropped the bag and flashed Ella Mae an electric grin. "My name means 'fiery and high-spirited,' but people always think of chicken when they hear it. That's me. A forty-year-old chicken." He shrugged in amused defeat while Ella Mae studied him. Ty's muscular forearms were tattooed with intertwined knots and swirls, he had a jagged scar on his forehead, and his eyes were the blue of an icy fjord. He had the confident bearing and the challenging stare of a Viking. And when he fixed his stare on Ella Mae, he made it plain that he liked what he saw. "Say the word, and I'll light up the sky."

Ella Mae jerked her thumb toward the entrance. "Outside? In the rain?"

He grinned. "Rain can't stop my rockets. In fact, folks will see them clear across the lake."

An idea came to Ella Mae, similar to the one she'd had when visiting Aunt Dee. "Jenny said that your fireworks can take any shape. Is that true?"

"Within reason, but yes."

Ella Mae quickly shared her vision and Ty's face grew

animated. "I like it," he said. "Let me go outside and make some adjustments. And after my show is over, I'll still be yours to command. I don't like folks threatening my family's friends, and Jenny said you've been a real good friend to her."

She thanked him, and he flashed his killer grin again. "You don't seem to be afraid of the storm or of this Nimue woman. That's good."

Ella Mae gestured at Suzy and the Upton siblings. "They give me courage." She then pointed through the tree branches toward the meadow where the bonfire burned. "All of them."

Suzy hooked Ella Mae's arm in hers and pulled her away from Ty. "We're not facing any foes without eating and drinking first."

Ella Mae laughed. "Feast away. Just go easy on the honeyed wine. I might need to call on that photographic memory of yours."

Fiddle music floated through the air and as Ella Mae and Suzy approached the meadow, they saw people dancing around the bonfire. The banquet had been laid closer to the orchard and the grass was littered with tables covered with yellow cloth and decadent dishes. After greeting dozens of people, Ella Mae ate a small piece of sliced beef in wild mushroom sauce and a forkful of golden potatoes seasoned with fresh rosemary. Having finished her meal, she inspected the objects she'd tasked a select group of men and women to make over the course of the week, and then sat down next to Aunt Verena and Leslie Conrad.

"I'm sorry I couldn't be of more help," Leslie was saying to Verena. "Hugh hasn't been in the office since Wednesday, and there's nothing on his computer. I think he realized I couldn't be trusted. But I didn't say a word to him, I swear."

Verena snapped a carrot stick in half. "Who else knew

that you were keeping an eye out for any communication between Nimue and Hugh?"

Ella Mae was just about to take a sip of wine when she froze with the cup halfway to her mouth. She knew the answer to that question. Only one other person outside Ella Mae's inner sanctum knew. "Lord, no." The words came out as moan.

"What is it?" Verena asked.

Instead of answering, Ella Mae's eyes darted around the meadow. "Where's Reba?"

"She's by the butterfly bush talking with the Drevers and their Scottish friends." Verena used a roast turkey leg to point at the bush. "What's happened?"

Leaving her cup on the grass, Ella Mae threaded her way through the press of people until she reached Reba's side. "I need you. I think I know who it is. Joyce and Kyran's murderer. The arsonist. The person who threw a brick through the pie shop window."

Fiona exchanged an alarmed look with Reba. "Is this vile creature here now?"

Ella Mae quickly found the person she was searching for and nodded. "Standing near the punch bowl."

Both Reba and Fiona frowned, clearly trying to comprehend how Ella Mae could call such an upstanding individual a murderer, but then the petite woman with auburn hair who'd been conversing with Carol stepped forward and said, "I'm Lundy. I've come from the Orkneys."

Ella Mae's eyes were locked on the figure by the punch bowl. "I don't mean to be rude"—she touched Lundy's arm without turning to her—"but I need to confront that woman. I believe she's a—"

"Selkie!" Lundy cried softly.

The word caught the attention of all the Scots, and Carol gasped. "Aye. Look at those dark eyes. Round as marbles.

I thought there was something familiar about her, but I never imagined a selkie would be so far from the sea."

Reba put her hands on her hips. "Are you tryin' to tell me that the woman we're all starin' at is a damned seal?"

Ella Mae, who'd been silently trying to accept that the world was even stranger than she'd already imagined it to be, whispered, "That makes sense." She grabbed Fiona's hand. "The night I showed up at your house uninvited, you said that selkies shed their sealskin when they come ashore. And if a person manages to steal that skin, they can control the selkie, right?"

Fiona nodded.

Without speaking, she and Reba began to move. Ella Mae was right alongside them.

"We'll flank her," Carol said to the other Scots from behind them.

Luckily, there were so many people in the meadow that the woman by the punch bowl didn't see them coming. At least not until Ella Mae raised her hands, signaling for a clear path. The music and chatter abruptly stopped. The crowd parted, and Ella Mae strode to the end of the banquet table and glared at the woman with the brown braid and the wide, dark eyes.

"You were right under my nose all along. You took our statements the night Joyce was killed. You were the first on scene the night of the fire. And you rushed to the hospital where Dee's life was dangling by a thread—undoubtedly to finish what you'd started—but you couldn't, because we beat you there." Ella Mae balled her hands into fists to prevent her fingers from wrapping around the woman's freckled neck and squeezing, squeezing. "How long has Nimue had your sealskin?" Her voice was a furious hiss.

The punch cup slipped from the woman's grasp and

dropped to the grass. Everyone waited in breathless silence as Officer Wallace gaped in astonishment.

Ella Mae expected a denial, but the young policewoman's shoulders sagged, and she said, "I've been her slave for two years." Her face crumpled and tears pooled in her dark eyes. "Everything she commanded me to do—all of those horrible things—I did while screaming inside. I would have died rather than hurt anyone, but Nimue refused to let me die. The only reason I can even speak freely now is because she's already in Havenwood. I've served my purpose."

"Why didn't you just kill me?" Ella Mae asked. "That would have been so much easier. Why go after Fiona? Why toss that brick or waste your energy torching the barn? You could have ended this months ago!"

Officer Wallace shook her head. "Nimue wants to deal with you herself. I don't know why. She doesn't tell me anything, she just gives me orders." She dropped to the ground and grabbed Ella Mae's pant legs. "Please end my suffering. I can't live with what I've done, but I don't have the power to take my own life. Not as long as she has my skin."

Reba's mouth curved in a cruel grin. "I'd be happy to volunteer."

As tempted as Ella Mae was to let Reba have her way, she shook her head. "Get Aunt Verena." She then put her hand under Officer Wallace's chin and forced her to look her in the eye. "What's your first name?"

"Marin."

Even her name sounded like the sea. Ella Mae studied the young woman's freckled face and tearful eyes and retreated a pace. "Stand up, Marin. If you've spoken the truth, then you're as much a victim as Joyce, Kyran, and Dee. But if you've lied, you will be punished." Ella Mae's stare was cold. "I swore to seek justice for Joyce and Kyran. One way or another, someone will pay a price for these crimes. My aunt, Delia LeFaye, may have something more to say about your fate. You burned her barn, her sculptures, and her body. Worse yet, you killed someone very dear to her and threatened the well-being of her beloved animals."

At the mention of animals, Marin let out an inhuman wail. "If I could have chewed off my human hands, I would have! It's against my nature to inflict pain on my fellow creatures. I've barely slept thinking of those poor cats and dogs."

Verena touched Ella Mae on the shoulder. "She's telling the truth."

Aunt Sissy jabbed a finger centimeters from Marin's chest. "Lucky for you. After what you did to my sister, I'd have gotten your sealskin back, flown you to South Africa, and fed you to the *biggest* white shark I could find." She backed away. "You remain a threat to us because you're still *her* creature. How does she communicate with you?"

"She has a blog. She posts assignments there," Marin said. "It's how she's recruited people over the years too."

"Is she headed for the island in the middle of Lake Havenwood?" Ella Mae asked.

Marin nodded. "Yes. She plans to flood the town using the lake water, starting with your house. That's all I know."

Chewie! Ella Mae thought but pushed the panic down. Fiona had said that throughout history, the women who'd held the title of Lady of the Lake had used islands to increase their abilities. Keeping this in mind, Ella Mae and the people who'd joined her had planned a defense around Nimue following this tradition. During her visit with Aunt Dee, the plan had fully bloomed in Ella Mae's mind and her people—those from Havenwood and from afar—had worked tirelessly to see her vision became a reality.

"If I can, I will get your skin back," Ella Mae told Marin. "But until then, you must be restrained. You can't control your actions and therefore are not to be trusted."

A local man on the other side of the table cleared his throat. "I can create a safe and secure place for her to, um, wait."

Fear flashed in Marin's eyes. "A cage?"

Ella Mae ignored her and focused on the man. "Show me, please."

The man walked to where a small copse of bamboo trees grew. He raised his hands and the trees creaked and groaned, bending over and intertwining until they'd formed a kind of cave. Ella Mae's mother placed a plate of food and a cup of wine inside and then beckoned to Marin. "When Officer Hardy returns and finds out what you've done, you'll be locked up for the rest of your life. You'll never swim again. If I were you, I'd climb in here and try to rest. It's quite comfortable. Nothing like the prison cell you'll face without our help."

Sobbing, Marin crawled into the cave and curled into a ball. Several bamboo stalks bent over and pushed themselves deep into the ground, blocking the entrance but still allowing for plenty of light and fresh air.

Ella Mae thanked the local man and then walked up the rise to the ash tree. She reached up into the branches and instantly came into contact with the cool metal of her crown. Placing the circlet on her head, she turned to find Alfonso waiting for her. After he'd touched her throat, she stood as tall and straight as she could and addressed her people.

"My friends, it's time for Tyson Upton to light up the sky. He's created a special greeting for those responsible for this and all the other terrible storms that have cause so much destruction over the past few weeks." She paused. "I don't want to declare war against those who decided to follow Nimue. I plan to invite them to join us instead. After we've done what we can to stop this storm, I'll go down the mountain to meet Nimue face-to-face. I will not return until I've dealt with her. And when I'm done and I've taken her sword, we'll gather again and discuss how to restore the ruined groves." Her voice sounded strange to her own ears. Where had she found this confidence? How could she be so certain of their success? But as she gazed at all the people standing shoulder to shoulder, she knew that she was borrowing courage from them.

In the stillness, the bonfire crackled, as if encouraging Ella Mae to continue. She spoke a little louder. "Are you ready to put aside your prejudices and stand with me, not as Gaynor and LeFaye, but as brother and sister?" She made a sweeping gesture with her arm. "Are we ready, at long last, to take our fate into our own hands?"

The crowd's roar was so powerful that the ground shook. People embraced and clapped and screamed as Ella Mae descended the hill.

She walked up to Ty and pointed skyward. "Burn a hole through the clouds and ignite the stars! Fill the night with rainbows of color! Show this woman that real magic is not about fear, but about beauty, hope, and unity!"

Cheers erupted in a fresh wave. The people followed Ella Mae as she made her way to the bonfire. She placed a branch from the ash tree in the center of the flames until the end caught fire. She then offered it to Ty. "In Beltane's of old, this fire had the power to mimic sunshine. People carried a burning stick into their homes to light their hearth fires. Now, take this flame, Tyson Upton, and light Havenwood's hearth fire. We will offer Nimue's people a place to call home."

Ty took the burning branch and followed Ella Mae out into the night.

Chapter 15

Ty had built a dome out of waterproof tarps at the edge of the parking lot to protect his pyrotechnics, and by the time he and Ella Mae ran down the trail and ducked beneath it, they were completely drenched. The wind slapped at the plastic roof and the rain sounded like machine-gun fire, but the fireworks were safe and dry and Ty promised Ella Mae that nothing would stop the show.

"My gift is a bit like Aiden's," he explained, checking a length of black cable. "I use an electrical firing system for my displays." He fiddled with a silver box housing a switchboard and wires. "That in itself isn't unusual. Lots of technicians use electrical firing systems. The difference is that I add a little magic to the electric charge. This transfers into each shell. When that shell is in the sky, the timer goes off, the powder ignites, and the stars inside explode bigger, brighter, and longer than normal fireworks. Not only that, but I can manipulate the patterns the stars form, which means I can make shapes other people can't. That's what will get the attention of the people by the lake. It'll be impossible for them not to notice the masterpiece I'm about to paint in the sky."

Ella Mae felt a thrill of excitement. If Ty could do what he claimed, she was on the cusp of witnessing something truly unforgettable.

At that moment, Aiden wriggled under one of the tarps and pushed the hood of his rain jacket off his face. Water dripped from the ends of his hair and ran down his cheeks. "Thought I'd lend you some extra juice," he said, smiling at his cousin.

Ty grinned. "Okay, then. Let's punch a few million holes in this storm."

The two men made their final preparations and then Ty asked Ella Mae to kneel behind a protective wall of sandbags. He handed her a pair of headphones with the assurance that they'd block out the worst of the noise. When she had them on, he lifted up the left earpiece, pulled a hunting knife from the inside of his boot, and shouted, "The second I cut a single tie, the tarp will be ripped off by the wind and Aiden and I will ignite the first round of shells. There'll be tons of smoke, but it should blow down the mountain. Are you ready?"

"Yes."

He signaled to Aiden and bent over a corner of the tarp. Suddenly, it folded like a bat wing and vanished, whisked away in a rush of wind. Ella Mae saw it melt into the dark clouds as the rain came pelting in on the three people and the fireworks.

Ella Mae didn't have the chance to wonder if the water would ruin their plans, because a row of rockets shot upward in a mighty whoosh of air and a series of shrill whistles. She craned her neck and, despite being pummeled in the face by pellets of rain, waited for the first detonation.

One Mississippi, two Mississippi, three—

Millions of white stars burst into the sky high above her, so high that she was sure the whole planet could see them. More rockets launched. Row after row of rockets, missiles, and shells raced upward. There were so many that it didn't seem possible.

What Ella Mae saw in the sky was too incredible to be anything but magic. The shells exploded and sparkling curlicues hung in the air as if they'd been spray-painted on a blank wall. Sparkling branches grew and forked, stretching and dividing, until the separate limbs and curling twigs united to form an enormous tree of dazzling white. It glittered in the sky, impeding the rain and burning the wind with unyielding light and heat.

"It's beautiful!" Ella Mae cried.

She'd chosen the tree symbol because it was an ageless connection between her people and the world. The ash tree was a recognizable conduit of magic. It had renewed their power for centuries. By creating an enormous image of a tree for Nimue's followers, Ella Mae was sending a clear message. She was offering them sanctuary.

"Show them the way, Ty!"

Ty gave her a thumbs-up and joined hands with Aiden. Another round of pyrotechnics spiraled and shrieked into the night. In what sounded like artillery fire, hundreds of shells blew open and a thousand leaves of blue, green, and gold appeared on the fading limbs of the white tree. They were so dazzling in their brightness that it was like witnessing the birth of a new galaxy. The entire tree glowed and throbbed like a living thing, and Ella Mae knew that no one who saw it could look away.

The wind and rain had completely ceased. Ty's tree had seized the attention of Nimue's people. Now Ella Mae knew for certain that people, not nature, were responsible for the monstrous storm. She could only hope that some of the people who'd joined Nimue out of fear or because they believed she could change their lives for the better, would see the invitation in the sky and accept the sanctuary Ella Mae was offering.

"Here comes the finale!" Ty roared, and flashed his electric smile. He released the last round of rockets, which flew skyward in lackadaisical spirals.

Ella Mae waited for more theatrical booms and a kaleidoscope of blinding light, but these bombs were almost gentle. They opened like flowers over the fading leaves, appearing to merge with them. Crimson, orange, and fuchsia fused with the other colors, creating a rainbow of flickering shapes above Lake Havenwood.

The shapes morphed into winged insects. Butterflies. Hundreds upon hundreds of starlit butterflies.

Thrilled, Ella Mae made her way to Ty's side. She reached for his hand while Aiden took hold of her other hand. The three of them stood there looking up as the cloud of butterflies drifted directly over the grove. The message couldn't have been more obvious.

In glimmering light and color, the butterflies were giving Nimue's people a chance. A chance to be forgiven. And to find peace.

And then they began to fall.

Their descent was slow and deliberate. They didn't wink out like spent matches, but faded, one by one, forming a path in the sky above the boulder wall leading to the grove. Even when the last butterfly was gone, Ella Mae could still see them when she closed her eyes. The imprint of their light remained, and she was certain the message was echoing in the minds of Nimue's people as well.

"That was the most amazing thing I've ever seen," she said to Ty in a voice choked with emotion. She then turned to Aiden. "This reprieve won't last long. Nimue will be furious and is probably screaming orders as we speak. Time for phase two."

Aiden grabbed Ty's elbow and the two men sprinted to the base of the muddy trail, where they called to a group of people holding metal objects.

Ella Mae waited for them at the edge of the precipice. Puffs of gunpowder floated over the treetops like dragon's breath and a veil of mist hid the surface of the lake from view, but Ella Mae knew that Nimue was down there. She suspected Loralyn and Hugh were as well.

As if in response, a wind swept up the mountain and shoved her with such force that Ella Mae reeled backward. She stumbled and was grateful to feel several hands reach out to steady her. Reba and Adelaide each slid an arm around her waist and stared out into the night.

"The wind's returning," Ella Mae's mother said.

"Let's see if our song lanterns can fly."

Straightening, Sissy morphed into her headmistress persona and beckoned for a cluster of faculty members and students from the Havenwood School of the Arts and a dozen visitors from other states to move forward. Sissy had chosen each and every one of them for the fragile beauty of their singing voices. They'd completed their assignments hours ago and were now ready to help the rest of the team launch the second phase of Ella Mae's initiative.

The next group of people were gifted in creating objects that could float or fly. For tonight's event, they'd made several hundred winged lanterns that would ride the violent air currents. They'd travel in a wide arc and inevitably circle back to the source of storm. Once they were over the island, the melody encapsulated in their mechanical hearts would be released and the haunting tune Ella Mae's mother had brought with her from another time and place would reach the ears of all of Nimue's followers.

The lanterns, which had been modeled after Dee and Kyran's metal birds, looked as delicate as origami cranes. Their long, steel wings and streamlined bodies made them both durable and aerodynamic, and the LED tealight candles in their chests glowed like tiny stars. Ella Mae had gotten the idea to build the bird lanterns while visiting Dee in the hospital, and she was sorry that her aunt wasn't there to see these exquisite music boxes fly.

"Let them go!" Ella Mae shouted over the wind.

Arms thrust outward, and the birds were released over the edge. The wind grabbed at them with greedy hands, spinning them around and around like pirouetting dancers. Ella Mae and her people joined hands and watched as the birds were whisked away, their candles bobbing like firefly lights.

The gale increased in force and Ella Mae could sense the rage in each slap of air. The cold tore at her skin, but Ella Mae didn't even blink. She was flanked by friends and family. She was upheld and supported by the people she loved and by those who loved her. She would not waver. She would stand firm.

Her hair whipped around her head in a whiskey-colored cyclone of mud, grit, and twigs. Her clothes were torn and soiled, but she didn't care. All that mattered now was the song.

Begin, she silently pleaded. *Hurry. Begin.*

Somewhere down the line, one of Sissy's students began to cry. The sound barely escaped her mouth before the wind snatched it away. Ella Mae worried that her people would be influenced by the girl's fear and would drop their hands and let the wind drive them back, but they didn't.

And then, Ella Mae thought she heard music. She cocked her head to one side and listened intently.

"Yes," she whispered, and then waited another moment. There it was again. That achingly beautiful melody that spoke of home. It filled the space around and inside her. It dispelled the wind and cold, instilling her with peace and warmth.

Ella Mae turned to her mother. "This was your gift. You brought this song to us. This old song from a time when we were united. You brought hope to us and to those people down there." She gestured at the lake. "The rain and wind have stopped. Havenwood won't be destroyed, because those people have been deeply moved by that song. You showed me that sometimes strength means making oneself vulnerable. Without you, we would have been lost." She released Reba's hand and wrapped her arms around her mother. Kissing her cheek, she held her for a long moment. "Take care of them, Mom. I have to go now."

"I'm coming with you," her mother said, pulling away.

Ella Mae shook her head. "No. Those people will need you. By the time we get them up here, they'll be weary in body and soul. They must be given food, rest, and compassion."

"I won't let you face Nimue alone," her mother protested.

"I'll bring Reba and Fiona, because I have no doubt that one or two of Nimue's priestess cronies will be hanging around, but you know that this confrontation comes down to me. Nimue had Marin leave clovers at two crime scenes to taunt me. She formed another clover out of the storm clouds to challenge me. I must answer her challenge, but I can't if I'm busy worrying about what's happening to the people who need sanctuary. You, Aunt Sissy, and Aunt Ver-ena have to take charge. There will be confusion and many questions."

The song continued, and the more it played, the less moisture-laden the air became. It grew lighter, like a person shrugging off a heavy coat, and here and there a star appeared in the night sky.

Ella Mae gave her mother's hand a final squeeze and then walked over to where Carol, Lundy, and the other Scots stood. "I'll go down first and then the rest of this group will follow. Every boat, dinghy, and raft we could appropriate is tied to the docks near my house. You'll be right on my heels. Carol, use Alfonso to speak to Nimue's followers. Many will be displaced Scots, and I'm sure they'll be comforted by a familiar accent. Lead them to the grove."

Ella Mae headed for her truck. All around, people rushed to their own cars.

"Wait!" Opal Gaynor suddenly blocked Ella Mae's path. "What about Loralyn?" Her face was etched with fear. "I have to go with you—I need to know that she's okay."

"If she's with Nimue, your presence will jeopardize your daughter's safety," Ella Mae said, and put a hand on Opal's shoulder. "Nimue will take the opportunity to pit the two of you against each other. Stay here and help"—Ella Mae searched for the right word—"the refugees. I'll do everything in my power to bring her back to you. I promise." Even though every second mattered, she held Opal's gaze as if she had all the time in the world. "Loralyn is one of us. She deserves a second chance."

Opal swallowed hard. "Thank you," she whispered, and turned to face the lake. Somewhere below, her daughter was either waiting to be rescued or to commit an act of treachery against people she'd known since birth.

The last thing Ella Mae saw before getting in her Jeep was her mother and her two aunts appearing at Opal's side. They surrounded her, forming a protective circle with their bodies. They bent their heads close to hers, offering her the kind of tender and wordless support that only women can offer another woman.

Ella Mae drove away with a warm glow in her heart.

She didn't remember the trip through the deserted downtown nor pulling to a stop in front of her garage. It seemed like one moment she was on the mountain and the next she was on the dock behind Partridge Hill, stunned by the sight of the coils of mist covering the lake. A new moon had burned through the remains of the storm clouds and laid a path of pale light over the shifting mist. The island was barely visible, but Ella Mae could sense Nimue's presence there.

This is my home, Ella Mae thought angrily.

Reba and Fiona boarded the little motorboat first, and tossed backpacks stuffed with weapons into the bow. Reba gunned the motor after Fiona had untied the lines. Ella Mae sat on the bench, twisting her head to look backward until she could see other people launching boats into the water.

Though the song could still be heard, it was no longer a reverberating echo, but a faint thrum, like a train whistle fading into the distance.

"Faster!" Ella Mae called to Reba.

Reba pushed the throttle and the light craft flew over the dark water. They passed several bird lanterns bobbing in the waves, their candles weakened by the mist, and Ella Mae's resolve wavered slightly. The lake she'd known her whole life had become alien. Up ahead, the island appeared to be lit by the ghost lights she'd read about in horror stories—blue-tinged illuminations hailing the arrival of evil spirits. In the worst tales, the lights belonged to the souls of the drowned, whose sole purpose was to lure poor swimmers into the water in the dead of the night.

Ella Mae shivered. The warmth she'd felt standing between her mother and Reba was gone. She glanced from the fog-fractured outline of the approaching island to the crossbow slung over Fiona's shoulder to her own empty hands. She'd hedged her bets on Nimue's magic being spent by this point, but what if it wasn't? Ella Mae knew nothing about what Nimue was capable of. As for her own powers? She didn't have combat training. She was a great shot, but her gun would be useless against someone who could freeze a bullet in midair.

I'll just ask the butterflies to carry her away, was Ella Mae's half-mad thought as they approached the island.

She blinked, trying to see clearly through the mist, because she didn't think there'd been so many trees growing along the beach before. Suddenly, she gasped. They weren't trees, but people.

"Look at all of them," Fiona said, reaching for her crossbow.

Reba unslung her gun and leaned it next to the steering wheel. "We're coming!" she called to the crowd. "Help is on the way!"

The figures, who'd been standing motionless and silent, suddenly surged forward. They waded into the water, shouting, "Please!" and "Get us out of here!" and "Save us!"

Ella Mae saw them plunge into the water. Men and women of all ages and colors, clearly desperate to escape the island. "Cut the motor," she told Reba.

The people headed straight for their boat. Reba tensed and shook her head. "There's too many of them," she whispered urgently. "They'll swarm the boat in their panic. We won't make it ashore."

Fiona stood, walked to the bow, and waved her hands. "It's all right, my friends. Here is the true Clover Queen." She pointed back at Ella Mae. "Let her pass so she can finish this. Look beyond us! Do you see all those boats? All those people? They're coming for you."

"Just as Ella Mae promised," Reba added. "They'll take you to our grove. There's a Beltane feast waiting for you. You can eat and drink and rest in the soft grass. Lord knows you must be tired." She paused. The people had stopped pressing forward. Their eyes shifted from the boat to Ella Mae to the approaching vessels.

"You're with friends now," Ella Mae said. "You're safe."

After a long hesitation, several people exchanged glances of relief. Another group began to murmur and gesture at the boats. A couple close to Ella Mae even managed timid smiles.

"Careful now!" Fiona called. "We're turning the motor on."

The boat moved slowly toward the shore, and as it passed, Ella Mae heard quiet cries of "Thank you!" and "Bless you!"

When the hull struck sand, Reba cut the engine and tossed the anchor onto the beach. A man who'd been standing nearby offered Ella Mae his hand and helped her disembark.

"What should I expect to find?" she asked him.

"It's just the Lady, a siren, a male water elemental, and three priestesses. The priestesses are air elementals. They're weak, but they'll die for her."

Ella Mae nodded. "And Nimue? Has producing the storm drained her?"

The man seemed reticent to speak, but he finally said, "As long as she holds the sword, she has power." He jerked his head to the right. "She knows you're here. You can't surprise her."

"That's not really our style anyhow. We like to rush in with our guns blazin'," Reba said. "Thanks, hon. You'd best hop aboard one of those boats now."

The man heeded her advice without delay, and the moment he was out of earshot, Fiona and Reba huddled together and discussed their next move.

Ella Mae closed her eyes. She'd been calling the butterflies for days. Though they were safely sheltered against the storm, she knew they were close by. Thousands of them. Swallowtail butterflies curled inside flower petals. Milkweed butterflies hidden beneath tents of grass. Angel moths pressed against tree trunks and tiger moths clinging to the underbelly of plant leaves. All awaiting her command.

Gather and prepare to swarm, she beckoned. *Swarm the woman with the sword.*

When she opened her eyes again, Fiona and Reba had sparkly goggles perched on their brows. They looked like a cross between Mardi Gras masks and x-ray glasses.

"Weeks ago, you asked Aiden to research how electricity travels through water. He used his findings to create light-pulse weapons. At first, it was just a precaution, but as soon as this storm hit the coast, he thought we might need them." Reba passed Ella Mae a pair of goggles and gestured at the gun in Fiona's hands. It was short and thick with a double-stacked barrel and a curved grip. "With both of us firing at once, we should knock out Loralyn and the air elementals. Maybe Hugh too. If we're lucky, it'll take them all down."

Ella Mae slid the goggles over her forehead. "What kind of injuries are we talking about?"

"Loss of consciousness," Reba said. "At least, that's what we're hoping for, but these haven't been tested on real people.

Only target dummies. And a cow." Seeing Ella Mae's frown, she assured her that the cow had made a full recovery, and then she turned to Fiona. "We'll shoot first and talk later, right?"

"Aye," Fiona said, and the pair marched forward.

The mist grew thicker as they entered the copse of trees lining the shore. With the branches blocking most of the moonlight, it was nearly impossible to see. Reba's eyes were sharper, but she was moving forward with care, her alert gaze seeking an enemy.

Show me the woman with the sword, Ella Mae told the butterflies.

A vision filled her mind. Nimue stood on a moss-covered rock in a clearing up ahead. She wore her crimson dress, and a short sword with a luminous green blade rested on one shoulder. She seemed completely composed, and the sight of her placid features frightened Ella Mae. Nimue's army had deserted her. She was left with Hugh, Loralyn, and three exhausted priestesses. Why, then, was her mouth curved upward in a smug grin?

Hugh's gray, glassy stare was directed right where Ella Mae and her two friends were headed. Loralyn's hostile gaze was also fixed on the same spot.

"Approach from the sides," she told Reba and Fiona. "They're gathered on a group of rocks in a clearing ahead. The moment I put my goggles on, fire."

Reba looked delighted, but then her smile faltered. "What about Hugh? What if he attacks you?"

Ella Mae shook her head in resignation. "I can't hurt him. The real Hugh is in there somewhere. He's a good man, Reba, and he has my heart."

"Damn it all," Reba muttered. "And Loralyn?"

"We need to bring her back to Opal if we can. Her siren's

song won't work on us, so let's just hope the light pulse will knock her out."

Fiona nodded. "If not, we have other ways of incapacitating her and trussing her up like a Christmas goose until we can get her to the grove. But what about Nimue? You heard the man on the beach. Her powers won't fade as long as she has the sword."

"Leave her to me," Ella Mae said, and strode forward.

Reba and Fiona vanished into the rising mist. It swirled in front of Ella Mae, squirming and wriggling like a pit of vipers, leading her to the Lady of the Lake.

The island was preternaturally quiet. No birds twittered. There was no insect buzz or the rhythmic croaks of frogs. The whole place was like a landscape painting, forever suspended in time, until Ella Mae stepped into the clearing where Nimue was waiting.

"At last, here you are," Nimue said in a honeyed voice with only a hint of Scottish accent.

Ella Mae planted her feet and met Nimue's bold, assessing stare. "You've traveled a long distance to meet me, ruining many lives along the way. Why didn't you just take a plane? It would have saved everyone a great deal of trouble."

Nimue threw back her head and laughed. Her red hair fell over her shoulders in fiery waves and the light from the sword blade cast a green pall on her hair and skin. She looked like a specter. "I didn't spend years studying, recruiting followers, and hoarding money to travel all this way just to kill you."

Ella Mae was taken aback. "Why else would you be here?"

"It's not your life that I'm after." Nimue shifted and her crimson gown pooled over the surface of the rock like spilled blood. She held out the sword. "Once I have what I came for,

I don't care whether you live or die." Gazing at Ella Mae with a studied casualness, she said, "It's your magic I want. Every ounce of it. I need you to pour it out until you have nothing left. When that's done, I'll be on my way."

"You've already abused your own powers beyond measure. You're not taking a thing from me," Ella Mae said. "Look around, Nimue. This place marks the end of your journey. You might as well put down that sword right now and spare yourself any suffering."

Nimue laughed again. It was a cold sound that swept over the glade like a winter wave. "No, Ella Mae. I won't suffer." She pointed the tip of her sword at the back of Hugh's neck. Because he was gazing at Ella Mae with a look of cool detachment, he didn't see the movement or how Nimue's face transformed. He didn't see the crazed smile and zealous gleam in her dark eyes or seem to understand what she meant when she whispered, "But *he* will."

Chapter 16

Ella Mae felt a stab of fear. Her gaze flicked from the three priestesses, who stood numbly at the base of Nimue's rock, to Loralyn's pinched face to Hugh's glazed stare.

"What does Hugh have to do with this?" she asked, returning her attention to Nimue.

Nimue lowered the green blade and scraped at a patch of moss with the tip. "Everything. He's the reason I had to wait so long for this moment. Initially, I'd planned on a complicated kidnapping scheme, but when you took away his source of power, which forced him to travel abroad, you saved me the trouble." She performed a mocking curtsy. "Thank you for that."

"What have you done to him?"

With an indifferent shrug, Nimue said, "Even elementals have their limits."

"Why are his eyes that color? They were bright blue when he left Havenwood."

"They've become the shade of the water he walked into with this sword." She gazed down at Hugh as if he were an obedient dog. "He had to drown to reclaim his powers. To become an elemental again beneath the surface of that cold, Irish lake, he had to die. That lake claimed part of him. He'll never be the man he once was, but such is the price of magic."

Though Ella Mae didn't want to believe what Nimue was saying, she sensed it was the truth. And yet she clung to the ever-diminishing hope that the Hugh she loved could still return to her.

"You don't know much about elementals, do you? In fact, you don't know much about any of us." Nimue gave her a wolfish smile. "I've studied for years and years. Ever since I first heard about the Clover Queen legend." She twisted her head to the right, baring her neck, and then raised the sword so that its eerie light illuminated the birthmark on her skin. It was the same distorted clover in the crime-scene photos from Fiona's house and in the burned grass near Dee's barn. "I fit all the criteria. Except one. My father wasn't one of the Fair Folk. He wasn't *aes sídhe*. He was just a small-minded man, and a mean drunk to boot. When he was lost at sea, I saw that as a sign. I could still rule, but I'd need to overcome a few obstacles."

"You can't rewrite a legend," Ella Mae said.

"Aren't there multiple versions to all of our stories?" Nimue asked, and Ella Mae had to nod in agreement. The tales concerning their kind varied from author to author, making it difficult to discern the truth in any of them.

"You found another Clover Queen legend?"

Lowering the sword again, Nimue began to spin the black hilt with one hand. Tiny sparks flew from where the blade bit into the rock. "Only after I became Lady of the Lake, which required a significant sacrifice."

"Your mother."

"Yes," Nimue admitted without a trace of remorse. "It was a necessary act. I had to prove my devotion if I wanted find the entrance to Avalon. I'm sure you're aware that the Lady of the Lake can create an Avalon anywhere, but the original place contains an unrivaled archive of magic. Scrolls and books penned by Morgan le Fay, the first Nimue, Myrddin—all of *their* predecessors. Diaries, alchemical formulas—a treasure trove of arcane wisdom—all housed in an ancient temple overlooking a subterranean lake in the Black Mountains of Wales. The cave entrance leading to this lake is surrounded by treacherous bogs and is eternally covered by a layer of glacier-thick mist. Avalon is down there. I found it, and I spent a decade absorbing every scrap of knowledge I could. Focusing on dead languages in school certainly paid off."

Ella Mae was a little daunted by Nimue's knowledge. Not only was she cruel and calculating, but she was also dangerously smart. Too late, Ella Mae realized that she'd underestimated this woman.

"Tell me of the legend you found in Avalon."

Nimue stopped spinning the sword and straightened. "Well, now we've arrived at the crux of the matter. The version you read was probably incomplete. Did it end with the usual lines about the Clover Queen breaking Myrddin's curse and uniting the *aes sídhe*?"

Reluctantly, Ella Mae inclined her head.

"That's the abbreviated legend. The longer one goes into detail about how the Lady of the Lake and Morgan le Fay were once allies. Friends, actually. Such was their bond that the first Nimue tricked Myrddin into surrendering his powers to her, even though she was in love with him. She put him in an enchanted sleep and sealed him away in a cave or inside a tree. Soon after, the non-magical began to take over the land. Nimue grew old and died, but not before penning the Clover Queen legend." She grinned. "You know the first bit. A woman would be born to two magical parents. She'd discover her gift later than was customary and she'd bear the mark of the clover. Her magic could be used to restore the old ways. Our glory days, so to speak. The extra lines state that it will take *all* of her magic to break the curse and that she must willingly sacrifice her power. In other words, you must give everything you have to save the life of another." She shrugged. "Who better than the man you love?"

Ella Mae waved off the idea. "You said yourself that he'll never be the same. Why would I give up my abilities for someone who's become a stranger to me?"

Nimue's dark eyes narrowed. "Because you're soft. You lured my misfit army away using fireworks and a song. From the second you knew I was heading to your pathetic little town you've lost sleep over how you could possibly protect every one of its insignificant inhabitants."

"This may come as a surprise, but you don't know every detail," Ella Mae said breezily. "After all, it's easy to conceal things from a spy once you've discovered their identity. If it were me, I'd be wary of information obtained by an envious siren and a pitiful selkie."

Nimue looked impressed. "So you've captured Marin?" She glanced at the priestess to her left, and said, "I guess you can have those sealskin boots, after all."

Ella Mae waved at Nimue. "We're talking about legends, not footwear. So let's say you get what you want and I mysteriously pour out all of my magic. What then?"

"I return to Avalon." She tilted her face skyward, inviting the moonlight to wash over her sharp features. "The Lady of the Lake is a title. So is Merlin. Once you give me what I came for, I can wake the Merlin. Together, he and I will elevate the *aes sídhe* to new heights. We both want the same thing, you and I," she added in a honeyed tone. "To break this curse. To live as we choose without fear."

"But to succeed, you'd destroy anyone brave enough to oppose you," Ella Mae snapped. "The original Nimue sacrificed her own happiness to protect us from being cursed any further. You're nothing like her. You shame every Lady of the Lake who's come before you."

"And you're a pathetic excuse of a queen," Nimue hissed, her mouth twisting into a snarl. "Like I said, you're soft. And because you're soft, you won't let me kill Hugh Dylan. I've bet my entire future on it."

Before she could raise her sword, Ella Mae pushed her goggles over her eyes, and yelled, "Now!" Jumping between two trees bordering the clearing, she covered her ears a second before a deafening boom accompanied by a searing light filled the clearing. Despite the protective goggles, tiny dots danced at the edge of Ella Mae's vision and she felt nausea rising in her throat. Struggling to regain her senses, she focused on the butterflies.

What she saw was a cloud of wings moving in the night sky. The butterflies were traveling over the strip of sand where Reba had beached their boat. In less than a minute, they'd be ready to swarm.

Ella Mae sat up gingerly, relieved that the dizziness and nausea had passed. She pulled off the goggles and glanced around. The clearing was deathly still. Loralyn and the priestesses were splayed on the ground, unmoving. Ella Mae had no idea if they were alive or not, but she was certain they were no longer a threat.

Hugh was glassy-eyed. A trickle of blood ran down his forehead from where it had struck Nimue's rock, and a dark bruise was already shadowing his skin.

As for Nimue, she was crouched like a panther above Hugh. Her lips were pulled back, revealing a flash of white teeth, and she clutched the sword so tightly that it was biting into her palms. Droplets of red dripped onto the stone, but she seemed unaware of the pain or her injured hands. Trembling with rage, she rose to her feet and glared at Ella Mae with undisguised hatred.

"I will take pleasure in watching you suffer." Nimue wiped her bleeding palms one at a time on her red dress and then grabbed the sword hilt with both hands. "Tell your friends to get out of here or I will kill them without a second's hesitation. As long as I hold *Caladbolg*, no one can defeat me."

Having moved closer, Ella Mae was now able to hear a dull hum coming from the sword. She remembered how the Flower of Life had hummed and pulsed with power. She remembered how its magic had coursed over the grove, permeating every stone, leaf, and blade of grass. Nimue wasn't making an empty boast. It was time to separate her from her weapon.

"Take Loralyn and retreat," Ella Mae said, looking first at Fiona and then at Reba.

Well aware of Ella Mae's plan, Reba scurried over to where Loralyn lay. After checking for a pulse, Reba shot Ella Mae a brief nod and then hoisted Loralyn's inert form over her shoulders. For such a small woman, Reba's strength was formidable, and Ella Mae felt a rush of pride watching her beloved friend disappear among the trees. She was relieved that Loralyn was alive and would be taken out of harm's way. Reba would carry Loralyn to the boat, secure her hands with plastic zip ties, and make her as comfortable as possible until they were all ready to leave the island.

Ella Mae wished the same could be done for Hugh. He

was slumped against Nimue's rock, having probably passed out while Nimue and Ella Mae were talking. He was completely vulnerable now and could do nothing to defend himself should Nimue carry out her threat.

There was a movement in the brush, and Ella Mae realized that Fiona had refused to fall back. She entered the part of the clearing where the moon acted as a spotlight and pulled off her goggles. "I wanted you to see my face before this night was over."

Nimue recoiled in shock. "Fiona?" She lowered her hands and gaped in disbelief. "Is that really you?"

Ella Mae heard the note of tenderness in Nimue's voice and suspected that, at this moment, Nimue was not the Lady of the Lake, but a little girl from a small village in the Orkneys.

"Aye, lassie. It's me." Fiona spoke very gently, as if trying to soothe a wild animal. She looked much smaller and older in the pale light—especially with Nimue towering over her from her rocky perch.

"I knew you were in Havenwood, of course," Nimue said. "And that you'd begun working for our baker queen, but I never expected to see you. It's been so long. So very long . . ." She stared at Fiona. "Have you come seeking vengeance?"

Fiona unslung her crossbow and set it on the ground. "I know better than most that I can't hurt you as long as you have *Caladbolg*. After all, who told you the tales about this sword, the Lady of the Lake, the Clover Queen, and Myrddin in the first place?"

Nimue allowed herself a tiny smile. "You did."

"I filled your head with too much nonsense," Fiona said contritely. "I should have taught you more practical things. As children grow, most leave their childish imaginings behind. But not you, Nimue. Your fantasies took over. They turned you into a different person. You could have had a happier life if you hadn't been born with that mark. And your mother would still be with us."

"But they weren't wild imaginings. The stories were true," Nimue protested. "The sword was at the bottom of Avalon's lake, waiting for a new Lady to claim it. It has the power to hurt and the power to heal, just as the legends say." She tilted the sword blade so that the moonlight danced along its beveled edge.

Fiona pointed at the weapon. "Something that powerful could be used as a permanent source of magic. We could create another grove like Havenwood's. Why don't we bring it home, you and I? Ours could be the most amazing grove in all of Great Britain."

"And limit myself to ruling a remote island populated by fishermen?" Nimue scoffed. "No thank you. I have far loftier goals. But we could still see my plan through together. It would be a richer victory with you by my side. You're the only family I have left."

Fiona looked away. "I can't be a part of your plans, Nimue. If you'd been willing to mend some of the things you've broken, I'd join you in a heartbeat, but it's clear that you're determined to walk this dark path. I will not follow. Your way leads to unhappiness and ruin. For others. And for you."

Nimue frowned. "Can't teach an old dog, can you?" She gestured at Ella Mae. "After I'm done with her, you'll have no purpose. What will you do?"

"I've spent half of my life wallowing in regret," Fiona said. "I'm through with that. I'm ready to go home. I'm just sorry that you'll never know what it means to call a place home. You always believed you were better than everyone else. It's why the other children avoided you. It's why you'll never ease the loneliness that has taken over your heart."

Fury washed across Nimue's face. "I will wake the Merlin and then I'll never be lonely again!" She raised the sword over her head and continued to yell at Fiona, but Ella Mae stopped listening. She sensed the butterflies hovering at the edge of the light, surrounding them.

Swarm! Ella Mae commanded.

A massive shadow of shifting wings descended from the sky, blotting out the moon and stars. Streams of butterflies and moths poured out from between the trees. Ella Mae had never seen so many at once. Without a sound, they formed a cyclone around Nimue's body, landing on her shoulders, her hair, her face. They crawled all over her, fluttering their wings to confuse her and massing around her eyes in an attempt to block her sight.

Nimue screamed in anger and thrust out a hand. Arcs of water vapor appeared, knocking the delicate creatures away from her face. Fuming, she lifted the sword over her head and spoke words in a language Ella Mae didn't recognize. Immediately, hail began to fall. The icy pellets struck the butterflies and drove them to the ground. Nimue began to laugh, and the hail increased in size. The louder she laughed, the harder the hail fell, killing hundreds of butterflies at a time.

Without warning, Fiona lunged forward.

"*No!*" Ella Mae cried, but too late.

Nimue cupped her hand and a baseball-sized chunk of ice appeared in her palm. She hurled it at Fiona, striking her shoulder. The older woman grunted but didn't stop.

"Don't!" Ella Mae tried to grab Fiona's arm, but she scooted to the side and kept reaching out for Nimue.

The hailstorm ceased as Nimue concentrated on attacking Fiona. She tossed big pieces of ice at Fiona, hammering her in the chest, the neck, and the head. She hit Fiona again and again, the ice making violent thuds upon impact. After a direct shot to the chest, Fiona dropped to her knees. She'd clearly had the air knocked from her lungs, but Nimue showed her no mercy. Forming an especially jagged lump of ice, she shrieked with rage and hurled it at Fiona. It smacked against her forehead and Fiona fell sideways—slowly, like a capsizing boat.

Ella Mae screamed. Not out of fear, but out of anger and helplessness. After weeks of meticulous planning, she was going to fail. She had no way to fight this woman, and once Nimue had what she wanted, she would continue on her twisted crusade.

"Enough!" Nimue bellowed. "It's time for me to get what I came for!"

The bodies of a thousand butterflies covered the clearing. Some had rent wings. Some had crushed abdomens. Others shuddered and tried to take flight but were too broken to fly.

The sight of them made Ella Mae's anger burn so brightly that heat filled the center of her chest. It felt like a sun had replaced her heart and was pumping liquid fire through her veins. Hot rays bloomed across her torso and raced down her legs and arms. And then, the hand bearing the clover mark began to glow.

Heedless of Ella Mae's transformation, Nimue resumed her stance over Hugh's unconscious body and raised the sword, preparing to plunge the blade between his ribs.

"You will not hurt him!" Ella Mae shouted. Her voice boomed across the clearing, reverberating with strength and authority. She thrust out her glowing hand, aiming it at Nimue, and willed the heat surge forth. A beam of pure white light burst from the clover mark on her palm. Ella Mae gasped, reveling in both the feelings of release and the consuming sense of power.

Nimue reacted immediately. She swept the sword in an

upward arc, shielding herself in green light and blocking Ella Mae's attack just in time. She then angled the sword across her body and grimaced as the green and white lights collided in a starburst of color.

"As soon as you're done playing around, I will kill him!" Nimue cried triumphantly. "Once he's gone, I'll finish off dear Fiona. Then Reba." Her dark eyes glittered with pin-pricks of green, and her skin and hair had taken on a green pall. Her mouth twisted into another animalistic snarl, making her look more like a goblin queen than the Lady of the Lake. "After Reba, it'll be your aunts, your mother, your friends, and anyone else foolish enough to speak your name after this night."

"Be quiet," Ella Mae commanded loudly. "Do you see the mark of the clover, Nimue? Do you see the light pouring out of it?" She took a step closer. "*That's* power. And do you know where it comes from? It comes from the love I feel for the people you would carelessly destroy. *Love* is power. You could never succeed because true leaders put their people first. Their happiness hinges on the happiness of others." She took another step. Her light beam grew wider, pushing the green back into the sword.

Nimue's brow was beaded with sweat and her arms trembled with exertion. She was losing her grip on the sword.

"No," she moaned. "It's not possible."

Ella Mae continued moving forward. The heat flowing through her was so intense that it filled her eyes. Her vision blurred. All of her senses were being taken over by the power welling inside her. Once, she thought she heard Reba screaming at her to stop. She didn't. She couldn't. She had to end this, so she coaxed every last ounce of magical energy to travel through her. Even when the green light was gone, she pushed one more time, completely emptying herself.

Again, she thought she heard Reba calling. She heard the words "a trick!" and "she needs Hugh alive!" but Reba's voice sounded so far away that Ella Mae couldn't focus on it.

Ella Mae took a final step. She saw the sword clatter to the ground. Its blade was now the color of moonlight and the hilt had turned white. The moment it left her hands, Nimue flew backward off the rock as if a colossal fist had struck her in the belly.

Nimue's fall was the last thing Ella Mae saw. The light filled her eyes and a buzzing noise roared in her head. The ground tilted, and her body, which felt as weightless as a dandelion seed, was unable to hold her upright.

Suddenly, her cheek was pressed against the cool earth and a woman was whispering her name. She sounded scared. Ella Mae wanted to tell her not to worry. She wanted to tell her that everything was all right and that she just needed to sleep for a little while. She wanted to tell her that she could hear the song her mother hummed when she was alone in her garden. The melody was very faint, but Ella Mae was certain that if she followed the butterflies floating just beyond her field of vision, they would lead her to a place where she could rest. A place of silky grass and sweet smells. A quiet, sun-dappled place. A sanctuary.

When Ella Mae opened her eyes, she knew that something about her had changed. Something significant.

She was in her own bed, dressed in a clean cotton night-gown, with Chewy fast asleep at her feet. Her curtains were drawn, but she could tell that it was daytime by the way the fabric glowed with a soft, yellow light.

Ella Mae's mouth and throat were incredibly dry, and she was glad to find a glass of water on her nightstand. Trying to sit up so she could drink, she let out a small groan. Chewy was awake in an instant. He rushed to the top of the bed and licked her cheek multiple times. Ella Mae buried her nose in his fur.

"I'm happy to see you too, boy," she croaked, and reached for the water glass.

As she gulped the water, she scratched Chewy's neck and watched dust motes dance in a shaft of sunlight. The light reminded her of the island in the center of Lake Havenwood. And of Nimue.

She looked at her hand, expecting to see her clover-shaped burn, but the skin of her palm was unblemished. Her mark was gone.

"You're awake," said her mother from the doorway.

Ella Mae held out her hand. "Have you seen this?"

Her mother nodded and sat on the edge of the bed. Chewy pranced back and forth between the two women, thrilled to have his favorite people sharing the same space. Ella Mae's mother gave him a quick caress and then took her daughter's hand in her own.

"What happened after I passed out?" Ella Mae asked.

"Reba brought you home. Others went back for Fiona, Nimue, and the three priestesses. Everyone is alive. Bumped and bruised, but alive. Nimue has taken Marin's place in the bamboo cage, and Fiona has Marin's sealskin."

Ella Mae was pleased to hear that Marin would never again be forced to do Nimue's bidding.

"What about Loralyn?"

Her mother sighed. "When Reba carried you to the boat, Loralyn was gone. She decided that helping you was more important than tracking Loralyn down, so she didn't look for her."

"Poor Opal. She must be beside herself."

"She's using every resource at her disposal to search for Loralyn, and she's grateful to you for trying to rescue her daughter."

Ella Mae couldn't imagine how Loralyn had managed to disappear, but she was still too groggy to think clearly. Resting her shoulders against the headboard, she closed her eyes. "I'm almost afraid to ask, but I have to know. Where's the sword?"

Her mother's silence was reply enough. "By the time our people reached the island, both the sword and Hugh were gone. No one's seen Hugh since that night."

Ella Mae opened her heavy lids and looked at her mother. "*That* night?"

"Sweetheart, you've been asleep for almost three days. After what you've been through, it's no surprise." Smiling, she reached out and tucked a strand of Ella Mae's hair back behind her ear. "But the storm is over. The sun is shining and it feels like summer outside. When you're up for it, Reba and I will settle you in a shady spot in the garden. You can watch Chewy and Miss Lulu play and see all the butterflies . . ."

Ella Mae touched her palm and then met her mother's troubled gaze. "I can see them, but I'll never call them again. My gifts are gone."

A tear slipped down her mother's cheek. "Reba tried to stop you. She knew that you were pouring out all you had."

"I couldn't stop," Ella Mae said. "Faces were flashing through my mind against a backdrop of white light: friends, family, Hugh. The people who are precious to me. I couldn't stop until I knew Nimue would be powerless to harm them or anyone else." She wiped the tear from her mother's cheek. "It's okay, Mom. Magic has always made my life so complicated. Maybe it can be simpler now. Maybe I won't miss it."

There was a soft knock on the doorframe, and Reba entered the room carrying a crystal vase stuffed with iris, bachelor's button, blue hydrangea, larkspur, periwinkle, and purple verbena. "It's good to hear your voice," Reba said, placing the vase on Ella Mae's dresser. "You scared the tar out of me. I thought I'd lost you."

"Just the Clover Queen part. The rest of me is fine." Ella Mae gestured for Reba to sit on the other side of the bed. "Where's Nimue?"

Reba managed a tight grin. "The Elders decided to frame her for the crimes she made Officer Wallace, er, Marin, commit. Officer Wallace and I planted evidence in a rental cottage near the lake, and then she led a bunch of cops to the site. Wallace brought Nimue to the station and arrested her on suspicion of murder. Officer Hardy, who returned to duty yesterday, was very eager to interrogate her. After she told him that she was the Lady of the Lake, he decided she needed a thorough psychiatric evaluation. She's been transferred to a high-security psych ward in Atlanta so that the experts can determine if she's fit to stand trial."

"Do you think she'll end up in prison?"

"A padded room is more likely." Reba was clearly delighted by the idea. "She told Hardy he couldn't keep her locked up because she needed to wake Merlin. She keeps telling him to find Hugh—that Hugh is supposed to become the Merlin and that he'll make sure she's released."

Ella Mae grew quiet. "What if she spoke the truth the night of the storm?" she asked after a time. "What if I played right into her hands? She wanted me to sacrifice myself for others, and I did. I poured out my magic to stop her, just as she predicted. That sword is more powerful than ever, and whoever has it could be even more dangerous than Nimue."

Reba patted Ella Mae's hand. "No need to worry about

that. Hugh's downstairs. He brought these flowers and begged me to tell you two things. First, his eyes aren't gray anymore. And they're not, I checked." Reba plucked a cornflower from the bouquet and placed it in Ella Mae's palm. "They look like this. Bright blue. Like they used to be."

Ella Mae gazed at the wildflower. Once, her heart would have leapt at the very thought of Hugh, but it beat somnolently in her chest. She was too weary to feel much of anything.

"What's the second thing?" she asked Reba.

"Hugh has the sword," Reba said with a radiant smile. "He's come to give it to you."

Chapter 17

"Can you send him up?" Ella Mae asked when she'd recovered from the shock.

Reba hesitated. "Do you want to brush your hair or put a little color on your lips?"

Ella Mae shook her head. "I don't care what I look like."

"Well, I'll fix you somethin' to eat while you two are talkin'. Three days without food is too long." She got to her feet and opened the windows. "You had far too much on your shoulders, but that's over with now. You should spend the whole day lying here. Listen to the birds. Smell the jasmine. Let the sunshine wash over your face. I'll run around and fetch whatever you want if you just promise to rest."

"What I'd really like is a shower, but that can wait. I need to lay eyes on that sword."

"I'll give you five minutes before I send Hugh up," Reba said left the room.

Ella Mae swung her feet out from beneath the covers and made to stand, but the room swayed and she nearly fell. She reached out, fumbling for the bedpost, but her mother grabbed her around the waist, and whispered, "I've got you."

The two women stood there for a moment while Ella Mae fought the dizziness. She then shuffled into the bathroom like an old woman and leaned against the sink. Chewy immediately took up his position on the bath mat, hoping Ella Mae was heading into the shower and that he could lap water from the floor and the sides of the stall when she was done.

"In a bit, sweet boy," Ella Mae told him. She splashed cold water on her face and brushed her teeth. She stared at her reflection in the mirror, stunned by the pallor of her skin, the puffiness around her eyes, and her dull, matted hair.

"Could I brush your hair?" her mother asked. "I remember how good it felt the night you freed me. You brushed and brushed until I finally fell asleep."

Ella Mae touched one of the limp strands sticking to her cheek. "A pair of scissors would be quicker, but yes, thank you."

Her mother helped her to the wing chair by the window and began to gently loosen the tangles. Ella Mae glanced out the window at the cloudless blue sky. All signs of the weekend storm were gone and the world was awash in sunlight. Across the lush green lawn, her mother's rosebushes were covered with plump, velvety blooms. Ella Mae's gaze roved over the sea of flowers in the garden, and she took in a deep breath of perfumed air. When she turned away from the window, Hugh was standing in the threshold cradling a sheet-wrapped bundle in his arms. Ella Mae could tell by its shape that it was the sword.

Without looking at her, Hugh placed the bundle on the

bed. Chewy rushed over to greet him, his little tail wagging wildly. Hugh ruffled the terrier's fur and scratched his back until Chewy flopped down, his tongue hanging from his open mouth.

Finally, Hugh straightened and met Ella Mae's eyes. "I rehearsed what I was going to say a dozen times, but now I can't remember a thing." He began clasping and unclasping his hands. "There are no words to express what I need to convey." Suddenly, he was on his knees before Ella Mae. "I've been such a fool."

"Please, don't do that. I'm not that person anymore." She showed Hugh her palm.

"I know," he whispered, his voice choked with anguish. "You gave your all to save everyone else. That's why I'm a fool. I thought I was half a man without my powers, but I was wrong. It took the light coming from your hand to burn the fog from my eyes."

Ella Mae gaped at him. "I thought you were unconscious."

"I did pass out, but not before I saw the *real* you. I saw the woman I'd known since childhood. Sure, you looked larger than life and it seemed like you were bathed in starlight, but it was you." He paused to collect himself, his face etched with pain.

Ella Mae's mother fastened Ella Mae's hair in a loose braid, set the brush on the nightstand, and put a hand on Hugh's shoulder. "I'll get you two some coffee." She whistled for Chewy and left the room.

"You told me that your abilities didn't define you," Hugh continued. "I should have believed you. It's always been your heart that's defined you, Ella Mae. When I saw you pouring your magic out, it became so clear. I wanted to shout out that I never knew the full extent of Nimue's plot—especially the

Merlin bit— but the world turned dark before I could make a sound."

"What happened when you came to?" Ella Mae still felt numb when she looked at Hugh. She wished it weren't the case, especially since he was laying everything bare, but she couldn't help it.

"Everything was quiet. I knew that you'd defeated Nimue and that I had a choice to make. I could either run or try to make amends." Hugh smoothed the quilt on Ella Mae's bed. "When I saw the sword lying on the ground, I knew that doing the right thing was going to be really hard."

Ella Mae immediately understood. "If you brought it to the bottom of Lake Havenwood, you'd have a permanent source of power again."

"I'll admit that I was tempted," Hugh said. "In my hands, that sword was like a living thing. My strength returned the second I touched it, but I wasn't blinded by it. Even when I swam off the island with the sword strapped to my back, I feared that my other form would take over and I'd lose sight of the choice I'd made, but I didn't. I thought of you and of what you sacrificed for the rest of us, and I stayed *me* up here." He tapped his temple. "I had command of my thoughts. I kept my eyes on Partridge Hill's dock lights, and I was more man than creature the whole time. I was your man. Your Hugh."

A sigh of relief escaped Ella Mae's lips. "This weapon will be used for good. It can heal. It can restore one of the ruined groves. It will bring hope to many people." She glanced at the bundle. "When my mother told me it was gone, I felt like we'd lost—that another enemy would take Nimue's place. Loralyn. Or one of the priestesses." Swallowing, she added, "Or you."

Hugh shook his head. "I'll never be vulnerable to magic

again. It's cost me what I held most dear." He gestured at the sword without taking his eyes off Ella Mae. "Nimue said this blade has a duplicitous nature. It changes depending on the person wielding it. If you use it, you can achieve amazing things." He stretched out his hand and carefully touched her palm. "You might even be able to heal yourself."

"I don't need healing," Ella Mae replied quietly. "If I could go back in time and do it all over again, I wouldn't alter the outcome. I can live without what I've lost." She took his hand. "Can you?"

Hugh gently pulled away and started pacing the floor, clearly frustrated that he'd failed to get his point across. "Don't you see? Nothing matters without you. The man who loves you is speaking, not the selfish, irrational water elemental." He stared at Ella Mae with such intensity that she nearly flinched. "You tried to convince me that you were the same girl I'd always known—with or without magic. Well, I'm the same guy you've always known. If we both shed those other selves together, there'll be no more secrets."

This created a tiny flutter of feeling in Ella Mae's heart. "No more secrets," she repeated. "Just a guy and a girl."

"*Yes.*" Hugh smiled at her, his blue eyes shimmering. "I've wronged you. I don't deserve you. But I will spend the rest of my days trying to be worthy of your friendship, if not your love. I will earn back your trust hour by hour, day by day. All I want is a shred of hope. If I can leave knowing you don't despise me, then I—"

"I could never despise you," Ella Mae said tenderly. "I couldn't hurt you that night on the island and I can't hurt you now." She held out her hands and Hugh was at her side in a heartbeat, his arms sliding under hers, effortlessly lifting her out of her chair. She gazed up at him. "We never seem to catch a break, do we?"

He traced the curve of her cheek and then raised her hand to his mouth and kissed each knuckle. "Will you give me chance?" His whisper was nearly inaudible.

"This might be our clean slate. A chance to start over," she said. "Or it might be the world telling us to let go. Maybe we're just not meant to be together."

"I refuse to consider that possibility," he said. "When I look at you, I still see my future. When I stand this close to you, I still believe in happy endings."

At this, Ella Mae smiled. She recalled her conversation with Aunt Dee and how Dee had laughed and said that Ella Mae had, and always would, believe in happy endings.

"Do you have enough faith for both of us?" she asked Hugh.

"I do," he said, his words sounding like a vow. "Enough to fill an ocean."

Ella Mae studied Hugh's familiar face. She saw her past in his eyes—the boy who'd climbed the tree to fetch her kite, the teenager who'd dived from the highest rocks into the cool water of the swimming hole, the man who'd fought raging fires. He'd always held a place in her heart. She couldn't imagine her life without him in it. "I can't make you any promises, because I need to sort out what's next for me. It wasn't easy adjusting to being magical, but no longer belonging to a group of people I care deeply for is going to be even harder." She squeezed his hand reassuringly. "But it'll be wonderful to know that I can talk to you about anything— that I don't have to hide things from you anymore."

"I look forward to those talks," Hugh said. "To any time that we spend together." He grinned and, for a moment, he was his old self again. "The pie baker and the fireman."

Ella Mae returned the grin. "I like the sound of that."

A light surfaced in Hugh's eyes, and Ella Mae knew she'd

given him the hope he'd been seeking. He leaned in, kissed her lightly on the mouth, and then enfolded her in his arms.

Ella Mae was surprised by the fierceness of his embrace, but she felt completely at home in his arms. Closing her eyes, she pressed her cheek against his chest, and thought, *There's still magic between us. It might be the only magic that ever mattered.*

Though Ella Mae took it easy for the rest of the day, she was concerned about The Charmed Pie Shoppe being closed for nearly a week. She knew she couldn't go back to work until she'd regained her strength, but that night, she asked Jenny to join her for a glass of wine in the garden so the two of them could come up with a plan.

"I can take charge of the pie shop until you're ready to come back," Jenny said, dropping into one of the wicker chairs on the back patio. "I'm not as skilled as you, but I can follow your recipes, and I already know how to prepare and plate the sides. You've taught me so much since I started working for you that I feel like I know what's best for our customers."

Ella Mae handed her a glass of sparkling wine. A trio of raspberries bobbed in the tiny bubbles. "Which is exactly why I wanted to know how'd you feel about becoming a partner."

Jenny's cheeks flushed with pleasure. "Seriously? I'd love it! I was hoping you'd let me take Fiona's place now that she's decided to return to Scotland. If I promise not to slap any of the bridezillas, can I be your partner and still handle the catering side?"

"Absolutely. Here's to new beginnings," Ella Mae said, and the two women clinked glasses. "We'll need to hire another server. Someone who can also double as a delivery person. You and I can trade off waiting tables whenever our new employee needs to leave the shop. Personally, I like the idea of getting out of the kitchen more. I miss chatting with our customers."

Jenny studied her over the rim of her glass.

"I know what you're worried about," Ella Mae said softly. "But I don't need magic to create amazing pies. Sugar, the woman who made the Sunshine Lemon Pie, reminded me of that. As long as we use the freshest ingredients and are passionate about the food we create, people will never know that our pies aren't enchanted."

"You really seem to be okay with this." Jenny shook her head in wonder.

Ella Mae smiled. "I am." She gestured around the bloom-filled garden. "I wake every morning to this paradise. The people I love are safe. I'm living my dream of owning a pie shop."

"The best in the country!" Jenny exclaimed heartily, and then grew serious again. "What will happen with you and Hugh?"

"To be honest, I'm not sure." Ella Mae turned her glass and the raspberries bobbed like buoys. "We're going take it slow. We hurt each other pretty deeply, and only time will tell if we can heal those wounds or if it'll take someone else to do that."

Jenny's brows rose. "Someone like Finn Mercer?"

Ella Mae had nearly forgotten about Finn and told Jenny as much. "Has he moved into his mother's house?"

"A couple of days ago. Since then, he and Aiden have been working like maniacs transforming that warehouse building. It's going to be part workshop, part storefront. Both of them are really excited about launching Finn's new lighting line." She smiled. "I haven't seen Aiden this fired up since Suzy first agreed to have dinner with him."

"That's great. And I'm really glad he and Suzy are happy, though I miss her. Between the History in the Baking events, preparing for Nimue's arrival, and keeping the pie shop running, I've barely seen my best friend."

"I've missed you too."

Ella Mae and Jenny turned to find Suzy standing beneath a metal arbor covered by blooming trumpet vines.

"Are you spying on us?" Ella Mae joked.

Suzy shrugged. "What can I say? I'm as stealthy as a ninja. A ninja bearing gifts." She pulled up a chair and, after giving Ella Mae a hug, handed her a box of gourmet truffles and a gift-wrapped package.

"Let's dig into these chocolates right now." Ella Mae told Suzy to help herself to wine and then bit into a truffle. A burst of sweet pineapple combined with the crunch of macadamia nuts filled her mouth. "How do they pack so much flavor into one candy?"

She passed the box to Jenny, who examined the flavor chart with interest. "I have to try the wasabi ginger."

"I'm going for the caramelized plantain," Suzy said, selecting a truffle with a yellow squiggle of icing.

The women sipped wine, ate chocolate, and talked. By the time they'd tried the French toast, cinnamon latte, peach rosemary, lemon lavender, blackberry sage, and peanut butter honey truffles, Ella Mae was feeling rather giddy.

"What's the present for?" she asked Suzy.

"Oh, I just thought you deserved a little something for saving our lives." She winked at Jenny. "Is there any more wine?"

Jenny jumped up. "There will be in a minute. Be right back."

Ella Mae tore the floral wrapping paper and examined the handwritten title on the cover of what looked to be a very old book. "*The Illustrated Cookery of Pastry Receipts*," she read. Very gingerly, Ella Mae opened the book and gasped in delight. Each page contained a watercolor painting of a pie, torte, or other type of pastry. Below every exquisite painting was a recipe for the item pictured, handwritten in delicate calligraphy. "Suzy, this must have cost a fortune! How old is it?"

Suzy shrugged. "Early nineteenth century. And yes, it's a rare, one-of-a-kind cookbook for a rare, one-of-a-kind cook." She grabbed Ella Mae's hand. "Lots of people pitched in. In fact, too many folks wanted to contribute. In the end, I created a fund to help those displaced by Nimue's actions. News of the Clover Fund spread like wildfire and people from across the globe have been donating like crazy. So much money's coming in that I truly believe we'll be able to restore all the material possessions lost in the storms." Suzy gazed at Ella Mae with moist eyes. "You made all of this possible. I am so incredibly proud to be your friend."

Ella Mae threw her arms around Suzy, and the two of them held each other and cried, laughed, and then cried some more. When Jenny reappeared with a bottle of prosecco, she shouted, "Enough of that nonsense, ladies! Dry your eyes and hold out your glasses. We have more toasts to make tonight."

The next morning, Ella Mae returned to The Charmed Pie Shoppe. The sun had barely risen when she tied on her apron, turned up the radio, and prepared the filling for the dessert special, a sumptuous chocolate cherry pie. Next, she made a dozen leek, pesto, and ricotta tarts and placed them in the oven. After setting the timer, she went out to the patio garden to enjoy a moment's peace before Reba, Jenny, and Fiona arrived for the day.

There were no tasks awaiting her in the tranquil space, as her mother had already tended the plants. The soil was moist, all the spent flower heads had been snipped, and every bloom was rich with color and scent. Ella Mae loved how her mother had blended flowers and herbs in this garden. One bed was crammed with basil, coneflowers, parsley, and petunias, while another was bursting with rosemary, thyme, salvia, and blue speedwell. The garden was both beautiful and utilitarian, and the customers could see exactly where the fresh herbs flavoring their food came from.

Ella Mae checked her watch. She still had ten minutes to relax before the savory tarts would be ready. Settling deeper into the chair, she smiled in contentment. She was looking forward to a day of baking. She thought of the sounds she'd soon hear. The subtle clink of flatware, the murmur of conversation, and the occasional outburst of laughter would float into the kitchen from the dining room whenever Reba or Jenny opened the swing doors. These noises were music to Ella Mae. A song of happiness.

Spotting a blue swallowtail perched on a yarrow blossom, Ella Mae put out her hand. The butterfly tiptoed up her pointer finger. From inside the pie shop, she heard Reba call out a boisterous good-morning. Aunt Verena and Uncle Buddy were coming by later for lunch, as were Aunt Sissy and Alfonso. As soon as Dee returned to Havenwood, Ella Mae's circle of family and friends would be complete.

"I'd better get back to work," Ella Mae said to the butterfly, and returned the insect to its flower. She didn't feel the slightest twinge of regret that the butterfly was just a butterfly and that she couldn't see through its eyes. She had pies to bake.

Later that afternoon, after serving a seemingly endless parade of customers, Reba and Jenny entered the kitchen with the last of the dirty dishes and sank wearily onto the stools next to the worktable. "Workin' for a celebrity is no picnic," Reba moaned. "I don't even have the strength to pull a Twizzler out of my pocket. That's how tired I am."

"You're such a drama queen," Jenny said, retrieving a licorice twist and sticking it in Reba's mouth.

Reba chewed her candy and looked at Ella Mae. "How are you holdin' up?"

"I'm fine." Ella Mae untied her apron and folded it over her arms. She glanced down at the embroidered rolling pin and smiled. "I'm happy to be back where I belong. In the kitchen, making magic."

Ella Mae had one last thing to do before she could put her role as the Clover Queen behind her. After closing the pie shop for the day, she went home, showered, and took Chewy and her cell phone down to the dock. Chewy barked an invitation to Miss Lulu and, within seconds, the feisty Schipperke was racing over the lawn, her brown eyes dancing with joy. The two dogs splashed about in the shallows while Ella Mae gazed at the blue hills above the lake and then dialed Dee's number.

She and her aunt exchanged pleasantries, and then Ella Mae explained the real purpose of her call. "I could bring the sword to you. This very moment. I believe it will heal your burns."

Dee was silent for a long moment. Finally, she said, "My sisters have made the same suggestion. I'll tell you what I told them. The doctor who saved my life the night of the fire must have given me a significant dose of magic, because my wounds seem superficial compared to what they should be. I don't need any more help."

"He took care of your internal injuries, but what about the burns on your arms and hands?" Ella Mae asked. "The graft surgeries must be difficult. And painful."

"They were," Dee said. "But they're done now. I've surprised everyone here with how well I'm progressing. As long as I can still work, I'll be content." She paused. "Besides, I don't want to erase the scars. They're a permanent reminder of the time I spent with Kyran. When I look at them, I'll feel sorrow, but I'll also feel gratitude and love. I don't want to forget any of those feelings. I don't want the proof of what happened to him to vanish because a magic sword healed my damaged skin. Can you understand that?"

Ella Mae thought of the sheet-wrapped bundle sitting on her kitchen table. "Yes, I can. Have you told Officer Hardy about Kyran?"

"Reluctantly. I didn't want Kyran's life to be overshadowed by his death, but I had to help Officer Hardy close this case so that Kyran's remains could be returned to his own country. He always said he wanted his ashes to be scattered in the river near his home because his favorite childhood memories were of playing in its water."

Dee's voice was surprisingly free of grief. "You sound really good, Aunt Dee." Ella Mae said. "I'm so glad. We've all been worried about you."

"And I've barely slept thinking about you, my sisters, and my sweet animals. Luckily, I've had August to distract me. Today, for example, we've been working on designs for my new barn. It turns out that August is as shrewd as he is kind. You should hear him talking to the architects and contractors. There are so many sides to him that I never knew existed." She fell quiet for several seconds and then continued. "I don't think I could have seen him this way if Kyran were still alive. As long as I knew Kyran was somewhere in this world, I couldn't love anyone else. And though I'll never stop loving him, I'm certain that he wouldn't want me to continue living like a hermit. He'd want me to be happy."

"So you're finally giving August a chance to court you?"

Dee laughed her soft, musical laugh. "He's been trying to do that for the past twenty years. The man has proved himself a hundred times over, so I've made it very clear that the next time he asks me out to dinner, I'll say yes."

Hurray for August, Ella Mae thought, pumping her fist in the air. "You're right, Aunt Dee. You have no use for this sword. You're going to be just fine."

"So are you, sweetheart," Dee replied. "You don't need special powers to lead a magical life. You never have. You've only ever needed to be yourself."

That evening Ella Mae drove her Jeep up the winding mountain road leading to the state park. Hundreds of people were waiting for her on the trail leading to the grove. As she ascended the hill, they all fell silent and stepped back to let her pass. Ella Mae fixed her eyes straight ahead and kept a firm hold on the sheet-wrapped sword in her arms. At the path's end, she reached out and touched the boulder wall with her hand. She felt nothing but warm stone. Nodding in acceptance, she gazed over the trees to where the sky was filling with striations of pink and orange. The sunset hues reflected in the glassy surface of Lake Havenwood and the air smelled of pine and honeysuckle.

Ella Mae took a deep breath and turned to Alfonso.

"Could I impose on you once more?"

"It would be my honor," Alfonso said, and then touched her throat.

Ella Mae looked down at the people crowded together on the narrow trail and felt an intense rush of affection for all of them. In every face, she saw courage and beauty, and for a moment, she was too overwhelmed to say a word. Finally, she composed herself and began to speak.

"My friends, I know that many of you are eager to return to your homes, but I'm glad that I had the chance to thank you for everything you've done before you go. I also want to share some incredible news with you. One of Nimue's priestesses had an ancient scroll in her possession. The scroll describes how the curse placed on our kind can be broken. If this sword is driven into a sacred ash tree, then we'll be free. Nimue's lust for power led her to both the sword and this scroll. Now, we have them both, and will use them for the good of all."

There was a collective gasp from the crowd and then a tumult of excited muttering.

"Fiona and Carol Drever will fulfill this task on their way home to the Orkneys. The Elders have decided that the sword should be taken to a grove on the Isle of Arran. Their ash tree was damaged by Nimue's storms, but it still stands. The moment the sword restores the tree and the grove, the curse will be broken. You can marry and bear children with another of our kind without fear of repercussion." She presented the sword to Fiona, who accepted it with a solemn nod. "The Elders have also pardoned Marin Wallace of any and all wrongdoing, seeing as she was forced to commit crimes against her will. Marin, I believe this belongs to you."

Ella Mae held out a duffel bag and Marin came forward

with hesitant steps. "Go on," Ella Mae whispered. "We all know you committed crimes against your will. You were one of Nimue's many victims, but you're free now."

When Marin opened the bag and saw her sealskin folded inside, she cried out in relief. "How can I ever thank you?"

"By accompanying the Drevers on a ship bound for Edinburgh," Ella Mae said. "The choice is yours, of course, but I'd feel better knowing you were with them. Do you want to return to Scotland?"

"With all my heart," Marin replied, her voice hoarse with emotion.

"Officer Hardy will be sad to see you go, but you've been away from home for far too long," Fiona said, and took Marin's arm in her own.

Ella Mae watched Fiona lead Marin back to where Carol, Lundy, and the rest of the Scots stood. With a pang, Ella Mae realized that she might never see any of them again.

Her gaze roved over the people gathered before her. Many would leave this night and never return. Those who lived in Havenwood would bump into Ella Mae on a regular basis—in the pie shop, the bank, the grocery store. But things would never be the same. This was the last time she could speak as one of them. From this moment onward, she would not be privy to their secret lives. She'd be restricted to small talk or a friendly wave as they passed on the street.

I can live with that, she thought.

What mattered most was their victory. A victory that could not have been achieved without the unity of these remarkable people.

"I wish those of you who are leaving a safe journey." She put her hand over her heart, which seemed to have swelled to twice its size. "You should be extremely proud of what you accomplished here in Havenwood. If you ever have a hankering for a homemade pie, come back and see me. I'll be delighted to serve you."

And with that, Ella Mae began to descend the hill.

She'd barely taken two steps when a woman standing to her left dropped into a low curtsy. "You will always be one of us," the woman whispered. Her eyes were filled with tears.

Ella Mae thanked her and walked on. As she progressed, every man and woman bowed or curtsied and repeated the same phrase. "You will always be one of us."

The echoed words were a gift. Through her tears, Ella Mae smiled. She continued her descent, certain that her heart would burst before she reached the trail's end.

"You will always be one of us."

"You will always be one of us."

By the time she reached the bottom, Ella Mae was too choked up to speak. She turned, looked back at the amazing people standing above her, and waved.

And then she got in her Jeep and drove away.

She didn't make it very far before she had to pull over. Putting her face in her hands, she let the bittersweet beauty of the farewell sweep over her. She cried hard for several minutes as joy, sorrow, gratitude, and grief poured out of her all at once.

Overhead, the first stars began to spark in the purpling sky, and Ella Mae rolled down her window to look at them. Calmer now, she wiped her face and eased the Jeep back onto the road. Thrusting her hand out the window, she let the spring air soar through her fingers and whip through her hair. As she neared the lights of town, she decided to spend the rest of the night snuggled on the couch with Chewie. She'd pour a glass of wine, flip through vintage cookbooks, and dream up amazing new pie recipes.

Ella Mae smiled. She felt lighter, like a great weight had fallen off her shoulders during the short journey from the mountain park to her home. She felt young and free for the first time in a very long time.

At a stoplight, she caught a glance of her reflection in the rearview mirror and was pleased with what she saw.

She saw a woman beginning a new chapter in what was certain to be a fascinating life.

A charmed life.

Recipes

Charmed Leprechaun Pie

20 chocolate sandwich cookie wafers, crushed
½ cup melted butter
2 cups marshmallow creme
⅓ cup crème de menthe liqueur
2 tablespoons white crème de cacao
Green food coloring
2 cups whipping cream
Andes Crème de Menthe Thins, finely chopped, for garnish
   (optional)

Preheat oven to 425 degrees. In a medium bowl, mix cookie crumbs and melted butter. Press crumbs into bottom and sides of a 10-inch pie dish. Bake for approximately 10 minutes. Remove from oven and cool. Once cooled, place crust in freezer. Also place large stainless steel mixing bowl and beaters in freezer to prepare to make whipped cream.

In large bowl, add marshmallow creme, crème de menthe, and white crème de cacao. Mix until smooth. Add food coloring until desired shade of green is achieved. For brighter green pie, add 5-6 drops.

Remove mixing bowl and beaters from freezer. Add whipping cream and whip with electric mixer until stiff peaks form. Gently fold whipped cream into marshmallow mixture. Pour into chilled pie shell. Garnish by sprinkling chopped Andes mints around rim of pie. Freeze for at least 3 hours.

Charmed Peach Blackberry Tart with Shortbread Crust

SHORTBREAD CRUST

¾ cup cold butter, cubed
⅓ cup confectioners' sugar
1½ cups all-purpose flour

Blend ingredients in food processor on pulse setting until your dough is crumbly. Pat into a 9- or 10-inch greased tart pan. Prick crust with fork or use pie weights to keep from bubbling. Bake in 350-degree oven for 15 minutes.

FILLING

3 or 4 medium fresh peaches
1 pint fresh blackberries
¾ cup sugar

3 tablespoons all-purpose flour
Pinch of salt
⅓ cup buttermilk
3 large eggs
½ teaspoon pure vanilla extract
6 tablespoons butter, melted and cooled to room temperature
1½ teaspoons lemon zest

While shortbread crust is baking, cut an X in the bottom of each peach with a knife. Fill a large saucepan with water and bring to a boil. Put peaches in water and boil for 45 seconds. If they're a little underripe, boil for a full minute. Remove from heat and immediately transfer peaches to a bowl of ice water. Drain water and peel skin from peaches. Pit and slice peaches. Wash blackberries and pat dry.

When crust is finished baking, remove from oven and allow to cool. In the meantime, make the tart filling by combining sugar, flour, and salt in a medium bowl. Next, add buttermilk, eggs, and vanilla and blend. Whisk in melted butter and lemon zest.

Place blackberries and peaches on shortbread crust. Transfer crust to a lined cookie sheet and pour filling over the fruit. The filling will reach the top. Bake until center is set, 55–60 minutes, depending on the strength of your oven. Cool tart, remove from pan, and enjoy.

Charmed Strawberry Muffin Pan Pies

   5 cups strawberries, chopped
   ⅓ cup granulated sugar
   ¼ cup packed brown sugar
   ½ teaspoon apple pie spice
   6 tablespoons cold butter, cubed
   1 package refrigerated piecrusts
   ¾ cup flour
   2 teaspoons fresh lemon juice
   1 tablespoon cornstarch

Preheat oven to 350 degrees.

Toss strawberries in sugar and let sit for at least 30 minutes.

Meanwhile, prepare the crumble top in a medium bowl by mixing flour, brown sugar, apple pie spice, and butter in a food processor. Pulse until you have a nice crumble topping.

Place piecrust on a floured surface and cut out circles using a circular cookie cutter or biscuit cutter. Press circles into the muffin tins so there are no air bubbles.

Next, strain strawberries to remove excess liquid. Transfer back to the bowl and mix in lemon juice and cornstarch. Spoon strawberries into cups and crumble topping over each cup. The cups should overflow with the filling.

Bake in the oven for approximately 45–55 minutes. Let the mini pies cool completely and then use a thin butter knife to loosen and remove pies.

Makes 12–16 mini pies, depending on size of your piecrust circles.

Charmed Sunshine Lemon Pie

30 lemon cream–filled vanilla sandwich cookies, finely
   crushed
¼ cup butter, melted
1½ cups granulated sugar
6 tablespoons cornstarch
1 pinch salt
1 cup water
⅔ cup fresh lemon juice (plus 1 tablespoon for whipped
   cream)
2 teaspoons lemon zest
3 drops yellow food coloring
2 tablespoons butter
¾ cup heavy cream
12 ounces cream cheese, softened
⅔ cup confectioners' sugar
½ cup finely crushed lemon drop candies for garnish
   (optional)

Preheat oven to 350 degrees.

Break cookies into pieces. Using the pulse setting on a
food processor, turn pieces into crumbly crust. Add butter.
Pulse until blended. Spread into the bottom and sides of a
9-inch deep-dish pie plate to form a crust. Bake for 10 minutes and then remove crust from oven and let it cool.

While crust is baking, place stainless steel mixing bowl
and electric mixer beaters in the freezer to chill. (This helps
produce a perfect whipped cream later on.)

In a saucepan, combine sugar, cornstarch, and salt. Stir
in water, lemon juice, lemon zest, and food coloring. Bring

to a boil over medium-high heat, stirring often for 2 minutes. Stir until mixture is smooth and thickened.

Remove saucepan from heat and let mixture cool completely.

Remove mixing bowl and beaters from freezer. Add ¾ cup heavy cream and 1 tablespoon lemon juice to bowl and beat until stiff peaks form.

In another mixing bowl, beat the cream cheese and confectioners' sugar until smooth. Using a rubber spatula, fold in the whipped cream. Remove ½ cup of this mixture to save for garnish. Spread the rest over the cookie crust.

Top with cooled lemon filling and chill in the refrigerator overnight.

If desired, garnish with dollops of whipped cream mixture and sprinkles of crushed lemon drop candy.

Look for the next Charmed Pie Shoppe Mystery
from Ellery Adams, coming 2016.

Turn the page for a preview of the next book by
Ellery Adams in the Book Retreat Mysteries . . .

Murder in the Paperback Parlor

Available August 2015 from Berkley Prime Crime!

"You expect me to break that with my bare hand?" Jane Steward, manager of Storyton Hall and mother of six-year-old twin boys, pointed at a piece of wood in disbelief.

"I do," replied Sinclair, Storyton's head librarian. He was looking at Jane with the fixed stare he reserved for guests who made too much noise in one of the resort's reading rooms or who had dared to mishandle a book.

Storyton Hall had thousands of books, and Sinclair knew the location and condition of every volume. He cared for the books as if they were priceless treasures. And to those who worked and visited Storyton, that's exactly what they were. People came from across the globe to spend a few days in the stately manor house tucked away in an isolated valley in western Virginia. Surrounded by blue hills and pristine forests, Storyton Hall was heaven on earth for bibliophiles.

Jane glanced around and for a moment, nearly forgot that she was standing directly beneath the carriage house in a room that didn't appear on the official blueprints. In fact, only a select group of people knew of its existence. Like Sinclair, they used the practice space to hone their martial arts skills. Butterworth, the butler, was particularly fond of attacking the seventy-pound weighted bags hanging from the ceiling. Sterling, the head chauffeur, preferred to spar with nunchaku, and Sinclair's preferred weapon was a set of throwing knives he kept hidden inside a hollowed-out copy of *The Art of War.*

Not too long ago, Jane would have found the idea of dressing in a *dobok* and practicing roundhouse kicks utterly ridiculous, but now, as she caught a glimpse of herself in the wall-length mirror, she knew that there was nothing amusing about her situation. It was also clear from Sinclair's expression that he expected her to break the board with her bare hand, and he expected her to do so without delay.

"It's easy, Mom! Fitz and I did it on our first try."

Displeased over the idea of being shown up by her sons, Jane frowned. "All right, I'm ready."

Sinclair held the rectangular piece of pine by its sides and braced himself for impact. "Check your stance," he ordered. "The power comes from your body. Whip your trunk around and you'll break the board without injuring your hand. Focus on a spot in the center of the board. See your hand going through the wood and continuing to move forward. Don't stop. If you think about stopping, you won't succeed. Lead with your palm, not your pinkie finger."

"Got it," Jane said. She adjusted her legs until she was in the proper stance and pretended not to notice the doubtful look on Hem's face or how Fitz was gnawing at his thumbnail. "I can do this," she said, unsure if she was addressing the boys or herself.

Taking a deep breath, Jane trained her eyes on the board.

She saw the grains in the wood and visualized the exact location she intended to strike. Raising her right arm, she pivoted her entire right side toward the back wall. Concentrating on whipping her hip and shoulder around as quickly as possible, she drove her hand, palm facing the ceiling, into the board. It parted with a satisfying crack and a large splinter of wood flew past Jane's cheek and landed on the floor mat near Hem's feet.

He picked it up, testing its sharpness with his index finger, and promptly jabbed it into his brother's side.

"Ow!" Fitz howled, and immediately retaliated by administering a front snap kick to his brother's wrist. The splinter came dislodged from Hem's hand and was snatched in midair by Sinclair.

"What have I told you gentlemen about martial arts?" he asked, his voice steely with disapproval.

Hem dropped his gaze and tried to appear penitent. "We should only use it for self-defense."

"Or if another person's safety is . . . threatened," Fitz added, looking pleased to have remembered the second half of the creed Sinclair recited at the end of every class. Too late, Fitz realized that he should have adopted a contrite expression as well. He opened his mouth to speak, but Sinclair only had to shake his head once and Fitz immediately clamped his lips shut.

I wish I could do that, Jane thought. *Give them one stern look and watch them fall into line.*

"Next class, you two will drill the entire time while your mother learns a new kick." He turned to Butterworth, who'd just finished pummeling a practice bag. It was still jerking on the end of its chain as if it had been electrocuted. "Mr. Butterworth? Would you be so kind as to demonstrate a spinning hook kick?"

"Certainly," said Butterworth. He leaned forward, shifting his weight to his left leg. In a flash, he whipped his right leg around in a sweeping one-hundred-and-eighty-degree arc. When he struck the bag with the ball of his foot, Jane was sure he'd knock it clean off its chain.

Sinclair tapped his own temple. "Because Mr. Butterworth has excellent flexibility, strength, and power, he aimed his kick high. If that bag had been a person, Mr. Butterworth would have made contact with his opponent's head. A well-aimed kick can unbalance your enemy and give you the chance to run."

"Or finish him off," Butterworth said. "Observe." He attacked the gyrating bag with a roundhouse kick and then swiveled and drove his elbow into its padded body.

"I will not be teaching you how to administer elbow blows until you are much more responsible," Sinclair told the sulking twins.

Jane decided she'd like to learn that particular attack sooner rather than later. Driving her elbow into someone's windpipe or solar plexus looked far easier than performing a spinning hook kick. She shared this thought with Sinclair.

"You need to train until that kick is second nature," Sinclair said. "I could call out a dozen different offensive maneuvers to Mr. Butterworth and he'd execute each and every one without pause."

Jane didn't think she'd ever achieve the level of mastery Sinclair was striving for, and though she was delighted that she'd broken the board, she was done training for the day. What she wanted most was a hot shower and a second cup of coffee. She and the twins had risen quite earlier than usual to get their training in. They had scurried across the back lawn, heads bent against the chill February air, before most of the resort's guests were even stirring in their beds.

"Perhaps that kick should wait until after the Romancing the Reader week," Jane said. "I don't want to pull a muscle before the Regency Fashion Show. I'd be a poor representative of the Grande Dame if I limped down the catwalk in the gown Mabel has toiled over for months."

Amusement glimmered in Sinclair's eyes. "Ah, yes, the fashion show. I'd nearly forgotten about that particular event—probably because every female under our roof can speak of only two subjects: the male cover model competition and the habits, interests, and whereabouts of Mr. Lachlan."

Taking the broken pieces of wood from Sinclair, Jane laughed. "Weeks before Lachlan first stepped foot on our property, you predicted that many ladies would fall in love with him."

Sinclair sighed. "Indeed I did. I also assumed that, after two months, his allure would have dimmed somewhat. Obviously, I underestimated Mr. Lachlan's appeal." He shot her a sly glance. "How do you find him?"

Jane made a shooing gesture at her sons. "Run home and change. If you get your chores done in time, I'll hand over your allowance before we drive to the village. A little bird told me that the Hogg Brothers are hosting an indoor picnic lunch and special contest for all kids twelve years old and under. The winner will receive a new bicycle from Spokes and a bike basket filled with treats from the Pickled Pig."

The twins exchanged wide-eyed looks and raced off. Butterworth followed at a more dignified pace, his spine straight and his shoulders squared. Jane recognized that Butterworth was leaving his role of combat expert behind in favor of his butler persona, and Jane wondered if such a marked change came over her when she finished one of her training sessions.

I doubt it, she thought. *I'm still getting used to living a*

*double life. Sinclair, Butterworth, and Sterling have been
doing it for decades. And now, Lachlan has joined our
secret circle.*

Once the sound of the boys' shouts and jostles faded, Jane
finally answered Sinclair's question. "I find Lachlan a bit of
an enigma. He's hardworking, courteous, and organized.
He's also a master salesman. For such a quiet person, I'm
amazed by his ability to talk people into sleigh rides, cross-
country-skiing ventures, and ice skating. Usually, wintertime
means less business at the activities desk, but not since Lachlan's arrival. He's certainly increasing our revenue."

"I'd hazard a guess that our female guests would happily
risk losing the feeling in their extremities if it meant spending time with Mr. Lachlan." Sinclair flicked a switch on the
wall and the practice bags began to rise to the ceiling. "Are
you immune to that shy smile, that roughish hair, or those
striking blue eyes?"

"He's quite attractive," Jane admitted. "But I have no real
sense of him. He doesn't volunteer an ounce of personal
information, and he'd rather traipse through the woods than
socialize with the rest of the staff. I know he's an outdoorsman, but I hadn't realized he'd be so . . . hermitlike."

Together, she and Sinclair walked to the door where
they'd left their shoes and socks. Once their bare feet were
covered and they'd bundled up in wool coats, Sinclair locked
the door behind them. "Mr. Lachlan was an Army Ranger.
He saw action in Iraq and Afghanistan as well as a host of
covert missions in between. I was well aware of his history
before casting my vote in favor of hiring him. I don't think
his past will impede his performance as head of recreation,
and he's an excellent asset when it comes to guarding you
and your family. However, he's unlikely to join the Storyton
Players in the near future."

Sinclair hurried up the stairs, checked to see that the coast was clear, and waved for Jane to step through the narrow gap behind a workbench. After she was through, he pushed a button obscured by a rusty saw blade and the workbench swung back against the wall.

Jane had only learned about the surprising number of hidden rooms and passageways located around Storyton Hall and its outbuildings during the past few months. Until last October, she'd been completely ignorant of the fact that certain people she'd known her entire life were a part of a group called the Fins. These men had pledged to protect the members of the Steward family with their lives. And since Jane had been born into a family that had been guarding a secret library and its treasures for centuries, she and her sons were also under the Fins' protection.

The first time Sinclair had led Jane to the attic turret and pushed open the door to the fireproof and temperature-controlled vault, Jane had nearly fainted. It wasn't every day that one discovered the existence of unpublished Shakespeare plays, gilt-covered Gutenberg Bibles, or the endings of famous but incomplete novels. Treasures entrusted to the Stewards for all sorts of reasons—to keep them from being stolen, damaged during wartime, or sold on the black market.

There were also books deliberately kept from the public eye—radical works filled with disturbing and dangerous ideas. Jane had read a few lines from one of them and was shocked and angered by the author's proposition that women were vastly inferior to men. The author went on to encourage mass sterilization of any female lacking a genius IQ. Considering the book had been written by a prominent English scientist during the first stirrings of the women's emancipation movement, its publication could have crippled an entire gender.

After that unpleasant read, Jane had stuck to perusing the secret library's incredible selection of rare fiction. A voracious reader since early childhood, it galled Jane that she didn't have enough free time to delve more deeply into the astounding collection stored in airtight containers in a nearly inaccessible room hundreds of feet above the ground.

It had taken Jane several weeks to reconcile herself to the fact that it was more important that she protect the library's contents than examine them. After all, to a lifelong book lover, the library was the Eighth Wonder of the World, and Jane referred to it as such when speaking to her great aunt and uncle or to the Fins.

Suddenly, the thought of her aunt made Jane start. She glanced at her watch and let loose a small cry. "I'm going to be late! Aunt Octavia will be furious if she doesn't get the best seat in the house for Edwin Alcott's soft grand opening."

Sinclair arched a brow. "Soft?"

Jane quickened her pace, striding across the brittle lawn toward her cottage. "It's practice for the real grand opening on Saturday. Sorry, but I need to run."

Jane jogged around the building that had once served as the estate's hunting lodge. The lodge was so spacious that Jane's uncle had divided it into two residences. Sterling, the head chauffeur, lived in the front half, while Jane and her sons inhabited the back. Jane loved the privacy this arrangement afforded her little family. She loved her side-door entrance that led into her bright, cheery kitchen. She loved the open living room with its comfy sofas and book-lined walls. She loved her herb and flower gardens, which were protected from prying eyes by a tall hedge. Most of all, she loved how the house had seemed to open its arms to her after her husband's tragic death. A pregnant widow, Jane had returned to Storyton Hall in search of comfort and a fresh start. She'd found both within its walls and in the hearts of its people.

Now, bursting into her cheerful, yellow kitchen, Jane cast a longing glance at the coffeemaker and then bounded upstairs to change.

"Boys!" she hollered as she ascended. "I hope you're dressed. I also hope your beds are made. If that room's a mess, you'll get a smaller allowance."

Indignant cries came from behind the twins' closed door, and Jane knew they'd opted to put off their chores and were now regretting that decision.

"And I *will* be checking under your beds," she added for good measure as she hurried through her bathroom and into her small walk-in closet. "What to wear? What to wear?"

Being a Friday, Jane would normally dress in a work suit, but since there was a teacher workday at the twins' school, Jane and the boys had a long weekend. Jane would love to pretend it was Saturday and throw on jeans and a sweater, but she knew casual attire wouldn't do. Edwin's guests were sure to wear their Sunday best.

"Especially Aunt Octavia," Jane murmured to herself. "She'll be dressed as if she were attending a luncheon for minor royalty."

After selecting a pencil skirt in gray wool, a cowl-necked sweater, and a pair of riding boots, Jane fastened her strawberry blond hair into a loose chignon, added a pair of hoop earrings, and then dabbed on gardenia-scented perfume. Satisfied by what she saw in the mirror, she exited the bathroom and yelled, "Fitzgerald and Hemingway! Prepare for inspection!"

There was a crashing sound from the boys' room, and when Jane pushed open the door, her twins cast guilty looks at the closet.

"We're ready, Mom!" Hem said, throwing his arms around her neck. "You smell nice."

"And you look pretty," Fitz chimed in.

Jane knew perfectly well that, should she peek inside the closet, a cascade of toys, books, and dirty clothes would tumble out, but she was running too late to do anything about it. Glancing down at her sons, she tousled their hair and said, "I will delay the inspection until this afternoon in exchange for a kiss."

Because the twins were in the "girls have cooties" phase, Jane knew she was asking for a significant boon. After a brief hesitation, her sons gave her a quick peck on the cheek and then immediately held out their hands.

"Can we have our allowance now?" Hem asked. "Please?"

"I don't keep dollar bills in my boots. I'm not a—" Jane stopped herself before the word "stripper" rolled off her tongue.

Fitz cocked his head. "Not a what?"

"A walking bank," Jane said, and ushered the boys downstairs.

Five minutes later, the trio arrived, red-cheeked and panting, in Storyton Hall's main lobby.

Aunt Octavia was already there, of course, looking regal in an indigo coat with a fur-trimmed collar, cuffs, and hem. She made a big show of examining her watch and then glanced across the room at the grandfather clock, and muttered, " 'I wasted time and now doth time waste me.' "

Oblivious of meaning of the reference from *Richard II*, Fitz tugged on one of her fur cuffs. "Is this from an endangered animal, Aunt Octavia?"

"That would be bad," Hem said, echoing his brother's stern tone. "Our teacher, Miss Bedelia, told us how people used to kill seals and otters to make fur coats. She was really upset."

Aunt Octavia bent over, leaning heavily on her rhinestone-studded cane, and whispered, "Miss Bedelia has no need to worry. This fur is one hundred percent fake. In fact, I'm probably suffering from chemical exposure. That's just what I need, following my diabetes diagnosis."

"I hope Mr. Alcott's café is a salubrious establishment," Butterworth said to Aunt Octavia as he held open the front door for their little party. "Mrs. Hubbard is most concerned that your healthy eating plan will be compromised."

Aunt Octavia glowered at the butler. "She's just put out because she wasn't invited. Mrs. Hubbard is a fine woman, but she'd like nothing more than to gossip about the event to anyone passing through the kitchens of Storyton Hall."

Butterworth was smart enough to drop the subject. Instead, he informed them that their car was ready and wished them a pleasant lunch. No one would have guessed that the butler, impeccably dressed in his blue-and-gold Storyton livery with his hair neatly combed and his shoes polished to a high shine, had been mercilessly pummeling a practice bag less than an hour ago.

The twins jumped into the back of a vintage Rolls-Royce Silver Shadow while Jane settled Aunt Octavia in the passenger seat. Behind them, Sterling was helping an elderly couple out of his favorite Rolls, a Silver Cloud II. He tipped his cap at Jane. She waved and then drove down the resort's long, tree-lined driveway.

At the end of the driveway, Jane slowed as the car approached the massive wrought-iron gates bearing the Steward crest—an owl clutching a scroll in its talons. The family motto, which could also be found on the guest-room key fobs, had been inscribed in an arch-shaped banner over the owl's head.

Aunt Octavia pointed at the crest. "Let me hear our motto, boys."

"*De Nobis Fabula Narratur*," the twins replied, doing their best to pronounce the Latin words correctly. "Their Story Is Our Story."

Aunt Octavia smiled. "Excellent. When we get to the village, you may see what I have in my change purse. If you can count the coins correctly, they're yours. I hear that the Pickled Pig market has a marvelous display of Valentine's Day candy."

Jane glanced in the rearview mirror and saw a gleam appear in her sons' eyes.

"Speaking of Valentine's Day, are the preparations for Romancing the Reader complete?" Aunt Octavia asked.

"For the most part," Jane said. "Our guest of honor, Rosamund York, is being a bit of a nuisance."

Aunt Octavia didn't seem surprised. "She's a diva. Wants fresh roses in her suite each day. Will only drink a specific brand of spring water. Prefers not to mingle with her fans outside of her scheduled events. Her publicist sees to her every whim and handles all of Ms. York's communication. Am I getting warm?"

Approaching a sharp curve known as Broken Arm Bend, Jane reduced her speed. "You're spot-on. How did you know?"

"Mrs. Pratt is a devout Rosamund York fan. I had the misfortune of running into her at the bookshop. When I foolishly mentioned Romancing the Reader, she turned positively giddy. I've never seen a fifty-something woman bounce in such a manner." She frowned. "It was rather disturbing."

Jane smiled. "Mrs. Eugenia Pratt is a devout fan of the romance genre. She reads three to four books a week, but I hadn't realized that she knew intimate details about her favorite authors as well."

"I'm sure she'd like to get *intimate* with the male cover models," Aunt Octavia said with a snort.

"What does 'intimate' mean?" Fitz asked.

"Being close to," Jane said as they entered the village. She pulled the car into the only vacant parking spot in front of the Pickled Pig and pivoted in her seat to address her sons. "Mr. Hogg is expecting you. Remember, he's providing you with lunch and will then introduce you to his new pet. You'll have a chance to enter the name-the-pet contest, and afterward you can fill a small bag with candy from the bulk bins." She held out a warning finger. "I expect you both to be on your best behavior. If I hear any unfavorable reports, I will hold your candy hostage until further notice."

The boys responded with the briefest of nods before Hem turned to Aunt Octavia. "Can we count your coins now?"

Aunt Octavia passed them her coin purse. "Just bring it into the market with you, my dears. I don't want to be any later for lunch than we already are."

Delighted, the boys jumped out of the car and ran into the market, nearly barreling into an older gentleman with a walker. Jane said a silent prayer that they wouldn't get into too much mischief and relocated the car to a spot in between Run for Cover, Eloise Alcott's bookstore, and Daily Bread, Edwin Alcott's new café.

Eloise must have been watching for them out the restaurant's window, because she whipped open the front door before Jane could reach for the handle. Jane's best friend was a lovely woman in her early thirties with chin-length dark hair that framed her heart-shaped face. Her gray eyes were kind and intelligent, and she smiled often. She was devoted to Storyton Village, her customers, and the Cover Girls book club. One would expect her devotion to extend to her older brother, Edwin, as well, but Edwin and Eloise weren't exactly close. Edwin was a travel writer and had spent most of his adult life journeying around the globe. He could be direct to the point of rudeness and didn't seem interested in getting to know the people of Storyton.

So naturally, Eloise was flabbergasted when her brother announced his intention to put down roots, buy the failing café next door, and completely transform the space in time for the Romancing the Reader week.

"You won't believe what Edwin's done," Eloise exclaimed as she ushered Jane and Aunt Octavia inside. "It's like entering another world. An exotic oasis right here in Storyton."

Eloise was right. When Jane entered the café, she gasped in wonder. Gone was the aging-diner look of the former establishment. The faded linoleum flooring had been replaced with dark, rich hardwood and an assortment of kilim rugs. Chairs with wicker backs and plump ivory cushions were pulled up to hammered copper tables. The walls were covered with antique maps and framed postcards. Potted palms stood like soldiers at regular intervals along the longest wall. At the back of the café, mosquito nets served as a divider between the main dining area and a lounge space. In this intimate alcove, British Colonial chairs with animal-print cushions were grouped around a black steamer trunk.

"Are people supposed to eat there?" Aunt Octavia gestured at the lounge area.

"It's a place for people to relax with a cup of tea or a smoothie. A conversation corner, so to speak," Edwin said, coming forward to greet his guests. He gave Aunt Octavia a deferential bow and then reached for Jane's hand. "I'm glad you could make it." He cast his gaze around the café, watching people take in little details that Jane had missed upon first glance, like the border of hand-painted tiles around the perimeter of the room, the antique birdcage, or the urn-shaped wall sconces. "What do you think?" he asked, turning back to Jane.

"It's wonderful," Jane agreed.

Edwin offered Aunt Octavia his arm. "May I escort you to the best seat in the house?"

Aunt Octavia inclined her head and thanked Edwin after he pulled out her chair, draped a napkin on her lap, and handed her a menu. After distributing menus to everyone, he disappeared into the kitchen and a middle-aged man wearing a white linen shirt and linen trousers entered the dining room. He flashed them a bright smile from beneath a splendid moustache, introduced himself as Magnus, and declared that he'd be coming around with mango-and-cardamom smoothies for them to sip while they studied the menu.

Jane was delighted to find that all the sandwiches had been named after famous poets and were far more interesting than the dry roast beef and Swiss melts the previous owner had served. She found it difficult to decide which one to try first.

"I'm having the Rumi," Aunt Octavia declared. "You?"

"The Pablo Neruda."

The food was delicious. When Edwin came out of the kitchen to check on his customers, he was greeted by a burst of applause.

"You're going to be mobbed by all the romance fans next week!" Mrs. Pratt, another member of Jane's book club, cried. "This setting is straight out of an Elizabeth Peters novel. Are you a romantic, Mr. Alcott?" She batted her lashes at Edwin.

"No," Edwin said. "That malady is for younger men."

"Come now," Mrs. Pratt pressed. "A man with such an obvious appreciation for poetry must believe in romance."

"Lord Byron understood. He wrote, 'the heart will break, but broken live on.'" Edwin smiled at Mrs. Pratt, but the smile did not reach his eyes. "And now, if you'll excuse me, I must see to the honey lavender crème brûlée."

As Edwin vanished into the kitchen, Jane wondered who'd broken his heart. And when.

"Dark, brooding, and handsome. He's a modern day Heathcliff," Aunt Octavia said, and then studied Jane. "You'd do well to stay clear of that one. Heathcliffs don't make good husbands or father figures for young and impressionable boys."

To her horror, Jane blushed. "What makes you think Edwin Alcott ever crosses my mind?"

Aunt Octavia barked out a laugh. "I may be old, fat, diabetic, and contrary, but I'm not blind. I've known men like Edwin Alcott. Indeed, I have. They're trouble, Jane. Trouble with a capital T."

"I had enough of that this past autumn," Jane said as the server appeared with their dessert. "But Romancing the Readers will be completely different than our Murder and Mayhem week. We'll be hosting a company of ladies devoted to happy endings. It'll be a lovely, festive, and harmonious time. Not a single dead body in sight."

At least, I hope not, she thought and plunged her spoon through the caramelized crust of her custard.

FROM NEW YORK TIMES BESTSELLING AUTHOR
ELLERY ADAMS

Charmed Pie Shoppe Mysteries

Pies and Prejudice
Peach Pies and Alibis
Pecan Pies and Homicides

PRAISE FOR THE
CHARMED PIE SHOPPE MYSTERIES

"The Charmed Pie Shoppe has cast its spell on me."
—Krista Davis, *New York Times* bestselling author

"Delicious, delightful."
—Jenn McKinlay, *New York Times* bestselling author

"[A] savory blend of suspense, pies,
and engaging characters."
—*Booklist*

elleryadamsmysteries.com
facebook.com/TheCrimeSceneBooks
penguin.com

From *New York Times* bestselling author
Ellery Adams

MURDER *in the*
MYSTERY SUITE

A Book Retreat Mystery

Tucked away in the rolling hills of rural western Virginia
is Storyton Hall, a resort catering to book lovers who
want to get away from it all. To increase her number of
bookings, resort manager Jane Steward has decided to
host a Murder and Mayhem Week, where mystery lovers
can indulge in some role-play
solving. But when the winner
Felix Hampden, is found dead i
realizes one of her guests is an a

PRAISE FOR THE
ELLERY A

"Enchant
—Jenn McKinlay, *New York T*

"In one word—A
—*The Best Reviews*

elleryadamsmysteries.com
facebook.com/TheCrimeSceneBooks
penguin.com

M1509T0614